NEVER

die

FOR A SINNER

NEVER

die

FOR A SINNER

ISBN-13: 978-1-964967-06-6

Cover Artist: Dark Heart Designs

First Edition: September 2025

10 9 8 7 6 5 4 3 2 1

To the girls who dream of being chased through the woods and railed by a psychopath . . . this one's for you.

<u>AUTHOR'S NOTE</u>

Dear Reader,

Thank you for choosing to read Never Die for a Sinner. Grab a glass of water and a fan because you're going to need it.

Levi and Ava's story will piss you off, make you laugh, and probably make you giggle and kick your feet. Maybe all in the same chapter.

That being said, this is not a clean romance. This is a dark adult romance with very real situations.

Please read through the trigger warnings carefully before you proceed. I have taken the liberty of listing them, so they are easy to read. Your mental health matters too.

- Explicit sexual scenes in great detail (like, a lot of them)
- Graphic violence and gore
- Explicit sexual scenes in great detail
- Graphic violence and gore
- Alcohol abuse
- Tortue
- Psychological abuse
- Emotional abuse
- Murder
- Mental abuse

- Physical abuse
- PTSD/CPTSD
- Vivid nightmares related to PTSD
- Organized Crime
- Breath play
- Rope play
- Spanking
- Degradation/praise kink
- Murder, again
- Kidnapping
- Someone gets fed to a bear (The bear's still a good boy though)
- Crude and obscene language
- Death by oxygen tube
- Sexy contracts
- Sexy forest frolicking
- Underground fight club
- Slight mention of human trafficking
- Horrible parents
- Torture
- Loss of a loved one
- Stalking
- Mentions of cancer

"Tell me every terrible thing you ever did and let me love you anyway."

—Edgar Allen Poe

PROLOGUE

Worthless . . .

My knuckles turn white from gripping the porcelain sink in front of me so hard.

Pathetic . . .

My hands shake—the empty bottle beside me a testament to my fading self-control.

Trash . . .

My eyes snap up to meet themselves in the mirror. The ice-blue is dull, rimmed in red from a lack of sleep.

It's been three days since I've slept through the night. Three days of torture from my mind that doesn't let me rest.

I fucking hate myself. I hate the voices in my head.

I hate the taste of whiskey, and I hate that I can't live without it.

I hate that he's still here. Still alive, clinging to his useless corpse in my mother's house.

I grab for the bottle, reminded that it's empty, while I stare at my own reflection.

I fucking hate them. I hate myself for looking like him.

I hate that I can't get the voices out of my head. His voice reminding me how worthless I am. Reminding me I'll never be more than what he's reduced me to.

Mostly, I hate that I'm out of whiskey.

In my sleep-deprived mind's eye, I don't see my face anymore. I see his. The same black hair. The same darkness hidden in blue eyes. The same monster.

In a flash, my fist snaps out, the glass slicing my skin as the broken shards rain down into the sink and over the rough cabin floor beneath me.

Seeing my broken reflection somehow offers a calming clarity that I wasn't prepared for.

The pain in my knuckles barely registers while my mind goes blank of all things except how to end this.

The same man who took my mother, my brother . . . Who almost took my entire fucking family from me, is alive in the same house where she sleeps.

The ghost that lives across the hall . . .

I won't let him try to take her, too.

And suddenly . . . the voices stop.

CHAPTER
One

LEVI

I t's with great sadness that we say goodbye to our dear old friend. A father . . . a husband . . ."

I fucking hate funerals.

Especially the cheap imitation of one.

My father's casket lies over a hole beside my mother, though if I had my choice, he would have been tossed into the ocean. The bastard doesn't deserve to spend eternity next to her.

I stand at the back of the crowd gathered around, listening to my sister and my aunt grieve a man who didn't give a damn about anyone but himself. The rain sprinkles down overhead, covering everything in a fresh coat of moisture, but I'm past caring.

I've waited for this day my entire life, only now that it's here, I'm finding I don't feel the retribution I had hoped for.

In fact . . . I don't feel anything.

The man who made my life a living hell is dead. He murdered my mother, tried to murder my sister-in-law, and with behind their backs with a smile on his face.

I'm glad the fucker's dead.

So why do I feel so fucking hollow?

"William was a good man. He was dedicated to his work. Loved his family . . ." *Or what we could provide him.* "His children will miss him dearly, and it's with that I want to say a closing prayer."

Oh, great. The fucking customary prayer that comes at the end of every service. Dad was never a religious man. In fact, I'm not sure any amount of praying could save him from whatever hell awaits him on the other side.

Still, it makes people feel better because they want to send off their loved one with as much hope as possible, no matter how shitty that person was.

My sister still refuses to believe it. My aunt is beside herself, faced with the fact that her brother-in-law murdered her only sister and tried to destroy her family.

I watch them bow their heads, refusing to do so because he doesn't deserve it. Death isn't an eraser. It can't wipe away your sins, no matter how you died.

I look out over the crowd, spacing out from whatever the preacher is saying. My gaze lingers on my brother, who stands across the tent from me, his gaze locked on mine. His wife has her head lowered beside him out of politeness, but Christian and I are on the same page.

Dad almost succeeded in taking Mila from Christian for good. He used our brother's mental illness to unleash a monster on our family that nearly killed us all. It actually succeeded in destroying our mother.

The man was a fucking asshole.

Let him be an asshole while he burns in hell.

Christian is the first to look away, to the little blonde beside him, when she raises her head at the end of the prayer.

He takes her hand and presses her fingers to his lips, and she softens only for him.

If you'd asked me five years ago if I thought my brother, FBI asshole extraordinaire, would be this fucking whipped for a woman half his size, I would have laughed in your face.

But when I look at the brunette beside Mila, whose soft green gaze finds mine across the tent, for the first time in my life, I'm finding myself jealous.

And I fucking hate it.

The Oak Ridge Lodge sits atop a cliff overlooking the valley below the Mount Baker National Forest. It's beautiful this time of year, but I grew accustomed to it a long time ago.

The Cross Estate rests on the same three hundred acres as the Oak Ridge lodge, and right now, I'm avoiding it like the plague. Parties were never my thing. They were Bella's, my sister. The dinner after my father's funeral is just another excuse to celebrate the life of a dickhead who didn't deserve it.

Call me crazy, but I have no desire to pretend any longer.

"Levi?"

I grit my teeth before I turn over my shoulder to find Bella standing at the edge of the terrace. She's the youngest of the Cross siblings, and the only girl, but she holds her own. Running the lodge and otherwise being a holy fucking terror in Prada, day in and day out.

We used to be close, but now, I'm finding I'm not close with anyone. Maybe Christian, but he only gets as close as I'll let him. Bella may as well be a stranger.

"What are you doing? It's freezing."

I shrug.

"I'm fine."

She winces, and I can tell she's trying to be gentle. Everyone has. Walking around me like I'm made of porcelain. Like I really give a fuck if the old bastard is dead.

He deserved to die. No one gets a free pass. Not me. Not Christian. Definitely not William Cross.

"Don't be like this. Please, come inside."

Fuck that. And listen to my Great-Aunt Marjory try to set me up with my cousins?

Absolutely not.

"I'm good."

She huffs, and I can practically feel her roll her eyes. Too bad. Right now, I'm focused on the slight tremor in my hands and the need burning in my chest.

Why can't she just walk the fuck away?

"Dad would have wanted you there."

Ice slips through my veins. I'm this fucking close to losing my shit, and she just won't let it go.

"Forgive me, but I don't give a fuck what Dad would have wanted."

"Levi—"

"I said, no, Bella. Fuck off." I'm not usually this harsh with her, but she needs to understand that not all of us had the loving, gentle version of our father. She was his favorite, and he doted on her while the boys got the beatings and various *other* punishments, he found fitting.

She doesn't know the man he was because he never let her see that side of him. Even when the veil did slip and she got a taste of just how much our father was capable of, she refused to see it.

Bella's quiet, and I can hear the tears in her voice when she speaks. I just can't find it in myself to care, right now.

"You don't have to be an asshole."

I don't respond. I came out here to be alone. It's not my fault she can't take a fucking hint.

"Fine," she says eventually. "But just know, you're driving the wedge between us. Not me."

And with that, she storms off back inside to play make-believe with all the rest of our family, who decided to spontaneously forget who William Cross *actually* was.

Alone again, I pull the flask out of my suit jacket and toss it back, drinking what's left. A burn slides through me. I barely notice it, numb to the effects, but it brings about a calm I'd been searching for the entire day.

Fuck Bella. She doesn't get to dictate how I feel.

If she wants to make a martyr out of the man who committed unspeakable acts against our family, then she's as stupid as he is.

Fishing the pack of cigarettes from my pocket, I stick one between my teeth and light it up. I quit smoking months ago, and what I actually mean by that is I've lied and told everyone else I have, so they leave me the fuck alone about it.

I blow out a cloud of smoke and watch it hang in the cool Autumn air. The sun is setting over the horizon, painting everything in shades of pink and orange. Sunset is my favorite time of day, usually because it means night will fall and there won't be a million fucking people wanting something from me.

Christian with his shit with Mila. Bella about Dad or the lodge. My Aunt Paulina about whatever the hell she can manage to come up with.

That *other* problem . . .

I've spent most of my life cleaning up other people's messes. It's what I'm good at. At night, I'm free.

I'm well and truly alone without a single fuck to give.

Except for when I catch a whiff of citrus in the air.

It's not five minutes after Bella goes inside that the door

opens again. My spine stiffens when I hear the footsteps behind me. I don't even have to turn around to know who it is. The scent of her perfume is enough.

Silence hangs in the air, and like the meek little ghost she is, she searches for something to say. I could almost chuckle, knowing if I were to turn around, I'd find her timid, her cheeks flushed a sweet shade of pink, and the prettiest goddamned eyes I've ever seen on the ground, instead of on me.

It's almost too tempting. I know a trap when I see one.

"What do you want, Ava?"

I'm harsher with her than I should be. She's gentle and soft to my rough edges. She wasn't built for this world like I was. This is new to her, but I'm not her teacher, and I'm not her friend. I'm not anyone to her but someone whose name is on the house she works and lives in.

"I just . . ." Her voice is barely audible over the wind whipping down the cliffside.

She's always so . . . submissive. Like she's afraid to be seen. Unfortunately, for her, I've *always* seen her, and it's turning out to be a real fucking problem.

"I know it's been a rough day," she continues, completely oblivious. "I wanted to check on you and see how you're feeling."

I can't help but chuckle darkly under my breath. The lamb worried about the big bad wolf.

I don't turn around for a long moment. When I do, I realize it was a mistake. She's fucking breathtaking. My cock's instantly hard in my slacks, and all manner of dirty thoughts slip through my mind about what I want to do to her.

The thought of pushing her down into the mattress, her legs clenching around my head while she cries out my name into the night—not God's—now that's something that could get addictive.

Fucking hell.

My gaze rakes over her prim and proper black dress. Soft waves fall down her back like rich chocolate. Perfect little body. Pouty lips.

Who the fuck am I kidding?

Ava Ryan is pure heroin. One hit is all it would take before I was hooked.

Which is exactly why I need to stay the fuck away from her.

A blush slips up her delicate neck and into her cheeks when my eyes meet hers. Instantly, she looks away—a bad habit of hers I can't wrap my head around.

I hate how fucking perfect she is. Like she was handcrafted to ruin me. It would be so easy to lose myself in her for a few days until I've had my fill. Maybe then I could get some fucking sleep instead of wondering what the little ghost across the hall is up to in the middle of the night.

I grit my teeth, blowing out a cloud of smoke around my cigarette.

She can't see this . . . side of me. This disturbed, broken, and unfeeling asshole that I try to keep hidden. The alcoholic former DEA agent, who spends his nights either drowning in whiskey or at the Tomb.

I know without a doubt, my jagged edges would be enough to scar her, and it's exactly why I need to keep my distance.

"I pay you to clean my house, Ava. Not play therapist."

The icy bite of my voice sends a shiver through her, and her mouth pulls into a frown. Hurt crosses her pretty face, and her cheeks flame. I ignore it before I do something stupid, like haul her over my shoulder and cart her upstairs to spend the night forgetting this fucking day. Forgetting who I am while I'm buried inside her.

Sweet little girls like Ava aren't good for men like me. I'm rough. Crude. I drink too much, and I smoke. She's too innocent. Too soft for a man like me. I'd break her and hate myself even as I couldn't stop because, like an arsonist to a flame, I'd be fucking addicted to the destruction.

Getting the good girl to be bad only for you?

Now *that's* real retribution.

Ava is silent, unmoving in her place on the muddy cliffside. Poor thing walked out here in her heels.

Not that I care. It's her fault. Always getting herself into trouble.

I've never met something so perfectly imperfect. Like something I wanted to break and cherish at the same time.

If she were mine, I would own Ava Ryan's every breath. There's not a thing on this planet I wouldn't give her to watch her eyes light up with stars . . . and that's a dangerous thought.

"Right," she says, almost cheerfully, like she's trying to cover up how much my words sting.

She still doesn't meet my gaze, her eyes on the ground at my feet. From the moment I met her, she's been this quiet, reserved girl. I want to see what it looks like when that timid shell shatters.

"I . . ." she chokes on her words, and I wait for whatever bullshit she's going to say about my father. It's been happening all day. Everyone offering their condolences. As if I didn't celebrate with a bottle of whiskey just last night.

Ava swallows thickly, and finally, those green eyes meet mine, the fading sun making them shine in a way that sends an uncomfortable burn through my veins.

"Just know . . . if you need someone to talk to . . . I'll listen."

I watch her leave; my gaze trained on the center of her back. When the door closes behind her, I actually scoff out loud, laughing under my breath when the cigarette falls to the ground where I'd bit it in half.

Ava may think she's helping me, but she doesn't realize there's more than one monster in this world she needs to be afraid of.

Soon, she'll figure it out, and I can only hope that when she does, her hate feels as sweet as her kindness.

CHAPTER
Two

AVA

Have you ever wondered what it must be like to be a ghost?

To have to watch the world move around you, knowing you're stuck in the same, stagnant place. Never moving. Never changing.

An extension of the background, translucent and silent.

Sometimes I feel like a ghost, hiding out in the shadows of the Cross Estate while others live their lives around me. Cleaning and cleaning and then cleaning things that have already been cleaned because that's my life.

My life has been a constant stream of trial and error and up until this point, I wasn't sure I'd even make it this far.

I guess I still don't know.

I'm the housekeeper and I see everything.

Like Bella Cross's silent tears when she thinks no is around because her father betrayed her in the worst way imaginable.

Or the way Christian Cross's hands tighten whenever he

implode on himself and everyone around him at any moment.

I see it all, though I'm not really sure anyone sees me.

"It's just a room, Ava."

I'm sure if any one of the Cross family saw me whispering to myself like a lunatic while staring at the door at the end of the hall, they'd throw me out in a heartbeat.

The door looms down the long corridor. The same corridor I travel to go to bed every night as my room is only three doors down.

I swallow over the lump in my throat, tightening my grip on the cleaning cart in front of me.

It's just a room. No harm ever came from cleaning a room.

I'm supposed to clean this room every Monday, but I've been avoiding it since the funeral. Every time I think about entering, my stomach ties up in knots and nausea pools in my stomach.

It's been three weeks, though, and it's time. If I don't clean it now, I never will.

Twisting my master key in the lock, I push the door open, the scent of stale air burning in my nostrils.

Everything is exactly as it was left. The curtains are drawn, shutting out most of the light outside the second-story windows. The air is stuffy, reeking of dust and age, while my mind makes me believe it's decay.

Like they left his body here for me to find.

Obviously, they did not. He's dead and buried. William Cross is gone. So are his beady black eyes that used to follow me around the room while he spewed all manner of vile, cruel things at me.

I blow out a breath through my teeth, ignoring the unease slipping through my veins and push my cart into the room.

I plan to strip the bed—something I'd rather not do, but it needs to be done.

I turn on the music in my headphones, letting the sound of Stevie Nicks wash away all the discomfort in my mind and focus on the task at hand.

People die. Whether it's too early or too late, no one lives forever. It's the people left behind to clean up the mess who are the real victims.

In this case, I'm not speaking about myself.

Yes, changing out the sheets of a dead man's bed is not high on my top ten things I'd like to do list, but I'm also not sad he's gone.

Even if he doesn't deserve it, people are grieving for William Cross.

The Cross siblings not only lost their mother when they were young, but now they've lost their father. All that's left is their mother's sister, Paulina, who raised them like her own when Elizabeth was murdered by her son and husband.

They've suffered so much, yet they all carry their burdens silently. It's just a reminder that my problems are just that. My own, and it's no one else's responsibility to help me.

Levi comes to mind. The way he buries everything so deep, I'm not even sure he knows it's there.

Regardless of how much of an egotistical playboy he is, I know there's a part of him he keeps locked away that won't let him rest.

The walls may be thick, but I can hear him, up at all hours of the night across the hall. I've debated on going over and asking if he'd like to talk so many times, it's become a nightly ritual.

I won't do it, though. After he essentially told me to mind my own business at the funeral, I've been avoiding him.

Levi Cross is not my problem.

The more time I spend cleaning the room, the more I feel like I'm being watched. Like someone is standing right behind me, just waiting for me to let my guard down.

I wouldn't put it past William Cross to come back to haunt this place, though I'm sure he'd be much better suited as a servant of hell.

I focus on one task at a time, dusting the furniture in the room, and cleaning the ensuite that William barely used. I even put all the belongings back exactly where they were after I finish, right down to the medicines on the bathroom counter.

Really, I'm just avoiding the bed, but that's neither here nor there.

Finally, accepting defeat, I tug the sheets off and shove them in a trash bag, trying not to think about why they're stained.

Bile slips up my throat and I swallow it down, tying the bag in a knot and tossing it to the cart like it had caught fire.

I blow out a breath, closing my eyes.

The hard part's over.

Time to get the hell out of here.

Unfortunately, when I turn around, I run right into a brick wall.

I scream, stumbling back until I fall onto the bed, only to be filled with horror and launch myself in the other direction until I crash to the floor.

When I look up, it's into the eyes of the devil himself.

We haven't spoken in three weeks. Not since the funeral when he treated me like I was Typhoid Mary, spreading the plague through all the lands.

He's so handsome, sometimes it's hard to look at him. In fact, most of the time, I can't. I've always struggled with eye-contact, especially with men. It was just a rule growing up in my family that you didn't make eye-contact, especially when you were in trouble. With Levi, though, it's worse. Like little electric shocks that sing across my skin where his gaze touches.

Now, I allow myself one glance at that perfectly carved face. The light, barely visible scar on his lip. The strong, tall muscles of his body hidden under a black hoodie and dark jeans. The icy blue eyes that seem to always follow me as if I'm doing something wrong.

Dark hair, broad shoulders, dark stare.

Levi Cross is sin personified.

His mouth is moving, but I can't hear him through the music in my headphones. Heart hammering in my chest, I reach up with shaky hands and remove them.

"What the fuck are you doing in here?" Levi snaps, his stare cold and his tone harsh. He towers over me, and I scramble to my feet, keeping as much space between us as I can.

"Cl-cleaning," I reply, stuttering from the adrenaline rushing through me. I use the dresser to drag myself up onto shaky legs, my heart beating rapidly against my ribcage.

"Get out."

My mouth falls open; the words caught in my throat. I can't look him in the eyes because doing so is like staring into the sun.

"I-it's Monday—"

"I don't give a fuck if it's Christmas. Get. Out."

My feet are frozen to the floor and I'm unable to move. I stammer through an apology, but Levi doesn't care, grabbing me by the upper arm and dragging me from the room. He grabs my cart, next, shoving it out the door and locks the room up tight behind him.

When he's done, he steps up in front of me, so close, I have no choice but to meet his gaze when he backs me into the wall.

His hand comes up to grip my chin and force my gaze to his. His eyes are all-consuming—deadly—and my heart bottoms out at the feral depravity in his gaze. "The next time I see you in that room," he murmurs darkly. "I'll spank your ass." He leans forward, his lips only inches from my ear and a shiver ghosts through me when his breath brushes over my bare skin. "And I'll make sure you like it."

And with that, he storms off down the hall, taking the bag of stained sheets with him while I try to remember how to breathe.

Night had swallowed Cross Estate whole.

I wake to the creak of footsteps on the wooden floor just outside my door—slow, deliberate, too measured to be accidental. Each step thrums in time with my pulse, a rhythm of dread counting down to something I can't yet name.

One . . . two . . . three . . .

He's come every night for the past three weeks. No one else knows. Not his family, not the staff. Only me.

He slips in under the cover of darkness like a ghost that never truly left. Always the same hour—two in the morning—when the house is asleep and even the walls seem to breathe softer.

Sometimes he opens my door. Just a crack. Just enough to watch me as I pretend to sleep. Then he closes it without a sound.

Other nights, he disappears into the room across the hall—his old room, still untouched—staying only long enough to remind me he's real.

But tonight is different.

Tonight, the footsteps don't stop at his door.

They keep going.

Past mine.

Past the others.

Toward the very end of the hall, where the air grows colder and the silence feels like it's holding its breath.

And somehow, without even seeing him, I know someone is going to die at Cross Estate tonight.

THUD

I jump awake to the sound of footsteps outside my bedroom door, followed by soft giggles.

"You're bad," a woman says, and it takes a moment for my eyes to adjust to realize where I am.

My heart pounds in my chest, chasing away the remnants of the dream.

It's always the same, but tonight it felt more lifelike.

"Are you going to be bad for me?"

I pause at the brooding voice, listening to the sound of people outside my door.

Oh great. Levi must be meeting someone from his fan club.

"I'm not that kind of girl."

Yes, she is, I mouth to the ceiling.

Look, I'm not bitter. I'm all for women having sex lives and hook-ups, so long as everyone follows the rules and no one gets hurt.

What I'm not for is being woken up for the third night in a row because Levi's trying to get laid.

"What happens here stays between us," Levi croons, and can't help but roll my eyes.

"Yeah, I've heard everything about you," she laughs softly. "Promise to call, and then you disappear. The eternal bachelor."

God, could he get any more predictable?

"It's not like that with you," Levi lies. I know it's a lie because he's said the same thing to the last three women he's brought home. Like I said, I see and hear everything. It's definitely not a blessing. "With you . . . it's different."

"It's different," I mock under my breath, rolling over and covering my head with my pillow. I can't hear what she says, but I'm sure it's something along the lines of Oh, please, Levi. Whisk me to your room so we can keep your housekeeper up all night howling like wildebeest in the wild.

Okay . . . maybe I am bitter.

I don't hear what else is said, but I do have the privilege of hearing the bedroom door slam shut and then something hit it a moment later.

Maybe it's his head, and with any luck, she's knocked him out.

Rolling back over, I stare at the ceiling in defeat.

1 . . . 2 . . . 3 . . .

I glance at the clock when the first moan hits.

Three in the morning. Looks like sleep is out the window for me . . . again.

Wonderful.

Slipping from the bed, I cross to the dresser on the other side of my rented room and open the top drawer. I don't have many clothes, but what I do have conceals the box hidden underneath it all.

"God, you're amazing," Random Woman #4 moans across the hall, and I reach for my phone resting on my nightstand, reading over the message again.

Unknown: One week.

The room feels smaller suddenly, the shadows in the corners creeping closer. I swallow hard, ignoring the sounds from across the hall while I try to quell the chill slipping through me.

Like I'm being watched.

Ava: Who are you?

The reply is almost instant, and it fills my heart with dread.

Unknown: You can call me Black.

I count to three, something I started doing not long after I started at Cross Estate. It doesn't help, but it's what the mentally sound people do when they're feeling anxious, so I like to pretend I'm the same.

One . . .

Two . . .

Three . . .

I shiver, even though my room is warm, and check the shadows in the corners for any ghosts lurking with oxygen masks and beady dark eyes.

Unfortunately, the chill is somewhere deeper. A part of me locked away that I refuse to access. Like a girl trapped in a closet screaming for someone to let her out.

Sadly, I don't think it will be me.

CHAPTER
Three

LEVI

There's nothing like waking up to the scent of citrus and lavender in the air.

Except for when the little brat wearing the intoxicating perfume barges through the door at noon with the vacuum on the *destroy the sound barrier* setting.

I groan, grab the pillow beside me, and hold it over my head.

It doesn't help, but at least I can compose myself before I have to look at her.

Ava doesn't stop, banging into shit and otherwise being a holy fucking terror while she vacuums my room.

"Jesus Christ," I grit, rolling over to find she's not even looking at me. Her headphones are in her ears, and she's sweeping as if I'm not lying right in front of her, dick swaying in the breeze, with a massive fucking hangover.

Without her realizing I'm here, it gives me a moment to check her out. My little housekeeper is something that men used to go to war for. Perfect little body, round ass, pr sound just as sexy moaning my name as it does when she's stuttering out some excuse for being in my father's room.

Ava Ryan is perfect in every way.

And that's why I can't fucking stand her.

Climbing from the bed, I go over to the wall, bend down, and rip the cord from the plug.

My head throbs in the silence that follows.

Ava spins around, letting out a yelp when she sees me there. I doubt the little vacuum tyrant even knew I was here. She's never been very perceptive, especially when it comes to me.

Fucking figures . . .

"Oh my God!" she blurts, her eyes wide as saucers and filled with horror.

I look down, following her gaze.

Oh, right. My dick's still out.

"You want an autograph?" It lacks any humor, because well . . . after being woken up like that, I'm not feeling very humorous.

Ava's cheeks flush a deep shade of crimson, and she looks past me, toward the wall instead.

I almost laugh. I would, were I not still on edge from her waking me up from a dead sleep. I rarely get sleep without strings attached.

"I-I-I . . ."

She's flustered. It's cute. Oddly enough, I've never found anything *cute* before in my fucking life.

Unable to resist fucking with her, I step closer, and she backs up abruptly until she crashes into the dresser behind me.

Yeah, just as I thought. I'd chew her up and spit her out before breakfast.

"If you wanted a peek, all you had to do was ask."

"I'm s-sorry," she stammers, feet still rooted in place

where she's pressed back against the dresser. "I-I'll go."

"Where's the fun in that?" She doesn't respond, though I can hear her sharp little intake of breath.

Fuck, I forgot how beautiful she is up close. Like she was handcrafted to ruin me.

"Come on, Ava. You woke me up for a reason. Might as well make it worth it."

Her eyes find mine for only a split second, and finally, fucking finally, she decides to fight back.

"Did I?" she counters. "Wake you?"

"What's the matter, sweetheart?" I know exactly what she's referring to, and I'm not sorry. No matter how much she's on my mind, some subconscious part of me needs to prove to her that it doesn't mean anything. Why else would I bring random girls home every night? "Lonely over there in your little prudish bubble?"

"You've woken me up for the last three nights with your . . . *fans*," she says haughtily, crossing her arms over her chest. Of course, my eyes follow, and she notices me checking her out, only making her glare at me more.

Grabbing a pair of boxers from the end of the bed, I slip them on. Forgive me, but fucking with her makes my dick hard, and the last thing I need is her knowing that.

"So, you were eavesdropping."

Her cheeks darken even more, and she looks away.

I want her to meet my gaze, but she refuses. Part of me wants to break that habit. The other half is grateful. Staring into her eyes is like staring into an eclipse. Fucking dangerous.

"I'm just asking you to at least be considerate that there are other people here that work for a living and have to get up early."

How could I forget? I've only been reminded of that simple fact every time I've caught a whiff of her intoxicating perfume in the last six months she's worked here. It's like that shit's hardwired to go straight to my dick.

Don't even get me started on the rest of her.

Suddenly, I'm acutely aware of the little brat standing in my space. Her scent. The little baby hairs blowing in the fan—the ones that frame her delicate face. Fuck, the blush on her cheeks. The fire in her eyes.

Bad idea, Cross . . .

Unfortunately, I'm full of those.

"So, you're jealous."

Her mouth falls open, and I chuckle low and dark under my breath.

"Of course not."

"When was the last time you got laid, Ava?"

"None of your business," she snaps.

Her cheeks flame when I take a step toward her. Then another until her perfect ass hits the dresser. She lets out a sharp intake of breath when I stop in front of her. Close enough that she can feel the heat of my body. Far enough away that she can't feel how hard my cock is. How my heartbeat's rocketing out of control in my chest.

. . . Just how much I enjoy these spats with her.

"You wish it were you in my bed at night? Making you come until you can't hold it anymore? Until you can't be quiet no matter what you do?"

Her lips purse, and she glowers at me. I still catch the shiver that rolls through her and the way her thighs tighten.

This is what I live for. She fires off at me. I fire back. The highlight of my day is fighting with Ava Ryan, and I'd be lying if I didn't fantasize about bringing her back to my room every single night, instead of the girls I bring home.

Fuck, I can't get her out of my head.

She's burrowed her way into my brain. In every single one

of my darkest fantasies.

It's fucking madness.

"You know what I think, little ghost?"

"Don't call me that," she grumbles, bending herself back over the dresser in an effort to get away from me.

The lamb and the big bad wolf.

I smirk, leaning forward and placing both my hands on the dresser beside her, effectively caging her in. She's so small, I tower over her, especially at this angle. She keeps her eyes on my chest, refusing to meet my gaze.

"I think you're pissed off because I'm not bringing you into my room at night. I bet if I slipped my hand into your panties right now, you'd be soaking wet for me." She swallows audibly, a tremor moving through her. She looks to the side when I press just that hair's breadth closer, nearly aligning my body with hers. "That what you want?" Her breath hitches when I reach up, dragging my knuckles down the side of her neck. "You want to be fucked until you don't have to think about anything but me and the things I'm doing to you, sweetheart?"

Fuck, she smells like heaven. Like salvation.

Like everything I can't fucking have.

"You're an asshole," she grits, her voice breathier than usual. "And I wouldn't sleep with you if you paid me a million dollars."

"Is that so?"

A throat clears behind us, and Ava launches away from me like I've just spontaneously caught fire. I don't move for a moment because I don't give a fuck who's at the door. I'm having too much fun.

"Ava, what are you doing in here?" Paulina's voice is stern, and I cock a brow in her direction. She's never been outwardly warm toward the housekeeper, which is strange to me. Usually,

Paulina loves the strays with as much heart as anyone else in the family.

I mean, fuck, she practically keeled over when Mila went missing the second time.

"I-I-I'm sorry."

There's that *I'm sorry* shit again. I'll break that habit if it fucking kills me.

"I'll just go."

"I think that would be wise," Paulina says, her cheeks flushed with irritation.

Ava rushes to grab the sweeper cord, but I beat her to it. Picking it up, I don't hand it to her. I look right over her head at Paulina, and judging by the way her lips tighten, she understands exactly what I'm saying.

I'm the only one allowed to fuck with Ava. Aunt or not, I won't tolerate her hostility.

"It's okay, Paulina," I murmur, stepping right into Ava's face. She glowers up at me, and the eye contact sears. "She can look if she wants. We both know she wouldn't know what to do with it if she got her hands on it."

And then I drop the cord in her hand and push past her into the bathroom to shower and jerk off to the image of the pretty little housekeeper on her knees for me, moaning my name.

My brother doesn't look up from his newspaper when I plop down in the chair across from him.

"Rough night?"

"Fuck off," I grumble, scrubbing a hand over my hair. It's getting long, but I have no desire to go to a barber and get it

26

cut. Barbers require small talk. I'm not one for small talk.

"Paulina came to tell me you were rude to her this morning."

Snitch.

"Paulina was rude to the housekeeper."

Christian smirks. "*Just* a housekeeper, or a particular housekeeper?"

My brother is turning into a gossip.

"Does it matter? She's staff."

"Funny how that only applies when you're trying to talk yourself out of fucking her."

"Please, tell me more, Mr. Psychologist. I'd love to hear what other theories you've got."

"Therapy might do you some good. Fix that loose screw in your head."

"Therapy's for bitches."

Finally, he folds the paper down and sits on the desk in front of him, chuckling under his breath.

"Must be getting old," I remark, nodding to the paper. "You're really stepping into this whole dad role, aren't you?"

"I'm not a dad," he grunts, grabbing a cigarette from his desk. The moment he pops it between his teeth and reaches for the lighter, the doorknob behind me turns, and he spits it out like a dog caught with something it shouldn't have.

I chuckle because Mila steps in, completely oblivious, while Christian shoots me a death glare, warning me not to tell her.

Fucking whipped.

"Oh, there you are," Mila sighs. "I've been looking for you."

"Me?"

My brother's wife has really ingrained herself in the lodge by now. She's been here a few months, and it's like she grew up here her whole life. Bella and Paulina love her. The staff love her. I've even grown a soft spot for her after everything that happened because I know, as much as I don't want to believe in it, she loves my brother with everything she's got.

"Yes, you. I need to know if you're bringing a date to the Christmas party."

The Oak Ridge Lodge is renowned for hosting the most extravagant Christmas parties for its affluent guests. There's live music, the finest foods, and enough eggnog to supply an army.

I fucking hate it.

"I'm not going."

"But you have to go. You're a Cross."

"So are you," I shoot back.

Mila smiles sweetly, though I can see the vinegar hiding beneath the surface. That smile says it all. *Come or else.*

"And I'm going." She nods to Christian, who's discreetly trying to recover his cigarette from the carpet below, before Mila sees it. He's been promising to quit for ages. I just think he says that so she'll still fuck him. He pauses, looking between us, clearly oblivious. "Christian's going."

"What's going on?"

"Your *brother* is trying to skip the Christmas party this year."

I don't know what she means by this year. I skip it every year. It's a tradition.

"Oh, how could you?" Christian smirks my way, and Mila glares at him.

"Christian . . . I worked hard on this."

He lets out a sigh and concedes. "She's right. You should come."

Whipped.

"Call me crazy, but I don't feel the Christmas cheer in the

air."

"Oh, come on," Mila grits. "It's my first year helping, and I worked really hard. Bella worked hard, too. The least you could do is be supportive."

"I am," I nod. "From afar."

"You can bring a date," Mila wags her brows, grinning like that's supposed to make a difference.

"I'll pass."

"You can bring Ava."

I swear to fucking God.

Why does everyone insist on bringing up that little brunette brat currently reigning terror on dust bunnies somewhere with the vacuum?

"Why would I do that?"

Christian chuckles behind his desk. Fucker's enjoying this entirely too much.

"I'm not bringing Ava to the Christmas party, Mila."

She places her hands on her hips, soft blonde ringlets flying around her in a huff.

"Why, because she's the maid?"

"Because I'm not going."

She glowers at me and starts to argue again when her phone buzzes in her hand. She pauses, staring down at the screen.

"Bella needs me," she growls, raising the phone to her ear. "But we're finishing this discussion later."

Christian's gaze follows her as she exits, like the girl hung the moon and stars.

"Does she let you wear your balls during the day, or is that a special occasion kind of thing?"

Christian places the cigarette back between his teeth and lights the end, blowing out a puff of smoke.

"Do you keep track of all the women you fuck by color-coding them by hair color, or their kinks?" he counters.

"The best part about being single is that I don't have to worry about them once they leave. No organization necessary."

He shakes his head, chuckling. Christian's always been a one-woman kind of man, and that one woman is Mila fucking Cross.

For six years, I watched him chase after her until he finally caught her. Now, I fear for the world if someone comes after her. He almost destroyed it the last time. I don't think it'll be standing if it happens again.

I'm happy for him. I really am. It's just not for me.

Women want to talk. They want to share secrets, chat about feelings, and otherwise look into your brain and figure out what makes you tick. I'd rather shut my dick in a car door than talk about what goes through my head, so staying single just makes sense. No fuss. No cleanup after messy break-ups. Just sex and the occasional dinner date.

It hasn't steered me wrong, yet.

"How's she doing, by the way?"

It's been almost two months since Mila was kidnapped and almost two months since I nearly lost what was left of my family. I watched my brother almost lose himself because he thought Mila had left him.

Why anyone would give another person that kind of power over them is beyond me. Just knowing there's another person walking around with your heart and sanity in the world? That shit sounds fucking terrifying.

Couldn't be me.

It will *never* be me.

"She's good. She's adjusting well. Fuck, sometimes I think she's handling it better than I am."

"She's resilient," I murmur, keeping my voice low. "She's been through this before. She's probably just ready to live a life where she doesn't have to be afraid anymore."

"I want that too," Christian says darkly, his eyes on a picture of him and Mila on his desk. "I'm just trying to decide if it's really over or not."

"Sebastian's dead. Talia's in jail. Dad's dead. It's over."

"I hope so." He's quiet for a moment. "What about you?"

"What about me?"

"What are you going to do now that it's over? Try to go back to the DEA?"

"I'm still figuring it out."

"Well, don't wait too long," he says, and I get the feeling the asshole's not just talking about work. "Sometimes the thing we want the most is right in front of us."

CHAPTER
Four

AVA

"Thank you for taking me to see the bunnies."

"Anytime, Ava from the main house," Alex chuckles with a smile. It's been our running joke for the last few months since I met him. Mostly because I live in the main house and he, who lives in an apartment in the small town a few miles away from the lodge, can't fathom what that must be like.

I hate to tell him, but it's definitely not all it's cracked up to be. You can't even get any sleep.

Alex works security here at Oak Ridge Lodge, and today, he found a nest of baby bunnies hiding out and waiting for their mother to return. He brought me down to see them, and they were the best thing I'd seen all week.

Over the last few months, he's become a good friend and someone I can talk to when I'm annoyed about something in the house that I'd rather *not* discuss with Mila. I love the girl, but she tells her giant husband everything.

"I'm sorry to say, the only bunnies I can show you are

"About that . . ."

"Uh-oh," I chuckle. "Don't tell me you've got another business proposal to discuss?"

He chuckles, scrubbing a hand through his dirty-blonde hair.

"No, nothing like that this time."

"Well, then what is it?"

"Bobby's holding a party next week," he says. "I was wondering if you wanted to go?"

I can't help but cringe at the thought of going to a party.

"I don't know if that's a good idea . . ."

"Come on, Ava. Come out with me and enjoy yourself. You can't let them keep you locked up in there forever."

"No one's keeping me locked away," I chuckle, though he's not that far off the truth. Escaping Cross Estate unnoticed is like trying to swim away from Alcatraz.

Suicide.

"Who's going?"

"Everyone from the lodge . . . Me . . . I was hoping you'd say yes, as kind of . . . like a date."

I freeze at the mention of the word *date*, my hands clamming up.

"We've talked about this, Alex. We're . . . friends."

He chuckles, but it's far from humorous.

"When are you going to stop friend-zoning me, Ava?"

"I'm not," I lie. "I'm just saying, what if things get awkward?"

"I'm not proposing. I'm just saying we have fun together. What's the harm in seeing where things go? I'm a nice guy, aren't I?"

I wince, my teeth digging into my lip.

"I don't know. I just—" I pause when a familiar dark cloud walks out of the house toward his car.

Two days ago, in his room, he basically told me I needed to get laid. I haven't been able to stop thinking about it since.

Levi Cross naked was something to behold, and I'm ashamed to say that I couldn't help but notice . . . *him*. Seriously, how is it that big?

A shiver moves through me, remembering the incident. The way my body reacted to his proximity. The cut of his hips where they form that little V that makes women go feral.

The scent of the forest, whiskey, and everything that makes up Levi Cross has been seared into my senses since.

Alex notices my steps falter, and his stare darkens when he follows my gaze.

Alex doesn't like Levi. Levi doesn't like Alex, but then again, Levi doesn't like anyone.

Least of all, me.

"Is this about Cross?" My cheeks flame at the mention of his name. I haven't spoken to him since he cornered me in his room.

"What about him?" I snap, my tone a little too defensive.

Judging by the way his shoulders tense, Alex picks up on it.

"Seems like a real dickhead."

I swallow past the harsh burn in my throat. Of course, Levi's a dickhead. He's crude, abrasive, and harsh.

He's also had a hard life, and I refuse to believe there isn't something good in him.

"He's had a lot to deal with."

"Yeah," Alex scoffs. "I'm sure that silver spoon doesn't taste great once it's tarnished."

"He's not like that," I argue, and Alex stops on the path, looking down at me. "His dad just died," I add, softening my tone. I'm the *last* person who should be standing up for Levi, but I've also heard his nightmares. Seen the shadows in his eyes when someone mentions his father. I know that pain, and as much as I don't like him, I can sympathize.

"So? Your dad's dead. You aren't walking around with a stick up your ass."

I bite back my retort and suck in a deep breath. I don't actually know that my father's dead, but after more than twenty years and not a single trace, I'd say it's safe to assume he's probably resting on the bottom of some lake somewhere, completely oblivious to the daughter he left behind.

"He's going through a hard time. Money doesn't make your problems go away." *It makes them worse.* "Have you even spoken to him?"

"Have you?"

"I have." *Not really.* "I'm just saying, don't be too quick to judge. People have a way of surprising you."

If you want the truth, as terrifying as he can be, there's a strange part of me that feels safe with Levi. Like nothing can touch me as long as I've got the big bad wolf on my side.

Yes, he's dangerous, but oddly enough, I know he'd never be dangerous to *me*. At least, not physically. My heart? Now that's a different story.

"Look," Alex starts, his voice quieter than before. "I'm not trying to be a dick. I know old man Cross just died. I'm just saying to watch yourself."

"What are you talking about?" I ask around the bitter taste in my mouth.

Alex's eyes darken, his jaw tense. "I've seen men like him get what they want far too many times."

"How would you know what Levi wants?" I challenge, but he's looking over my head. I don't have to turn around to know who he's looking at. Still, I do and find that frosty stare lingering on mine across the path.

Levi's expression is unreadable. His gaze dark and

haunting as always, but there's something else there in the tension in his shoulders.

Alex stiffens, and he chuckles dryly, shaking his head.

"You're right," he concedes when Levi climbs in his car and drives off. "I haven't got a clue what he wants.

Since I was a kid, reading has been my escape. Mainly romance, now, but as a kid, I loved anything fantasy. Bonus points if there were vampires, because I was one of *those* kids. You know . . . the ones that fantasized about starring in their own personal *Twilight* hell.

Anything to take my mind off what life really was. The constant stream of men my mother brought home every few weeks. It was always the same. She'd profess her undying love for Bill, or Jim, or John, and even Hector, the antique she met at a bar, but after a few weeks, that undying love would fizzle out late at night in the form of three a.m. screaming matches.

Because I couldn't sleep over the cursing and fighting and broken glass, I took to reading to keep myself occupied until her boyfriends either left or dissolved into acts no ten-year-old kid should ever have to hear.

That habit bled over into my adult life, and now, I'm sitting in the window nook in my bedroom, reading to take my mind off things.

It's late, and I should be getting ready for bed, but I can't sleep. It's not that I'm not tired. I've barely slept more than a few hours a night all week, even *with* Levi being quiet, for once. I would like to think maybe he took what I said to heart, but I have a feeling it's more about the fact that he's barely been home than anything remotely respectable.

He seemed . . . different today. Darker. Stressed, even.

I can't help but wonder what goes on behind the scenes at both Cross Estate and the Oak Ridge Lodge that I'm not privy to. I hear a lot, but mostly tidbits, and though Mila and I are close, I know she doesn't tell me everything. I'm not even sure *she* knows.

I'm afraid that if I know the full story, I'll no longer feel the slight sense of security I've come to find in my mundane life of cleaning the Cross Estate.

I've got enough problems to worry about without adding the Cross's and their killer family members to the list.

Not to mention the brooding psychopath that sleeps across the hall . . .

It's not that I'm afraid of Levi. I just . . . don't know how much I should trust him. Since I came here, he's been nothing but cold or rude, right up until the other morning when I stumbled into his room to find him completely naked and nearly had a heart attack.

That morning . . . he was *hot*. A bully ready to humiliate me because he enjoyed the way I blushed at his crude words.

I wasn't lying when I told him nothing could get me into his bed.

Forgive me, but I actually have to *like* someone before I'll sleep with them, and Levi hasn't given me any reason to. He thrives on intimidation. He sleeps around, and he's got the mouth of a seasoned sailor.

Never mind that what he said the other day has been replaying in my head since.

A rush of heat slips through me, remembering his dirty words. Men like Levi don't make idle threats. I fully believe if I found myself in his bed, I wouldn't come out of it in one piece.

Blowing out a breath, I sit up straighter and reread the

same paragraph for the fourth time. Unfortunately, I can't stop thinking about the little lines in Levi's hips that make women go feral.

Is it bad that everything he described made my knees feel weak? Or that the growl in his voice made my thighs slick with need.

Or that I'm maybe picturing him in place of the man in this book?

As if he's standing over my shoulder, I pull the book closer to myself, reading a few lines where the man is spanking the woman. Then a few more because now that I've started, I don't want to stop.

Even in my fantasy, he's as handsome as sin.

The universe must be mocking me, because a thud sounds outside and I pause, peeking out the window, my heartbeat rocketing in my chest.

Levi stalks from the house, barely visible in the black he's wearing, but I see him. Broad shoulders. Black tousled hair that I would love to run my fingers through. Impossibly long legs and a butt that taught me male butts can be hot, especially in dark denim.

Oblivious to me watching from above like a creep, he stalks to where his fancy black car has been sitting out front and takes a drag of the cigarette in his mouth, blowing out a cloud of smoke, before tossing it to the side. I can't help but roll my eyes at his littering.

Figures. It's always the hot ones.

I huff and flip back to my book, ignoring him, but I can't focus on anything else when the engine roars to life.

He's leaving again. He always leaves late and comes back home around three or four in the morning. I can't help but wonder where he's sneaking off to. Especially when every night he comes home, I hear him open my door and peer in quietly before he shuts it again.

Looking back out the window, the headlights cut on, and he doesn't move for a long moment, as if he's watching me through the dark tint of his windshield.

I can practically feel his gaze searing into mine, reminding me of what he'd said about having me in his bed.

"You want to be fucked until you don't have to think about anything but me and all the things I'm doing to you, sweetheart?"

"God, Ava. He's just a man," I growl under my breath, and turn my head away, making myself look busy by pretending to read instead of anything productive because I can't focus.

It's no use. The blonde male main character in this book isn't the same.

Why are men with messy black hair always so attractive?

After a long moment, Levi revs the engine once, then, like a demon in the night, he speeds off down the drive.

Finally, when the sound of the car disappears, I let out the breath I'd been holding, leaning my head back against the wall behind me.

Okay, maybe he's right.

I do need to get laid.

CHAPTER
Five

LEVI

I've found heaven in the blood I can spill in underground street fighting.

I slip through the crowd of men and the few women that find themselves here, the scent of weed and sweat overpowering as I pass the cage in the center of the room.

Two men are in the ring, each one battered and bruised. Some might find it horrifying—taking joy in bashing another man's face in. I think it's exactly what this world needs more of.

The ability to let go of all social constructs and fight shit out like grown men. Release the pent-up frustrations that we all face on a day-to-day basis without having to worry about the repercussions.

It's why I found this place. The adrenaline rush it gives me. I come alive the moment I step through the door.

No one knows I'm DEA. Well . . . former DEA. No one knows my family is one of the richest in the state. No one knows Christian Cross, my FBI big brother, or his twin,

Here I'm just me. Whatever version I want to be.

I slide up to the bar and take a seat. The place used to be a dog-fighting ring until Diego, the man who owns the Tomb, "bought" it for the low price of two .45 bullets and a whole lot of bloody mop water.

"Back again, I see."

I glance up at the bartender with fire-engine red hair.

"Tough crowd," she says, slipping a beer across the counter toward me. "Sure you want to fight tonight?"

I take a swig of the beer, ignoring the bad taste on my tongue. I've always hated beer, but you'd have to be an idiot to come into a place like this completely sober, and my flask isn't allowed.

"Tough crowd every night," I muse, and Cherry comes around the bar, falling onto the stool beside me.

Cherry's sweet . . . ish. I may or may not have spent a few drunken nights, maybe at her place, but not in a while. Don't get me wrong. She's a nice girl. She's lived a rough life, and she deserves to get out of this place. I'm just not the one who's going to give her that. I can barely keep myself alive.

Not to mention, those soft green eyes that seem to be burned into the back of my fucking eyelids lately.

"What are you doing here, Cherry?"

She cocks a delicate brow at me and takes the beer out of my hand. I let her because it tastes like ass.

"What else would you suggest I do, Black? Sell cookies outside the local nunnery?"

They call me "Black" for my hair. And for my black heart. When I get in the ring, I don't hold back. Everything fades away, and I don't have to think. I can just let go.

Not to mention, giving them my real name is suicide.

"Beats slinging beer to lowlifes."

"You forget *you're* one of the lowlifes I sling beer to?"

"No, I didn't forget."

She shakes her head, laughing under her breath.

"Where've you been, anyway? I haven't seen you around in the last couple of weeks."

"Been busy."

She smirks, wiping away a drop of beer that slips down her chin.

"By busy, you mean hiding out in some poor girl's apartment, don't you?"

"Jealous?"

"Nah," she chuckles. "I know I was your favorite."

"Or maybe I was just that drunk."

"Right back at you, Black."

We both turn around to watch the ring when a whistle's blown. Whistles mean someone got hurt, and when I say someone got hurt, I mean someone's either broken or someone's dead.

A guy gets dragged out by two men, blood oozing from his mouth, while the crowd cheers on the man who did it to him. That's just how it is here.

I once saw a man get stabbed with a broken bottle. He nearly bled out before his girlfriend managed to drag him out of the ring and presumably to a hospital.

The only rule is that your identity gets left at the door, and no one runs their mouth about what really goes on in the Tomb.

Anything else is fair game. Except for bottles. Diego said there was too much blood.

"You should think about it," Cherry says without missing a beat, and I cast a sideways glance at her. Cherry's good at confusing the fuck out of me. "I mean, find a nice girl and settle down. You know, instead of doing whatever the hell it is you're doing."

Here we go.

"Why would I do a fool thing like that, when I can just come here and see you?"

She rolls her eyes, not buying any of my bullshit.

"Because contrary to popular belief, I don't actually like you. I just think you're pretty."

Never in my life have I been called pretty, but coming from Cherry, I know it's best to just take it as a compliment.

"I mean it, Black," she says, her voice quieter. As if talking about life outside the warehouse around us is forbidden. She glances back at the ring, where a couple of men are mopping up the blood from the last fight. "I see people get hurt in here every night. People die. This . . . isn't the place for you."

My number is called, and Cherry winces when I move to stand.

I appreciate her concern, but she's wrong.

This is exactly the place for me.

Plucking my beer back from her, I down the rest of it before setting it down with a grin.

"Hope you bet on me."

She doesn't return the smile.

I hear her growl as I make my way to the ring in the center of the room. There's a few bigwigs on the sidelines. Mostly businessmen who come to bet on these fights like we're animals in a cage, but . . . then again, isn't that what we really are?

The degenerates of the world who can't live without violence. Who need the pain to feel alive and take comfort in knowing places like this exist.

A few of them eye me when I walk to the ring, slipping my hoodie off as I go, along with my T-shirt.

A few people holler my name when I step into the ring, but I ignore them. I'm not one to make friends, and I'm not taking any of the women here home tonight.

Wouldn't want my little housekeeper to miss any sleep.

I toss my shit on the stool right outside the ring and take my place in the center of the cage. The guy who enters on the other side of me is notorious for pulling switches out mid-fight, but I'm not afraid of him, nor am I afraid of dying.

Shit comes with the territory. Don't get in the ring if you value your life. I couldn't give a fuck less about mine.

"You both know the rules," Diego says over the noise of the crowd cheering around us. I nod, as does Spinner, the long-standing champ grinning in front of me.

He's only the champion because he hasn't fought me yet. To win at this game, you've got to have a lot of pent-up rage, and I've been saving mine for the last two decades.

At twenty-seven, I've watched my mother burn to death. Watched my brother meet the same fate after he tried to kill the rest of my family. I've survived things that I would rather have let kill me, and yet, here I am, carrying on, though every day feels like a struggle to understand who the fuck I am.

Am I a Cross? A DEA agent? Just some scum of the earth lowlife who hangs out at underground fighting rings and enjoys how it feels to fight?

For a month, I've been coming here, and yet every time feels like the very first time. When I found an outlet that didn't come from a bottle and shut off the voices in the back of my mind, even if only for two minutes at a time.

"You get two minutes. No weapons. Just pure adrenaline," Diego instructs, grinning back and forth between the two of us.

Diego lives for this shit, just like the rest of us. We come here because we're what society can't understand—just pure rage simmering beneath the surface with no real outlet.

"Any questions?"

"Yeah," Spinner grins, licking his lips like a fucking psychopath. "When this is over, how long do I have to wait before I go home and fuck your bitch for you, too?"

I chuckle under my breath.

That statement's going to cost him.

"On three."

The crowd cheers, but I let the blood rushing in my ears drown them out.

"One . . . Two . . ."

Spinner lunges for me, and I duck his first strike, grinning through my teeth when he stumbles to the other side of the cage.

This is what I was born and bred for. This is why I'm not cut out for the formal Christmas party or white picket fences. In a world where it's either kill or be killed, I will always come out on top.

Spinner growls through his teeth, whirling on me. I let him circle me in the ring, keeping my back away from him because I know the first chance he gets, he's going to try to get me on the ground. I've seen the asshole fight enough to know what dirty tricks he's got up his sleeves.

The first punch he lands is like the first shot of whiskey in the morning.

I fight back, and though I feel blood coating my teeth, I keep going.

Fighting has become my narcotic, and with each hit, I feel more alive. It's what keeps me coming back here and keeps me from doing something stupid at home, like making the pretty little housekeeper mine.

Everything rushes to the surface. Watching Sebastian die. Watching the life bleed from my father's eyes. The lies. The DEA. The alcohol.

I slam my fist into Spinner's jaw, and I feel a crack. Spinner fights back, and I don't know how much time is left on the clock, but I could do this all night.

Rushing him, I bend down, wrap my arms around his legs, lift him, and drop him. We land in a heap, and the sound that whooshes out of him is agony. He takes the chance and slams his fist into my side, and though I don't feel it now, I'm betting I will later.

Rearing back, I bring my fist down on his face, and time both slows down and speeds up all at once. The adrenaline courses through me like pure oxygen, fueling the fire that's burning in my veins until all I can feel is the rush.

The blood roars in my ears, my body vibrates with energy, and finally, I feel alive.

I punch him over and over again, and when the buzzer rings, I don't even hear it.

Two men pull me back, dragging me away from Spinner, who looks up at me through swollen eyes and spits blood through his teeth. My chest heaves with each breath, and I can't even hear what the men above me are saying as Diego grabs my hand and declares me the winner.

Spinner grins at me, even though he lost, because that's what this place is.

One of us will always lose. Tonight, it's him.

The house is quiet and dark when I get home. I slip through the garage and make my way into the kitchen, getting a bottle of water and downing it before I head upstairs.

When I lost my job, I was living in my own apartment in the city. Nothing big, but it was enough for the little time I was there. I was an undercover agent, so I spent a lot of time away from home. The apartment was really just a place where I could crash when I was off-duty, so I wouldn't have to come here and deal with my father.

Since I was forced into a leave of absence, I moved back home. Those four apartment walls seemed to swallow me the more time I spent there. The ringing silence was enough to drive me fucking insane. It's how I found the Tomb in the first place.

I can't say I regret it. Not completely, at least. As much as I don't want to admit it, being close to my family has helped me forget the complete and utter failure I was when I lost my job. It gives me something else to focus on rather than how fucking pissed off I am that I let shit get to me.

That I let *him* get to me.

I start toward the stairs when a glow from the den catches my eye, and I pause. Stepping over to the door, my sister is curled up in front of the fireplace—a habit of hers since we were kids—while she stares into the flames.

"You're up late," I murmur, leaning against the doorway.

"Couldn't sleep," Bella murmurs, her eyes finding mine. Whatever else she was about to say is lost when her gaze rakes over me, no doubt seeing the blood on my cheek. "Oh my God. What happened?"

"Nothing," I lie. "Just nicked myself shaving."

Christian and I have tried to keep Bella as far away from the dark parts of our lives for as long as possible. And for good reason. She nearly had a breakdown when all our father's secrets came to light. I can only imagine how she would react if she found out I was visiting an underground fight club because it's the only thing that makes me feel alive.

Well, one of the *two* things that makes me feel alive. The other has brown hair, pretty green eyes, and a knack for pissing me off.

"Are you drinking again?"

"Nope, never acquired the taste," I lie, the flask seeming heavier in the back pocket of my jeans.

"You must think I'm really stupid if you think I'm going to believe that."

I shrug. "Believe whatever you want. I'm fine.

She shakes her head, drawing her knees up to her chest. She looks at the picture above the mantel, and I can't help but follow her gaze, locking eyes with my father.

"I wish we could just paint over him," she says quietly.

A pit forms in my stomach. How many times have I thought about burning that fucking picture, only to talk myself out of it because Mom's in it, too?

I watch my sister. She's always been six years old in my eyes. My kid sister, who follows me around and demands I play with her dolls or make-believe. I always did, even if I suffered the consequences later because "boys don't play with dolls," even if it's just to pacify their little sisters.

Looking at her now, I can see the woman she's become, and that scares me. Knowing someday she's going to get married and have a family, just like Christian. Knowing some dickhead's going to come along and say something smooth and eventually, she'll fall for him, not knowing what I know. That he could rip her heart to shreds, and there's nothing I can do to stop it.

Shit feels powerless, and I fucking hate it.

"Why are you really down here, Bella?"

She purses her lips, her dark eyes turning back toward mine. They shine in the glow of the fire, and something like lead fills my chest.

"I told you, I couldn't—"

"The real reason."

She sighs, hugging her legs to her tighter, and looks away. "I just . . . had a nightmare, okay?"

"About?" I already know. I've known since we brought her home; I just have no fucking idea how to talk to her about it.

"You know," she starts, looking down at her hands in her lap. "When Sebastian came and kidnapped me in the middle of the night, I thought I was losing my mind. I had no idea he was even alive, and then all at once, I was learning he killed Mom. He was working for Dad, and Dad was actually a raging narcissist hellbent on stealing everything from us. Then, I realized this is just our family. What's next, Levi? What big secret am I going to learn later on that everyone else knows but me?"

I shake my head. "There are no secrets. Not anymore."

She scoffs.

"Yeah, I'll remember that when it comes out. Paulina was looking for you tonight, by the way."

Of course, she is. She's been trying to talk to me for the last week, and I've been avoiding her.

It's not that I don't care for my aunt. It's that I'm really not in the mood to explain myself right now. She wants to talk. I don't. Simple as that.

"I'll talk to her tomorrow."

"She's worried about you," Bella says, eyeing me. "We all are."

"Why?"

"You have to ask? You're different."

I shrug. "No different than I've always been."

"You're drinking a lot."

"Shit happens."

"Don't be like that. I'm only trying to help. Are you having nightmares again?"

Jesus Christ, why can't anyone let it go?

"When you can get your bad dreams under control, we can

talk about mine."

Her face drops like I'd slapped her, and her eyes shine with tears.

Well, shit.

I should apologize for being a dick, but sometimes, Bella doesn't know when to stop pushing. I won't apologize for not wanting to share my feelings. I'm not one of her girlfriends. I'm not Paulina. I'm also not required to share anything with fucking anybody, at least not here.

She wants to be pissed off, so be it.

"Fine, Levi. Have it your way," she murmurs coldly, and stalks to the door, pushing past me and leaving me to stare after the fire for a lot longer than I think even I realize.

Bella's smart. She knows there's more to the story I'm not telling her. That doesn't mean she's entitled to my nightmares. The shit that haunts my brain every night isn't her problem. Especially not when she's dealing with her own shit.

Heading upstairs, I scrub a hand over my face as I go. I'm exhausted, but I know I won't sleep. Not really.

I'm just about to enter my room when I pause, staring at the door across the hall.

Pushing it open just a hair, I peek my head in, looking at the small form in the center of the large canopy bed.

She doesn't stir at my presence. In fact, she looks peaceful for once.

Soft light filters through the windows, casting her in shadows. My chest clenches watching her. Soft dark hair creates a chaotic halo around her face. Pouty lips parted over her slow, even breathing.

She looks like a goddamned angel, and I'm the devil who stole her away to keep her locked in my cage.

I ignore the nagging thoughts in the back of my head and close the door.

One thing I've learned about angels in the past twenty-seven years?

They lie, and sooner or later, the truth always comes out.

CHAPTER
Six

AVA

Well, bless my stars, is that *my* granddaughter standing before me?"

"Hi, Nana." I grin through the sting her words leave behind and lean down to wrap her in a gentle hug.

"Oh, you can hug me better than that. I'm sick, not made of porcelain."

I can't help but chuckle when she hugs me tighter, and her familiar comforting scent envelops me.

It's been a few days since I've been able to make it out, and the guilt weighs heavily on me. I sink down in the chair beside her while she mutes the TV. "I'm sorry I haven't been by to visit more often."

"Nonsense," she waves a hand, settling back against the over-fluffed pillows behind her head. She looks different. She's paler, like she's not seen the sun in days. Her eyes betray how tired she is, though I can see she's putting up a brave face for me. "I know how busy you are."

out and takes my hand.

I try not to notice how small her fingers are compared to mine. If I think about it too much, I'll cry, and I make it a point to never cry while I'm here. I'll save that for the twenty-minute drive back to Cross Estate while I'm alone with nothing to do but think about my life decisions because my car doesn't have a radio.

"Don't be sad for me, Ava Lynn. I know you have a life to live. I don't expect you to be here every day."

The backs of my eyes sting, but I push the emotions down, intertwining my fingers gently with hers.

Her gaze sweeps over me, taking in my messy braid and the stain on my old hoodie. I'm sure I look like I just climbed out of a sewer, but she only smiles softly.

"Tell me about your life, sweetheart. Meet anyone special recently?" she prods. "A man, perhaps?"

I know where she's going with this, but I don't have the desire, nor the words, to tell her that, apart from a few spicy dreams involving the very hot, very psychotic man that sleeps across the hall from me, I have no desire to mingle with anyone. Opposite sex. Same sex. Nothing.

"I have a couple friends. Mila and Alex. I've told you about Mila, but Alex works at the lodge with me."

Nana gives me a knowing look.

"A friend?"

"*Just* a friend."

"Well, what about this Mila girl? Anything special there?"

I chuckle and roll my eyes. I've only ever been into guys, but Nana's all-inclusive. It wouldn't matter who I brought home; she'd love them all the same if it meant she could have great-grandchildren.

"No, Nana. Mila's married."

"Well, you can't blame me for asking."

"How's the medicine working?" I ask, brushing past the topic of my love life.

She smirks, seeing right through me, but she moves on.

"The same as always. Sometimes I wonder if it's worth it."

My heart drops in panic at the thought that she might not be here someday. Instinctively, my fingers tighten around hers, and she winces. Immediately, I loosen my grip.

"Of course, it's worth it. Does it at least make you feel better?"

"I guess," she yawns. "Though I'm exhausted all the time. I feel like all I do is sleep."

"Sleep is healing."

"Ava," she says softly, her smile sad. "We're going to have to talk about it at some point."

I shake my head.

"There's nothing to talk about, Nana. You're going to keep taking your medicine, and soon the cancer will be gone. I know it."

She's gracious enough to smile at me, though I can almost read her thoughts.

The medicine is pointless. Brain cancer is nearly impossible to come back from, but advanced brain cancer?

Every day I wake up wondering when it will be the last. If I'll be too late visiting her and find her permanently asleep.

"Have you spoken to your mother lately?"

I grit my teeth so hard my jaw aches.

"No . . . Have you?"

"No," she says, her eyes heavy. The medicine wears her out. Especially on the days following her treatment. "Not in a few weeks."

I bite my tongue because what I really want to say isn't conducive to helping her feel better.

So, I say nothing at all.

"Have you thought about speaking to her?"

"No. Why would I?"

It's been years since I last spoke to my mother, and I'd still prefer a dozen more.

"I just . . . I worry about you, Ava."

"No need to worry about me. I've got everything I need."

It's a lie, but Nana doesn't need to know that.

"Well, you promise me if things get tough, you'll speak to her?"

I wouldn't ask my mother for a paper towel, let alone her support.

"Of course."

"Good. You're a good girl, Ava. I just want you to be okay."

As her eyes start to grow heavier, I watch her. It's hard to believe the same woman who used to braid my hair and watch cartoons with me every morning is the same one who lies in bed day in and day out, unable to do any of the things she used to love. Just . . . waiting. Waiting for the next round of medicine. The next meal . . . waiting for death.

Slowly decaying while I can't do anything to stop it.

Sometimes—and I'd never tell another soul this—it's like she's already gone.

"I'm sorry, Ava. I'm just so tired," she yawns, her eyes heavy. "That treatment this morning wore me out."

I pat her hand, sitting silently beside her. This happens more often than not. Nana will fall asleep before I leave, and I'll tuck her in and sneak out. It's become a tradition, at this point.

"It's okay, Nana," I whisper, and despite myself, a tear slips down my cheek. At least she's not awake to see it. The last thing she needs is to worry about my pain, too.

I'm not sure how long I sit there, but eventually, when

she's fallen asleep and all that fills the air is the sounds of her even breathing, and the whir of the machines in her room, I force myself to rise from the chair.

Gently, I stoop down and press a kiss to Nana's cheek, committing her scent to memory in case it's gone the next time I visit.

"I love you, Nana."

I've always hated storms.

The kind that shakes the house when lightning strikes.

Every time the thunder rumbles, my heart squeezes in my chest just a little bit tighter.

Loud sounds have always bothered me. From arguing to fireworks, there's always been that shot of fear that rushes through me, making me sick to my stomach.

Tonight is no different, and it's why I'm still awake, padding down to the kitchen at two in the morning to get a glass of water.

No one's awake, so I don't bother changing out of the giant T-shirt I wore to bed and take the back stairs down to the kitchen. The house is dark and silent. I can't escape the feeling of being watched. Like William Cross's ghost is silently plotting my demise.

The Cross Estate has always given me the creeps. Just thinking about how anyone or any*thing* could be hiding around the corner or watching me from the shadows sets me on edge.

Stepping into the dimly lit kitchen, I cross to the cupboard for a glass, then fill it with water from the fridge. In my haste to get a drink and get the hell out, though, I knock one of the grapefruits off the counter that Paulina insists on force-feeding everyone every single morning, and I have to bend over to pick it up.

"I hate this fruit," I grumble when it rolls away, forcing me to chase after it, ass in the air with nothing on but a black lacy thong.

I manage to grab it and toss it back in the bowl before I turn around to leave.

And stop short when I see none other than the devil himself sitting at the kitchen table, a glass of whiskey in his hand and his eyes trained on my bare ass with a hint of amusement.

I just bent over bare-assed in front of Levi Cross.

I JUST BENT OVER IN FRONT OF LEVI CROSS.

"What are you doing hiding in the shadows like a creep?" I snap, wrapping my arms around myself so he can't see my nipples through my T-shirt.

Levi cocks a brow at me, his gaze sliding over me until it reaches my eyes.

I burn up like I'm gliding into the center of the sun.

Scratch that. That may be enjoyable compared to this.

God, those eyes . . . they could fracture the ozone.

"Are you awake?"

Still, no response.

No, of course not. I'm not one of the bubbly blondes he brings home. Instead, he stands and stalks across the kitchen toward me, forcing me to fall back into the island.

The heavy scent of whiskey settles over me, and my mouth waters. Tingles shoot up my toes, and I grip the edge of the counter behind me for support.

I definitely need it when he leans closer, until his face is mere inches from mine, his hands placed on the marble on either side of mine, effectively caging me in.

It's been a week since that day in his room, and I can't deny my body hums in his presence despite the trickle of fear that slides through me.

His lip is busted, and he's got a bruise forming on his cheekbone like he was in a fight. Unfortunately, it only makes him look more devastating, especially in this light.

Oh, I am so screwed.

"What's the matter, little ghost?" he asks, his voice a heavy mixture of pure seduction and straight danger. The tenor slips through my bloodstream, and my thighs tighten over the aching sensation there. "Couldn't sleep?"

"I wanted water." I don't know why I'm bothering to tell him. It's not like he owns me.

He smirks, his gaze studying me. My skin sears from the eye contact.

"You think you're safe in your secrets, little ghost?"

"Whatever game you're playing, I don't want any part of it," I manage, even if my voice is slightly shaky. He picks up on it, of course, and raises his fingertips to brush them down my cheek.

My skin burns where he touches me, like the flames of hell have crawled up to seduce me to sin.

"And what game would that be, Ava?"

The game where he tries to prove what I already know. There's something about Levi Cross and that devil-may-care smirk that does something for me.

I swallow over the lump in my throat at the way he says my name. My hands grip the countertop harder when his fingers glide across my jaw down to my throat. Gently, he wraps those fingers around my throat, not constricting, but like he's reminding me that he could squeeze the life out of me at any moment.

"If you're trying to scare me, it's not going to happen," I

lie. My tongue darts out to lick my lips, and his gaze follows the movement, darkening like he's deeply disturbed by something.

Leaning forward, the stubble on his cheek brushes against the skin of my neck when neither of us moves. My heart feels like it's going to beat right out of my chest. My thighs are damp with need, and my mind is so scrambled, I'm having a hard time forming a coherent sentence.

It's just a man, Ava. One who has made it perfectly clear from the moment you arrived that he wants nothing to do with you.

I freeze when his lips skate over my racing pulse, leaving a trail of fire in their wake. I grit my teeth to silence the sigh that threatens to leave me, my eyes fluttering closed when his fingers tighten around my throat, just enough to remind me they're still there.

"Your body's begging for me, sweetheart," he murmurs, almost like he's angry about it. I'm not even sure he realizes he's said it out loud.

"I don't want anything to do with you," I whisper, though my core tightens with his words.

My heart hammers in my ears when he grabs my hand off the kitchen counter, slipping it between us and raising it to my throat, before closing his on top of them. He squeezes lightly. Enough for me to feel my pulse racing.

"Feel that?" he breathes, barely above a whisper, and a shiver ghosts through me at the darkness in his gaze. "That's all I need to know you're lying."

"Am I?" I challenge myself to meet his gaze head-on, though it feels like staring into a black hole and trying not to get sucked into its gravitational pull.

Something flashes across his features, and then his fist tightens. I glare back at him, refusing to back down. Fuck him. He doesn't control me.

My heartbeat skitters under my fingertips. Levi notices, his lips tipping up at the corner in a devilish smirk that does something to my body that I'm powerless to stop.

Shame rushes in, my cheeks flaming. The ache between my thighs is embarrassing, reminding me that only two men have ever been there and that to Levi Cross, I probably am a prude. I may as well be naked underneath him right now, with how exposed I feel under that icy blue gaze.

Maybe that's why I'm so excited by it. The idea that a man like Levi Cross could look at me the way he looks at other women. Like I'm something to be desired, not a pest or a puppet.

Not that it matters. Levi has never shown any interest in me. Least of all, sexually. Whatever he's doing right now is a ruse to get me to get under my skin because I bruised his ego when I told him I'd never sleep with him, and I'll be damned if I fall for it.

"What about your secrets, Levi?" I breathe, and he doesn't move for a long moment, continuing to stare down at me with that dangerous black gleam in his eyes. Like he could rip me to shreds with his teeth, his lips pull back into a slight snarl, and if he weren't already devilishly handsome, he would look monstrous.

"Run back to your bed while you can." He releases me, that familiar coldness returning to his gaze. Finally, he looks away, and whatever spell he'd had me under is broken.

I don't stick around to ask what that means. I'm not sure I want to. Instead, I grab my glass of water on unsteady legs and hurry past him toward the kitchen door.

"Oh, and Ava," his voice rings out in the darkness behind me.

Begrudgingly, I turn and find him watching me, something demented in those eyes.

His lips tip up in a smirk.

"Hope you sleep well."

I blink, staring at him and trying to piece together what *that* means because it's absolutely terrifying.

He's just trying to scare me, but I'm not willing to be manipulated.

So, I plaster my sweetest, fakest smile on my lips, clutch my water tighter, and spin on my heel, even though I know he's looking at my ass.

And just because I know he hates it, "Goodnight, *Mr. Cross*."

CHAPTER
Seven

LEVI

The house is quiet as I slip through the back door. It's three in the morning, and my family is asleep. They don't even know I'm here as I step up the stairs to the second story.

It's been three weeks since I left, and every day, I've been quietly plotting. Stewing.

Making my way upstairs, I pass my sister's room, then Ava's. Finally, I pass Paulina's, and the room at the end of the hall beckons to me like an old friend.

Like it knows why I'm here.

The machines around the four-post bed in the center of the room ring quietly in the night. It smells like a hospital past the door, and my chest fills with disgust. I've always hated the scent.

He's asleep in his bed, but when I rip the cord keeping the machines on out of the wall, it only takes a moment before his eyes open. He reaches for the oxygen tube in his nose, confusion on his face.

"It won't work," I say from the shadows, and his eyes go wide as I step into the moonlight. He stares at me in shock, and I grin.

I've been waiting for this day all my life. How many times have I

Now that we know he kept my brother locked away and alive, knowing that he murdered my mother, there's nothing that could stop me. Knowing that the longer he's alive, under the same roof as her . . . *well . . . I just can't let that slide.*

He opens his mouth to speak, but without his precious oxygen tube, nothing comes out but a raspy breath. Stepping forward, I grab a spare oxygen tube from the end of the bed, wrapping it in my hands while I approach.

"Christian wants you to suffer. Tomorrow, you would have been moved to a new facility where you'd probably be kept alive for another few months." I shrug. "I think that's too kind."

And then I lunge for him. We struggle, but I'm bigger than him now. Stronger. Wrapping the tube around his throat, I pull it tight until it's cutting off what little oxygen he can get.

"Le—"

"Shhh . . ." I tighten my hold on the tube, silencing the sound of his gurgling cough, begging for air.

It won't come, though.

It's time for us to move on. Be a family.

Looming over him in the darkness, his eyes are wide with fear and pain.

Good. Now he'll finally know what it feels like to wonder if you're going to die or not.

He struggles feebly underneath me, his bony hands clawing at my wrists to pry me off, but it's no use.

"I always liked Mom better," I murmur, though I'm not even sure he hears me. His hands fall away from mine to the bed with a thud, his eyes glazing over. I listen to the sound of his wheezing breath until it fades, and even then, I don't let go.

I won't stop until he's dead.

When I'm sure he's gone, I release my hold, cracking my knuckles in the silence of the room. The machines keeping him alive start to beep frantically, and I take that as my cue to leave.

I move to stand, only something catches my eye. When I step back, the body isn't my father's.

No, this is much, much worse.

Pale green eyes stare back at me, lifeless under heavy dark lashes. The soft skin that used to glow is now pale, fading away just like the life that once rested inside it.

"Ava."

My voice is strained. My chest tight.

No. No. No. This is all wrong.

Why is she here?

I call out her name. I shake her small form, but she doesn't acknowledge me. She doesn't even blink.

The roar in my ears grows louder. My blood pumps harder.

I killed her. I fucking killed her.

"Murderer," a soft voice whispers. "You're a murderer."

"I'm not—I didn't mean to."

"Murderer. Murderer. Murderer," the voice sings, repeating the word over and over until the roar grows louder and I can't help but cover my ears.

"Murderer, murderer, murderer."

"Stop," I growl.

Everything falls silent. The room around me vibrates. Or maybe that's me.

I look down at the form in the bed and she's just . . . gone.

And then the whispers are right behind me.

"MURDERER."

The moment I sit upright in bed, I'm in my room.

Everything is dark, and the roar in my ears is gone. So are the whispers.

"Fuck." I scrub a hand over my face and try to shake the nightmare off. I'm drenched in sweat and tangled in the sheets like a maniac.

I'm twenty-seven years old. Way too fucking old to be

having nightmares like a child, but still, even as I collapse back to the sheets, I can't wipe the image burned into the backs of my eyes.

It's not real, right? Who cares? It's not like dreaming this shit means anything.

It's just my mind playing tricks on me because I haven't been sleeping enough, but fuck . . . I fucking hate it.

I suck in a shallow breath, staring at the canopy above my head.

The vision of the girl with the lifeless eyes clings to the corners of my brain.

I shouldn't . . .

Fuck it.

Quietly, I slide from the bed and exit my room. Across the hall, I silently twist the door handle and push the door open just enough to peek at the bed.

Still there.

I only allow myself a second, and the scent of citrus washes over me like an aphrodisiac.

Then, I glance at the door at the end of the hall.

I fucking hate that door.

Stalking toward it, I test the knob.

Still locked. Good.

If I had my way, I would have gutted that entire portion of the house, just to get rid of it.

The hair on the back of my neck stands up, almost like the brush of cold fingers sliding down the back of my neck.

Figures. Should have known I'd never really escape him.

Goosebumps rise on my skin, and I swear I feel someone standing behind me.

Only . . . when I turn around, no one's there.

"Go back to hell," I mutter under my breath to whatever unseen force is hovering over me, and head back toward my room.

After all . . . the dead can't hurt you.

Fortunately, neither can nightmares.

"How are you feeling today, Levi?"

You want the truth? The therapist in front of me would shit himself if he knew how I was really feeling.

Suppose I told him I'd spent most of the night lying in bed and staring at the ceiling. My mind alternates between thoughts of the pretty little brunette across the hall and my father's vindictive ghost haunting the space between us.

Suppose for a second, I told him that I can still feel the way his body went slack underneath me when I choked the life out of him.

How when I close my eyes, all I see are his glassy ones, staring back at me.

Do you think I'd be sitting in his plush Seattle office, listening to some bullshit classical music that's supposed to make me feel calm when really it just makes me feel like a fucking idiot for even coming here?

No. I'd be down the street where they throw all the other degenerates and lowlifes who don't deserve to walk the streets.

"Good, I guess."

Dr. Proctor readjusts in his seat, raising his ankle to his knee and showcasing his obnoxious-ass purple socks.

"Why don't you expand on that for me?"

Jesus Christ.

I scrub a hand over the back of my neck, glancing at the

clock on the wall. I've only been here for a bit, but it feels like five fucking years.

"I don't know what you want me to say," I shrug. "I guess I just don't have any complaints."

Proctor nods, though I can tell he's not convinced.

"Tell me, how are you sleeping at night?"

Like shit.

"Good. I get about six or seven hours most of the time."

"And have you been staying away from alcohol like we discussed in your last visit?"

Not at all.

"Yeah. Haven't had a sip."

Listen . . . I know therapists are supposed to help, but I can handle my own problems. Whether I tell him the truth or not, I'll still be lying awake tonight thinking about them.

There's not a doctor in the world who could make sense of the shit in my head. Fuck, I can't even do it, and I've been stuck in it for twenty-seven years.

"And your family? How have things been going there?"

"Good. All is well."

Proctor sets his notebook down on his lap and clasps his hands in front of him expectantly. I don't like the way he looks at me. Like he can read my thoughts before I even know what they are.

Like he can pick out my lies faster than a bee can find honey.

"Levi . . ." he starts, and I can feel the dad-speech coming before it even leaves his lips. "Life is honest. It's brutal and unforgiving. It's harsh, but it also forces us to be truthful with ourselves in the end. The truth isn't meant to be easy, and I think you and I both know you're avoiding it."

Fuck.

I glance at the clock. Another five minutes have passed. I

thought for sure it felt like ten.

"Why don't we start with the basics?" Proctor resumes, opening his notebook and scribbling something down. "Why don't you tell me something easy. Like your childhood?"

I chuckle under my breath.

This fucker has no idea.

"It sucked," I shrug. "Not much else to tell."

"Why don't you walk me through your family? How many siblings did you have?"

"Three."

"And they are . . .?"

"Two boys and a girl."

"And you?"

"And me," I nod. I don't know why the fuck it matters. I don't see Christian sitting beside me. Or Bella. Sebastian's only fortunate that he doesn't *have* that opportunity.

"So, we have a mother and a father, three boys and a girl . . ." Again, I nodded. "How did that work out?"

Jesus, this is painful.

"I don't know. Like any other family, I guess."

"What is your happiest memory from back then?"

When Mom kicked Dad out for a week, and he wasn't there to fuck with me.

"Mom sneaking me out at night to go to this all-night family diner."

"And what would you order there?"

"Is that relevant?"

"Everything we discuss here is relevant, Levi."

I hate it when he says my name. Like he knows some shit I don't.

I blow out a breath between my teeth, willing my composure to slip into place. "We'd get waffle sundaes."

"Can't say I've heard of those before. What are they? Ice

cream and waffles?"

"Yeah, with shit—*stuff* sprinkled on top."

"It's perfectly fine to curse in here. I'm a grown man with three teenage boys. I can assure you, I can handle it." He scribbles something else down in his pad, and I fucking hate it that he's taking notes on me. "And why was this the happiest time for you?"

That one's easy.

"Got to spend time with Mom without everyone else."

"I see. You wrote in your onboarding packet that your mother passed when you were sixteen. I'm very sorry to hear that."

Something is humming in the room, and it's starting to annoy the fuck out of me. Proctor and I sit in silence for a moment before I blurt it out.

"Twelve."

"I'm sorry?"

I suck in a deep breath. "I was twelve when she died."

"My mistake, you're correct. That's a young age to lose one's mother. Can you tell me how she passed?"

The trickling irritation that had been slowly festering in my blood finally flares up, and before I can stop myself, I snap.

"My brother murdered her and burned the family cabin down with her in it because my father put him up to it."

Proctor pauses, and I think for probably the first time in his career, he's at a loss for words.

Good. Teach the fucker to write notes about me.

"So, yeah. I guess you could say it was hard," I murmur, tugging the collar of my hoodie away from my neck. Why the fuck is this room so stuffy?

Proctor is quiet for a long time before he scribbles something else down in his pad. Probably some bullshit about how fucked in the head I am.

"And was law enforcement ever involved?"

"Only after the fucker was dead."

Proctor nods, taking off his glasses and setting them down in his lap.

"And when was that?"

Here we go.

"Two months ago."

Proctor nods like he's got it all figured out. Fucker doesn't know anything about that night, and neither does anyone else.

Only Christian, Sebastian, and I really know what went down that night, and well . . . one of us is dead.

"I think what you're feeling is entirely valid. To go through so much at the hands of a family member is unspeakable. But . . . you aren't telling me what happened to *you*, just the facts of what your family went through. I won't push you more on it today, but I think it's important to remember why you're here."

"Because it was either this or the DEA would send me to prison?"

"No," Proctor corrects. Bullshit, we both know that's the only reason I'm here. "To clear your mind of the guilt that's holding you back."

I think back to the thousands of dollars' worth of equipment I destroyed three months ago when everything came to a head.

They said it was some kind of mental break.

I think it was more along the lines of a mental rewiring.

Breaking that shit felt good, and even if I have therapy or prison looming over my head, I'd do it again if given the chance.

"I don't feel guilty for anything."

Lie.

Proctor eyes me over his glasses like the guy with a beard in *Harry Potter*. "Now, Levi . . . Are you being truthful with yourself?"

Does it matter?

Like a saving grace, the buzzer chimes, and I can breathe a sigh of relief.

Fucking finally.

Instantly, I'm rising to my feet.

"I want you to do some homework," Proctor announces from behind me when I stride toward the door.

"I'm not a kid."

"No, but think of this as an experiment. If you can pass, I'll sign you off to go back to work."

I grit my teeth. "And if I don't?"

"Then we will continue our sessions until you are ready to return to work."

Fucker is backing me into a corner.

"It's either this, or we can call the DEA and tell them you aren't capable of recovery."

"That's a dick move."

He doesn't argue.

"Fine, what do you want?"

"I want you to write down five things you want for yourself in the next year. I don't care what it is, but I don't want any of those things to be monetary in nature. You have money."

"So, what the fuck do I put down, then?"

Proctor smirks, and it's the first time I've seen any ounce of emotion on his face since I've been coming to see him.

"When you allow yourself to stop focusing on what you've lost, you'll figure it out."

CHAPTER
Eight

AVA

I t's nights like tonight where I find myself lost in my thoughts. My head is foggy, like I never really woke up this morning, and I can't shake the unmistakable feeling of dread.

Of course, that could be because I just left Pleasant Oaks. I stayed with Gran as long as I could before I knew I had to leave. The sun had set already by the time I made it out to my old, beat-up car—Judith—and I practically ran to get in and lock the door like the literal devil was hot on my tail.

Not that it's in any way valid. No one's watching me. As far as boring goes, a wet paper bag is probably more interesting.

The night is chilly, and a shiver ghosts through me. The heater's barely existent, but what can you expect when you buy a five-hundred-dollar car from a man named Chester?

Reaching over, I try to turn it up, but it's maxed, so I fall back, my mind wandering to ignore how cold my fingers are.

The holidays were Gran's favorite, starting with Halloween. We'd always hand out candy to the local trick-or-treaters, and she *always* forced me to dress up with her.

I'd pretend to be annoyed for the longest time, but truthfully? I'd give anything to go back to those days right now. Just to have her healthy and happy again, even if we never celebrated another holiday again.

She seemed . . . different tonight. Tired, yes, but more withdrawn. I can't escape the devastating feeling that she's right. She's dying, and there's not a damn thing I can do about it.

No amount of fresh-baked goods from Mila, my visits, or even her favorite old TV shows will help her. In the end, I have to say goodbye, but what's worse is not knowing. This waiting game is something I've never experienced before because instead of excitement for what's to come, it's pure and utter dread.

Gran has been my rock for the last twenty-three years. When she's gone, I'm alone in the world.

Tears start to brim in my eyes, and I push them back, refusing to cry. I've cried every night this week, and right now, I need all my eyesight to watch for deer on the back roads leading toward Cross Estate outside of Seattle.

It's not like it will make a difference. Ultimately, fate awaits everyone. The rest of us are left to pick up the pieces.

"Come on, Judith," I growl under my breath when she makes a detrimental sputtering sound.

That *can't* be good.

"I just want to go home."

Judith doesn't seem to give a shit.

The entire car lurches, a loud grinding coming from under the hood, and I'm forced to surrender, pulling to the edge of the road.

As soon as I put the car in park, the battery cuts out, casting me into complete darkness.

Great. Just. Freaking. Great.

I force a calming breath past my lips and hunt for my phone in the pitch black that surrounds me. I find it in my bag, but there's no service this far out in the wilderness.

There are no cars. Nothing but trees and deer and that existential dread that comes from staring into the darkness for too long.

The universe *has* to be mocking me.

I check my phone.

—Nothing.

I try the key again.

—Also nothing.

Smacking my hand on the steering wheel does nothing but bring tears to my eyes. Once they start, I can't get them to stop. Finally, I accept my fate, laying my head on the steering wheel and letting out a sob.

"I really hope to God this is rock bottom because I don't want to know what comes after this."

Judith offers no support.

Big, ugly tears fall down my cheeks, and for the first time in a long time, I let them.

I don't know how long I sit there, but it doesn't matter. I cry for Nana. For the bills piling up around me, threatening to swallow me whole. The worthless cancer treatments. I even cry for the dog I had when I was a kid because I can. Who's here to stop me?

I'm well and truly alone out here.

Or so I thought.

Someone knocks on the window beside me, and I let out a screech that could break the sound barrier. A dark figure looms outside the window, and when it bends at the waist, peering in at me, I realize rock bottom is a figure of speech.

It can always get worse.

Levi waits patiently for me to roll down the window, casting that same bored look my way when his gaze slides over my face.

"There a reason you're crying on the side of the road?"

I swallow past the lump in my throat, turning away so he can't see me wipe the tears off my cheeks.

"I'm not crying." *Lie.* "My car broke down."

He steps back and looks at Judith, and the distinct sinking feeling of dread fills my stomach.

"Pop the hood."

I stare at him for a moment when he steps around to the front.

In this light, with his headlights shining brightly behind us, he looks devastating. Like a creature of the night that climbed out of the woods to take pity on—or murder—the poor, unsuspecting girl on the side of the road with her shitty car.

"Unless you'd like to spend the night out here."

Oh, whoops.

Hurriedly, I reach down, hitting the latch, and he opens the hood. I climb out, keeping my distance, though I have no idea what he's looking at when he messes with wires and metal pieces under the hood.

A shiver moves through me, and I wrap my arms tightly around myself, ignoring the scent of his cologne as it washes over me on the breeze.

"It's fucked."

I pause, unsure what to do when he shuts the hood and stalks toward his car without another word.

I stare after him, my feet rooted in place when he opens the driver's door.

"Are you going to stay there, or are we going home?"

Home. With Levi?

Absolutely not.

"I can wait," I say, though my voice sounds akin to what I would expect a mouse to sound like if it could speak. "I need to have it towed home."

He cocks a brow at me, and I half expect him to accept my answer and drive off in the night without me.

"Get in the car, Ava."

Fuck.

It takes a moment for my feet to register what my brain is telling them, but I manage to break free under his heavy gaze and grab my bag from my car, hugging it to me tightly and sliding into his passenger seat when he holds the door open for me.

Inside, the leather smells like him, and it's warm. He shuts the door behind me and stalks around the front before dropping into the driver's side without a word.

If I thought sleeping across the hall from him was intense, sitting in the front of his Aston Martin is even worse. I can practically *feel* my blood teeming with electricity from being so close to him.

I stay silent, and so does he as he pulls the car away from Judith and starts down the road.

It's as tense as you would expect, and the air practically hums around us. I get the feeling he's pissed off, but I don't know why. Levi and I have never been anything more than tolerant (barely) acquaintances.

"Why were you out tonight?"

My skin bristles at the sound of his voice, and I shiver. He reaches over and turns the heat up.

"I was visiting my grandmother," I answer quietly, keeping my eyes trained on the dash.

"This late?"

This feels like a breach in some unspoken contract. A moment of truce in a never-ending battle between us over who can get further under the other's skin.

"She lives in a nursing home. I visit her a few times a week."

I cast a glance in his direction and notice his hand on the steering wheel, the other on the shift knob in the center.

Why is watching him shift his fancy car the hottest thing I've ever seen?

And why have I never noticed the veins in his hands?

I readjust in the seat, suddenly hot in the small space, and tear my eyes away.

"I take it you're close."

I pause, trying to clear my head of the Levi-induced haze.

"She raised me . . . When I was twelve, I came to live with her. She's the only family I have."

I don't know why I'm telling him this. He doesn't care.

It's Levi freaking Cross. If it's not a vagina attached to some leggy blonde or a bottle of whiskey, it's beneath him.

I'm beneath him in his eyes. Probably why he goes out of his way to be a flaming asshole nearly every second of his life.

I clear my throat, readjusting in the seat to give my mind something else to focus on other than the vortex of a man beside me.

Levi is quiet, his fingers gripping the steering wheel tight enough that his knuckles start to turn white.

Guess I pissed him off, again.

"You shouldn't be out so late," he says after a long moment. "Especially in that piece of shit you call a car."

Irritation and embarrassment flood through me in waves. I shove it down, propping my elbow on the door and laying my head in my hand while I continue to watch the Washington forest pass outside.

"Not all of us can afford Aston Martins, Levi."

"Maybe you should think about saving your money a little better." I hate it when he speaks to me like I'm a child in need of guidance.

"I'll get right on that," I reply coolly. "Right after I pay for the nursing home—"

"You're paying for it?" He has the audacity to cock an eyebrow at me.

I'll rip that eyebrow off in your sleep, Mr. Cross.

"How much does it cost a month?"

"Enough," I reply curtly.

I don't know why he cares so much. It's not like I'm stealing from his family. I'm paying my dues by working six days a week at their fancy mansion to afford it.

"I should have walked home," I grumble.

"I'd be happy to stop the car if you'd like."

An electrifying silence settles between us, and we both stare each other down. I'm the first to break, looking back at the road.

"Levi!"

We smash into the deer standing in the middle of the road, and the car jolts sideways on the slick pavement. Levi tries to regain control while we spin on the slippery road.

It's not until we skid to a stop that I realize I hadn't breathed the entire time we were spinning out of control.

I'm also only aware of my hand on Levi's thigh when a burning sensation slips through my blood.

He cocks a brow at me, his breathing as ragged as mine from the adrenaline, and I look down to where my hand is resting on his leg.

Dangerously close to his dick.

Instantly, I rip my hand away.

"You alright?" he asks when I scrub a hand through my

hair.

The deer is gone, lying in the brush somewhere. There's no way it survived that hit. We were doing well over the speed limit.

My hands are shaking, and my chest feels tight, the adrenaline enough to steal my breath away and my asthma enough to render me speechless. Frantically, I reach for my bag as my throat closes. It's like someone sucked all the air out of the car.

"*Ava.*"

Levi tugs the bag out of my hands, opening it and looking inside while I struggle to catch my breath.

He finally produces the inhaler, popping the cap off and placing it to my lips. He keeps his hand on the back of my head while he pushes the medicine into my lungs, and it's strangely . . . comforting.

"Breathe." He says it as if I've forgotten how. Not as if I have asthma and we just killed a deer and probably shattered his fancy car.

But . . . there's also something else in his gaze. Is he worried about me?

Levi Cross, worried about the little maid he was just interrogating FBI-style.

Who would have thought?

I take another breath, laying my head back as my chest relaxes. He doesn't release me, his fingers winding through my hair at the back of my head to hold me up.

"I'm okay," I breathe, though my voice is shaky. I'm not sure if it's from looking up into his eyes or from my breathing condition.

"You didn't say you had asthma." It's an accusation.

"Levi . . . I have asthma."

He shakes his head, finally releasing me, and grabs the

door handle.

"Wait," I jump, and he pauses, looking back at me. Reaching out, like I'm trying to comfort a wild bear, I touch a spot on his forehead. He doesn't even wince, though there's a sizable gash in his skin right above his brow. "You're bleeding."

"Not the first time," he says, looking at his blood on my hand as if something about it disturbs him.

"You need to get it looked at."

He glances at the rearview mirror.

"I'm fine, Ava. I've had worse."

"It's not fine," I argue. He looks down to where my hand rests on his forearm. "Please . . . At least let me look at it."

He stares at me for a long moment before something hardens in his gaze.

"Fine. I'll let you stitch it when we get home."

And with that, he's pulling away as if I'd burned him.

"Where are you going?"

"To make sure it's dead."

I watch him disappear into the treeline while my breathing slowly returns to normal. It's not long before I hear a loud *pop,* and sorrow washes over me.

I don't know whether it's for the deer or the man that had to kill it, but it's there, and it makes my chest ache.

And unfortunately . . . I'm realizing I'm not as indifferent to Levi Cross as I thought.

Levi drops the first aid kit down on the coffee table in the den, while I fidget nervously with my hands.

"Have you ever given stitches before?" he asks, cocking a brow at me despite the blood oozing from his head.

"No, but . . . how hard can it be?"

He just shakes his head, stalking toward the door.

"Where are you going?"

"Give me a minute," he replies gruffly.

He disappears from the room while I open the kit and look through the items, pulling out what I think I'll need, though I really have no idea.

By the time he comes back, he's got a bottle of whiskey in his hand and a grim look of determination in his eyes.

"Really?" I shoot him a look when he settles on the couch in front of me. It's entirely too close, but I'm about to get a whole lot closer when I stitch his head shut.

He doesn't say anything, popping the lid off the bottle. He raises it to his lips while eyeing me over the top, as if he's challenging me.

Fine. We'll see how cocky he is when I've got a needle in my hand.

I grab the thread and needle—why does the needle look so weird?—and start the painstaking process of trying to thread it with his gaze on me.

I chance a glance at him, and it's a big mistake because once I do, a shot of electricity shoots through me.

"Stop staring at me."

"Just wondering when you're going to figure it out or let me do it."

"I don't need your help. I'm competent."

He cocks a brow at the threadless needle in my hand.

"Looks like it."

"You know, I could have just let you bleed out."

Lifting the bottle of whiskey back to his lips, he takes a drink, a devil-may-care glint in his eyes.

"You wouldn't."

"Why, because you're my boss?"

"Because you've got a soft heart."

I pause, and he smirks, while my chest flutters uncomfortably. Just when I think I have him figured out, he surprises me again.

Finally, I manage to thread the weird needle and hold it up for him to see.

"I told you I was capable."

"You're going to have to sit on my lap."

I'm sure if my cheeks get any hotter, NASA will label me as a second sun.

My stomach dips to my toes. "That sounds nefarious."

"Don't worry, sweetheart. You're not my type."

Ouch.

"Right, how could I forget? You prefer leggy blondes with a black hole personality."

"Or I prefer women who won't get clingy."

"Okay, that was rude," I quip, my cheeks flaming. "I do not get clingy."

"No?"

"No. Least of all with someone like you."

His eyes flash with that cocky indifference that I've come to both loath and crave at the same time.

"Let's go," he says, gesturing to his lap. "I don't want you stabbing me in the eye because you're unsteady."

Asshole.

"Should have just let you bleed out," I grumble under my breath.

I don't know what it is about this man that makes all my inhibitions and morals jump out the window, but nevertheless, when I place my hand on his shoulder, pushing him back into the couch, my heart skitters in my chest at the look in his eyes.

It was there. That fleeting glance. Like he'd gladly fall to his knees and worship me if that's what I asked for.

I almost laugh, picturing a man like Levi Cross being so consumed by a woman that he'd give up heaven and earth to make her the queen of his hell.

As if he would be that consumed with *me*.

Carefully, I slip onto his lap, holding the needle above my head to keep from stabbing him. His eyes never leave my face, his tongue running over his teeth when I settle over him, my legs straddling either of his.

My core warms as his gaze slides down my body, toward the center of my thighs, where I rest just over top of him, hovering in an effort to save myself.

"All the way," he says, and if I'm not mistaken, there's a slight rasp to his voice that slips through my blood, warming me from the inside out.

He doesn't touch me even when I rock unstably on his lap, gripping his shoulder to steady myself, but the heat of a thousand suns burns on my skin when I settle over him, feeling the hard length of him pressed against my core.

Oh my God . . . is this turning him on?

He cocks a brow.

"Problem?"

"No problem at all."

He readjusts his hips, and his cock brushes against my center, unfortunately reminding me of the ache between my thighs.

"None?"

I grit my teeth. He's trying to toy with me.

"None at all," I sigh. "Fortunately, I can get cheap dick anywhere. Yours has no effect on me."

He chuckles darkly, and the sound goes straight to my core.

"We'll see about that."

Shaking my head, I place my hand on the side of his face to steady myself. I move forward, and right when he's about to say something that will probably make me blush, I pierce the skin with the needle.

He hisses out a breath through his teeth, his hand shooting to my hip and his fingers tightening to near bruising strength, but I don't stop. I've sewn up holes in clothes before. Stuffed animals when I was a kid. This can't be all that different, right?

"Punishing me, little ghost?" he asks. Despite the needle slipping through his torn skin, the pain doesn't seem to have much of an effect on him.

"Something like that," I murmur curtly, my lips pursing as I work. I can't look at him because if I do, I know I'll screw this up, and call me crazy, but I have a desire to prove myself.

I finish the stitches, and although they look choppy, they hold. When I settle back, attempting to get off his lap, his grip tightens, locking me in place.

My eyes go to his for only a second, and I find him staring at me with something so far from indifference, it makes my stomach do cartwheels around my organs.

"I'm done," I say softly, and his jaw clenches. My eyes stay on the lines of his T-shirt where it stretches over his skin.

"Are you?"

I nod, my tongue darting out to lick my lip. Levi's gaze follows the motion and darkens.

"Ava . . ." he says quietly. "Look at me."

I suck in a shaky breath and force my gaze to his. It's a mistake because once I look at him, I can't look away. Ice-blue eyes, the color of an Arctic tundra. Only, instead of sending a chill through me, my blood heats with fire.

His gaze flicks from the whiskey bottle, then back to mine, dark and so consuming, it feels like swallowing a live grenade.

"I think I should go up to my room now," I breathe, and neither of us moves.

"I'm thirsty." His voice is dark and deadly calm, like a gentle breeze before the storm of a lifetime. I blink at him, not understanding.

And then realization hits.

Sucking in a shallow breath, I place the needle on the stand beside us, taking his bottle instead and holding it out for him, but he doesn't take it.

He nods at the bottle of amber liquid.

When I don't move, his voice is stern and calculated. Controlled.

"I said I'm thirsty, Miss Ryan."

A shiver moves down my spine when I realize what he wants.

"You're insane," I whisper. He doesn't try to deny it.

Leaning back, he readjusts underneath me and settles back into the couch.

"It shouldn't be a problem for you. As you've said, you can find cheap dick anywhere. I have no effect on you, remember?"

Asshole.

Why did I have to say that?

Cocking my head to the side, I smile sweetly at him and hope he can see the hate flashing in my eyes.

"Whatever you say, *Mr.* Cross."

His chin tips up, his gaze taunting. He thinks I won't actually do it, which only spurs me on more.

Lifting the bottle to my lips, I gather some of the whiskey in my mouth, and the smooth burn coats the back of my throat, nearly making me choke.

God, how does he drink this?

Leaning forward, I press my lips to his, my stomach fluttering when I taste the whiskey on his lips from mine. Levi doesn't move, his arms over the back of the chair like a damned God, while I, the poor girl obsessed with him, practically pant on his lap.

The liquor passes from my tongue to his, and with the barest touch, all my senses come alive.

Levi tastes like sin. Like warmth and darkness and everything mothers warn their daughters about, when he lazily slips his tongue against mine, capturing the liquid. Like he doesn't need to. Like he's doing it as a favor and not because he told me to.

It should turn me off. Unfortunately, it only makes me want him more.

I *want* to see his control slip. I want to hear my name in his brooding voice. I want to *feel* the effect I have on him, even if he's too stubborn to admit there's some part of him that wants me.

Armed with a light buzz from the lack of oxygen in the room and a whole lot of ambition found in my new mission, I lean back enough to break the contact and put the bottle back to my lips. This time, my pulse leaps when I lean back down, aligning my lips to his. Our tongues tangle and the whiskey passes between us, getting lost somewhere amongst the heavy pants that I'm not even sure are mine or his, at this point.

Everything sharpens to a point, coalescing directly between my legs until my clit throbs behind the lacy material of my panties.

I repeat the motion, and this time, something deep rumbles in his chest when the whiskey flows into his mouth. Something unhinged. Unintentional. Like he wants my taste so bad he can't fucking stand it.

That makes two of us.

A breathless whimper leaves my lips when his hands finally leave the couch, his fingers hovering over my ribs as they slip up my sides, over the sides of my breasts, then along my shoulder blades. He's barely touching me, but it brings about a desperation I hadn't known I could feel.

I take another drink, and when I meet his lips with mine, something in him snaps. He grips the back of my head, forcing my lips against his and pulling me in deep with his tongue. He may as well be licking between my legs with the lust that slips through me.

His tongue tangles with mine, and I suck on the end of his, drawing out his sharp breath. His hands slip down to cup my ass over my jeans, his fingers tightening to a near-bruising strength as my arm wraps around the back of his neck.

He shifts and his erection brushes against my core, drawing out a moan as the friction brushes over the sensitive bundle of nerves, and Levi stops, his face inches from mine and his eyes dark as night.

Watching me with a calculating look in his eyes, he uses his hand on my ass to move my hips against his erection again, and this time, a shiver rolls through me, my blunt nails digging into the flesh at the back of his neck.

It all combines into a dizzying wave of euphoria I'm not sure I ever want to come back from.

Abruptly, he grips my chin, forcing my lips back with a rough growl, and I nearly topple off his lap. My heart hammers in my chest, beating out of tune, and my lips burn where he'd kissed me.

"Go to your room, Ava," he says darkly. It's a warning. One I'm not sure I even want to understand the meaning of.

The moment he releases me, reality rushes in, bringing with it all the self-doubt, the insecurity, and the shame that were easy to ignore with his lips on mine.

Shakily, I climb to my feet, and like the prudish good girl I am, I leave the room, not daring to glance back.

Never Die for a Sinner

CHAPTER
Nine

AVA

Hell hath no fury like Paulina when she sees a single speck of dust anywhere in Cross Estate. And today? She's on the warpath.

"You must do better," she scolds, her voice sharp enough to slice through glass as she shifts her gaze back and forth between me and the other, older housekeeper, Magdalene. Her tone is firm, disapproving, the kind of tone that makes grown men check their shoes for mud.

Magdalene bows her head with practiced calm. "Of course, ma'am. We'll get right on it."

I hover near the doorway, holding a tray of folded linen napkins and fighting the urge to roll my eyes. The Cross family may have money, but they're not exactly aristocracy. Half the rooms in this place are just for show—more furniture than function. And Paulina treats each one like it's a damn cathedral.

"Oh, leave them be, Paulina," Bella Cross says breathlessly as she breezes into the kitchen.

bottle.

"The house is damn near spotless."

"It can be better," Paulina replies flatly, not even sparing her niece a glance.

Bella raises an eyebrow and tosses her long, dark braid over her shoulder. "Why don't you scold Levi for all those greasy car parts littering the garage? Now that's a real crime."

Paulina's eyes twitch. For a second, I think she might combust right in front of us, veins in her neck straining with the effort of not saying something truly incendiary. Then she huffs like a bull preparing to charge and stalks out of the kitchen with the force of a hurricane in heels.

"Those boys will be the death of me . . ."

Bella and I wait a moment. Then we look at each other—and lose it.

I slap a hand over my mouth to stifle my laugh. Bella grins and shakes her head, cracking open a water bottle and taking a long drink like she didn't just stir the pot and set it to boil.

"Thank you," I say through a sigh, setting the napkins down on the counter. "She was two seconds away from giving me a mop and a toothbrush."

Bella smirks, leaning against the marble island. "Of course. I know how my aunt can be."

"A dust bully?"

"You know what they say. If she's hard on you, that means she likes you."

"Could've fooled me," I mutter, sliding onto one of the barstools. Bella sets a plate of grapes between us, and I take one, chewing slowly.

Bella grins wider and tosses a grape into her mouth. "What happened to your car, by the way?"

The question slams into me out of nowhere. I freeze. My fingers curl around the edge of the stool. "What do you mean?"

"It showed up on a tow truck this morning," Bella says casually, reaching for another grape. "Levi said it broke down."

My mouth goes dry. My cheeks heat instantly, and I fight to keep my expression neutral.

"Oh. Yeah. It just kind of . . . stopped working," I say, forcing the words out.

Bella frowns. "Why didn't you call me? I would've come and picked you up."

My heart starts beating faster. "Your brother saw me on the side of the road. He stopped. It wasn't a big deal."

But it was.

I can still feel the ghost of his lips on mine when he drank whiskey from my tongue. Still hear the rasp in his voice when he said my name like it meant something. And no matter how many times I've brushed my teeth today, I can't seem to erase the taste of him.

Bella raises a brow, clearly reading more than I meant to reveal.

"No big deal, huh?" she says slowly, a knowing gleam in her eyes.

I look away, focusing on a random speck of flour on the counter and willing myself not to smile. Or blush. Or unravel completely.

"I don't know what you're talking about," I grumble under my breath, trying to sound casual, but the sound of footsteps behind me forces me to snap my mouth shut.

Oh, no.

"I'm just saying," Mila's voice floats down the hall, in some heated debate with Levi and Christian. "A bakery could really take things to the next level."

"I think it's a good idea," Bella chimes in, her tone far too smug for someone pretending to be neutral. There's a glimmer in her eyes—mischief, or maybe just too much awareness—and it makes my stomach flutter with nerves.

They dissolve into conversation, discussing the possibilities of adding a café to the lodge, while I try to wrangle my heart beating frantically in my chest.

A brush of awareness slides through me the moment Levi steps up to the kitchen island beside me, his presence like static in the air—undeniable and far too close. My pulse stutters, betraying me, like my body hasn't quite forgotten what it felt like to have his hands tangled in my hair, his mouth hot and hungry against mine last night.

I keep my eyes on Bella, but I can feel him—every inch of him. The way he leans casually against the counter, just barely brushing my arm. The faint scent of his cologne mixed with the essence of hot man.

Heat flares in my chest and races straight down to my core. I shift in my chair, crossing one leg over the other, trying to ignore the way my skin prickles with warmth. The silence stretches, thick and loaded, and I swear I can still taste him on my lips, while he acts as if nothing ever happened.

Like I imagined it.

Like he doesn't remember every second the way I do.

I chance a glance up, quick and quiet—and he's already looking at me. Our eyes lock. The air pulls tight between us. His smirk is slight, barely there, but it slices through me like a blade. Then he turns his attention casually back to Bella, like he didn't just set fire to my entire nervous system.

"Well, I have to go," Bella announces, breaking through the haze and snapping me back to reality. "I've got a meeting with a travel agency in half an hour, and I want to show up before them to make them look bad."

I snort a laugh before I can stop myself, shaking my head at her unapologetic villainy. She grabs her water bottle with a grin and struts from the room like she's walking a runway.

"Please," Mila's voice draws my attention back to the conversation. She looks up at Christian, her brows raised in mock exasperation.

Christian tries—and fails—not to smile. His lips twitch like he's holding back something warm and fond. I catch the subtle look between them and smirk to myself. The man is absolutely whipped, and it's kind of adorable.

"Fine," he relents with a sigh, looking to Levi. "We'll be right back."

"Sure you will," Levi mutters with a chuckle as the couple disappears, leaving just the two of us in the room.

Well . . . this is awkward.

He shrugs, leaning back against the counter beside me like he owns the air between us. He crosses his arms, and my traitorous eyes dip to the way the muscles in his forearms flex beneath his skin. My mouth goes dry.

"Couldn't leave it sitting there," he says simply. "You really need to consider getting a new car."

"Yeah," I scoff. "As soon as you show me where the money tree is around here, I'll get right on that."

His smile tugs at one corner of his mouth, the kind that's quiet but dangerously charming. And somehow, it makes my heart pound even harder.

Unsure what to say or do, the first thing that comes to mind comes tumbling out of my mouth like a runaway train.

"Why is your aunt so obsessed with grapefruit?" I ask, swallowing thickly past the lump forming in my throat.

Levi shrugs, a slow, devious smirk curving across his lips like he knows exactly what game we're playing—and how to win it.

"What's the matter? Don't like it?" he asks evenly, reaching forward and grabbing one from the bowl in front of me. He peels it with deliberate slowness, his strong hands working over the fruit like he's trying to torture me with citrus.

"It's disgusting," I blurt, shifting in my seat as my body scrambles to recalibrate around his nearness. Why does he have to be so close? So casually, dangerously close?

"It's good for you," he counters with a maddening shrug, like he's being reasonable.

I roll my eyes, resisting the urge to groan. This family is so freaking weird.

"You eat it then."

He only smirks harder.

Challenge accepted.

He cocks his head slightly, eyes glittering with mischief, and slides the plate of grapes Bella left across the counter. With maddening calm, he sets the grapefruit down and scoops a generous amount of sugar from the sugar bowl nearby. Then, without breaking eye contact, he dips a piece of fruit into the sugar and makes a show of taking a piece and dipping it in, before he tosses it in his mouth.

"Isn't that cheating?"

He cocks a brow

"What's fun about life," he says smoothly, grabbing another piece, "if you don't cheat a little to get what you want?"

His gaze is fire and smoke and warning bells all at once. And then—just when I think the moment can't get any more unbearable—he dips another segment into the sugar and holds it out for me.

Right between his fingers.

I reach to take it, but he pulls back just out of reach.

Oh, you have got to be kidding me.

I glance back toward the doorway, silently shaking my head.

He grins down at me with the kind of expression that should come with a warning label. The glint in his icy blue eyes is anything but innocent.

"Open, Ava," he says, voice dipping lower, rougher. Commanding.

My breath hitches. "Make me."

His hand is on my face in an instant—fingers curling beneath my chin, thumb pressing against my cheek, pinching gently until my lips part in shock.

I don't move. I can't. His eyes are locked on mine, and I'm rooted to the spot like a puppet strung too tightly.

Then, with excruciating slowness, he slides the sugar-coated segment across my tongue. My lips close instinctively around his fingers, and I swear the whole world narrows down to this moment.

"Suck," he murmurs, voice so dark it coils low in my belly like heat struck from flint.

Holy. Shit.

My brain short-circuits. Heat travels through my veins, and I shift awkwardly in my chair at the rough tone of his voice. I swirl my tongue around his fingers in my mouth in a momentary lapse of judgement, I'm not sure I'll ever recover from.

"That's it. Good girl."

God, save me.

Defiantly, I nip the pad of his finger in protest. His grin only deepens, satisfied and thoroughly unbothered, before he finally, slowly, drags his fingers from my mouth.

The way he looks at me... like he's already imagined a thousand more ways to ruin me.

And God help me, I might let him.

He trails his thumb along my lower lip, watching it glisten. My whole body is on fire.

This is Levi Cross. The man who's made it his personal mission to torment me since the day I set foot on Cross Estate.

I do not want him.

Not in the real, meaningful sense. Not in the let's-ruin-our-lives sense.

. . . Right?

Just like I said: I need to get laid. Maybe then my body will stop throwing itself at the human equivalent of a hurricane in dark jeans.

"Baby girl..." he drawls, leaning in close. "You make it really hard not to ruin you."

I blink at him. "W-what?" I stammer. My brain has officially entered blender mode.

He smirks, and it's devastating. That kind of smile should be outlawed.

"Oh no," Mila's voice giggles from the doorway, and I nearly fall out of my chair.

I jerk back so fast I nearly crash to the floor, heart hammering like it's trying to escape my chest.

Mila raises a brow, barely hiding her delight, while Christian lingers behind her looking—well, like Christian. Slightly scowling. Perpetually unimpressed.

All eyes are on me. My cheeks go up in flames.

Fantastic.

I glare at Mila's too-wide smile. No doubt she's already inventing some elaborate story where Levi and I are secretly star-crossed lovers instead of combatants. The throbbing in my core? Probably just indigestion. Has *nothing* to do with Levi. Or the way his jeans hug his stupid perfect—

God, I sound like an idiot.

I hate grapefruit. I hate *him*.

But the way his fingers tasted—sweet, tart, sinful—I'm scared I'd do it again tomorrow if he asked.

Levi leans back like nothing just happened, casually stealing the air from the room with his presence alone. Mila looks like she just found out Santa's real. Christian still looks vaguely bored, but that's nothing new for him. If it doesn't have to do with Mila, it may as well not exist.

I can't do this.

"I have work to do," I mutter, already halfway out of my seat, and heading toward the door before I let Levi feed me any more sinful fruit.

I need to put some distance between us, especially if I'm going to follow through with my end of the deal.

Right now, I want to be anywhere but here.

Anywhere but near *him*.

I listen to the sound of his door closing while I silently pace through my room.

This is either a really stupid plan, or—no, scratch that. It's just stupid. Maybe even suicidal.

Levi Cross isn't one to fuck with, and here I am, plotting grand theft flash drive while I listen to the sounds of his footsteps retreat downstairs.

What if he catches me? Maybe he'll just kill me on the spot. Maybe he'll drag me out of here by my hair.

A shudder slips through me at a creak down the hall.

That damned room. I swear it haunts me, plaguing my dreams with thumps and thuds in the night. Why can't the dead just stay dead? Why does he have to torment us from the afterlife? Was one lifetime not enough?

"Shut up, Ava," I grumble to myself, flexing my sweaty hands. "You sound insane."

Maybe I *am* going insane.

Blowing out a breath, I try to calm my breathing and focus on the plan. Get in and get out. He's leaving for the night, so that means I'll have a few hours to find what I'm looking for before he gets home. By then, I should be long asleep. Maybe then I'll be able to breathe a little easier.

Who am I kidding? There's always something else.

I just hope next time, it's not something impossible.

My heart beats unsteadily in my chest when I step over to the door, listening for any sounds of anyone awake.

I know for a fact: Bella is out with her boyfriend, Rob. She probably won't be home tonight. Paulina is down in the den reading one of her monster pornos she thinks no one knows about, so she'll be busy for the next few hours. Mila and Christian are at their house, and Javier is doing whatever Javier does when he's not cooking the best food on planet earth.

Levi . . . well, who knows where he goes most nights?

Carefully, I twist the knob, and the door creaks when it opens. Instinctually, I shush it, like a kid trying to sneak out of their room at night to grab a cookie.

The hall is dark, and I don't waste any time, hurrying across and knocking tentatively on the door.

I don't know what I'll do if he answers. I didn't think that far ahead.

I knock again, and when no answer comes, I try the handle, pushing the door open to the dark bedroom beyond.

His room smells like him.

Like whiskey and tobacco, mixed with that little bit of the forest beyond these four walls. My mouth waters, and I inhale instinctively as I step into the room and carefully shut the door behind me.

Then, I stop.

"Well, shit."

Now what?

With no time to waste, I shake myself, hurrying over to his dresser. I pull open the top drawer, blushing when I see the boxers lined up neatly in a row.

Levi Cross needs some color in his life. All his boxers are black.

Steeling myself, I root around the bottom of the drawer, and when I find nothing, I shut it tight, blowing out a breath.

Why is it so hot in here?

I move on to the next, searching through every T-shirt, sock, or pair of jeans I can find, but every drawer is empty.

I search the closet, the dressers. Under the bed, and I even go so far as to look in the bathroom. It's nowhere to be found, and the more time that ticks by, the more desperate I become.

Where the *hell* would he hide it? More importantly, *what* is he hiding on it?

Why is this little piece of plastic the balance between life and death?

I suck in a deep breath, my hands shaking, as panic slips over me.

I scrub a hand over my face, turning back toward the bed.

Throughout the time I've worked here, I've learned things about that bed. I've heard the moans of the women he brings home. I can't stop the bitter stab of something dark and envious swirling in my gut when I step over to the edge of the Alaskan King bed, looking down at the carefully made sheets from when I made it this morning.

I hate him. I hate him because deep down, I know I don't. I hate him because he's the reason I'm here and because he made me care, even though he's given me no reason to.

I grab the mattress and lift it as best I can, inspecting underneath it.

Nothing.

"Goddamnit," I growl. "Where the *fuck* is it?"

I fall to the bed, running my hands through my hair.

I'm fucked. I'm fucked. I'm fucked.

And then, movement to my left catches my attention, and I nearly collapse when my heart falls to my toes.

Oh, I am sooo *fucked.*

Levi smirks at me from the door, leaning against the frame with a sinister grin on his face like he just found out his favorite toy is broken.

. . . And now he gets to destroy it.

"Hello, little ghost."

CHAPTER
Ten

LEVI

It's cute . . . the fear in her eyes.

She backs up against the wall, jumping when she hits the chair in the corner.

She shivers, trying to come up with a reason as to why she's in my room, and, even in the dim glow of the bedside lamp, I can see that she's gone pale.

"Looking for something?" I step into the room, and I swear she jumps with every thud of my boots on the ground.

"I-I-I . . ." she stammers, her eyes darting for any possible exit she can find.

There isn't one. There's no way out for her. Not unless I allow it, and now that I've got her cornered, I'm feeling anything but generous.

She's going to regret the moment I caught her sneaking around.

"You know it's rude to go through people's things."

"I was just looking for something," she lies. "I thought I lost an earring."

She backs into the corner, as far away from me as she can get, and secretly, I'm fucking begging for her to give me a reason to hunt her.

I've never cared much to play with my food before I eat it, but prissy little Ava Ryan . . . that's a different story.

For the past year, my thoughts have been plagued with what I'd like to do with her. How badly I want to hear her scream for me. How I want to hear her moan my name and beg me for more.

After this afternoon, I'm strung tight and barely restraining myself from throwing her onto the bed and showing her how good it feels to give in to me. I wasn't lying when I told her she needed to get laid.

I just left out the part where I would cut the dick off any man who tried.

"You see, little ghost . . . I think that's a lie."

She swallows nervously. Poor thing is even shaking as if I'd hurt her.

She's not wrong. I do plan on hurting her. I just plan on making it feel like fucking heaven when I do.

She shakes her head, tongue darting out to lick her soft pink lips.

"N-no. I thought I lost it when I was dusting."

"Really?"

I step closer. She realizes she has nowhere left to run.

"You see, the funny thing about that, sweetheart?" I stop right in front of her. She flinches when I raise my hand, brushing the soft chocolate hair back from her face and leaning close. Fuck she smells like heaven. "You don't wear earrings."

She freezes for a moment before cold, harsh clarity washes over her, and her eyes widen to big pale-green saucers. I chuckle darkly under my breath, and just when I'm about to press against her, she darts.

She doesn't make it far before I catch her around the waist, dragging her down to the bed. Her stomach hits the mattress, and a gust of air pushes out of both of us when I fall over her. I keep most of my weight on my knees and hands, using one to wrap around her throat from behind.

Dragging her head back, I press my lips against her ear, a mix of lust and anger at her snooping washing over me.

"I'm sorry," she rushes, clawing at the comforter beneath her.

"Not so fast, little ghost. Let's talk about this. Why were you snooping through my room?"

"I already told you I wasn't," she growls, her throat bobbing under my hand.

"And I don't believe you. What's the matter? Didn't get enough in the closet the other day?"

"Fuck you," she seethes, and I can't help but laugh wickedly.

If only she fucking knew . . .

"I prefer my girls with a little more passion in them."

"And I wouldn't touch you if you were the last man on the fucking planet."

I drag my hand around to her hair, fisting it over her shoulder. I trail my lips down the smooth skin of her neck, and she shivers at my touch, wiggling underneath me. I flip her over and push myself between her thighs, pinning her to the mattress, and my cock brushes against her center. I grit my teeth at the friction.

Fucking hell, she feels so fucking good.

"Come on, Ava," I murmur low in her ear. At the same time, I roll my hips into her, and she lets out a quiet gasp when the hard notch in my jeans brushes against the leggings covering her pussy. "I know you've thought about me."

"A momentary lapse in judgement."

"Is that so?"

That earns me a snort. I roll my hips into hers again, and she fights to roll me off of her. Fortunately, I'm a whole head taller and at least a hundred pounds heavier than her tiny stature.

With her underneath me, I get a better feel of her body than what she normally allows me to see. Soft curves. Round ass. Fuck, I could devour her.

"Just let me go, Levi," she growls, fisting the sheets in her delicate fingers.

"I don't think so, baby girl." She shivers at the nickname, and I smirk deviously. "You're going to tell me why you're snooping through my room."

"I'm trying to find your personality," she grits, and I actually chuckle, nipping the side of her neck where it leads to her shoulder. She yelps, and I soothe the sting with my tongue, groaning at the taste of her.

Like fucking cotton candy.

"I love the fight in you when you're cornered," I breathe in her ear. I tighten my fist in her hair, dragging her head to the side so I can see those pretty green eyes.

"What do you want?" she whispers, her lashes fluttering. I can almost see her heartbeat racing, her breathing as ragged as mine.

"I want a lot of things from you, sweetheart. Starting with what you were looking for."

She wiggles underneath me, struggling against my hold in her hair.

I'm finding the longer she's underneath me, the less I give a shit about what she was looking for and the more I want to stick my fingers in her leggings and see if she's wet for me.

"Did you honestly think I wouldn't find out you're hiding something, Ava? You think I didn't realize you were watching me? Waiting for me to leave?" I press a kiss to the tip of her nose, and she shivers underneath me, a soft whimper slipping through her teeth.

"I don't know what you're talking about," she growls, fighting my hold once more.

"No? You really made it so easy." I nip the side of her neck, drinking her in. "You played right into my hand. All I had to do was close the door and wait down the hall. I'll give you props; you waited longer than I thought you would. I almost gave up, but you, Ava, you don't disappoint. You marched right in and went through my drawers without so much as a care. What is it? Some kind of fetish? Need money?"

"Fuck you," she growls through the tears in her eyes. "And fuck your money. I don't want it."

"Then what is it, Ava. I've got a lot of steam to blow off, and you feel really fucking good right now, grinding against my cock.

"I'm not doing anything," she lies. I look down the length of our bodies to where she's arching against me. I roll my hips into her again, and her lashes flutter, her cheeks turning a pretty shade of scarlet.

"No?" I taunt, doing it again and hissing through my teeth. "Fuck, Ava . . . feel that?"

"You're insane," she grits.

"You want me to stop?"

I can smell the fear rolling off her, but I can *feel* her lust when she pushes back against me.

"Why are you such an asshole?" she grits.

"Why are you such a brat?" I counter. "You never answered my question, Ava. Do you want me to stop?"

"Fuck you."

"If you insist," I purr in her ear.

I keep up with her pace, letting her rock against me.

Allowing her to take what she wants. When a soft whimper leaves her lips, I bite back a curse, leaning my forehead against hers.

This is fucking madness.

"Last chance, Ava," I rasp, gripping her hip to still her movements. "Or do you want me to fuck you until you're willing to tell me every secret buried in that pretty little head?"

When she doesn't respond, I stand, grip her hips, and tug her down the bed. I'm about to climb back between her legs when she stops me in a breathless rush.

"Wait, wait, wait . . ."

I roll my neck, my control in fucking pieces from the little brat underneath me.

"What? Have something you want to confess?"

She pauses, soft green eyes staring up at me in the moonlight, and for a moment, I lose my train of thought.

Fuck, she's pretty . . .

That's when she chooses to strike, her sneaker connecting with my dick. I stumble back, allowing her to scramble off the bed, and curse under my breath.

"Fuck!"

Pain shoots through me and up into my stomach, but it's momentary when the thrill of her hurriedly backing toward the door catches up to me.

Oh, little ghost, you have no idea what you've just signed up for.

"If you can catch me, you can fuck me."

And then she runs.

I chuckle low and sinister.

"Game on, baby girl."

I give her a momentary head start, listening to the sound of the door closing downstairs before I start after her.

Exhilaration courses through me. This is exactly the kind of excitement I've been searching for. This high I only feel when I'm with her. Only now, following her out of the house and toward the woods, it's amplified.

My cock is rock-fucking-hard, pressing against the zipper in my jeans. Anticipation teems through me, my hands nearly vibrating. It's dark and with no light, I know she doesn't have a single chance in outrunning me. I know these woods like the back of my hand.

She was mine the moment those pretty little words left her tongue.

The forest is loud around me as I step through the trees, filled with the sounds of animals scurrying off. Owls in the trees. Leaves crunch under my boots with each step, and I drink in the scent of her lingering in the air.

Fuck . . . this is going to be goddamned glorious.

I pause just inside the treeline and listen, waiting.

To my left, a twig snaps, and I chuckle under my breath, stalking in that direction until I see her ducking under low-hanging branches and stumbling in the dark up ahead.

Watching her, I keep back, letting her think she's getting away, when really, it was never even a possibility.

The moment I found her sneaking around my room, something in me snapped.

Ava Ryan is *mine*.

The closer I get, the harder my blood pumps, and the more she looks like prey.

I've been denying the urge to claim her for months, and now, she's offered herself up to me on a silver platter, and I'm practically fucking salivating, knowing I'll soon own her.

I could fuck anyone in the world. Nothing would compare to watching my prissy little housekeeper turn into a slut for me and only me.

The ultimate fucking prize.

She must sense my presence lingering in the darkness behind her, because when she reaches a clearing, she whips around, scanning the trees for me. I stay back, out of her line of sight and watch, a feral grin tugging at my lips.

"Little ghost . . ." I call out from the darkness, watching her turn around in a circle, searching for me. She can't see me, and her eyes gloss over me as she searches the trees, her breathing ragged.

I stalk through the forest as quietly as possible. I'm strung tight, the adrenaline pumping through me pounding in my veins. My cock is begging to take her up on her little offer, but I'm enjoying this far too much to let it end so soon.

"Fuck off, Levi."

A wide grin spreads across my face.

Fuck, she's going to be *fun* to break

"You done running?"

She huffs angrily, scanning the trees, while she tries to catch her breath.

"You haven't caught me yet," she snaps back.

I can't help but chuckle.

She's already caught, and she doesn't even know it yet.

Her head snaps to where I'm standing just out of sight, and she darts in the opposite direction. I listen to her crash through the trees before I stroll along behind her, whistling through my teeth.

She's fast, but I'm faster. It doesn't take much to keep up with her. The more we play this game, the harder my cock gets, and her words continuously ring out in my mind.

If you can catch me, you can fuck me.

Oh, baby girl. You should know better than to tempt a hunter like that.

I take off after her, running now. It's really too easy. Her legs are shorter than mine, and I'm used to pushing myself. I have the stamina to run through these woods until daylight, but I know she'll tire out before then.

I stay back just enough to scare her and have her turning around every few feet to look for me.

Unfortunately, she doesn't see the log until she's clambering over it and crashing face-first into the dirt.

I fall back, hiding in the shadows while she sputters on her hands and knees.

"Giving up so soon, little ghost? I thought you were better than that."

"Fuck you," she growls, out of breath. It's cute. Her anger. It'll make catching her all the sweeter.

"Soon. But first, I'm going to let you wear yourself out a bit."

She surges to her feet, rushing into the brush, and I smile with pride.

That's my fucking girl.

I knew the moment I laid eyes on her, there was more to the timid girl than she'd let on. She just needed someone to bring it out of her.

"Run, run, little ghost. There are monsters in these woods that would love to eat you for a midnight snack."

"You're sadistic," she calls back at me from up ahead.

"I prefer *creative.*"

I'm not even running. Just stalking after her. It's nothing to keep her in my line of sight.

I can practically smell the fear rolling off her as she runs as hard as she can. She didn't expect me to catch her, and certainly not once she ran into the trees.

I don't bother staying quiet. I want her to know I'm right behind her. I want her fear and panic and all those other delicious things that make her fight that much sweeter.

After all . . . she invited this chase. Not me.

For a split second, I lose sight of her through the darkest part of the forest, and when the sounds of her footfalls through the fallen leaves stop, so do I.

I hang back, listening for her rough breathing, but she's silent.

A smile spreads across my face.

She thinks she can hide from me.

"Tired, baby girl?"

As expected, I hear her quiet gasp, just past the few trees blocking my view of her. I sneak through the trees, avoiding the brush until I'm only a few feet away.

She looks around, hugging her arms tight around herself and shivering in the cool October air. She won't be cold for long. Soon, I'll have her burning up underneath my fingertips.

For a moment, I just look at her. My gaze rakes over her from head to toe. In the moonlight, I can see the way her chest rises and falls rapidly. The way she presses herself back against a tree.

I almost chuckle. Poor thing wore herself out.

It's about damned time. I've finally got her right where I want her.

Now it's time to claim my prize.

CHAPTER
Eleven

AVA

I am an idiot.

I'm not a runner. I'm not even athletic.

So why did I tell Levi that if he caught me, he could fuck me? I mean, what sane woman does that? I *knew* he'd love the challenge just for the simple fact that he's hellbent on punishing me for going through his room.

I should have known it wouldn't be that easy. Nothing with Levi Cross ever is.

Now, I'm pressed against a tree, a hand covering my mouth to silence my ragged breathing while I listen for the sounds of his footsteps.

It's pitch black, save for the streams of moonlight through the thick treetops. I can't see more than a few inches in front of me. I have no idea where I'm at or how far away from the house I am. I've never ventured this far into the woods, and now a complete psychopath is chasing me, determined to make me eat my words.

The thought of Levi catching me and pinning me down

expected. His rough words in my ear, his cock buried inside me, while he finishes what he started.

A shiver ghosts through me at the way he'd called out for me in the dark.

What does it say about me that the sound of his voice, leering from the darkness like a predator, makes me wet? Maybe it's just him, or maybe it's the fact that I haven't slept with anyone else in a long, long time, but I know a masochistic part of me, buried deep, deep down, wants him to catch me, so that I can see if he really lives up to the hype.

And maybe then we can move on and forget about this little cat-and-mouse game we've been playing for the last year.

My heart beats unsteadily as I strain to hear him. He's gone silent and call me crazy, but I feel like that's not a good sign.

Abruptly, something crashes a few yards off in the opposite direction, and I let out a quiet sigh of relief.

Maybe he won't catch me, after all . . .

But of course, I never get that lucky.

I turn and run right into his hard chest, letting out a screech in the night.

His hand snatches out, his fingers wrapping around my throat when I attempt to spin and dart away. At the same time I try to run, he grabs me, and we both stumble over the roots of a tree, crashing to the dirt. The wind is knocked out of me, and his weight pins me down on the rough forest floor beneath us.

"Please," I whimper when he rolls me onto my back.

"Please, what, my little thief? Let you go?" he taunts, his fingers gripping my wrists and shoving them to the ground above my head. I thrash in his hold, kicking and screaming, but I'm only hurting myself in the process. Levi's huge, and I'm a whole foot shorter than him. Not to mention, probably a hundred pounds lighter. There's no way I'm getting out of this.

Levi has the audacity to look bored with my antics in the pale glow of the moonlight overhead. I can barely see him, save for the wicked gleam in his eyes that tells me he's enjoying this. His breathing is heavy, mirroring my own, but it's his cock, hard and nestled against my thigh, that makes me pause.

I guess I'm not the only one turned on by our little chase through the woods.

"What were you after in my room?"

"You don't understand," I growl, arching against him, but it's useless.

"Were you searching for something in particular, or are you just a little klepto?"

"Neither," I pant, trying to roll him off of me, but my body is tired. After running through the woods for what felt like four hours, I can't imagine why.

"Stop," he commands, pressing himself between my legs. "You're just going to hurt yourself."

As if he cares.

"What's it matter? You're going to hurt me, anyway."

"You think so?" Levi chuckles darkly, and a tremor rolls through me at the sound.

My nails dig into his hands, holding mine, and I hope I draw blood. Serves him right for the stick digging into my back.

"Now that hurts my feelings. I've been nice to you. Let you get a head start and everything."

"You don't have feelings," I bite back.

"You're the one who came up with this little game, sweetheart. 'If you can catch me, you can fuck me'? You really think you stood a chance?"

For a moment there, yeah, I did.

Like I said. Stupid.

"Now, the question is, what am I going to do with my prize?"

At the same time he speaks, he shifts against me, rolling his hips against mine.

I grit my teeth to silence the sigh that threatens to rip free, the friction enough to draw goosebumps on my skin.

This is wrong. I should *not* want this. I shouldn't want him. He chased me through the trees like a maniac, hunting me like prey, and yet I can feel my thighs growing slick with need.

He thrusts against me again, and this time, my breath catches, my eyelids fluttering at the delicious heat overpowering every other sensation in my body.

"That's it," he grins wickedly when I let out a soft whimper, shifting underneath him. "It turned you on to get hunted, didn't it?"

"Fuck you," I bite, and he laughs, the sound filling the clearing and silencing everything else around us. Figures. Even nature knows not to fuck with Levi Cross.

It would be nice if my vagina could get the memo.

Levi sits back, releasing my hands and takes my hips in his instead.

"Oh, I plan to."

My pussy throbs in response to the rough edge in his voice, my heart beating unsteadily.

Looking down the length of my body, he slips his fingers under my T-shirt, over the planes of my stomach until he reaches my breasts. I didn't wear a bra for this endeavor because I thought I'd be in bed by now, the flash drive tucked away carefully until I could get rid of it.

The moment his fingers graze my bare nipple, I let out a quiet hiss through my teeth. This shouldn't feel good, but even as I think about how badly I hate him, I'm arching into his touch.

I try to fight it. I swear I do. Unfortunately, my body has other ideas. A gasp slips free when he rolls the hardened peak under his thumb. He grins savagely, thinking he's won.

God, hasn't he? He *has* won because now I'm not begging for his mercy. I'm begging for his touch.

"Fuck, look at you," he murmurs, rolling his hips against me. He drags his denim-covered cock over the notch in my leggings, and I swear I see stars. At the same time, he pinches my nipples, and I drag my teeth across my lip. "I'm going to enjoy this, sweetheart."

He shifts against me again, and I can't hold it any longer. A moan claws its way up my throat, something fluttering low in my core. God, it's awful, but I want to come so bad. With the way he's grinding against me, the friction is impossible to ignore.

"What's your safeword, Ava?" he rasps, his fingers tightening on my hips. He drags me closer, teasing me until I'm right on the edge.

"W-what?"

"Safeword. Surely, you've had one in the past?"

I can't even form a coherent thought, much less worry about whether I had a safeword in the past.

I shake my head, sticks and leaves digging into my hair. "I didn't have one."

My pussy tingles with the sudden lack of friction, but it's my skin that feels like it's on fire from the way his eyes glide over me.

"Excuse me?"

I swallow heavily over the lump forming in my throat. Levi stares down at me, seeming to put the pieces together slowly.

"Never?"

Gingerly, I shake my head.

Something in his gaze softens, but only for a moment.

"Not very safe, sweetheart. Give me a word—anything you can say, and that will be your word if you want me to stop."

He releases my hip and looms over me in the darkness, his frosty blue gaze searching mine. I can barely see him, and I'm glad. I'm sure if it were bright, this would be far more terrifying than it already is.

Being alone with Levi in the house is one thing.

Being alone in the woods with him is like volunteering to spend the afterlife in an eighty's slasher flick.

"Ava." A shiver ghosts up my spine at the bite in his voice. Almost like he's pissed off that I'm making him wait.

"Purgatory," I rush, without even thinking.

He stares at me for a moment before he nods.

"Purgatory." Both hands slide under my T-shirt, over my waist, then higher. "Fuck, you're so soft. I could break you. Make you bend to my every whim."

"Screw you," I breathe, but it's lost on him. His fingers slide higher, twisting my nipple, and I bite my lip to silence my moan.

He knows exactly what he's doing, because he does it again, his gaze locked on mine.

"Give me your sounds, Ava. Don't try to hide from me."

Asshole. He doesn't deserve them.

Bending down, his lips latch around my nipple and he sucks, drawing his tongue over the hardened peak. I arch into his mouth, the pleasure forcing me to bite back the desperate cry that threatens to break free.

He watches me under his lashes, nipping the hardened peak between his teeth before moving to the other side.

"These are perfect," he grunts, almost like he's pissed off about it.

At the same time, his lips latch around my other breast, his hand slides between us, gliding under the waistband of my leggings. His fingers cover my pussy, and he slips my thong to the side to drag his finger through my folds.

"Fuck," he rasps, his lips breaking free. Looming over me in the dark, he slides that finger inside me, and I'm powerless to stop the quiet gasp that escapes.

Levi grins, slowly pumping that finger inside me.

"There she is. Let me hear you, baby girl."

I shake my head, and his eyes light with a challenge. Sinking down, he presses kisses along my breasts and torso, stopping to run his tongue up my stomach before he moves even lower. I shiver under his touch, my body tightening around his finger slipping in and out of me. Wet sounds fill the air, and I know I should be embarrassed, but I'm not. It feels too good.

"What are you doing?" I ask nervously when he leans back, withdrawing his hand from my panties. He fists my leggings on either side of my hips and drags them down, completely exposing me to him.

His eyes light with fire when they slide over me, leaving a searing path in their wake.

"Fucking perfect," he breathes, and I get the feeling he didn't mean to say it out loud. "Fuck, I'm going to ruin you."

In a flash, he's flipped me over until I'm on my stomach. Hiking me up by my bare hips, he drags my panties down around my knees before he pushes my shoulders down to arch my back.

Then he licks me from clit to ass, and I nearly jerk out of my body.

He groans in satisfaction, his hands tightening to near-bruising strength on my hips while I let out a startled sound.

"Easy now, little ghost," he chuckles against my skin. He circles my entrance, teasing me, and all I can do is dig my nails into the dirt and take it.

My eyes flutter closed, his quiet growl enough to make my stomach dip.

He licks me like a man starved, dragging my hips back to meet the thrust of his tongue inside me. It feels so good that I can't help but rock against his tongue. His lips seal around my clit, and I can't silence the whimper that slips free.

"Fuck, yes," he grunts against me. In a flash, he throws me onto my back before he dives back between my folds. My head thuds back into the dirt, my back arching to get me closer to his mouth, and my skin hot, despite the cool night air.

He looks feral in this light. Like a monster come to rip me to shreds, and with the way his lips latch around my clit. He flutters his tongue, and I actually think that might be true.

No woman could survive Levi Cross. That's what makes him the unobtainable. Especially not when he growls in satisfaction when my thighs tighten around his head. It's too much. Too powerful.

"Please . . ." I don't even know what I'm begging for, at this point. Mercy or an orgasm. Somehow, they seem like the same thing.

Levi slips a hand between us, his finger sliding back inside me. My body sucks him in greedily, betraying how badly I want this.

"Look at you," Levi purrs. He curls his finger up before slipping it back out to add a second. "So wet and willing for me. Your pussy is begging for my cock, Ava. You feel that? Feel how wet you are? It's dripping into my palm."

My head falls to the side. I can't look at him when he's saying such dirty things to me. His mouth is filthy, and the fact that it only makes me want him more is shameful.

"Tell me, baby girl... why would you agree to give me free rein to play with this body without any rules? You knew I'd catch you."

Because I've wanted it for months . . .

"Momentary lapse of judgement," I breathe, and he

chuckles, dipping his head back down. He licks and sucks my clit until I'm not sure if purgatory is my safeword or the world I must have fallen into in my jaunt through the woods.

My hands fist in my hair, his hair. He growls in acquiescence when I roll against his tongue, his fingers pumping harder. He brushes them over some dark part inside me that only drives me closer to the edge.

So close. I just need . . . God, I don't know what I need, but I know he does, and judging by the wicked gleam in his eyes, he's withholding it from me.

"Tell me what you were hunting for?"

"Nothing," I growl, but the sound is breathier than I'd like.

"Tell me, Ava, and I'll give you what you want."

"No, you won't. You'll just hurt me."

"Tell me what you were after, sweetheart, and I'll make you come."

God, I want to come so bad. With the way he's grinding against me, the friction is impossible to ignore, but I can't. If I tell him, there's no chance for him.

"Come on, Ava. Give me all your secrets, and I'll make you come for me. Your pussy is begging to come, isn't it? You can feel yourself getting hot. Fuck you're so beautiful."

A sob wracks up my throat while he keeps my body suspended right on the edge. I'm so close, I need a little more, and this *need* I've felt growing over the past year can finally fade away, but he's not letting me.

"I can't tell you," I breathe. Tears slip down my cheeks, and I'm not sure if it's from the overwhelming pleasure radiating through me or the knowledge of what he'll do when he finds out.

"Why, Ava?"

"Because they're going to hurt me," I whisper, and that's when everything comes to an abrupt halt.

My pussy tingles with the sudden lack of attention, but it's my skin that feels like it's on fire from the way his eyes glide over me.

"Want to run that by me again, baby girl?"

I shake my head, pinching my lips together. I feel like I swallowed a softball.

A shiver ghosts up my spine at the bite in his voice. Almost like he's angry that I didn't tell him sooner. Why would I? He's made it clear from the moment we met that he wants nothing to do with me. At least, until now, when his cock is pressing against me.

I shake my head. "I don't know."

I suck in a shaky breath. I'm trembling with the adrenaline from my lost orgasm mixed with the fear of telling the man between my legs what they wanted me to steal from him.

"I don't know," I repeat. I swipe at the tears on my cheeks, and his eyes narrow. I can't read the look in his eyes, but I bet it's akin to the same look Julius Caesar gave Brutus.

He's right. He is going to ruin me.

Abruptly, he leans back, grips my hips, and flips me back over onto my stomach. Hiking me up until my ass is in the air, he leans down, sealing his lips around my clit with a growl. He flutters his tongue until I come with a hoarse cry, my head buried in the dirt.

"Fuck, I've waited ages to hear that fucking sound," he grits against my skin, raising up behind me. His hands roam over my bare skin, and I shiver with the aftershocks of my orgasm.

And just when I think he's going to let me get away, he holds me even tighter.

"Not so fast, baby girl. We're just getting started."

CHAPTER
Twelve

LEVI

She's lying.

I believe that she may not know who sent her after me, but there's more to the story than she's letting on. Oddly enough, I'm willing to bet it has everything to do with the flash drive hidden in a very unreachable place. What I don't believe is that she's telling me the whole truth.

She tries to crawl away from me, her body still vibrating under my hands. For a moment, I worried I broke her with how hard she came against my tongue.

My pretty little thief.

Finally, with the truth out in the open, I can take her the way we both desperately need. I wasn't lying when I said her pussy was dripping for me. I draw back, running my fingers through the come slipping through her folds and swirling it around her clit.

I knew there was more to her than the stuck-up, prudish demeanor she likes to portray. I knew once I got my hands on her, she'd turn into my perfect little slut.

forest.

Maybe then, this fascination with her will have faded, and I can move on with my life.

Unfortunately, something tells me it won't be that easy.

After her orgasm, her body went slack in my hands, and she fell to her stomach in the dirt. I hike her body up, pulling her back against my chest. My nose skims along the side of her neck, drinking her in, and I shiver at the feel of her in my palms.

My hand slips down between her legs, and I roll her clit in circles, slowly edging her toward another orgasm. She drips down my fingers, her pussy practically begging for me to slide inside.

"Fuck, look how ready you are, Ava," I rasp in her ear, and she shivers. "This body was made for me to fuck."

She whimpers, adjusting in my grip while my hand slides over the smooth, creamy skin above her pussy.

Fucking hell, she's perfection. Everything I've been dreaming of since the moment I laid eyes on her. All soft and warm skin dipped in the scent of citrus. I've never cared what perfume a woman wore until I caught a whiff of my little housekeeper.

"That what you want? Want me to fuck you? Fill up this pretty little cunt until you're begging for more."

"I want you to go to hell," she breathes, and my lips kick up in a smirk.

"Baby girl," I whisper, brushing the hair back from her face. "I've been there. I found it boring."

Before she can mouth off again, I push her forward, adjusting her so her knees are spread wide. In the barely visible moonlight overhead, I can just make out her glistening folds, shining from my mouth on her cunt.

She jumps when I lower the zipper of my jeans, and when I tug my cock out, I bite back a groan at the friction.

I've been rock-fucking-hard since the moment I found her in my room.

Made running through the forest pretty fucking difficult, but it was worth every second.

"Last chance, Ava." I stroke my cock through her folds, and her pussy flowers open for me. Her juices coat my dick, and I use it to stroke myself, my eyes fluttering closed at how fucking good it feels to finally get some relief. "You going to safe word on me?"

"As if I have a choice," she snorts, and in a rush, I swat her ass. Not hard, but she gets the point. She yelps, falling forward onto her stomach, and reaches back to cover her exposed skin.

I don't give her any time to recover, dragging her back to her knees. I fist her hair in my hand and tug her head back until she's forced to look at me.

"You always have a choice, Ava. Whether or not you like the outcome is up to you."

She bares her teeth, and I grin, releasing her.

"Fine, little ghost. Have it your way."

I pull her back to me, fisting my cock and dragging it back through her folds. She falls down to lay her head against her arm, arching her ass into the air. She's attempting to look like she's given up. She doesn't realize she's only enticing me more.

She's so wet and ready, I push in the first inch, and my body tightens, feeling her squeezing around me.

Fucking hell . . .

"Wait," she jumps, attempting to push herself up. When I don't let her, rocking my hips into her, she whimpers, falling back to her hands and arching against me. "No condom."

"You're not on birth control?" Oddly enough, this isn't enough to make me stop.

"Of course, I am. I still don't want whatever you might be

carrying," she growls back, yet she wiggles her hips, allowing me to slip deeper. My hands tighten on her ass, and I push in further, drawing a quiet gasp from her when I push in halfway.

"This may come as a surprise to you, sweetheart," I bite, clenching my eyes shut. "But you're the first girl I've ever fucked without a condom . . . and I'm afraid you just created a monster."

My head kicks back to the stars, a shudder running through me. Every clench of her tight muscles has me gritting my teeth, holding myself back from rutting into her.

When I pull back, only to thrust back inside her, she lets out a moan.

"Fuck, Ava. You have the tightest cunt. Like a virgin, squeezing the fucking life out of me."

I look down to where my cock is sliding in and out of her, agonizingly slow. The animalistic urge to claim her is the only thing I can think about. The desire to fuck her into the dirt until she walks out of these woods knowing she will never find another who will fuck her the way I do.

I need her to beg for me. Her whimpers and soft sighs aren't enough. I want her moaning my name and clawing at the dirt when I make her come for me over and over again until her legs are shaking uncontrollably.

To say she's stolen my sanity is an understatement. I'm full-on fucking deranged.

I should savor this, but fuck, I'm too far gone to care. I want her too fucking badly.

My hips hit her ass, the sound of our skin meeting filling the dark clearing. Black dots appear in the corners of my vision every time she tightens around me, her body greedily sucking me back in.

"Goddamn, baby girl," I grunt, my pace quickening. "You take it so fucking well. Like you were made for my cock, sweetheart."

She shudders at my words, moaning when I bottom out inside her.

"Oh my god," she gasps when I drag my cock back to stroke my head over her G-spot. She arches against me, letting me slip deeper.

I could come right now. I've fantasized about her for so long, it doesn't seem real.

"Please . . ." she begs, and I groan.

That's it. That's exactly what I need.

"You're close, Ava. I can feel you tightening around me," I rasp as I fuck her, not stopping. I reach under her, swirling her clit with my fingers again, and she jerks in my grasp. "You're going to come for me like a good girl, aren't you?"

When she doesn't answer me, I smack her ass again. She yelps, but follows it with a moan, her back arching further, welcoming me. Running my hand up her spine, I feel her pressing back against me, eager to take what I'm giving her. I fuck her harder, matching the pace with my fingers on her clit until she's nearly crying with the building pleasure.

"So close . . ." she breathes, laying her head down on the ground. Her eyes are closed, and from what I can see, there are wet streaks slipping from the corners of her eyes. I slide my hand up her neck, fisting my hands in her hair, and use it as leverage to fuck her deeper.

"Come on, Ava. Be a good little slut and come on my cock."

Her moans grow louder, her pussy tighter, and when she comes, it's with a cry that fills the air around us.

I grit my teeth, damn near seeing stars with how hard she clenches around me.

"That's my fucking girl."

She shivers, her eyes rolling back in her head, and her hair stuck to her face. I fuck her through her orgasm and force myself to pull out before I can come. I'm close, but I'm nowhere near finished with her yet.

Once we walk out of these woods, she'll no longer be my plaything. One night is all I'm giving myself before I let her go because I know the moment I don't, I'll be too addicted to stop.

I rip my hoodie over my head, tossing it to the ground. Then, I take her hips in my hand and lift her onto it, rolling her onto her back. She peers up at me through her lashes, and she looks so utterly fucked covered in dirt and a small spot of blood where she must have hit a tree branch, that for a moment, I think I'm fucking dreaming.

Then, I slide back inside her, and I'm reminded just how real this is.

"Fuck, Ava," I bite. I place my hands on either side of her head and pump inside her, punishing her with each thrust. Leaning down, I run my nose up the side of her neck, drinking her citrus straight from the source. "Your fight is intoxicating, sweetheart. I could watch you struggle with how bad you need my cock all day."

"I hate you," she breathes, but any anger she had is lost when she tightens her legs around my hips. Her hands slide down my sides, the blunt ends of her nails brushing against my bare skin where my T-shirt rides up.

I fucking hate the shiver that ghosts through me. It's fucking ridiculous.

"Keep talking, little ghost. Tell me how much you despise me and let me prove you wrong when I make you come again."

Her head kicks back, and I fall over her, fucking her harder. The base of my cock brushes against her clit, and her nails dig into my shoulders. Her heels press into my ass, urging me for more.

I wrap my arms around her, holding her tightly. One of my

hands hooks underneath her knee, bringing her leg up so I can hit her deeper. The other fists the roots of her hair to drag her head back.

She's panting, her breathing mirroring my own. I bury my face in the side of her neck, nipping and sucking a path up to her jaw. I feel her heart pounding in the pulse point in her throat. Taste the perspiration clinging to her skin. These aren't things I normally notice, but somehow, all it makes my chest tighten irrationally.

I skim my lips over her ear, my voice rough. "Who fucks you, baby girl?"

"Do you have to talk?"

I'd love to punish her for that, but for now, I let it go because I know how bad my filthy mouth turns her on.

"Answer the question, little ghost."

Her tongue darts out to lick her lips, and suddenly, I'm acutely aware of how she tastes.

"You do."

I shake my head, heat sliding down the base of my spine as my cock grows thicker. Ava's lashes flutter, her desperate little whimpers driving me fucking insane.

"Wrong answer, Ava."

Her brows knit together in confusion, dissolving into one of pure desire when I change the angle of our hips, allowing me to brush over that sweet spot inside her.

"Levi."

The sound of her saying my name sends a rush through me that rivals any narcotic on the market.

"Again."

"Levi," she breathes, her voice airier. A groan rumbles through me, and I roll my groin against her clit, drawing out a soft moan that does really does it for me.

I skim my lips down the side of her face, dangerously close

to her mouth. Fuck, I want to kiss her. I've never wanted to kiss another soul in my life. Kissing breeds feelings, and where Ava and I are concerned, there are none. Nothing more than contempt and this maddening desire to fuck her that I can't seem to control.

"Again," I demand, knowing I sound like the fucking psychopath she claims I am, but I don't give a fuck.

"Levi," she moans, her eyes growing heavy and her breathing shallow.

I fist her hair tighter, and she rolls her hips against mine with every thrust. Her little moans fill the night air, spurring me on.

"Levi . . . I'm going . . ."

I grab her hands, pinning them to the ground above her head, and give her what she needs to come for me, again.

She explodes underneath me, crying out my name like it's a Hail Mary into the night.

"*Levi* . . ." she cries, her tight pussy strangling my cock. She steals the breath from my lungs, and I fuck her through her orgasm with quick, harsh thrusts. It feels so fucking good, I swear I black out for a moment.

I slam into her, my vision blurry and my chest tight. And then I fucking explode.

"*Fuck, Ava* . . ." I grip her with bruising force, a white-hot light shooting through me when I come so hard, it steals my breath away.

The moment I float back down to earth, it's to find her watching me through half-lidded eyes. I pause, a tremor rolling through me from how hard I'd come.

Prissy little Ava Ryan made me come harder than I ever have in my life.

Fuck. What has she done to me?

She's shivering underneath me. Whether from her orgasm

or the cold, I don't know. I draw her closer, pressing her against me to warm her up.

She shakes in my arms, and when I pull out of her, I hiss at the loss of her wet heat.

Slowly, I climb off her and rise to my feet, holding out a hand to pull her up. She stands on wobbly legs, her hair mused and filled with leaves and sticks from the forest floor.

A better man would take her home and clean her up. Run a bath for her and massage the kinks out of her neck from fucking her on the forest floor.

I'm not a better man, though, and the sooner she figures that out, the better.

"I can't believe I let you do that to me," she grumbles.

Not to be mistaken with, *I can't believe I let you fuck me in the woods.* That's slightly less insulting.

She tugs her leggings back up her hips, and I'm almost pissed that her ass is gone. I was enjoying staring at it.

"Well, believe it or not, sweetheart. It happened," I murmur, grabbing my hoodie off the ground. I toss it to her, and she tosses it back.

Fine. She wants to be a brat; she can be a *cold* brat.

She starts walking, not even bothering to make sure I'm with her.

"You're going the wrong way."

She pauses, her shoulders tight.

I see my little prude is back.

Without another word, she turns and stalks in the other direction. I chuckle under my breath and follow behind her.

We make the trek back to the house in silence, and she ignores me when I hold my hand out to help her. That's fine. She can pout all she wants. I don't owe her anything. She wanted it just as bad as I did.

Yet . . . somehow . . . I still feel like a dick when I catch sight of the scratch on her cheek.

Fuck that.

Why the fuck should I feel guilty? She broke into my room. Snooped through my shit. She was going to steal from me. She's lucky she's still got a job and a place to live.

It's not until we make it up to the house that I've decided I've had enough of her little attitude.

Fuck it.

Before she can make a mad dash into her room and slam the door in my face, I grab her, shoving her back into the wall, my hand wrapped around her throat.

She lets out a startled gasp, her pretty green eyes going wide, and a look of fear on her face. As if she actually thinks I could hurt her.

My thumb brushes over her rapid heartbeat in the side of her throat, and she swallows heavily, a shiver moving through her.

"Don't think I won't find out what you're hiding, Ava. And when I do, you'd better hope to God you have a good excuse for sneaking around my room."

I watch the gears turning in her head, as if she's trying to come up with a new lie to spin. It won't work. I can see right through her, and the moment I find out who she's working with, I'm going to enjoy punishing my new little toy.

Because she may not know it yet, but the forest wasn't the end of this arrangement. It's not over until I say it is.

And I've barely gotten a taste.

I shove away from her before I can drag her back to my room for the night, stalking across the hall. Before I shut the door, I turned back and found her still pressed against the wall, watching me under heavy lashes.

"Until next time, little ghost."

Jessi Hart

CHAPTER
Thirteen

AVA

I'm officially another statistic.

Just another poor, pathetic soul left shattered after a night with Levi Cross. Shattered because I no longer know who I am.

I look down at the dirt caked in my nails in the shower. I've tried scrubbing, but I can't get it all. My pussy feels like I had sex with the *Incredible Hulk,* and my back and tailbone are sore from the hard ground.

The worst part?

I can't even be angry. I asked for it. Hell . . . I *wanted* it.

Who tempts a wolf with a fresh, juicy steak?

Someone who has a death wish, I think dryly.

Every time I move, I'm reminded he was there. While I'm not a virgin, the ache between my thighs is new. Before Levi, I'd slept with a grand total of two guys. Levi feels like the equivalent of *six* of those guys all mashed together into one dangerously handsome psychopath.

And now . . . I'm screwed.

have a feeling they'll be back. It's only a matter of time before they come to collect whatever the hell is on that elusive flash drive.

Something tells me the excuse that Levi caught me isn't going to fly.

I take a deep breath, trying to steady my nerves. I have to think. I can't panic.

—Who am I kidding? Panicking is what I do best.

The truth is, I'm out of options. Every step I take feels like walking a tightrope over a pit I can't see the bottom of. Who knows what happens after I fail to deliver what they've requested?

That thought alone terrifies me more than anything else.

When I cut the shower off and step out into the steamy bathroom, I catch a glimpse of myself in the mirror as I wipe the steam away.

I *look* shattered. How do you go back to the mundane after a night like that? Will I ever even walk comfortably again?

After we made the long trek back to the house, and he promised to find out exactly what I was up to in his room, I wobbled to my bed and passed out, exhausted from the night's activities. I'd woken up dirty, sore, and confused before I was forced to reconcile that last night wasn't a fever dream. I really did that.

What kind of person hunts someone down in the woods and fucks them in the dirt?

What kind of person *asks* for it?

Growling at my own reflection, I storm back to my room. People have sex every day. Some have even kinkier sex than I could ever dream of. A romp in the woods is like foreplay for those people.

So, why am I so upset over one night?

Is it the way he called me *baby girl*? How my body seemed

to react to the nickname like he was some kind of sex god. Or maybe it's how even when he was rough, his hands were gentle, like I was made of glass.

Maybe it's just because I've been thinking about him for so long that now that I've had a taste of him, I'm not sure which way is up, let alone how to regulate these strange, tender feelings blooming in my chest.

Unfortunately, as much as I'd like to pretend otherwise, I'm not indifferent, and that's a problem.

Despite how crude he is. Despite the way he acts like I'm beneath him half the time, there's this little voice screaming in the back of my head that he's not a bad man. He pretends he is to hide the fact that he can't sleep at night because the nightmares wake him. That he's an alcoholic, still struggling with his childhood and his father's death, and that he cares a whole hell of a lot more than he lets on.

Levi definitely cares. He just hates himself for it.

Luckily, today is my day off, so when I put on some clean clothes, no one is expecting me. I take my time—totally not hiding in my room to avoid the man across the hall—and clean. I change my sheets because they're stained with mud and littered with bits of leaves and sticks. I vacuum and I even sort through some of my clothes before I'm forced to acknowledge the fact that my stomach is literally eating itself.

Silently, I make my way downstairs to the kitchen to look for something to eat. I find some leftover pasta that Javier had made the night before and grab a bowl, sliding it into the microwave. While I wait, I cross to the far cupboard to fetch a glass for water.

Only to run right into a hard wall of muscle.

Uh oh.

Levi catches me with an arm around my waist and a devious glint in his eyes.

"God, do you moonlight as a brick wall?" I snap, and he cocks a brow. I fall back a step when he steps forward, then another and another until my back hits the wall and all the air whooshes out of me.

He towers over me, his frame blocking mine until all I can see is him. He leans on his arm above my head, his front so close to mine, I can feel the heat of his body against my skin. My breath catches in my throat, my pulse skyrocketing as that familiar scent of whiskey washes over me like a drug.

"Hello, little ghost," he greets so quietly, I can barely hear him over the pounding of my own heart.

His eyes burn with amusement. His free hand comes up, brushing a lock of hair back from my face, and my skin burns where his fingertips touch.

"You seem tense, Ava," he says, his thumb lingering on my cheek for far too long to be considered appropriate.

"Not that it matters to you, but I'm hungry."

"Last night work up an appetite for you?" His gaze flicks down my body. In response, my core tightens. "Are you sore?"

"I don't know why you're pretending to care," I bite, and dry amusement flickers across his gaze.

He readjusts, and my hands press further into the wall when his lower half brushes against mine. For a striking moment, I feel . . . *him* pressed against my stomach before he readjusts.

Last night comes flooding back to me, and warmth travels down my spine. It's madness, considering how this will only end one way. I'm nothing more than a distraction for him. Eventually, he'll get tired of me and leave me alone.

I'm merely enticing now because it's something new. He practically hates me, yet, for some sick reason, he wants me, and that pisses him off. Even if he won't say it, there's a part of Levi Cross that can't ignore me any more than I can ignore him.

"I couldn't care less. I won fair and square."

Rude.

"Oh, so fucking me was a challenge?"

"Perhaps . . . I always did love giving to charity."

What. A. Dick.

I shove at him, but he doesn't budge, and I'm this close to stabbing him with my bare fingers, if that's even possible.

"Little Ava, so afraid to live her life. Tell me, is that why Mendez is so fascinated with you? He thinks you'll be easy to control?"

"His name is Alex," I correct, looking at his lips. It's a mistake because I can't stop thinking about the way they felt against my skin just last night. "Don't you have something better to do? Like steal virgins in the night?"

His lips tip up in a smirk, and he inches even closer

"I'd love to hear how you lost your virginity. I have a feeling you weren't inviting some little frat boy to chase you through the woods?"

"Still thinking of last night? I thought you weren't interested?" I breathe, accidentally looking at him for a split second.

Unfortunately, it's long enough to send a shot of desire through me.

My entire body is humming with approval at having him in my space while my mind races a mile a minute trying to combat the shame of wanting a man so inestimably that it's burning through my veins.

"Mmm . . . I find you *very* interesting, baby girl."

My heart flutters uncontrollably; my stomach drops to my toes.

"Pity. You must have fallen and bumped your head if you think anything between us will ever happen again."

A twinkle of something dark and repressed flashes across

his gaze, before it's replaced with a calm clarity that stirs something unsettling in me. Stepping forward, he aligns the front of his body to mine, his knee pressing between my legs, and I let out a quiet gasp, trying to shove him back. I may as well be fighting with a brick wall because he doesn't move.

His lips curl into a snarl, and I can feel his erection digging into my stomach.

God, this man is insane. Any one of his family members could walk in, and here I am, practically grinding against his thigh in the kitchen.

"There will come a time when you will learn not to play these little games with me, Ava. I'm not the good guy you want to pretend I am. I'm not pining after you. I'm not waiting around for you to fuck me. You are nothing more than my prudish little housekeeper. Last night meant nothing."

Alarm bells scream in my head, telling me to run, but my body begs to drag him closer. Beg for more friction, the brush of his hands on me, anything to quell the raging inferno in my blood.

There's a breath of silence where neither of us moves. Both of us lost to the feeling of each other's bodies, and if I didn't know any better, I'd say the hardness pressed against me proves he's not at all indifferent to my effect on him.

In a bold move on my part that surprises even me, I reach between us, cupping his erection through his jeans, and force myself to meet his gaze.

"This is all I need to know you're lying."

His jaw tenses so much I fear for his teeth. I brush my thumb over his length—his overzealous length, might I add— and his nostrils flare.

And then I let go of him, place both my hands on his chest, and shove him back with all my might. The air is cold where his skin was touching mine, and I ignore the goosebumps pebbling on my flesh.

Levi glares at me. Or maybe he's looking at me in awe. Honestly, with him, they look almost the same.

"Oh, and a word of advice," I say, pausing in the doorway to the kitchen with my bowl of pasta in hand. "The next time you decide to chase a girl through the woods and fuck her, maybe bring a condom. I'd hate for you to have to deal with the consequences of your own actions for a change."

CHAPTER
Fourteen

LEVI

I pull on my cigarette, letting out the cloud of smoke and watching it hang in the air of night. A ship horn blasts somewhere out in the bay, signaling it's coming into port, but it's not why I'm here.

A noise catches my attention, and my gaze shoots back to the docks to where a ship is being unloaded a few yards away.

They can't see me where I am, hidden in the brush across the street. They do this under the cover of night. Not many are awake at three a.m., but I am.

I've been here for an hour, just watching. Waiting for the proof I need.

A black SUV pulls through the gates, heading over to where they're unloading the remaining cargo from the small ship. I pull out my binoculars, zooming in on the back of the car.

A worker crosses the dock, heading toward the back window. They exchange words, but the glass is tinted, making

My hands shake with uncontrollable rage.

My blood roars in my ears.

All this time, it was right there in front of my face, and yet, I didn't want to believe it.

I still don't.

I'm about to turn away when I spot him. The back door opens, and he climbs out, smoothing down the lines of his suit. He looks around, his gaze sliding over me where I'm standing in the shadows. He doesn't see me . . . but he can sense me.

His gaze lingers in the shadows surrounding me for only a moment before he starts walking toward the warehouse off the docks, presumably where they store all the drugs that come in on the ships.

I watch him disappear through the doors as the last bit of cargo is placed on the dock.

In the blink of an eye, everything goes silent.

The men on the docks disperse—the doors to the warehouse slam shut. Even the waves of the ocean fall silent.

Silently, I slip my flask out of my back pocket, raising it to my lips.

I let the whiskey coat my senses, drowning out the noise in my head, telling me to go in there and put a bullet between his eyes.

Slowly, I roll my shoulders, cracking my neck.

My day will come. When it does, Trailblazer Corp, the DEA, and all of Seattle will know not to fuck with what's mine.

My father may have been a sick, sadistic mother fucker, but one thing he taught me before I killed him?

No one fucks with the Cross's.

Least of all, him.

"Starting a mechanic's business now?"

I glance up at the sound of Christian's voice as he steps through the open garage door. I've been out here since the moment I got back this morning, hands deep in the guts of Ava's beat-up Oldsmobile.

The damn thing barely qualifies as a car. Tires worn down to threadbare rubber, the heater gasping like it's on life support, and the engine rattling like bones in a coffin. Hell, it would probably make a better boat anchor than a vehicle.

Christian stops beside the gold monstrosity Ava has named Judith, and leans down, his nose wrinkling at the fuzzy, purple seat covers as if they might be contagious.

"Cute. Purple's really your color."

"Yeah, fuck you," I grunt, slamming the hood shut with a satisfying clang that echoes off the garage walls. "Thing's a piece of shit."

"Thought you didn't care?" he tosses back, amused.

"I don't," I snap, a little too quickly.

He raises both hands in mock surrender, lips twitching. "Right. Must've been imagination."

It's not entirely a lie. I didn't fix it *for* her. Not exactly. I just needed something to do. Something to keep my hands and brain busy while everything around me unravels. I've always been good with cars—took apart and rebuilt my first one before I was sixteen. I even fixed my Aston's front grill after we slammed into Mega-deer the other night.

Christian watches me for a beat longer, the amusement in his eyes softening into something else—concern, maybe, or curiosity. I don't care enough to figure it out, and that's probably for the best.

"You're avoiding something," he says quietly, almost casually, but there's an edge there I can't ignore.

I snort, wiping grease-streaked hands on an already filthy rag. "Yeah," I grunt. "You."

He shrugs. "Or her."

Jesus fucking Christ.

"Don't you have something better to do?"

"Nah, I'm avoiding Bella and her Christmas demands."

I round the car and slide into the driver's seat. The scent of her perfume hits me instantly. I can't fucking escape it.

Warm citrus and a hint of vanilla. Light, sweet. Unmistakable. It clings to the fabric, to the steering wheel, to everything. My mouth waters, and the memory of her pressed against me in the woods crashes over me like a tidal wave.

So soft and warm. The way she moaned my name. Fucking hell, she was perfection.

Fucking hell.

I hate it.

I hate that I crave her.

"So, where'd you go last night?" Christian asks, voice casual—but I know him too well.

I open my mouth to tell him about the information I'd learned, but fall silent. I don't need to implicate him any further in this mess. He's finally able to relax and settle down with his wife. He doesn't need to be a part of my problems.

"Met a girl," I say instead.

He tilts his head. "Yeah? Only to come home and fix another girl's car?"

"Am I being interrogated?"

Jesus Christ. "You're being asked."

I scowl. "I've got shit to do."

He shrugs. "I don't give a shit who you're seeing. Just don't bring—"

"Don't bring shit home. I know."

We stare at each other for a long beat, tension like static in the air. Then he leans back against the counter, jaw ticking. Watching me.

"You don't need to worry about me," I grunt, turning the car over before he can say anything else.

The car coughs, sputters, then miraculously roars to life. I rev the engine a few times, listening to the uneven tick like a time bomb counting down. There's no way this thing survives the winter.

Where the hell did she even find this car? A junkyard? The ocean floor?

"I've been thinking," Christian says suddenly, "about this lodge. This house."

"What about them?"

"You really want to spend the next fifty years doing the same shit?"

I shrug, scrubbing my hands in the sink. "Wasn't our decision. Mom and Dad did that."

"Yeah, well, there's nothing saying we can't change it."

"You want to change the lodge?"

"Just a thought."

"If you want to change it, change it. You won't hear any complaints from me—"

I freeze.

Across the gravel path, Ava is walking toward the house, her laugh soft, head tilted back—and standing next to her is that smug, fuck-faced security guard, Alex Mendez.

My vision narrows.

Christian must feel the air change. He follows my gaze, and when he sees her, then me, he lets out a knowing breath.

"Definitely just my imagination."

"Fuck you," I mutter.

A rush of something pissed off washes over me.

"Have fun with that."

Christian slaps my shoulder with a smirk and disappears inside, but I barely notice. My attention is pinned to the woman outside and the man who doesn't know just how much I would enjoy slicing every one of his fingers off for touching her.

She doesn't notice me lurking in the shadows of the garage, but Mendez does. The fucker looks over her head while she's completely oblivious, and winks my way, a twisted grin spreading on his lips.

And then, she does something that's going to cost her.

He's brushing something—leaves?—from her hair, and she thanks him with that sweet, innocent smile she has *never* given to me. My stomach twists—my pulse pounds.

Ava walks away, toward the house, and Mendez has the audacity to turn my way, winking.

My grip tightens on the wrench until pain shoots through my fingers, and suddenly, I'm thinking of all the ways I can punish her.

I tell myself I don't care. Who gives a fuck if he touches her? I have no claim to her.

Then something in me snaps.

Fuck it.

Ava Ryan is *mine*. She just doesn't know it.

I toss the wrench onto the bench and stride toward the house, boots echoing against the tile. Every step calculated. Measured. I round the corner, eyes locked on the dark-haired girl at the other end of the hall.

She spots me and freezes.

Her gaze widens. She knows something's changed. Maybe it's the look in my eyes. Maybe it's the air thick with tension. I see the fear flash across her pretty features. It's quick—but it's there.

She smiled for him.

I'm not letting that shit slide.

She takes a cautious step back. I cock my head to the side, waiting to see what she's going to do.

She surprises me, spinning on her heel and running in the other direction.

I actually chuckle under my breath.

Fine, baby girl. Let's play.

CHAPTER
Fifteen

AVA

He's lost his mind.
Levi catches me around the waist, tugging me into the storage room.

"Running off again, Ava?"

"Let go of me, you *psychopath*," I growl.

He chuckles, forcing me back into the wall. His body covers mine, and liquid fire slips through my veins.

"Who's your friend?" he asks, a devilish grin on his face.

"Why do you care?"

Levi only smirks, bending down and pressing his lips to my ear.

"Your first mistake is thinking I do . . ." A tremor moves through me at the scratch of his stubble on my skin, and the heat that was already gathered between my legs amplifies to a scorching flame.

I surge in his grasp. "I'll scream."

He shoves me back against the wall, his big body boxing me in.

I stare at him blankly, my mind reeling at the near-feral look in his eyes.

Oh my God . . . Levi's jealous.

"Alex is my friend," I grit. I shouldn't care. The man is an actual psychopath, though I can't lie and say there aren't butterflies swarming through my stomach when his lips tip up in a sinister grin.

"Does he know that?"

Gathering all my strength, I place my hands flat on his chest and shove, but I may as well be shoving at the wall. He's at least a foot taller than me, and a whole lot stronger.

A soft, humorless chuckle escapes his lips.

"You've been hiding from me."

He's right. I have. After the other night, I haven't been able to get him out of my head.

The way his hands felt on my skin. The brush of his tongue against mine. The way he tasted like danger and sin and safety and everything I want to consume me, all wrapped up in one devilish man.

I'm no fool. A man like him would ruin a girl like me.

"Haven't you, little ghost?"

Slowly, I nod, unable to tear my gaze from his.

"I—"

"Shh . . ." he hums softly against my temple, his thumb tugging my bottom lip from between my teeth. He watches me like I'm the most fascinating thing in the world. Like a toy, he wants to take his time ripping apart.

My heart thunders in my chest, my clammy hands pressed to the wall behind me.

We shouldn't be doing this. I should shove away from him and go about my day. I *should* forget he exists and move on with my life.

Unfortunately, I've never been good at following the rules.

"Let me go," I breathe, warring with the demons in my head telling me not to let this man touch me and the fire burning my body to a crisp telling me he's the only one who can quench it.

He leans closer, boxing me in, making sure I feel every inch of him pressed against me. My nipples are drawn to tight points. My clit is throbbing in my panties. My heartbeat skitters to a stop when his lips meet the shell of my ear.

His hand snakes into my hair, fisting the strands and tugging my head back. He leans in, pressing his nose into the crook of my shoulder and inhaling, like he's memorizing my scent.

"You can't stop thinking about it, can you?" His other hand slips down my side, over my hip, and to my thigh, teasing at the hem of my shirt. His finger traces over the smooth flesh peeking out beneath, and heat slips through my veins. "How it felt when you were grinding against my cock. How bad your pussy ached to have me inside you."

God, he's filthy . . .

"I don't want anything to do with you," I lie, breath trembling when he chuckles darkly.

"See, baby girl . . . I think you're lying." My stomach dips at the nickname, and I hate it.

He presses his lips to my neck right over my racing pulse. His gentleness, mirrored by the roughness in his voice, throws me for a loop. As if he wants to rip me to pieces, but he's barely holding on to his self-control.

Something tells me Seattle couldn't handle Levi Cross unhinged.

"I think you're salivating for my fingers in your cunt. Teasing you until you come all over them." I bite my lip, a shaky breath managing to slip free when he traces the hem of my jeans, up to the center of my thighs. "That what you want? You want me to touch you?" His fingers stroke up and down my thigh as if he's taunting me. Testing me to see just how far he can push me before I break.

The pressure in my core expands, and I can barely breathe from the weight of it. Like I'm going insane.

"My pretty little prudish housekeeper, hooked on the touch of a man she hates. Is that it, Ava? You're afraid of what everyone will say when they find out you're just as attracted to me as the women you claim you're nothing like?"

"Fuck you," I growl, surging in his hold. He shoves me back, harder this time, and his lips skate across my racing pulse.

"I can make you feel good, sweetheart," he whispers, and a shiver slides through me. The man is a walking red flag, yet I'm addicted to the attention he's giving me. The knowledge that someone is jealous over *me*. Let alone Levi Cross. It makes me feel wanted for the first time in my life.

But . . . unfortunately, I didn't realize it always comes with a price.

"You won't get what you need unless you tell me," Levi says in my ear, nipping my earlobe between his teeth, and for some reason, I feel it in my nipples. I bite my lip between my teeth, trying to work up the courage to walk away from him.

God, I can't believe I'm doing this.

"Yes."

He chuckles in my ear, and it's the scariest sound I've ever heard. My core pulses with need, burning hot when he flicks the button of my pants and slowly eases his hand inside.

Am I really about to let Levi Cross touch me?

"You've been dreaming of this, haven't you, Ava?" He slips my panties to the side, and I bite back a moan when his thumb slides through my folds, gathering my wetness. He releases a sharp breath, his fingers in my hair tightening and jerking my neck up to meet his gaze. "Say it."

"Only when I want to come," I admit, voice cracking, and he groans like he's been waiting to hear it his entire life.

"Suck." He raises his fingers to my lips. I don't get the chance to deny him, because when I open my mouth, he presses them against my tongue. I choke, tasting myself on his fingers. I've never experienced anything so . . . erotic in my life as the darkness in his gaze and his rough curse under his breath when he watches me suck my own flavor from his skin.

He pushes further into my throat, making me gag around his hand. Tears well in my eyes, clouding my vision, and all I can think about is what it would be like if it were his cock.

"Fuck, that's a good girl."

Pleasure zips straight through me, his rough approval stirring something inside me I didn't know existed.

And then, I realize I'd do anything to hear this man call me a good girl, again.

When he pulls his fingers from my mouth, he reaches down, swirling over my clit once, before he's sliding one long finger deep inside of me with a sharp hiss through his teeth.

"You're fucking drenched, Ava. Is this for him, or me?"

I don't respond, clamping my lips shut to keep the moan on my tongue from slipping free. My stomach tightens at the growl in his voice, the throb in my clit matching the whir of the pool cleaner in the room behind us.

He leans forward, pressing a hand over my mouth to silence me while he slips a second finger inside, watching my reaction.

"Fuck, that's tight, baby girl." Levi tightens his hold on my hair, tugging my head to the side, nipping the side of my neck. My pulse races beneath his teeth, and I gasp against his hand, biting it to silence the sound when he adds a third finger. "You're so sweet when you want something."

The pleasure in my stomach tightens when he swirls his

thumb up to my clit, rolling my wetness over the sensitive bud and clamping his hand tighter over my mouth to silence the moan that threatens to claw free.

I don't want to give him the satisfaction of knowing he's getting to me . . . even if the evidence is all over my inner thighs.

Somehow, I know if Levi were to know how much I *really* think about him, he'd use it as a weapon.

"Feel me, Ava?" he asks, his voice rumbling through my chest and going straight to my pussy. His lips travel up to my ear, his tongue dipping inside and rimming the shell. "Feel me filling your sweet little cunt? Imagine how good it'll feel when it's my cock."

"Levi," I breathe against his palm, my voice shaky and my skin damp with perspiration. I grind against his hand, chasing the pleasure as everything in my body tightens, right before it shatters.

And then his hand drops away.

I sputter at the loss of his touch, tears welling in the corners of my eyes out of frustration.

Fucking asshole.

Levi chuckles darkly, pressing his lips to my cheek with a rough kiss.

"You going to let that little prick touch you?"

He's freaking insane.

"I told you, he's just a friend," I grit.

My head knocks back into the wall when his fingers find me again. He releases his hold on my hair, only to move those fingers around to grip my throat and roughly force my gaze to his. They tighten enough to steal my breath away, and my own hand shoots up, wrapping around his as a momentary shot of panic courses through me.

It's very quickly replaced with a fever when his fingers find me again, and this . . . this is new.

He laughs under his breath, pride in his eyes when I let out a garbled moan, the pleasure doubled as my body comes alive under his fingers. My pussy clamps down when he slips two inside me, curling them up to brush over a spot that has me seeing stars.

I arch into his palm, my eyes clamping shut as the first waves of my orgasm start to tear through me.

He removes his hand completely. "Answer the question, baby girl."

"No," I hiss between my teeth.

He chuckles, the sound dripping with malice. He presses closer to me, his hard cock digging into my stomach as he lowers his lips back to my ear.

I let out a growl, tears slipping down my cheeks, when he stills his movements.

"No, what?"

"Screw you, Levi," I seethe, but he just chuckles, dipping his fingers back inside me, and this time, his thumb circles my clit. My eyes cross, my hands digging into his shoulders in an attempt to hold myself up. I'm sure there are little half-moon crescents from their blunt ends.

Good. He can have something to remember me by.

He sucks the flesh below my ear, nibbling and marking me. I arch my neck to give him better access, my hips arching into his rough thrusts as he picks up his pace.

"So fucking beautiful," he breathes in my ear. "Riding my hand while I keep you just on the edge of coming."

He withdraws his fingers.

"You going to hide from me, again?"

"I fucking hate you," I seethe, clawing at his wrist. Tears well in the corners of my eyes, my sanity slipping away just as fast as my orgasm.

He chuckles in my ear.

Jessi Hart

"If your hate looks like this, I'd hate to see what your *love* looks like."

He resumes his ministrations, and my knees wobble, threatening to give out. He's practically holding me up while I shake in his grasp.

"Say it."

I'm both furious and so turned on I can't think straight. I'm pretty sure I'd call him daddy right now, if he wanted me to. That's how far gone I am.

"No."

"No, what?" he taunts.

"No, I won't hide from you again," I growl.

"Fuck," he rasps against my skin. "That's my good girl." I whimper, closing my eyes, but his hand tightens in my hair painfully.

"No, don't look away from me, Ava. Let me see how bad you need it, sweetheart. You want to come, don't you?"

I shake my head, but it's a lie. He's unlocked a need inside me I didn't know existed.

"Ask me nicely."

I bite down on my tongue, fighting it. My body is strung tight. He's dangling my orgasm in front of me, but he won't let me come until I give him what he wants. Like some kind of sick punishment.

"I'll stop," he warns, his patience hanging on by a thread. "If you think I won't walk out the door right now, and leave you fucking breathless and wanting, you're dead fucking wrong, little girl."

My pussy clamps down at the rough threat, and something in me breaks.

"Please make me come," I beg on a shaky breath, and finally, with a sinister chuckle, he gives me what I'm dying for.

It only takes a couple of brushes of his fingers on my clit, and my knees are buckling. A moan claws its way up my throat, and he presses his hand over my mouth to silence it as the entire world comes crashing down around us.

God, the Pope, Mother Theresa herself could walk in and catch us right now, and I'd be powerless to stop the pleasure coursing through me.

"That's it, Ava. Come on, my fingers like a good little whore," he growls in my ear.

"Levi," I gasp, my eyes screwed shut and my voice muffled by his palm as every nerve ending in my body feels like it's become a live wire.

The orgasm that rips through me is the most intense, earth-shattering feeling I've ever experienced. Like a thousand volts of electricity shooting through my body at once, rendering me nothing more than a puddle at his feet.

I cry softly, my body arching into his until there's not a single inch of space between us.

"That's it. Good fucking girl." A tremble moves through me as he draws my orgasm out until I'm squirming under his hand. He leans into me, slowing his movements until my pussy vibrates against his hand, his lips at my ear. "I told you I'd make you beg for me, sweetheart."

I don't have the brainpower or the stamina to try to figure out what that means, right now. Everything in me has been turned to mush.

I let out a shaky breath, the aftershocks of the most intense orgasm I've ever had rattling through me.

He watches me, a darkly disturbed look on his face. Like I ruined his plans and now, he's not sure what to do about it.

"Don't call me a whore," I mutter through my teeth.

He releases me, and I open my mouth, but before whatever nonsense that was on the tip of my tongue, he spins me around, pressing my front to the wall and stealing my breath away for an entirely different reason.

I clear my throat. Now that the deed is done, I feel . . . shaken. Maybe he ripped my plan to shreds, too.

A shiver moves through me from his lips at my ear, his voice rough and his words demanding.

"Let me catch you with his hands on you again, and I'll remove them while you watch."

Leaning back, he drops my keys in the palm of my hand.

"Car's fixed."

And then he releases me, stalking out of the supply closet without another word.

CHAPTER
Sixteen

LEVI

I park my car and drag my hood up over my head, making my way to the old warehouse to the south of downtown Seattle.

It's late, almost three in the morning, and there's not a soul in sight. Usually, I'd be drunk or dragging a pretty girl into my bed, but since that night on the couch a few days ago, I haven't felt like doing either.

—Not unless it involves the one thing I can't have.

Fucking figures.

My instincts told me to ignore the call I got earlier today, asking me to come here, but I must be a masochist.

Why else would I insist my little brunette housekeeper take the room across the hall from me and not the perfectly open one down by Javier's?

I step through the side door they told me would be unlocked into the dark warehouse. The only light is one in the center of the room.

The place looks abandoned, with a few old crates and nothing more. The silence is loud, ringing in my ears with each scuff of my boots on the broken concrete.

"You brought me out here at two in the morning. The least you could do is show your face."

see here tonight.

"Marks."

"Hello, Mr. Cross."

"Levi," I correct. *I fucking hate being called Mr. Cross. Reminds me of my father.* "Just Levi."

"Very well," Marks says, stalking into the ring of light in the center of the old, decrepit warehouse. "I trust you came alone?"

"I know you didn't."

He chuckles under his breath, shoving his hands in the pockets of his overcoat.

"On the contrary, you won't find anyone here but me."

"Scared?"

"Opportunistic," he retorts.

Marks has always been "opportunistic". He's older, in his early fifties, with a penchant for being ruthless as they come. I guess when you've got more money than God, you can afford to be a dick.

"I appreciate you meeting with me on such short notice."

I stand back and light the end of my cigarette. No need to stand on formalities. I already lost my job.

"Yeah, well, I have somewhere to be, so if we could make this quick."

I know I'm being rude. I don't give a fuck.

I don't like him. He doesn't like me. No use pretending any different.

"Of course. Time is precious. I imagine you have loads of it now that you're not working."

Fucking dick.

He smiles, knowing he won.

"What's this about?" *I gesture to the warehouse around us.* "You bring me out here to kill me?"

"On the contrary, I came to make you a deal."

I can't help but scoff.

"I don't make deals with criminals."

Marks smirks, ignoring me. "I recently came into some information."

"Good for you. What's that got to do with me?"

He chuckles under his breath.

"This is why I've always liked you, Cross. You don't like to fuck around.
I shrug. "Like it even less, now."

He chuckles under his breath, eyeing me. "Funny thing, loyalty. One minute, you're one of the best agents on payroll, then the next, you're cast out to the wind with charges hanging over your head."

"You going to keep being an elusive dick all night, or are you going to explain what the fuck you're talking about?"

"What if I told you I know who's been stalking your little girlfriend?"

I freeze.

Well, fuck.

"What the hell are you talking about?"

"Senator Johathan Wright ring any bells?"

"You're lying."

"Am I?" he cocks a brow.

"He's dead. You shot him."

"He is . . . but does that mean he's no longer a threat?"

I narrow my eyes, searching his face for a tell, some flicker of uncertainty that might give away the bluff. But Marks doesn't flinch—he never does. He's the kind of bastard who could stare you down while stabbing a knife in your back.

"You're saying Wright's alive?" I ask slowly, the smoke from my cigarette curling between us.

Marks tilts his head, a faint smile tugging at his mouth. "No . . . Capable from beyond the grave? That's another story. I've seen ghosts before, Levi. This one happens to be pulling strings from the shadows—and those strings lead straight to Wright."

My stomach tightens, but I keep my face blank. "If that's true, you'd have taken it straight to your people."

"Not this." His eyes glint. "There's a leak in the DEA. I don't know who I can trust—except, ironically, the last man I should."

I narrow my eyes. "And that would be me?"

Marks spreads his hands like it's obvious. "You're already out. No badge, no leash, no stake in the game. That makes you dangerous—but it also makes you useful. You're the fork in their plan they didn't see coming."

"Or maybe you're just setting me up again."

His smile twitches. "If I wanted you gone, you wouldn't be standing here."

I can't help but chuckle darkly.

"Why me?" I ask.

He steps into the light, the shadows cutting sharper lines across his face. "Because the person I'm hunting has a very personal interest in something of mine. Wright's not the one you should be afraid of."

"Then who?"

He steps closer, his shoes crunching on the grit-strewn concrete, and lowers his voice like the walls might be bugged. "There's someone else. Someone inside. Clever. Careful. Invisible when he needs to be. I don't have a name yet . . . just whispers."

"Then why should I believe you?"

"Because," Marks says, his gaze boring into mine, "Two nights ago, one of my informants turned up dead. And the last thing they sent me before they disappeared was a single word."

I arch a brow. "Which was?"

"Black."

Interesting.

"That's it? That's your smoking gun?"

"I'm going to tell you something, and I want you to listen to me. Really listen." He lowers his voice, glancing around the empty warehouse. For the first time since I met him, Marks looks nervous.

I don't fucking like it.

"Your life isn't the only one in danger."

"What the fuck is that supposed to mean?"

Marks smirks and steps closer, finally tossing me the folder he's been holding the entire time. I take it and open it up to the first page.

The blood rushes in my ears when I look down into the soft green eyes in the photograph staring back at me.

You've got to be fucking kidding me.

"She's got nothing to do with this?"

"No," Marks agrees, though his stare darkens when he looks down at the photograph in my hand. "But do you think they'll care about that?"

"So, what? You're threatening her?"

I'll fucking kill him.

"Not at all," Marks says. "Though, I think you and I both know that's never really mattered."

She doesn't know I'm here.

She *hasn't* known I'm here all week. Watching from the shadows. Waiting for her to slip up.

I've watched her . . . memorized her routine. I've gone through every detail of her life with a fine-tooth comb.

She's younger than I thought, at twenty-three. The only child of her addict mother, with whom she's been estranged for some time. Her father was never in the picture, though I already knew that. She lived with her grandmother until six months ago, when she took this job. She graduated from high school with straight As and a scholarship to Brown, where she didn't attend because her grandmother fell ill.

Her grandmother's in debt. Massively. Ava's been covering most of the bills, but she's falling behind, and now, her grandmother's spot at the nursing home is in danger.

She works. Visits Gran, as she calls her. Goes for walks along the hiking paths that fill our forest, and otherwise, is a good little girl who follows all the rules.

Ava Ryan has to be the most boring person I've ever met.

On the surface.

Behind closed doors, well . . . I already know that's a lie, but it seems not many know that secret side of her. The one that craves the darkness as much as breathing. Who loves to be chased in the woods and fucked in the dirt like a slut.

I won't lie and say it doesn't fill me with a dark sense of joy to know that she's only bad for me. Only I know this side of the prudish, gorgeous little housekeeper.

Or so I thought.

She's hiding something. I'm not a fucking idiot, but what I am is patient. I've followed her for three days now, but she's yet to make a phone call, speak to someone, or even breathe a name I haven't heard.

I just need one name. One, and I'll have all the evidence I need.

Either she's lying, or she's already become a pawn in this game. Either way, I'll get to the bottom of it.

Ava's a smart girl. She knows how to hide behind the crowd well. Unfortunately, she's never been able to hide from *me*, and my little ghost will soon come to learn I'm the only one she can trust in this world.

I told myself I wasn't going to let it get this far, but staring out into the woods surrounding my cabin, I know I can't stop. I'm too fucking gone.

I can't get her moans out of my head. Her desperate little whimpers and that sweet voice crying out for me while I made her come.

Not to mention the dirty looks she shoots my way whenever I see her. They're fucking addicting. She's exactly what I've needed and everything I can't have.

Until now . . .

Fuck . . . I've jacked off three times in the last twenty-four hours, and even if my cock is sore from how many times I've come, it's not enough.

The need to unravel her secrets one by one until there's not a single thought in that pretty little head I don't consume gnaws at me.

It's so far past a desire at this point, even I can't help but wonder for my fucking sanity.

If I thought I understood this . . . *obsession* before, that ship has sailed. I'm officially losing my goddamned mind, and the little brunette brat that sleeps across the hall from me is the culprit.

I down the glass of whiskey beside me, letting the burn coat my throat and push away the disturbing thoughts that have been swirling through my head since I chased her through the forest.

I set my empty glass down on the desk beside me. I don't come out here often—not anymore—but I needed to think.

It's a stupid plan. One that's only going to make this harder in the long run.

Most people would recommend committing me.

Most people don't have little Miss Ava Ryan living across the hall from them, with her pretty fucking smile, either.

All I need to do is get her out of my system, and when I'm done with her, she'll move on, and I'll be free of this . . . burden eating away at me. I can detach myself once she's not the unobtainable prize.

I'll hold up my end of the deal. Then, I'll let her go.

Looking up at the wooden beams that run across the cabin, I can't help but chuckle.

Ava has no idea what's coming, but I meant what I said. I gave her three days to think I'd forgotten about her sneaking around in my room.

Unfortunately for her, I'm a Cross. We don't forget.

She'll tell me her secrets and if I have to fuck them out of her, well then . . . I guess I'm willing to take one for the team.

CHAPTER
Seventeen

AVA

Y ou know that feeling of being watched?

It's been a week since Levi chased me through the woods, and three days since that little impromptu closet tryst, and I'm starting to think I won't ever return to normal. My body isn't sore anymore, and some of the bruises have healed, but there's this strange new . . . ache between my thighs whenever I think of him.

I've caught myself staring into space more than once, daydreaming about that night. Quite frankly, it's embarrassing. It was just sex. Not a damned marriage proposal.

I can't help but wonder if this is how all the girls he sleeps with feel? Or am I just that pathetic that I'm secretly pining after his attention, even if I actively shun him whenever I see him, like he's the walking plague.

More times than I can count over the last three days, I've felt that strange tingling sensation on the back of my neck. Like he's watching me, waiting for his moment to strike. I know he hasn't forgotten about me searching through his room, and the longer I nursing home. I'm starting to get the feeling he's toying with me. Maybe he'll send one of his big gargoyles to strangle me in the forest one day, leaving my body to rot like the leaves that cover the ground.

My only peace is my daily walk, and even that is turning out to be anything but. Like today. I'm alone and out later than normal because Mila and Christian went to the city, and Alex is out doing whatever it is Alex does. It's a nice day, slightly warmer than it has been, but the sun is quickly setting over the horizon, and soon, everything will be cast in shadows.

The last thing I want to do is be caught out in these same woods again, so I'm rushing to get back to the house before nightfall.

I feel like someone's watching me, and my heart is beating more and more unsteadily with each step.

They wouldn't send someone here, would they? I mean, I'm on a pretty popular path. I'm sure someone would notice something. Furthermore, he made no mention of what he would do to *me*. Only Levi.

And then I'm right back to where I started. Anxious. Overwhelmed. Sick to my stomach.

And all this over a man who doesn't even care about me.

I walk faster, a sudden chill skating down my spine.

I hate feeling vulnerable.

Like I'm just a toy in someone else's game.

Since the last time I was in these woods, I've been going about my days like nothing happened. Like I didn't have the most mind-blowing sex in my life. The words he'd said after still sting, echoing back to me with each step I take.

What happened between us was nothing more than sex.

I actually find myself laughing bitterly. As if it could be anything else.

Falling for Levi Cross would be suicide. I would have a better chance of surviving a ten-story drop.

As I push through the trees, the shuffling of leaves sounds behind me, and I whirl around, coming to a full stop on the path so fast my hair whips me in the face.

Something tells me that was *not* an animal.

It all happens so fast.

One minute, I'm staring at the brush that's too dark to really see through, and the next, someone is wrapping something around my head.

My scream gets lodged in my throat, and a gag is shoved into my mouth. A second later, a black sack is dragged over my head, and I'm fighting tooth and nail with the arms that wrap around me.

Panic is the first thing to slip into my veins.

Then, full-blown terror when my hands are ripped behind my back and cuffed.

I scream behind the gag, but I'm hauled off my feet without a word and tossed over someone's shoulder. I try to kick and fight, but I'm powerless to stop him when he carries me away. Seconds later, I'm thrown backward, and my ass hits a leather seat, before a car door shuts and I'm carted off into the night.

Tears wet my cheeks, and my sobs are muffled by the gag. Not that it would matter. I'm out in the woods alone, and I know it will be hours, maybe even days, until someone notices I'm missing.

Which means I'm trapped.

I don't know how long we drive but it feels like a lifetime. The seconds tick by, and I can't do anything but stare at the inside of the black sack over my head and listen to the crunch of the tires of gravel. The ride is bumpy, and at one point, my shoulder digs into something hard behind me, making me whimper around the gag in my mouth.

Okay, this is bad.

When the car finally comes to a stop, I wait, listening to the sounds of whoever it is exiting before the door shuts, and I'm thrust into complete silence. I force myself to breathe, even if it is stuffy inside the sack, and try to wiggle around in the seat.

My hands ache behind my back. My shoulders are sore and stiff.

I'm sure I'll have a permanent divot in my hip from the damned seatbelt buckle under my ass.

Adjusting my feet, I try to kick at the door, but I can barely move. He must have my ankles tied too, because why wouldn't he?

Way to go, Ava Lynn. You've gone and gotten yourself kidnapped.

Sagging into the leather, I let out a quiet sob because I can. Because I've been kidnapped by an actual psychopath who's probably going to string me up and murder me in the Washington version of *The Hills Have Eyes.*

This fucking sucks.

When the door finally opens, I let out a squeak behind the gag, jumping in the seat. Someone grabs me and, like a ragdoll, I'm hauled out into the cool night air and thrown over someone's shoulder again. I wriggle in their grasp, and the man slaps my ass hard enough to draw a cry from my lips at the sting.

I listen to the sounds of his footsteps, squirming in his arms, but he only tightens his hold. He doesn't say a word, even when I scream at him to put me down. I don't care if it's unintelligible. I do it anyway.

Warmth hits me, and I shiver, my head spinning from all the blood rushing to my brain at this angle. The sound of the footsteps changes, and I realize we're inside somewhere. It's silent, save for the crackle of a fireplace when I'm ripped over the man's shoulder and dropped to my feet without a warning.

My knees threaten to give out, but he holds me up, ripping me around and taking my cuffed hands. There's a click, and the cuffs fall off, and instantly, I flex my sore wrists. It's only a split second, though, before my arms are ripped over my head.

I stumble forward, groaning against the gag when a rope is wrapped around one, then the other above my head, forcing me up onto my tiptoes to keep my footing.

It doesn't feel good, and tears well in my eyes, slipping down my cheeks. I bite the gag, whimpering at the material in my mouth and wishing that I could be literally anywhere but right here with whoever the crazed lunatic is that just kidnapped me from the woods.

A dark chuckle sounds, and the bag is ripped off my head, making me clench my eyes shut at the light around me. It's dim, but after being in the dark for God only knows how long, it stings.

And finally, when I can open my eyes without feeling like they're going to burn out of my skull, my heart falls in my chest.

None other than the devil himself stands in front of me, grinning ear to ear and holding the black sack that had just been on my head.

"Hello, baby girl."

I growl through the gag, lurching in the rope holding my wrists. It burns against my skin when I fight its hold, but he clearly went to Boy Scout camp because it doesn't budge.

Levi smirks, his eyes flashing wickedly in the warm glow of the fireplace cackling behind him.

Okay. This is worse than I thought.

We appear to be in a cabin, though I'm too disoriented and utterly fucking shocked to notice much other than the man in front of me.

Levi circles me like a caged tiger, the muscles of his bare chest shining in the light. My gaze runs over the tattoos inked into his skin. From a rose to something in Latin I can't understand, right down to the bear growling on his chest.

Unfortunately, I make the mistake of glancing lower, noticing the way his abs shine in the light.

The man was built to break things. Probably women like me, if you want the truth.

With the gag in my mouth and the rope forcing me to stay suspended in the air, I have no choice but to simply glare at him as he stalks back and forth in front of me.

"Surprised to see me?"

"*Asshole*," I say, but it comes out sounding more like "ashdkghd."

His wolfish smile makes my heart drop to my aching toes, and I shift uncomfortably, whimpering as the rope drags against my skin.

"Ava, Ava, Ava . . . what am I going to do with you?"

If this is some kinky sex thing, I'm going to kill him.

"My beautiful little thief."

I knew he didn't forget. I could never be that lucky.

He stops in front of me, reaching up to brush a lock of hair back from my wet cheek. I hadn't even realized I'd been crying. "You see, I thought you were this sweet, naïve girl. Never hurt a fly. Imagine my surprise when I found out you were lying."

My brows knit together in confusion. I try to say something, but it's useless. Not that I think he'd believe me anyway. If he's gone to these lengths to get me out here, he's already convinced himself he's right.

"I asked you in the woods who sent you to steal from me. You told me you didn't know." He continues pacing again, and my eyes follow him. I slip on the wood floor, groaning when the rope digs into my skin. "You lied to me."

I swallow thickly, but my saliva tastes coppery. I must have bitten the gag so hard, I made myself bleed.

Levi circles me like a predator until he's at my back. In a flash, his hand digs into my hair, and he tugs my head back, his lips at the side of my throat.

"I'm going to give you one chance to tell me the truth."

The gag falls from my mouth, and I sputter, my lips dry and sore from the material. I cough and tears slip freely down my cheeks when he releases my hair, letting my head fall forward.

"I told you," I croak. "I don't know."

"You're still lying to me, sweetheart," he purrs, and liquid heat slips through me at his voice in my ear. Is it normal to feel turned on when you're terrified? Because I get the feeling maybe I'm just fucked in the head. "You should know I don't like liars."

Levi grips my hip and kneads the flesh of my side where my shirt has ridden up. I close my eyes, a whimper escaping my lips when he slips his hand into the waistband of my jeans, teasing the skin beneath.

"I think you like pushing me. I don't think you're as innocent as you claim to be, little ghost." He removes his hand, circling back to the front. I feel him in every step.

I'm clearly in need of a good therapist and probably a straitjacket, because when he comes back into view, my first thought is how hot he is.

He stops in front of me, his fingers stroking through the tears on my cheeks.

"Tell me the truth, Ava." He steps closer, his fingers slipping under my jaw to cup my throat. He tilts my face up to his, crowding me. I whimper, and his fingers flex against my racing pulse, his eyes dark and absolutely terrifying. "Tell me who you're working for."

"I'm not working for anyone," I grit. Why can't he just believe me?

Because you've been acting shady, the voice in the back of my mind chimes.

Bitch.

"You're so goddamned pretty," he says, like it pisses him off. His fingers tighten just a hair, like he knows he could choke the life out of me if he wanted to. "Pretty *and* deceitful. I told you I would find out, sweetheart. Why can't you just tell me the truth?"

Fuck. He knows . . .

Fresh tears sting in my eyes, and Levi notices, leaning forward and catching one on his tongue. My heart hammers in my chest, my breathing ragged with both fear and the effort to hold myself up.

"I've been so patient with you, Ava, but that patience is wearing thin. You'll either tell me who you're working for, or I'll keep you here until you do."

"You're a psychopath," I spit, and he grins, pinching my cheeks together.

"Oh, baby girl. You have no fucking idea."

Reaching between us, his thumb circles the button of my jeans. I shiver, unable to do anything but hold on and wait for him to decide what he's going to do to me.

"You don't tell me the truth; I'll leave you here wanting and waiting."

"Please, not that—" I rush, panic slipping through me. He chuckles, nipping the line on my jaw at the same time he flicks the button of my jeans.

"It sucks, doesn't it? Wanting something so badly and not being able to have it."

"You're an asshole," I growl when he slides the zipper down.

"Do you remember your safeword, Ava?"

"Fuck you."

He grins. "Good."

He hooks his fingers in the loops of my jeans, slipping them down my legs. Kneeling down, he looks up at me, sliding them off me completely.

I don't even recognize myself. The man is a certified psychopath. He's tied me to the rafters of some cabin in the middle of the woods, and yet, my clit throbs with desire. My nipples are hard, poking through my t-shirt and bra. My pussy is wet, coating my thighs. All I can do to relieve the ache that's been steadily becoming harder and harder to ignore is rub my thighs together.

Levi notices and presses my knees apart, holding himself away from me, so I can't grind against him.

"I think you like this, sweetheart," he taunts, his nose trailing up the side of my face. Leaning down, he buries his face in the crook of my neck, inhaling me like he's breathing in my scent. "You like being at my mercy. Just begging to get fucked."

"I hate you," I seethe, angry tears burning in my eyes. I pull on the rope, but it must be made with diamond thread, because it doesn't even *budge*.

"Not enough to use your safeword, though."

Fuck. I hate that he's right.

More importantly, I hate that I still want him.

Levi circles me, slipping around out of sight again. I feel him at my back, his presence overpowering, even if I can't see him.

"Who did you think I was when I found you in the woods, Ava?"

"You." *Lie.*

With a loud crack, his hand connects with my ass, striking me. I gasp at the pain, surging in the binds as tears sting in my eyes.

"Did you just spank me?"

Levi's lips are at my ear, his hand tugging my head back.

"You're lying. Again." His hand slides over the sensitive skin, and I clench my teeth, my breathing ragged. "You must not want some relief. If you think I won't keep you here all night, wanting and begging to be fucked, you're wrong."

"Who says I want you to fuck me?" I growl, even if the evidence is plain for him to see.

"You haven't told me to stop."

I think if he did right now, I might succumb to the dark side and start a riot.

"I'm going to ask you again, Ava. Who are you so afraid of?"

"You."

Again, his hand strikes my ass, right over the first mark. Pain erupts from the spot, but it's the *other* feeling that slips through me that's absolutely devastating.

I . . . like it.

Heat floods my core, and I groan, hoping he can't see my thighs shaking with need.

Of course, he does.

"Never thought you'd be one to enjoy your punishment, Ava, but I can't lie and say I'm not impressed."

Another strike comes, and I mewl, leaning my forehead against my arm. My entire body is trembling with the effort to hold me up while I fight against the desire to push back against him.

"You like the sting of it," he whispers against my ear. "You like how bad it feels. You hate that you want it, but you can't ask me to stop because it's got you so worked up, you're ready to tell me the secret to life, aren't you?" His voice is husky, and I get the feeling I'm not the only one enjoying myself.

As depraved and insane as this is, it's also . . . freeing. Being out here where no one can hear me. Judging by the complete and total darkness outside the windows, I can scream as loud as I want.

That thought both terrifies me and turns me on.

"Please—"

"I know what you need, baby girl. You just have to cooperate. Your body is. Why can't your mind?"

"Because you won't understand," I gasp, unable to hold the words back any longer. Tears leak from the corners of my eyes, and he rewards me with his fingers. Slipping between my folds, he swirls my wetness around lazily, circling where I need him so desperately.

"Tell me what I won't understand," he rasps, his fingers continuing to tease me. I shake my head, and he withdraws them. I cry out at the loss of him, my body teeming with desire. "You won't get what you want if you don't tell the truth."

I could safeword, and this would end. I know he would untie me and put me on my feet. He would stop if I just asked him.

What does it say about me that I don't want him to stop? That this is the most alive I've felt in years—maybe even my entire life.

"Tell me, Ava," he says in my ear. "Who sent you?"

Fuck. Fuck. Fuck.

I can't do it.

The fight leaves me, and I arch back into him when he tugs my head back.

"Last chance, sweetheart, before I sit down and watch you struggle. What do they want?"

I'm going to hate myself for this.

"A flash drive," I pant, licking my lips. They're salty from my tears. "He wanted a flash drive."

"Who, Ava?"

I shake my head. "He calls himself Black. He's been following me for weeks." I swallow nervously, my mouth parched and my body sore and exhausted from holding myself up. "I swear that's all I know."

The silence in the room is deafening.

I wait for the blow to come—either his fist or his words. My eyes clench shut, and I hide my face as much as I can, knowing this is where things turn ugly.

Only . . . the blows never come.

"Fucking finally."

Levi presses tender kisses along the side of my face. It's a stark contrast to this entire situation, and it only serves to confuse me even more.

He doesn't care. He's only trying to get information out of me, but I can't help but revel in his softness, even if it's only just for a moment.

"That's my good girl," he purrs in my ear, and I shiver at the praise. Am I really that far gone that a few words will have *this* effect on me? "Just one more question, and I'll let you go, baby girl. What does he want you to get?"

"A flash drive . . ." I breathe. "They wanted a flash drive."

There's a deafening silence I can't even begin to dissect.

Levi's hands leave me, and he stalks around until he's standing in front of me again. His expression is indifferent, even if I can see the hardness in his jeans.

"Please, I'm not working for them. I was scared. They said they would come after you if I didn't give it to them. I just want to take care of my grandmother," I rush, panic ebbing through me. "She's all I have left."

I'm not sure if it's adrenaline, combined with the sexual frustration or the sheer panic in my veins, but I bury my face against my arm, a sob wracking through me.

I flinch when he reaches for me, his hand finding my hips. My eyes fly open when he picks me up, relieving the pressure on my wrists. My legs lock around his waist, and he reaches between us, undoing his jeans and fisting his cock.

Swiping himself through the wetness at my core, he aligns his cock at my entrance.

Then he's pushing me down on his length.

My head falls back, and I cry out at the intrusion, my still roped arms around his neck for leverage.

My pussy sucks him in greedily, and I don't think I've ever been this wet before. It's a shame because this is the most depraved, erotic experience of my life.

If my nana knew what I was doing right now . . .

"Levi," I groan, wincing when he hits that deep-seated spot inside me that has him pushing against my barriers. "Please . . . I need . . ."

"I know what you need, sweetheart." I know I'm imagining it, but there's a tenderness in his voice. It's not real. Levi doesn't care past what he can get from my body, but I can't help but revel in the desire in his voice. He wants to fuck me. He's been holding back, forcing me to tell him the truth when he wanted me just as badly.

My thighs tremble around his hips, and he's deep enough that his groin brushes over my clit with each stroke. It hurts, and it feels so damn good that I can't think straight. I arch against him, completely powerless when my mind goes blank and I finally, *finally* get the release I've been craving since that night in the woods.

My orgasm hits me harder than it ever has before. Black spots dot my visions, and I know I scream. I can't tell if it's his name or unintelligible gibberish, but Levi doesn't stop, drawing out my pleasure as the orgasm lasts forever.

"Fuck, you're so perfect, Ava. You were made to take my cock. Weren't you?" I can barely make out what he's saying, let alone answer him with the mind-numbing orgasm stealing every one of my senses.

I can't help the soft, needy sounds on my tongue, and I can't even beg him to stop when he continues fucking me, jerking me down on his cock so hard, the sound of our skin meeting fills the room. He buries his head in my neck, his teeth grazing my sweat-slicked skin, and his groans fill my ear. Before I know it, I'm coming again, or maybe it's just one long orgasm that's meant to kill me.

"That's my girl," Levi growls in my ear, his lips quirking up in a smile. "Taking my cock so well. I knew you'd come so hard you couldn't think when you finally gave in to me. You become so mindless with pleasure that it steals your voice away."

He's panting, his abs slick with sweat as he fucks me. Changing his angle, he pulls back, forcing my arms to release him, and holds me by the hips.

"Come on, Ava. Come for me again. I know you can. You're squeezing the life out of me."

At this angle, it allows him to fuck me hard and fast, taking everything I have and giving me nothing but pleasure in return.

I wonder if the rope will snap, even if I couldn't even get it to budge. My body responds to his harsh fucking in ways I didn't know were possible.

I shouldn't want this. I shouldn't be begging for it, but even as I realize all these things, I know it's pointless. I want him like my next breath. I want this side of Levi. The demanding, powerful side that gives me so many orgasms, I can't think, let alone be afraid.

"Yes, yes, yes . . ." I whimper when he hits that perfect spot, dragging the head of his cock over it again and again. "Levi," I gasp, my entire body trembling in his hands. "Please, I'm going to come. I—"

Dragging me back to him, his lips find mine, and he kisses me hard. He bounces me on his cock, and that's what sends me over the edge. I gasp and writhe against him, and he curses under his breath, his hand tightening on my ass.

The moment I come, the orgasm tears me to shreds. I'm not sure if I even breathe when the euphoria washes over me, my entire body vibrating and spent. Levi growls against my throat, fucking me through it, and my chest heaves with each breath as I cling to him. He fucks me once, twice, three more times, and snarls, his hips colliding sharply with mine one last time before he stills.

His come fills me, and I come harder, clinging to him with my last shred of sanity as both of us silently float back down from whatever ethereal plane we made it to.

I expect him to release me immediately, but he doesn't; instead, he presses his damp forehead against mine, his eyes closed as we both try to catch our breath.

"I'll take care of it, Ava."

I open my mouth to snap back at him, but nothing comes out but a quiet, exhausted groan.

I've been told that before.

CHAPTER
Eighteen

LEVI

The Columbia Club.

I've always hated the place.

"How quaint," Christian remarks, following behind me. I'm not stupid enough not to bring a second.

Christian and I get yearly invites to join, despite rejecting them every time. Now, standing in front of the old brick building located in the heart of Seattle, I find my skin is crawling like I've been swarmed by a thousand fire ants.

The air feels . . . pompous. Thick with expectation and pansy-assed men who would rather pay someone to hold their dicks for them when they piss than get their hands dirty.

The Cross's prefer the dirt and grime. The Columbia Club is for men like our father, who hire men like us to do the dirty work for them.

I don't belong here.

I stride up to the front door, and the doorman holds out a hand to stop me.

Of course he does. I don't fit the part.

pomade shit in my hair, so it's wild and unkempt. The scar on my lip, ironically, from Dad's Columbia ring, which he was so proud of.

I'm exactly the type of man this club was created to avoid.

"Can I help you, gentlemen?"

Both of us answer in unison. "No."

I move to step past him, but he remains determined to be in the way.

"Ten o'clock meeting with Palmer," I grunt.

He glances at the Rolex on his wrist. "It's fifteen after."

"Which is why you need to get the fuck out of my way."

If he were wearing pearls, he'd be clutching them, judging by the shocked expression on his face. How dare I use a curse word on the great steps of douche?

"I can't let you—"

Fortunately, Christian's only knocks him out.

The guard dog hits the ground like a bag of bricks. I look at Christian. Cock a brow. Christian shrugs.

"He was in the way."

He's not wrong.

I stroll through the front doors, whistling under my breath. The club is situated in an ancient brick building in the heart of downtown Seattle. Men from all over the country come here to join its ranks, but few are actually let in.

Surprisingly enough, you can walk right through the front door if you know how to fight.

I've never understood the need for the extravagance that this place is made of. As if the world didn't know they were rich, the men who created this place needed somewhere to come when they wanted to cheat on their wives with each other. To bring their mistresses or to discuss business that the public can't hear.

It's all a bunch of bullshit, and from the moment I enter, I'm on edge.

I pass by a few rooms off the main foyer, ignoring the prying eyes that follow me as I walk. Most are gathered in a large room lined with plush couches and oversized televisions showing the game. I've never been one to care about football. I've always had more important shit to worry about, I guess, but the sound drifting out the French double doors reminds me of a different time when life was simpler.

You know, back when I had shit figured out and someone wasn't investigating me for murder.

I make my way through to the back, where I was told he'd be, nodding to a man whose eyes follow me as I go. He nods back once, his expression guarded, before he walks away.

I push through the double doors at the end of the hall and step into a den filled with smoke. Men have cigars hanging from their mouths, and the air reeks of booze and elitist ideology. They're all gathered around a pool table, while a few of them cheer on Palmer and another douche I don't know.

They don't notice Christian and me when we walk in, too immersed in watching Palmer stroke his ego to see me join their group.

That's fine. I've learned how to be patient.

I merge into the crowd while Palmer lines up his shot. The fucker grins when he sinks the six ball into a corner pocket and takes a bow for his posse of undulating scrotums.

"What did I tell you?" Palmer drags the poor girl next to him under his arm. "I'm the fucking best."

Jesus, I fucking hate this guy.

Man, let me tell you. The silence in the room when I start clapping is something to be reckoned with. Everyone turns to look at me, their eyes going wide. It's even better to watch the smile fade from Palmer's face when he sees me standing across from him.

"Looks like someone's been practicing."

Palmer's glare intensifies.

"What the fuck are you doing here, Cross?"

I smile, holding out my hands with a shrug. "Just came to have a little conversation. It's been a long time, buddy. We should really catch up."

Palmer's jaw tenses, and his little lap dog, Swanson, steps up to bat first.

"You aren't welcome here."

I can't help but chuckle under my breath.

"You think that's funny?"

"The thought that you think you've got enough balls to throw me out is." I round the table slowly, my hand gliding along the felt. One look at Christian and he knows what I'm going to do. Fortunately, he doesn't try to stop me. "How tall are you now, Boy Wonder? Five-one, five-two?"

"Better yet, how has your life been since you left the Lollipop Guild?" Christian chimes, and I'm reminded why I love my brother.

Swanson's face turns red, but luckily for him, Palmer stops him from going any further.

"Enough," he hisses. "What do you want, Cross?"

"Now, is that any way to talk to your best friend?"

"You've got five seconds to tell me what the hell you want before I tell Matt you're causing a disturbance."

Alright, dickhead, if that's how you want to play it. . .

"Right," I smile. "How could I forget. Lying is your specialty."

I look at the camera in the corner of the room. The light is still red.

"You see, Palmer, the other day, my girl came home and said someone was following her. She couldn't tell me who it was, so I did some digging. Turns out, they're saying their name is Black. You wouldn't happen to know anything about that, would you?"

He stares at me coldly for a moment, his eyes taking on that sinister gleam that not many get to see. Then he makes the mistake of laughing under his breath.

"Should have known you'd go after the little mistake," he says darkly.

A few of the men chuckle in the group, following Palmer's lead. I chuckle right along with them.

Three . . . two . . . one . . .

The light turns off on the camera in the corner of the room.

And then I swing.

The number eight-ball in my hand smashes into the side of his head, sending him stumbling back.

"*Fuckkk . . .*" He groans in pain, doubling over to clutch the spot. Too bad we're just getting started.

"Don't even think about it," Christian warns Swanson, when everyone else backs away from Palmer.

Walking over to Palmer, I grab his hair, yanking him up, and drag him to the pool table. He's still disoriented when I shove him face down into the slate, his slobber coloring the felt.

"What the fuck?" he curses, trying to fight me off, but I'm bigger than him. Funny how now that the shoe's on the other foot, he's not so tough.

I stoop down in front of his face, close enough so only he can hear what I have to say. To be honest, I wanted to string him up by his balls when I read those messages on Ava's phone earlier tonight. What I'm going to do to him is child's play compared to what will happen if he goes near my girl again.

"That was for thinking you could fuck with her."

I drag his head back, shoving his face harder into the slate.

"That was because you're a lying piece of shit."

Yanking his head away from the table, I bring my knee to his face, ignoring the pain when I hear the sound of his bones crunching fill the air.

Yanking his head away from the table, I bring my knee to his face, ignoring the pain when the sound of his bones crunching fill the air.

"And that's just because I don't fucking like you."

He collapses to his knees, his nose gushing blood down the front of him. He glares at me, his entire body shaking with rage when I crouch down in front of him.

"The next time you come near her, I'll rip your throat out with my teeth."

I shove away from him and stand, reaching into my back pocket and pulling out the flash drive he sent her after.

"So you don't have to send any more girls to my house to do your dirty work for you."

"You think she's safe in your castle, Cross?" he cackles from behind me when I stalk towards the door. I turn, my gaze locking on his. There's blood seeping from his nose down into his teeth, making his smile all the more sinister. "It doesn't matter what you do to protect her, sooner or later, someone's going to come for her, and there's not a damned thing you can do to stop it."

All I can do is laugh under my breath.

"Good luck."

CHAPTER
Nineteen

AVA

I'm just saying, once the beast transformed, he was *not* the growly man I expected, and I'm disappointed," Mila says, washing a plate from tonight's dinner while I dry. It's difficult because I have to keep pulling my long sleeves down, so she doesn't see the bandages around the rope burn on my arms.

I woke up this morning in my own bed, cleaned up with bandages on my wrists. Part of me was surprised, and I'll admit, grateful to know he took care of me after . . . whatever *that* was last night.

The other half is angry that I even let myself get into this predicament in the first place.

Levi now knows whoever Black is sent me to find information on him, and that I did it only because they threatened him. He said he'd take care of it, whatever that means, but I still have nothing to go on when they approach me again.

"Did you hear a word I just said?"

Whoops.

"Yeah, you were talking about the Beast and how un-beastly

"That was ages ago. What's the matter with you? You've been staring into space all night?"

"Nothing," I lie. "I'm just tired."

"I get the feeling you're not telling me something," Mila says, eyeing me with that knowing look. As my best friend, she's come to learn how to see right through my lies, and I've got to say, it's a nuisance.

"Well, I don't know what it would be. I have nothing to hide."

Mila shrugs, going back to washing the dish in her hand.

"If you say so. Just know, I'm here to talk if you need it."

"Thanks, Mila."

She smiles. "So, how's Levi?"

I shake my head, lost in thought. "I haven't seen him since last n—"

Fuckkkkk.

Mila grins, wagging her brows at me.

"I knew it."

"I don't know what you're talking about," I grumble, cheeks hot enough to fry an egg. "I was just going to say I haven't spoken to him since the other day."

"Is that when he left that giant hickey on your neck?"

Dammit.

"I shouldn't have come here," I grumble, and she laughs.

She only smirks triumphantly.

"I think it's great. You both deserve someone worth a damn."

"It was nothing," I lie.

It was definitely something. In fact, I can still feel the brush of his hands on my body. Under my clothes, my skin is marked with his touch. His hands. The hickey on my neck is a constant reminder of what we did, and every time I see myself in the mirror, I can't decide if I should be ashamed or turned on by the memory.

Not that he cares. I haven't seen hide nor hair of him all day.

Complete radio silence.

I won't lie and say I didn't contemplate running the moment I woke up.

It wouldn't do any good, and I know it.

"So how was it?"

"Shhh . . ." I growl under my breath, listening to make sure I can still hear Christian in his office. I can just make out the deep baritone of his voice from here.

"Fine," Mila grumbles, dropping her voice to a whisper. "How was it?"

My mouth runs dry, and the rope burns on my wrist sear underneath the bandages.

"It was fine."

"Just fine?" Mila taunts, staring at my neck balefully.

"Okay, fine," I huff, tossing the towel in my hands down. "It was amazing."

She grins. "Define amazing."

Might as well let her have it. She's going to come to her own conclusions if I don't.

"He may or may not have chased me down in the forest. Is that what you want to hear?"

"Actually . . . yeah. How did you convince him to play naked tag in the woods?"

"It wasn't naked tag," I correct, dropping my voice. You never know who could be lurking around here. "I just . . . maybe, may have told him if he could catch me then . . . well, he could fuck me."

Mila's jaw hits the floor.

"Ava Lynn Ryan. *You* told Levi Cross—*my brother-in-law*, might I add—that he could fuck you if he caught you?"

"That's what I said," I grit, a little too aggressively. I scrub a hand through my hair, ripping out my ponytail holder. I don't know why. Maybe it's because I think I'll be able to hide the blush on my cheeks behind a blanket of hair.

"I'm surprised at you, Ava. I'll be honest, I didn't think you had it in you."

"Rude," I remark, and she shrugs. "It was a total lapse in judgment. I shouldn't have said that. I'm surprised he didn't laugh in my face." *Or murder me for going through his room.*

"Can you blame him? I mean . . . look at you. You're a walking wet dream."

"Ew."

She chuckles, tugging my hand when I attempt to walk away.

"I'm just saying, you're shy. I get it. I am too, if it's not with Christian."

"You literally handcuffed your husband to a chair and gave him a lap dance," I point out, and she blushes.

"Okay, but that was with him. With anyone else, I would *never* be able to do that. Besides, that was to prove a point."

"That you could do it?"

"That he doesn't control me."

Damn . . . She has a point.

"Well, it doesn't matter. Levi is—"

"Charming?"

Both Mila and I freeze before a wide grin spreads on her face.

I don't have to turn around to know the literal devil is standing in the doorway behind me.

God, I hope he didn't hear any of that.

"What are you two up to?" Christian asks, completely oblivious to the obvious tension in the air when he steps into the kitchen behind Levi and places a kiss on his wife's forehead.

Levi, on the other hand, stares straight at me, a knowing smirk on his face.

He heard everything . . .

Asshole.

My entire body vibrates with irrational desire. I can't stand him, and yet, I also can't get the feeling of his hands out of my head.

There's also the trickle of fear sliding through me, reminding me that he knows my secret and there's nothing stopping him from making me disappear somewhere on the Cross's some three hundred acres.

Is there a kink for being scared, but also turned on?

I hope so, because if not, I'm defective.

"Just girl talk," Mila says, but I know she's going to tell Christian everything the moment they're alone.

God, why did I open my big, fat mouth?

"I think I'm going to head out," I say, clearing my throat past my heart that's somehow taken root there. "Busy day tomorrow."

"So early?" Mila asks. I don't know what she's talking about. It's nearly ten at night.

"Yeah, you know. I like to get up early."

I actually hate it, but I'm betting on no one in this room knowing that.

"I picked you up. Let me take you home," Mila says, releasing Christian and looking around for her keys.

"I'll walk back," I say, but no one listens to me because Levi interjects.

"I'll take Ava home. I was just on my way."

The wink he shoots in my direction may as well be a threat.

He's either going to kill me or fuck me again. The worst part is, I would welcome the latter, though I know it would only be a mistake in the end.

"That's a great idea," Mila beams, and Christian stares between the three of us curiously. Poor guy. "Is that alright with you, Ava? I really am tired."

I shoot her a narrowed look. She's a terrible liar.

"Then, it's settled," Levi says, grinning wolfishly at me. "Grab your things, Ava. I'll make sure you get home safe and sound."

My heartbeat thunders in my chest from the wicked gleam in his eyes.

Something tells me that won't be the case.

Levi Cross is going to kill me.

The moment we step out into the night, and the door shuts behind us, I take off in the other direction down the path, but of course, Levi's faster than I am.

He wraps an arm around my waist, dragging me back into his hard chest with a sinister chuckle. "Not so fast, rope bunny."

"Don't call me that," I snap, heat rushing to my cheeks.

He doesn't acknowledge what I said, instead pushing me back into the side of his fancy black car and looming over me in the darkness. I can't help but glare up at him through my lashes, though when his lips tip up in that devil-may-care grin, I can't stop the shiver that slips through me.

Of course, he notices that too.

"What do you want, Levi?"

He reaches up, and I jerk in his grasp when his fingertips brush along my lip. Moving lower, he pushes the hair back from my neck where I applied a pound of concealer to hide his mistake— unsuccessfully. I know he's looking at the marks he left, as if he's proudly inspecting his handiwork.

Knowing Levi, he probably is.

He boxes me in with his body, looming over me in the darkness. His lips hover inches from mine, and my heartbeat skyrockets at the simple thought of kissing Levi Cross—a man I'm supposed to hate.

"Have you been thinking of me?" he asks, his voice taking on that husky rasp it did last night. The slightest touch of his fingertips on my skin has my heart beating out of tune and my core clenching. I'm already wet, and he's barely touched me.

"No." *Lie.* "Why would I?" *Because last night was the most intense orgasm you've ever had in your life.*

"What's the matter, baby girl?" he murmurs, and his voice may as well be his tongue brushing between my legs.

Warmth slips through me, straight to my core, and my traitorous body begs for his touch. His hand brushes over the bandages on my wrist, as if he's reminding me of last night.

As if I even needed to be reminded. It's all I can think about.

"Afraid of people learning you like to be tied up and edged until your face is soaked with tears and you're begging to come?"

Desire washes over me at the same time as shame. A shiver ghosts through me, and I look away from his prying eyes.

Whore.

"Absolutely not," he breathes, gripping my chin in his hand and forcing my gaze back to his icy blue one. "Don't do that. Don't look away from me. You enjoyed it, didn't you?"

Enjoyed it? That's the problem. I did, and it's fucked up. What kind of person likes that?

"It was . . ." My throat threatens to close over my voice. "I've never done anything like that before."

I'm ashamed to admit my lack of experience, especially with a man like Levi who probably knows things I couldn't even begin to fathom.

It just proves him right. I am a prude.

"That didn't answer my question, Ava. Did you enjoy it?"

"I didn't use the safe word, did I?"

He chuckles under his breath, his lips lingering over mine.

Kiss me, I want to beg, but what kind of loser begs a man to kiss her? If he wanted to, he would have done it by now.

Finally, he steps back, releasing me, and I shiver in the cool night air.

"Get in the car, Ava."

"Levi, I'm sore—" I breathe, cheeks flaming hotter than the sun when he fixes me with a look.

Uh-oh.

"No one said anything about sex." He opens the door, a wicked smirk on his face. "Get in. You and I need to talk."

CHAPTER
Twenty

LEVI

I can't explain it. It's like I come alive when she's near. She makes me think all kinds of crazy shit, I shouldn't. Like how I can convince her to give herself over to me completely. Get her to agree to come to my cabin and never leave. Let me spend the rest of my days worshiping her in every way possible.

Then I give myself a reality check.

Ava is a passing fantasy. It's exciting because for the first time in a long time, she's different. She's not throwing herself at me. She's using me to get what she wants. It's fucking exhilarating.

Soon, I'll get bored and give her up. Until then, she gets to deal with the monster she created when she invited me to chase her through the woods.

Silly girl. She had to know it wouldn't end there. Hunters don't stop hunting just because they caught their prey.

"Where did you bring me?" Ava asks when I pull to a stop at the diner that sits on the outskirts of the city.

I cock a brow at her.

"You didn't get out much as a kid, did you?"

before I climb out. She doesn't move from the door when I come to her side, eyeing me warily.

"It's a diner, Ava. Not a sex club."

"I know that," she snaps.

"Then let's go. Unless you'd prefer to sit out here by yourself?"

"Fine," she grumbles, and without thinking, I take her hand in mine. It's a big fucking mistake because once I do, I don't want to let it go.

The papers in my pocket threaten to burn a hole in my leather jacket the moment her soft hand fits into mine. Her skin is smooth and perfect, and so fucking tempting, I drop it the moment she's out of the car.

She follows me up the front sidewalk and inside, where the air smells like it always used to. Like fried food, butter, and everything the media swears is bad for you.

"Take a seat wherever you'd like," the nice, older woman on shift smiles at us, and I give her a nod, leading Ava to a booth near the back of the room.

What I want to discuss with her isn't something I want everyone to hear.

"Cold?" I ask when Ava shivers, slipping into the seat opposite me.

"No," she lies, and before I have a chance to call her on it, the waitress comes to take our order.

"Waffle sundae, please," I answer before Ava can even get her mouth open.

She looks across the booth at me like I've grown an extra head.

"Good choice," the woman smiles. "Anything else?"

Ava shakes her head, and she walks away with a smile.

"What the hell is a waffle sundae?" Ava asks the moment she's out of earshot.

"You'll see."

"You brought me here for ice cream?"

"Who says it's ice cream?"

"God, you're impossible," she rolls her eyes.

"I'm not the one who asked to be hunted down and fucked in the woods like an animal. Then pretended like I was too high and mighty to say I enjoyed it."

Our waitress returns before Ava can answer, and she glowers at me over the plate as it's lowered to the table between us with two spoons.

"You kids enjoy."

"Thank you," Ava says, ever polite, even when plotting my death. "It was a lapse in judgment," she says, snatching the spoon out of my hand when I hold it out to her.

"Must have been a pretty good one. Considering how many times you came."

She rolls her eyes, her cheeks flaming a thousand degrees.

"What are we eating?" she huffs, staring at the monstrosity on the plate. I get the feeling she's desperately trying to change the subject. It's fine. We'll be circling back to her "lapse in judgment" later.

"A waffle sundae," I answer.

"You eat this?"

I shrug. "I thought we'd just stare at it."

I take a bite, and it's like the last twenty years didn't happen. Like Mom's sitting here with us and cracking jokes. Smiling and happy and not bones in a grave that I haven't visited in entirely too fucking long.

"It's delicious," Ava muses, taking a bite.

"Have I lied to you yet?"

Heat bristles up my spine at the dry look she gives me.

I guess I deserve that.

"Why did you really bring me here? I know it's not just so we could get ice cream."

I cock a brow at her.

193

Inquisitive little brat.

"And if it is?"

"Then I'd say you've fallen and hit your head."

"Can't a man take his employee out for a treat every now and then?"

"You wanted to talk, so talk. Enough of this taunting crap," she snaps quietly, and I refrain from chuckling, my cock hardening at the bite in her voice. I've always known I enjoyed her fire. Now, I'm finding it fucking addicting. "You and I both know why you brought me here. I told you everything I know."

"Oh, I believe you."

"And if you're expecting me to beg or grovel—wait, what?"

"Just what I said. I believe you don't know anything more than you've already told me."

She sinks back in the seat, utterly confused.

"Then, what do you want?" she hisses, fear shining in those pretty green eyes.

Pulling the papers out of my jacket, I toss them onto the table in front of her.

She pauses, looking from the contract that landed dangerously close to a drop of ice cream on the table, back to me.

"What is this?"

I lean back in the booth. This is the part where she either tells me I've lost my mind, or she finds out just how fucking crazy I am.

"It's a contract."

"For?"

I brush back the smirk on my lips, keeping my gaze indifferent.

"For you."

I'm not even sure if Ava breathes when her gaze roams over the front page.

Poor thing looks like she might pass out. I don't blame her. I'm sure it's a lot to process, but then again, she's the one who got herself into this mess. I'm simply giving her the only real option she has.

"This . . . this is . . . *are you crazy?*"

I can't help but grin. She has no fucking idea.

"Think of this as a gift."

"A gift," she scoffs, crossing her arms over her chest. "You're asking me to be your sex slave."

"It's not a question. It's a choice. You either agree to the contract, or you're free to deal with whoever's stalking you on your own. Your piece of shit car. Grandma's medical bills . . . The choice is yours."

"How do you know about that?" she snaps.

"Funny what you can find when you go through someone's room."

She looks like she might try to stab me with her spoon.

"This has to be a fever dream."

"The terms are simple. You want to take care of your grandmother. I want to fuck you without worrying about you growing attached." She glares at me, her cheeks burning brighter than the sun. "You will be available to me whenever and wherever I want. In return, I will make sure you're both protected, take care of the bills at the nursing home, and you'll receive an allowance."

"Like a child?"

"Like a woman in my bed."

She blushes a deep shade of scarlet, peeking up at me through her lashes. "You say *a* woman. As if there will be multiple."

I hadn't given it much thought. Of course, there would only be Ava because once she's mine to use, there would be no room for anyone else in my head. Fuck, there hasn't been for months. Every woman I bring home is just a reminder of the thing I can't have, sleeping right across the damn hall.

With this contract, that becomes null and void.

"We would be exclusive."

"But not dating."

"No dating."

195

"So, we'd be exclusive fuck buddies without the buddy part?"

I ignore her little jab and point to a new line in the contract.

"When we're done, the contract will be terminated, and you'll receive a hefty severance package." I point to a line at the bottom of the contract, and her eyes go wide.

"One million and *one* dollar?"

I smirk and shrug. "You said one million wouldn't be enough."

She rolls her eyes and shakes her head, her cheeks darkening.

"When this ends, I'll let you go, and you're free to move on with your life. You don't say a word to anyone, and I'll make it worth your while." I force her to meet my gaze, though hers are greener than I've ever seen them before. Like the inside of a gemstone. Oddly enough, my chest aches. "When the time comes . . . you won't fight me on it."

"So basically, you can throw me to the side whenever you feel like it, and I don't get a say in my life being completely uprooted?"

Fair point.

"You have the liberty of ending the contract whenever you see fit. Though the moment you develop feelings, the deal is off. I'll end it immediately."

She studies me for a moment. Probably trying to figure out what's going through my head.

Good luck, because even I can't figure that shit out.

"So, you wrote up a contract because you want to have sex with me without your conscience getting in the way?"

"Incorrect. I wrote up a contract because I want to fuck you without *your* conscience getting in the way."

"Sounds like prostitution."

"Think of it more as friends with benefits."

"But we aren't friends," she points out.

Ouch.

"Then just benefits."

She sits forward and lets out a huff, angrily scooping ice cream into her mouth. My gaze lingers on the way her tongue slips along the spoon, and instantly, visions of her on her knees, doing nearly that exact same motion with my cock flash through my mind.

"And whoever this Mr. Black is? What do you plan to do about him?"

"He won't come near you again."

"Bull," she grumbles with a roll of her eyes. I swear I'm ready to bend her over this worn leather seat if she doesn't fucking stop licking her spoon. "A whole contract. I guess I should feel special."

"Wrong. Nothing about our arrangement will change, other than when I want you, you're mine. When it's over, as I stated, you'll be released with the severance listed at the bottom. I don't want any feelings. No fighting. No strings. The moment you try to demand more of me than what I'm willing to offer, the deal is off, you'll be let go *without* your severance package."

She's quiet throughout my entire speech, chewing on her lip. I hate that I can't see what's going through that head of hers, but I hate even more that she's not already agreed. This fucking maddening obsession will only go away if I give it exactly what it wants and let myself get bored with it.

"Can't accuse you of being romantic," Ava grumbles finally, setting her spoon down.

"There is nothing romantic about what I want to do to you, baby girl."

She chews on her lip, looking anywhere in the room but at me while I wait.

"And if I say no?"

I can tell by the look in her eyes she's not going to. She wants this money as much as I want her to take it.

Now, if she'd get out of that pretty little head of hers.

"Then I take you home, and you can be free to do whatever it is you plan to do about your grandmother and the man following you."

She chews on her lip, looking anywhere in the room but at me while I wait.

Then finally, she sits forward and grabs the contract.

"You don't even have a pen."

I bite back my smirk, pulling one from the inside pocket of my jacket and sliding it across the table to her.

"I have your word?" she asks, and for once, when she meets my gaze, it's head-on. I can't deny it hits like a thousand watts shooting up my spine. "You'll take care of her?"

Fucking finally . . . She's mine.

"Consider it done."

Ava's silent when I shove the car in park outside Cross Estate. The moment the engine is off, she's out the door and storming toward the house. I can't do anything but chuckle and follow her.

Little brat's on a warpath.

She attempts to shut her bedroom door in my face, but my boot stops it, sending it rebounding back into the wall.

Ava's eyes go wide as she spins at the edge of her bed, then they narrow on me when I step into the room after her.

"I want to be alone."

"Too bad," I grunt, closing the door behind me.

It's a bad idea because there's nothing stopping me from fucking her with the door closed.

Well . . . nothing but her, but I don't think it would take much to get her ready and begging for me again.

"Let me see."

She looks at my outstretched hand like it's crawling with maggots.

"Why?"

I cock a brow and fix her with a look. She blushes deeply and begrudgingly lays her fingers in mine so I can tug her over to the bed. My cock pulses against my jeans. It's ridiculous. A simple touch of her soft skin against mine, and it's all I can think about.

Spreading her out underneath me to see what she'd feel like, nothing separating us, so I could use her entire body to draw those sweet little whimpers from her lips.

Fucking hell.

Ignoring the burn in my chest, I slowly unwrap the bandages covering the burns on her wrists. They look a lot better than they did this morning, but they still need to be covered.

"I can do it," she argues when I grab the ointment and bandages I'd stashed in her nightstand last night.

I don't even give her an answer. I just push her back on the bed. She lands on her ass, bouncing, and looks up at me, her mouth falling open.

I shrug, drag a chair from the corner, and sit in front of her, dragging her until she's in between my legs. She blushes with my hands on her thighs, as if I haven't already seen all of her.

She's silent while I clean the burns, gritting her teeth to hide her grimace when I swipe an alcohol pad over the wounds.

"Can I ask you a personal question?" she says softly, watching me work.

I know I'm going to regret this. "You can."

"Why did you lose your job?"

Well, fuck.

"Are you asking if I did something wrong?"

She looks over my shoulder, and it's answer enough.

"Look at me, Ava." Her gaze flicks to mine, and I study her face. "Sometimes, the people who claim to be good have the dirtiest hands of them all. I think you probably already know that, don't you?"

She lets out a deep breath, and the silence in the room hums.

"So . . . you tell me. Do you think I did something bad?"

"If I did, do you think I would be here right now?"

Touché.

"I'm just confused as to why he's after you. And why is he using me? I have nothing to do with this."

"I told you, he won't be a problem for you anymore."

"You say that as if you know who it is."

When I don't respond, she pounces.

"You do. Who is it?"

"No one that you need to worry about," I mutter gruffly. "Now, stop moving."

She falls silent while I work, tossing the old bandages to the side and pulling out new. Is it overkill? Probably. I don't care. I never intended for her to pull as hard as she did, and a part of me feels guilty for that, even if she enjoyed it.

"Why did you bandage my wrists?"

"Why are you so damned stubborn?" I retort.

"I'm not," she argues, and I cock a brow at her.

"I don't try to be." She shrugs. It's the most honest she's ever been with me. "I think you bring it out in me."

I chuckle, and she watches me slather her wrists in the same cream I used last night.

"You didn't answer my question," she says softly.

A tension settles in the air between us. I've fucked her in the woods. I've tied her to the rafters in my cabin. Fuck, I brought her home and cleaned her up last night after she fell asleep and bandaged her wrists. Still, somehow, this is the most intimate we've ever been. This silence between us feels almost comfortable.

I fucking hate it.

"I'm not going to."

When she doesn't speak, my gaze flicks up to hers to find her watching me, a curious expression in her eyes.

Last night when I brought her home, she was so soft, and warm, and fucking out of it. I won't lie and say I didn't think about keeping her at the cabin, but shit always has a way of finding clarity in the daylight.

Like the fact that the little brunette housekeeper I can't stand means a little something more to me than I had originally planned, and it's really starting to piss me off because I feel fucking powerless to stop it.

And maybe because I know someday, she's going to wake up and regret ever meeting me. When she learns who I really am, and that I'm so much worse than she thought.

God fucking help me on that day.

"You had burns from the rope."

When I got her into her bed and cleaned her up, she wouldn't open her eyes. I was sure I'd pushed her too hard, and for a split second, I was this fucking close to losing my shit.

Then, she shot me a glare and grumbled something unintelligible, and the relief I felt was unlike anything I've ever experienced before. I'd bandaged her wrists and covered her up, watching her sleep for a few minutes before I forced myself to leave.

"That's what happens when you tie someone up to the rafters in your cabin with rope," she says softly, watching me work on slathering ointment on the rope burn. It'll be gone in a few days, but I'm not leaving her like this.

"Fine, baby girl. You win. Next time, I'll use silk."

"Next time," she scoffs, rolling her eyes, but I can see her cheeks flame, remembering it.

I wrap each wrist in a new, clean bandage, making sure it's tight enough that she won't rip it off in the middle of the night, before I cap the cream and slide it back into her nightstand. When I'm done, there's a heavy silence in the air, like something between us has shifted.

"Next time you'll be begging me to tie you up," I smirk, my

finger sliding up her thigh. She shivers, shifting, but she doesn't pull away. "I didn't realize how hard you were pulling when you were begging me to fuck you."

"I didn't *beg*," she argues.

"Why are you so afraid to admit you enjoyed it?" She doesn't respond. "Why are you ashamed?"

"Because I shouldn't have enjoyed it."

"Why not?"

"Maybe because it makes me feel like a whore," she snaps, and the ringing silence that follows is loud.

Abruptly, I lean over her, forcing her back into the mattress. She stares at me wide-eyed and confused, and so fucking sweet.

My fingers wrap around her throat, and now that I have her attention, I bring her gaze to mine.

"Let's get one thing straight, sweetheart," I murmur darkly, my lips hovering over hers.

Fuck, what is it about this girl that makes me lose my damned control?

"Nothing about what I will ever do to you makes you a whore. Liking to be tied up and pushed to the edge doesn't make you a whore. Getting off on my spanking that perfect little ass doesn't make you a whore. And liking sex *definitely* doesn't make you a whore."

She's speechless, and her throat bobs under my hand with a rough swallow.

"So don't ever let me hear you call yourself that again. Not unless I'm buried inside you, making you scream it for me before I'll let you come. Understood?"

Her lashes flutter when I tighten my hold ever so slightly, and she finally nods.

"Let me hear you."

"Yes," she breathes. When she opens her eyes, they're full of something different that she's trying to fight. Something I don't think either of us is ready to acknowledge.

"Good girl."

I chuckle, pulling back enough to look down the length of her body. I'm so fucking hard.

"What is it about you that is so fucking addicting?"

My hands roam down her sides, over the soft skin of her ribcage, and then lower, to her hips, where I knead the flesh and tug her closer until she's settled right between my legs.

Her eyes grow wide, her breathing shallow in the space between us. My cock is so fucking hard, but even I know she's sore after last night.

Her lips hover inches from mine, and I swear I can feel her heart beating where I'm touching her. It's fast. Like a hare, and I raise my fingertips to her throat, just to feel the steady pulse that proves my little ghost wants me more than she'd ever be willing to let on.

"Your pulse is racing, baby girl," I breathe, my lips quirking up at the corners in a smirk.

Her tongue darts out to lick her lips, her soft green eyes wide. *Fucking hell, those eyes.*

Those eyes could make me do shit that should terrify me.

I move closer, and for a long moment, we breathe each other's air. She looks from my mouth, up to my eyes, and my cock rages in my jeans to feel her delicate fingers wrapping around my length.

Lowering my head, I take what I want and push my lips against hers. My tongue slips into her mouth, my hand wraps in her hair, and I just fucking feast on her like I should have done in the forest.

Like I should have done last night.

She even tastes like fucking citrus, and my mouth waters the moment her tongue dances across mine. My fingers tighten, and I lean forward, crowding over her on the bed, and fisting the comforter beneath her. I keep her pressed against me with my hand in her hair, and growl at the soft little whimper that slips free.

Her hands fist my shirt, and I can't tell if she's trying to pull me closer or shove me away. I fucking love it, and it only makes me want to fucking devour her.

I've never given a fuck about another person's lips until Ava Ryan withheld hers from me, and now?

Fuck her. She's not getting them back until I say so.

Slow . . . I remind myself. *Savor it.*

This isn't just a kiss. It's a goddamned claiming. Kissing her does nothing but prove to her I can have her however I want her until I'm bored with her.

Eventually, her hands slide up the back of my neck, her fingers tugging at the dark roots of my hair. A shiver slips through me that leaves me both mildly disturbed and fucking irritated that the little brat has so much control over me.

My hand leaves the bed, going to her lower back, and I grip her hip to keep her from wiggling closer to me when she lets out a soft moan.

Fucking hell.

When the heavy petting and desperate grinding get to be too much, and I'm too close to losing every ounce of self-control I have with her, I break the kiss, leaning my forehead against hers while we both breathe heavily.

I've got to get the fuck out of here before I spend the night trying to figure out just how many times I can get her to moan my name.

Abruptly, I stand from the bed, ignoring the way my chest tightens at the little shiver that slides through her.

"I'll see you tomorrow."

"Levi?" she calls softly.

I pause, hand on the door handle, and look back at her.

She looks so fucking soft and warm, a part of me hates myself for all the ways I'm going to use her.

"I believe you," she says finally, and I grit my teeth so hard my jaw aches.

I stare at her for a minute, unsure what to say because no one fucking believes me.

No one ever believes me.

Why should it matter if she does?

"Goodnight, Ava."

CHAPTER
Twenty-One

AVA

The two days following my . . . *agreement* with Levi are the most confusing two days of my life.

He ignores me almost as much as he did before, to the point where I start to question myself as to whether or not the whole diner-contract meeting was a fever dream.

He's barely home, and when he is, he leaves shortly after. He doesn't stay the night, and I can't help but wonder if he's out sleeping with other women again despite what he said, or if he's somewhere else, avoiding me because he regrets ever making the deal in the first place.

Why does he have to be so confusing?

Why do I have to care?

To top it off, my phone goes silent. Not so much as a whisper from Mr. Black. I can't say I'm not relieved. I also can't say I trust this silence. It all just seems too perfect.

The more I think about our agreement, the more I question my morals.

Sex for money, no matter how you paint it, could be

agreeing to his terms, but it sits heavily on my shoulders, reminding me of what I agreed to.

The pros are great sex with the object of my fantasies. Nana would be taken care of. I wouldn't have to skip meals to pay for the nursing home. I could save up enough to get out of here and maybe finish school. I could move and find somewhere quiet and peaceful and just breathe.

The cons?

Everything else.

My morals have taken a major hit. My sense of self. I've never been overly sexual. The incident in the woods was a one-off thing that backfired majorly.

What if he finds out I'm boring in bed? That I've only ever slept with two men and have the experience of a teaspoon?

There's no doubt in my mind he'd end it immediately if he deemed me too boring, and, in that regard, I have to worry about my self-esteem.

I've read through my copy of the contract so many times that it's become wrinkled. I found it on my bed the day after I'd signed the original. It just seems surreal, and I'm still not sure what I'm doing.

Especially when he hasn't "requested" my presence.

I know he's playing some sick game. Stringing me along to build up the anticipation until I've stressed myself out enough to quit.

I let out a sigh that's not audible over the sweeper I'm running in the den.

What the hell is a girl to do?

I cut the vacuum off, and only then do I realize my phone is ringing. I jump, tugging it out of my pocket to see the nursing home's name flashing on the screen, and answer it instantly.

"H-Hello?"

"Hi, this is Patrice from the Pleasant Grove Senior Care Center. Is this Ava Ryan I'm speaking to?"

I swallow over the lump in my throat.

"It is."

"Good, I'm just calling because it appears as though we're two months behind on payment for your grandmother's account. Do you have time to discuss this?"

Fuck.

Fuckkkkkkk . . .

"Yeah, umm . . . I have the money. I just need to come in and pay."

"That's great to hear. I just have to inform you that if this month's payment is missed, the account will fall into default, and we won't be able to continue housing your grandmother."

Tears burn in the backs of my eyes, and a rush of anger washes over me.

He said he'd take care of it. It's been three days, and I haven't heard a single word from him. Not a fuck you, fuck off, or even a simple hello.

More than that, though, I'm pissed at myself.

How could I let things fall behind this far? I've paid as much as I can, yet it still isn't enough. My account is at five dollars even with my paycheck coming in, and I know it won't be enough.

Scrubbing a hand over my face, I know what I need to do.

A pit forms in my stomach, filling with acid, but I start toward the stairs anyway.

"I'll see it gets done."

"Thank you," Patrice says, all smiles on the other end of the line. "Have a great day."

I hang up my phone and don't stop on my way up to the second story. Levi's door is unlocked when I turn the knob, and I don't bother knocking because I can barely remember to breathe, let alone my manners.

"You asshole!"

I freeze when I see he's on the phone, standing in front of the windows at the far end. He turns around, his gaze locking with mine, and gives me a disinterested once-over before he resumes his conversation.

Well, this is awkward . . .

"Tomorrow," he replies coolly, his gaze still on me.

Maybe I should have knocked.

I stand in the doorway, arms crossed over my chest uncomfortably, while his stare continues to bore into me like two lasers determined to turn me to ash.

"I have something that needs my attention," he murmurs gruffly. "I'll call you back."

He hangs up the phone and turns away from me as he moves about the room, shoving things in his pockets.

"I'm not in the mood, Ava."

My temper flares because I'm not in the mood *either*.

"I just got a call from the nursing home. They said if my grandmother's account isn't paid by the end of the month, they're kicking her out." He slides a hoodie over his head, and despite the brief glimpse of his perfect abs, I keep ranting. "I don't know what the hell you're doing, but *you* approached *me* about your little contract of sin, and if you expect me to put out without paying up on your end, you'd better think again, Levi Cross. I'm not one of those girls who's just going to fall for your lies and not expect you to uphold your end of the bargain."

I'm panting by the time I fall silent and still angry. It only gets worse when he raises his brows, a hint of amusement in his eyes.

"Feel better?"

I'm going to beat him with the toilet brush.

Screw him. I square my shoulders, meeting his gaze head-on. "I'm serious. If you can't be bothered to hold up your end of the deal, then there will *be* no deal."

The thought of losing the opportunity is crushing, but I shove my chin high, anyway.

Stay strong, Ava. He can smell fear.

"Well, as fun as this was, I really don't have time for your games today, sweetheart."

He turns away from me, and I gawk at the back of his head.

Fucking asshole . . .

Without thinking, I grab the closest thing I can find, and twenty-five years of pent-up frustration come out when I wing a pillow from his bed at him.

Unfortunately . . . it hits him square between his broad shoulders.

For a brief, shining moment, everything feels like glorious triumph. Angels sing. Doves do dove things. Levi Cross gets what he deserves.

Then he turns around, and those icy eyes lock on mine.

Uh-oh.

"Baby girl. . ." His voice sends a shiver down my spine. "You're going to wish you hadn't done that."

I bolt, rushing from the room and nearly fall to the ground, and beg for forgiveness when I hear his footsteps thundering after me.

I don't pay attention to where I'm going. I just run, ending up in my bedroom across the hall. I try to slam the door on him, but his heavy boot kicks it back, sending it rocketing into the wall behind it when he fills the frame.

"I-I-I'm sorry."

"No, you're not."

I rush toward the bathroom, but it's useless when he catches me around the waist, hauling me back and pinning me between the wall and him.

His breathing is heavy, and his eyes are on fire when he fists a hand in my hair and drags my face up. His other hand hits the wall beside my head, and I jump, cowering instinctively.

I don't mean to flinch. I really don't. But it's not a voluntary response.

He's quiet for a moment, and my breathing comes out shaky. Tremors slide through me, and I know he can feel them.

His hold in my hair loosens, and his hand slides down to grip my jaw.

"Open your eyes, Ava."

I force myself to meet his gaze, and it's like looking into a black hole, devoid of emotion.

He searches my face for a moment, like he's reading a book and it's the worst one he's ever had the displeasure of picking up.

"I'm not going to hurt you, Ava."

I don't have a response for that, so I don't say anything.

He waits for me to speak up, but I can't.

After a moment, Levi slides his free hand into his pocket and pulls something out, depositing it in my fingers. I don't look down, but I know it's paper and part of me wonders if it's our contract with a big *VOID* right through the center.

He leans forward, his lips only inches from my ear, and a shiver slides through me. His breath fans across my neck, drawing out tingles on my skin that feel like electric zaps.

What am I doing? I threw a pillow at the man.

I'm really in over my head with this man.

"If you had asked, you would have found it's already been taken care of," he says so quietly, I barely hear him.

His lips touch my neck ever so softly in the lightest of kisses . . .

Then he steps back and leaves me pressed against the wall, staring at the spot he just vacated.

It's not until I hear his footsteps retreat down the stairs that I unfold my fingers and look at what he'd placed in my hand. My heart drops, my mouth running dry at the check he'd given me.

And the hundred thousand dollars it's made out for.

"Oh, fuck."

I was wrong.

Hell really does exist. Right here at Cross Estate.

"You're weak."

"Oh, fuck you," I huff in between heavy breaths, my hands on my knees and my back hunched. My heart races in my chest, and I feel like I just tackled a grizzly bear and barely lived to tell the tale.

"You haven't been eating enough," he mutters like a disappointed father.

Speaking of, how long is this torture going to last? We've been down here for hours, and my stomach is starting to digest itself.

"Nothing gets by you, does it?" I grumble.

This evening, he woke me up from a truly great nap by pounding on my door and telling me I had five minutes to get dressed and meet him in the hall.

I ignored him, only to be ripped from my bed and thrown over his shoulder like a ragdoll when he dragged me into the bathroom to get dressed before I was forced down to the gym.

We've been here ever since, and let's just say, I think I'd rather raw dog a root canal than spend another ten minutes being tackled by Levi Cross in his fancy little home gym.

"Do you think a man who's after you is going to give you a moment to catch your breath?" he taunts, circling me like the asshole he is. "When they attack, it will be with force."

"Can't you put a shirt on?"

I swear it's impossible to focus on anything with his abs glistening like they are.

"Distracting you, sweetheart?"

I roll my eyes. "No." Yes. "You're just sweaty."

"All the more reason for you to try harder."

"Why are we doing this?" I grumble, wiping the sweat off my brow. "They're after you, not me."

He ignores me and motions for me to ready myself.

"Again."

"I don't want to."

I'm done. My back and legs are on fire from being thrown around like Levi throws around the word *fuck*. I'm hot and sweaty, and I have a strong feeling my ass will be imprinted in the mat beneath us for years to come after how many times I've landed on it today.

"What you want doesn't matter much, does it?"

Wow, rude.

"Oh, right," I scoff, rolling my eyes. "How could I forget? Whatever his majesty wants, he gets."

He lets my little comment go and nods, signifying for me to take the position.

I think I'd rather lick a dirty foot.

"Try. Again."

"Fine," I grumble, hunkering down into the position he'd taught me before immediately straightening. He shoots me a look, and I have a feeling I'm starting to get on his nerves.

Good.

"Why not just give me a gun?"

He cocks a brow at me, and instant awareness slips through me.

"And watch you shoot yourself by accident?"

My cheeks flame, and I bite my cheek to keep from spouting off with more nonsense that will just piss him off and take my place.

"The problem with relying only on a gun to save you," he murmurs, keeping his voice low. It bounces off the room, making it hard to pinpoint exactly where he is while he circles me like a shark hunting for blood in the ocean. Something about the darkness in his tone sends a shiver up my spine, and I have a feeling it's nothing to do with how dangerous I know he is.

God save me.

"When the bullets run out, time does too."

In the blink of an eye, my legs are swept out from under me, and I land *hard* on my tailbone on the mat beneath us.

I wince, sputtering from the impact, and collapse there, accepting defeat.

"Get up."

"Get a life."

"That's rich coming from the maid." He leans over me, his face upside down over mine, and I glare up at him.

"So, how the hell am I supposed to fight them off? Magic? Some Harry Potter shit?"

He holds out his hand to me. I choose to stand on my own. I don't need his help.

"You're small. You can move faster. Move in ways they can't."

"The bigger they are, the harder they fall," I mock. He can't honestly believe that.

"Size is nothing but a different set of steps, Ava. If you allow it to, your helplessness will control you."

"Noted," I huff, and he starts to stalk me again.

I don't like it when he does this.

"Why are you even bothering to teach me anything? I thought I was just here until you were done using me?"

"Can't very well fuck you if you're dead, now can I?"

God, he's an even bigger dick than I originally thought.

"And to think I was starting to believe you actually liked me."

He smirks . . . and then he kicks my legs out from under me.

God, I hate him.

"You're a walking canker sore," I grumble, and a spark of amusement lights his gaze.

"I'm not the one on the dirty gym floor, now am I?"

"Don't let Magdalene hear you say that. She'll put a hex on you."

"Wouldn't be the first time." He holds out a hand to me, and this time, I take it, allowing him to pull me to my feet.

And pull my front into his.

It's a mistake because the moment we're in each other's space, it's like all the air gets sucked out of the room. My heart beats faster—not that it wasn't already racing. My mouth runs dry at the scent of him around me. My head gets foggy.

And then I have an idea.

He looks down at me, studying me when I place my hand on his stomach to right myself. His very muscular stomach with abs that I may have dreamed of last night, might I add.

I allow my touch to linger for a moment, my tongue darting out to lick his lips, and his expression darkens. His gaze slips down over my body, and my blood heats in my veins.

Then, I swipe his legs out from under him.

"Take that, asshole," I cheer the moment he hits the ground, but before I can dart away, he's got me around the waist and is hauling me down to the rubber mat beneath him.

Okay, I fucked up.

I let out a yelp that dissolves into a laugh when I land, rolling over and attempting to scurry away. His big body crowds over mine, his length pressing against my leg through my shorts. Something hot slips into my core, but before I can register it, he's gripping my hips and hauling me back to him.

"Running off again?"

"Levi . . ." I fight against his hold, unable to hold back my laugh when his fingers tickle against my skin. "Stop," I gasp as the uncontrollable laughter takes over.

It's been a long time since someone's tickled me, and the fact that Levi now knows my kryptonite means he's going to use it against me any chance he can.

He rolls me until my back is against the mat and he's looming over me, a wicked grin on his lips.

"Are you ticklish, baby girl?"

"No," I lie, but he doesn't believe me.

"No?" he taunts, a devious look in his eyes.

"Levi," I warn when his hands slide up my thigh. Heat slides through me, mixed with the urge to shimmy away from him when he brushes over the inside of my thigh.

"Where are you most ticklish, baby girl?"

Oh. My. God. That voice should be illegal.

"Here?" His fingers brush over my sides, his eyes glinting with dark amusement.

I shake my head, my tongue darting out to lick my lips.

"Here, then?" His hand slides lower to cup the back of my knee, and I can't help but wonder if there's an erogenous zone there I didn't know about.

I swallow over the lump in my throat.

"No," I breathe.

"Then, it must be here." He moves to my inner thigh, and though I'm most ticklish there, I can't say that's the feeling I get with Levi Cross touching me there.

"Maybe," I breathe, and his smirk widens, his breathing growing heavier. My heart hammers in my chest, and my mind goes blank to anything but him touching me.

It's the most glorious feeling in the world.

At least for a moment.

"*Levi!*"

Both of us snap up, looking toward the doorway where Paulina is standing, shooting daggers in my direction. I sit up, drawing my knees to my chest while embarrassment floods through me.

Well, shit.

"If you're done, the police are here," she grits, shooting me a warning look before she turns on her heel and stalks back out of the gym.

"The police?"

Levi tugs me to my feet, his playful mood all but gone.

"Go upstairs. I'll handle it."

"But—"

"I said I'd handle it," he snaps, his tone warning me not to argue with him.

I swallow thickly, stepping back when he releases me.

"We're done for the day," he says, and without another word, he grabs his shirt and strides out the door, leaving me suddenly cold while I stare after him.

I stay rooted in place for a long time, debating on going up to my room like a good little girl or snooping.

You can probably guess which one wins in the end.

Sliding up against the wall, I listen to the sounds of the muffled voices from within.

"We believe the Burelli crime family is linked to the death of Patrick Wright," a young cop says, while another stands beside him. "You were there that night, were you not?"

"I don't know," Levi counters. "You tell me." I can just barely see him leaning against Christian's desk, his arms crossed over his chest. He's put his T-shirt on, but his hair is a tousled mess from our day down in the gym.

My breath catches in my throat. Who are they talking about?

"I was off-duty that night."

"Off-duty. So, what did you do?"

There's a moment of silence while my heartbeat thuds unsteadily.

"Saw a girl," Levi says finally, and a pang of jealousy hits me in the chest.

I don't know why. It's not like anything we're doing is exclusive.

Still . . . whoever she is. Fuck her.

"And what did you and this girl do, if you don't mind me asking?"

I grit my teeth. This guy is an idiot.

217

"You want a play-by-play?"

"Levi," Christian growls, silencing his brother. "The girl doesn't have anything—"

"Cherise," Levi cuts him off.

"Last name?"

"Don't have one."

The detective sighs, clearly annoyed.

"And how do you know Cherise?"

"I think we established that," Levi replies smoothly.

"She a prostitute?"

"Bartender."

"Same thing," the snarky detective murmurs with a nasty grin. Asshole.

"Would this Cherise be able to vouch for you, were we to fact-check some of your statements?"

"If you can find her, sure."

"Where do you think she might have gone?"

"Your moth—"

"*Enough.*" The look Christian throws Levi's way sends a chill down even my spine. Levi, fortunately, has the good sense to shut his mouth for once.

"Where did you meet Cherise?"

"I would reckon that if she's a bartender, I met her at a bar," Levi sighs.

"What bar?"

"Don't know. Just went to a bar."

"You went to a bar, but you don't remember which one?"

"You want a list?"

"I get the feeling you're feeling defensive, Mr. Cross."

"I get the feeling you've overstayed your welcome."

"You know, death seems to follow you, Mr. Cross," one of the detectives says, and a humming silence falls over the room. "First, your mother. Then your father. Now, it's seeped into your work.

Who's next?"

"Guess we'll find out."

"We've been told someone showed up uninvited at the Columbia Club last week and broke Donovan Palmer's nose. That ring a bell?"

"Can't say it does."

"He's lying," the other detective growls, but I'm too busy going over what he just said.

Suddenly, my heart's beating like a drum.

"You got evidence?" Christian asks, kicking back in his chair. I get the feeling he knows more than he's letting on.

"Camera had an outage at the same time as the attack. Oddly convenient, isn't it?"

"Sure is," Levi retorts.

"Mr. Cross—"

"It's Levi," he interrupts. "And if you have nothing else to assume, I've got somewhere to be."

There's a moment of silence before the polite-ish one speaks up.

"No. Nothing else."

"For now," the other adds. "We're going to find out what happened to Senator Wright one way or another. No matter who we have to take down along the way."

"Be my guest."

Heavy footfalls sound on the other side of the door, and I jump back in a frenzy, rushing to the spare bedroom beside Christian's office and ducking inside.

"Oh, and Cross," the second detective calls, and the footsteps stop. I imagine Levi turning back to them.

"We're going to need that list."

Seconds later, I hear them pass over the sound of my racing heart.

Senator Wright . . . As in the Senator whose body just washed up in Seattle a month ago? My mind races a million miles a minute, trying to process the information.

The Burelli crime family sounds serious.

. . . So what does Levi have to do with them?

The detective's words echo back in my head, setting a chill in my bones that has nothing to do with the crisp October air outside.

"First, your mother. Then your father. Now, it's seeped into your job. . . Who's next?"

When I finally ease the door open, the hallway is empty. A sliver of cold evening light spills through the blinds, striping the floor in pale gold. I pad toward my room, my bare feet silent on the floorboards.

Silently, I shut my door behind me, nearly jumping out of my skin when I turn to find Levi leaning against the wall behind it.

There's no trace of the easy smirk he usually hides behind. Just a darkness I've only seen once before—when someone threatened me.

He finally lifts his gaze, and it pins me in place.

"You heard all of that, didn't you?"

My throat goes dry.

Well, shit.

"Who are the Burelli's, Levi?"

His jaw flexes, and I see the war behind his eyes—between telling me the truth and keeping me in the dark.

"They're the reason Senator Wright's dead," he says finally. "And if we're not careful . . . they'll be the reason we are too."

CHAPTER
Twenty-Two

LEVI

"What are you saying?" Ava asks, her brows knitting in concern. She steps further into the room, dropping her voice. She glances toward the closed door as if she can still feel Tweedle Dee and Tweedle Dum loitering just outside.

"The Burelli Crime family," I say slowly, "The one case I wasn't able to finish before I left my job."

Her head tilts. "Left?"

I give a single nod, my jaw locking. "Left."

Her eyes search mine. "Why would you leave?" She shakes her head, still piecing it together. "Furthermore, what could they want from you now?"

"The Burelli Crime family has been linked to a string of deaths. The most recent being Senator Wright. To top it off, we believe they control the ports."

"Meaning?"

"Meaning they control the drugs on the streets of Seattle."

She blows out a breath through her teeth, wrapping her arms tightly around herself.

some stupid little flash drive. I mean, if you were no longer a DEA agent, why would they still be coming after you?"

"Because I know their secrets."

"Like?"

"That's not important," I murmur, the edge in my tone making it clear the subject's closed. "What is important is that they're dangerous."

She groans and throws her head back, as if I just told her she was grounded for life.

Little brat.

"I haven't gotten a text in a week."

"And you think that means they've stopped watching you?"

Her gaze sharpens. "Why do you care?" she snaps, but the bite in her voice sounds more like deflection than anger.

I give a lazy shrug that's anything but casual. "You signed a contract stating it's my job to protect you. That means whatever I say goes."

She scoffs, folding her arms in a way that pushes her shoulders back—whether she realizes it or not. "Well, I think you're overreacting. So, they got my number because I live here. It could have been anyone."

I take a slow step toward her, letting the space shrink until she has to tilt her chin up to keep looking at me. "You really think so, baby girl?"

The nickname rolls off my tongue like a warning and a promise all at once.

Her cheeks flare hot, a blush that blooms fast and betrays her before she can look away. I see it. I feel it. And it's enough to make me smirk.

"Thought so," I murmur, not breaking eye contact.

"You're impossible," she growls under her breath.

"And you're a brat," I counter.

"So, if this is the Burelli's, then who is Black?"

Lead fills my chest, but I shake the feeling off. I don't have time to dwell on it.

"There's a place I go to. Called the Tomb." My voice flattens. "I don't go by Levi or Cross there, Ava."

She stares at me, the silence stretching long enough that I can almost hear the gears turning in her head. Then her eyes narrow with dawning realization.

"Let me guess . . ." Her voice is quieter now, colder. "You go by Black."

I don't answer. I don't have to. She knows.

"This is getting far too confusing," she mutters, sinking onto the corner of the bed and scrubbing a hand over her face. "I mean, why would someone be pretending to be you to blackmail me into stealing . . . from you?"

"Your guess is as good as mine," I grunt. I lean my shoulder into the doorframe, the wood cool against my arm. "Though, if they're pretending to be me, I don't think it's so much of a coincidence that you were being followed."

Ava's lips flatten, the kind of tight line she makes when she's holding back more than she's saying. "Then that would mean they know about . . . us." Her cheeks flame, and she looks anywhere in the room but at me.

"Exactly." My voice is low, clipped. "And if they know about Black, they know about the Tomb. That means they're not just some random street hustler with a vendetta. They've been inside my world. They've seen the shit that doesn't make it into police reports."

Her gaze lifts to mine, something like fear—or maybe recognition—flickering there. "So . . . what happens now?"

I push off the frame, crossing the short space until I'm standing in front of her. The air between us feels warmer here, charged. "Now? I find out who's playing dress-up with my name. And when I do, they'll wish they'd picked anyone else."

Her jaw tenses, but she doesn't break eye contact. "You can't do it alone."

"I'm not asking you to help me," I say, though the words taste like a lie the second they're out. She knows it, too.

Her gaze hardens. "Then you're an idiot. Because if they're after me, Levi, then we are already in this together—whether you like it or not."

Something coils low in my gut, dark and unshakable. She's right. I hate that she's right.

I sit beside her, elbows resting on my knees, our shoulders almost touching. "Then start telling me everything they've said to you. Every word. Every threat. No holding back."

She hesitates only a beat before nodding. "You're not going to like it."

Her voice is brittle, quiet in a way that makes my pulse slow.

"Try me," I murmur, watching her closely.

Her fingers twist in the hem of her shirt, knuckles whitening. "The last message they sent . . . it wasn't just about the flash drive. They said if I didn't get it, they'd take something from me."

My chest tightens. "Something?"

Her throat works as she swallows. "They said—someone." She finally looks up at me, and the weight of her stare lands like a fist to the ribs.

The room is so still that I can hear her breathing—shallow and controlled.

"They won't get to you," I say, my voice low and dangerous.

She lets out a short, humorless laugh. "I'm not worried about me, Levi. I think they meant you."

The words land cold and sharp at the base of my spine.

I lean back, jaw grinding. "Then they've just made their first mistake."

Because anyone stupid enough to put themselves in my crosshairs won't walk out of them.

Ava studies me like she's trying to decide whether I'm about to run headfirst into a trap or burn the whole city down. She's not wrong on either count.

The air hums between us, charged with something volatile.

"You think they're bluffing?" I ask.

"I think…" she says slowly, "…whoever this is, they want us chasing the wrong thing. They want to keep you distracted while they get whatever's on that flash drive."

I stand and start pacing, the movement keeping the tension from boiling over. "Then we stop playing defense."

Her brow furrows. "Meaning?"

"Meaning I'm done waiting for them to make the next move. If they know about the Tomb and me as Black, then they've been close. Too close." My tone hardens. "So we draw them out. Make them think we're giving them exactly what they want."

Ava blinks, torn between thinking I've lost my mind and wondering if it might actually work. "And if they take the bait?"

A slow, humorless smirk tugs at my mouth. "Then they meet the real Black."

Her breath hitches almost imperceptibly, but she hides it well. "So . . . what now?"

"Get dressed."

"Why?"

I chuckle under my breath as I head towards the door.

"We've got work to do."

CHAPTER
Twenty-Three

AVA

I f you had told me a month ago that I'd be walking into a secret, underground street fighting ring hand-in-hand with Levi Cross, I would have laughed in your face.

Now . . . it's just another peek into the man I sold my life to.

The Tomb is an underground street fighting club. It makes sense. Now, I understand why Levi always comes home with bruises and cuts.

The moment we walk through the door, my hand in his, the scent of blood, sweat, and booze hits me like a punch to the face.

People are everywhere, and the place is as loud as a nightclub with just as many drugs. There's a cage in the center of the room where almost everyone is gathered, watching two men completely annihilate one another like this is a WWE wrestling match.

My steps must falter, because Levi looks back at me over his shoulder, and his hand tightens around mine.

"Stay close," he says, though I can barely hear him over the crowd cheering for Cheddar, whoever the hell that is.

Heads turn as we walk past, and people whisper to their

move out of his way as we pass.

I must admit, I like being on his arm like this. His hand holding mine like he's afraid of losing me. Like he wants the world to know I'm his girl, even if it's only for now.

We step up to a bar, and the bartender turns, her eyes wide and locked on me.

I feel a twinge in my gut with the look in her eyes, because I know that look.

She's in love. Or at least . . . she cares. Enough that she doesn't like that Levi's here with another woman.

She's beautiful, her fire-engine-red hair piled up on top of her head. She's the type of girl I would expect Levi to be hooked on because she doesn't fit into a box, just like him.

I can't deny I'm jealous because he smiles at her, and I can see they have an easy relationship.

"Cherry," he greets, tugging my hand to drag me closer to him.

"Black . . . Long time no see," she says, and there's an air of grievance in her tone. "Who's this? A friend?"

"Mine."

My cheeks flame, my heart fluttering in my chest at the possessiveness in his tone.

Cherry, on the other hand, nods solemnly, her gaze rebounding between the two of us.

"Black," someone calls from behind us, and I jump at the sudden intrusion of the man, Cheddar, grinning ear to ear with blood coating his face like the extra-large male version of Carrie. "Getting in the ring tonight?"

"No," Levi hums, his arm tightening around my waist. "I'm here on business."

Cheddar grins, showcasing a broken set of teeth. They look painful, but he doesn't seem to notice.

"Unfortunate for you. I've got at least two more good rounds in me."

Levi chuckles, patting him on his overly sweaty shoulder.

"You lose any more teeth, you're going to be eating smoothies for the rest of your life."

"Hello, pretty lady?" Cheddar asks, smiling at me. He reminds me of a gentle giant who doesn't realize how big he is when he holds his hand out. His unfortunately very *bloody* hand.

Levi and I both turn, locking eyes with a different, much cleaner man. He's handsome, and the most notable thing about him is how he doesn't look like he belongs here at all, save for the bruise across his cheek. His green eyes sparkle with indifferent amusement as he flashes a grin at me.

"Donovan Palmer, though everyone here calls me Diego. You must be Ava. Welcome to my Tomb."

I move to shake his hand, but Levi steps in the way.

"We have an appointment."

Something unspoken passes between them. A warning, maybe? A threat? I can't tell over the hum of the tension radiating in the air.

"Come back to my office. We'll chat. You can even bring your pet."

"She'll stay here, where Cheddar can keep an eye on her."

The man smirks, chuckling under his breath.

"Have it your way."

He stalks off toward the back, and Levi turns back to me. Pulling me into his chest, he leans close, like you might when you're pressing your lips to someone's cheek, only in his case, it's so he can whisper sweet threats in my ear.

"You leave this bar, and I'll spank your ass until it's as red as Cherry's hair. Understood?"

My cheeks burn when he pulls back, only to lean in and press his lips to my forehead. It's soft and gentle to the outside world, but to me, I can feel the threat lingering.

He would. I know he would.

The terrifying thing is that I know he'd make me like it.

"Fine," I grumble, and he swats my ass when I turn to climb onto a bar stool.

"Cherry, whatever she wants. Ava, give me twenty minutes," he says, and then he disappears down the hallway behind the other men.

Cheddar, who returns with a shirt on and substantially less blood, slides into the stool opposite me.

He looks like a giant beside me, and I'm sure the view is comical from behind.

"What will you have?" Cherry asks, and I can tell she'd rather serve me sewer water than anything from this bar.

"Um . . . a Coke, please."

She stares at me like she's bored, but nevertheless, grabs a can and slides it across the counter toward me.

I take it, feeling like a child who's waiting on her father to conduct business while the unwilling employees look after her.

"So . . . is Cheddar your real name?"

Cheddar, who takes a big swig of a beer, smiles at me.

"No. My real name is Hector."

"Hector. I like that." *Better than Cheddar.*

"What's your name?"

"Ava," I answer without thinking. Everyone here calls Levi Black. I don't know if that was intentional or if they just aren't supposed to know his real name. Maybe I'm supposed to be undercover, too.

"Miss Ava," Cheddar smiles. "Happy to meet you."

"You Black's new watchdog, Cheddar?" Cherry asks from the other end of the bar.

"Mr. Black asked me to look after his lady friend, so that's what I'm going to do."

"What a fine babysitter you are," she says sweetly, though Cheddar doesn't realize it's anything but sweet.

"Sooo . . . Hector. What is this place?"

"This is the Tomb," Cheddar announces proudly. "On account

of it being a place where people can fight to the death if they want. No rules."

"Sounds like anarchy," I mumble.

"Sounds like a place not fit for someone who drinks Coke at a bar," Cherry chimes.

I grit my teeth to keep from spouting off at her and chalk it up to jealousy.

I get it.

I'm jealous too. I shouldn't be, but a part of me hates that Levi comes here and spends time with her. She obviously cares for him, and in turn, hates me because of it.

I can't fault her for wanting the man, any more than I can fault Cheddar for going in the ring.

Some things are just inevitable.

"How long have you been coming here?"

"Three years," Cheddar says.

"And you always fight?"

"Only on days they tell me I'm allowed. They won't let me fight no one smaller than me."

Judging by his Goliath size, I'm imagining that's not very often.

"Why do you fight, Hector? Surely, it must hurt."

"Pure adrenaline, Miss Ava. That's what Mr. Black calls it."

"I take it you and Mr. Black are friends."

Cheddar stares at me for a moment, his smile fading. I hadn't expected such a serious look from him, but I get the feeling I struck a nerve.

"Cheddar, I'm sorry if I upset you."

"Mr. Black saved my life," he says darkly, and a shiver runs down my spine. "Whatever he needs from me, he'll get."

I pause, my heart beating faster.

"How did he save your life?"

"Cheddar," Levi snaps from behind us, and I can't deny the anxiety I'd felt without him melts away.

It's annoying, because this is Levi. A man I'm literally contractually obligated to have sex with. Not a damned saint.

A moment later, strong arms cage me in, his hands pressing to the counter on either side of me. His breath, warm on the side of my neck, sends chills down my spine.

"Careful, baby girl . . ." he murmurs, so low only I can hear him. My pulse quickens, my skin heating with the warmth of his body washing over me. "Remember what happened last time you stuck your nose where it didn't belong."

"Miss Ava didn't leave, Mr. Black," Cheddar says, completely oblivious. "I made sure of it."

Levi straightens, though his hand slides around to wrap around my waist. My stomach dips with his touch, a dull throb roaring between my legs.

Damn, he's good.

"Yes, you did, Cheddar," Levi says, handing him something I can't see. "You did well."

"I'm not a child," I growl at him, but he ignores me, in true Levi fashion. He tosses a twenty down on the counter for Cherry, and she gives him a look I can't understand when he takes my hand in his.

He nods at her once, and I stare at him in confusion, but of course, he doesn't tell me anything. He hauls me off the stool and claps Cheddar on the back.

"Come on. We're going home."

"Good night, Hector. See you next time."

"Night, Miss Ava," he calls with a wave.

"Did you make friends with Cheddar?" Levi asks over the loud music as he leads me back through the throngs of people.

"Everyone deserves a friend," I say with a shrug, and something flashes across his face before it's quickly gone. "Even the damaged ones."

My blood is teeming with electricity when we return home.

I feel like I ran into an electric fence nipples first, with the energy radiating through me.

The ride here was quiet. Tense, even. Levi seemed lost in his thoughts, so I decided not to prod him. I wasn't even sure he was going to bring me home and fuck me, though I can't lie and say I haven't been thinking about it.

It's like he came into my life and screwed up my libido. Before, I was content, focusing on surviving. Sex wasn't even on my radar. Now, all I've been able to think about tonight is how to get his hands on me again.

I've found that when he's touching me, I forget the outside world. I forget about my problems, the financial pit I've fallen into. My grandmother's looming cancer diagnosis. Whoever is after us. All of it dissipates, and for a few brief shining moments, euphoria takes its place.

Honestly? It's not even the mind-blowing orgasms.

Okay, it's not *all* the mind-blowing orgasms. It's something deeper. The desire to feel craved. Wanted.

Knowing that *this* man wants me so much, he was willing to create a contract so he could fuck me. I actually want him bad enough that my blood feels like it's laced with fire. My inner thighs are slick with need, and there's a dull throb radiating through my core when we make our way inside the mansion and up to the second story, where our rooms are.

The sounds of his heavy boots on the carpeted hardwood floor underneath us seem to mimic the sound of my heart, beating loudly against the inside of my ribcage.

He doesn't even seem to notice the fact that he's stolen my breath with the simple touch of his hand on my lower back when he leads me down the hall.

He pauses at my door, and both of us turn, stopping when the other opens their mouth to say something. His eyes flash, roaming over my body, and just like that, my morals take a swan dive out the window.

I throw myself at him, lips landing against his. I didn't expect him to catch me and haul me up against him, but his arms lock around me, lifting me to wrap my legs around his waist. He groans into my mouth, and his tongue slips against mine, teasing. Tempting.

He's only really kissed me one time, but it's all I've been able to think about since. The taste of him on my tongue, the brush of his stubble against my skin. The dizzying haze Levi Cross seems to create in my brain.

Levi kisses with everything he has. Somehow . . . I still need more.

"Please," I breathe against his lips. His hands knead the bare flesh of my hips, under the flowy material of my sundress. I want him to rip it off me, push me down into the mattress, and make me his good girl. In fact, I'm craving it.

"Fuck," he grits when I grind against the length of him resting heavily against me. It's not enough. The tightening of his fingers on my ass tells me he feels the same way.

He hauls me inside his room, not bothering to put me down when he shuts the door behind us. My hands roam over him, lips finding his pulse racing in the side of his throat, and I ignore the pang of something deeper, kissing there instead. My lips trail over the stubble of his jaw, nipping and sucking a path back down his skin.

"What's gotten into you today, baby girl?" he rasps, placing me on top of his dresser, just inside the door. He fists my hair, his other hand sliding between us to palm my breast through my dress. I bite my lip against the moan that threatens to slip free, needing him closer.

My hands instantly go for the button of his jeans, and he lets me, hissing out a breath through his teeth when I manage to slip my hand inside and fist his cock.

"I want you," I breathe, my voice breathless as I stroke him. His hand in my hair tightens painfully, dragging my face back to look at him. There's something dark in his gaze, but I can't place what the feeling is.

"You want me to fuck you, Ava?"

"Yes," I breathe, my tongue darting out to lick my lips. His gaze follows the movement, and for a split second, he looks torn. "Please? This is why we're here, isn't it?"

Like a whip cracking, his demeanor changes. He's no longer gentle and sweet, but demanding and rough, just like I need him.

In a flash, he drags me off the dresser, spinning me around to the bed. He pushes me over the side and hauls my hips back when I fall forward.

I can feel his hardness pressing against my rear, teasing me when he slips his hands under the hem of my sundress and raises it over my hips. I shiver in the night air, but seconds later, when I feel his fingers sliding over the soaking wet material of my thong, I don't much care.

"Mmm . . ." he hums, and the sound goes straight between my legs. "Soaking wet, Ava. Is this for me?"

"Y-yes," I breathe, arching my back when he moves my panties to the side and slips his fingers through my folds.

"Tell me what you want, Ava."

My cheeks flame, but I know I'll never get what I want if I don't tell him.

"Fuck me," I beg, my fingers digging into the thick comforter of his bed. "Please."

"Whatever you want, baby girl."

He knocks my legs apart, widening my stance and moving between them. It's almost too far, but one look back at him over my shoulder makes me completely forget how uncomfortable it is. He looks like a madman. One as desperate to touch me as I am for him.

He aligns himself at my entrance, pushing inside, and both of us moan, the sounds of heavy breathing filling the room.

He presses his hand to the center of my back, forcing me to arch for him and let him slide inside. I grip the bed underneath me, my eyes fluttering closed at how freaking good it feels to finally get him inside me after thinking about it all night.

When he finally reaches the hilt, I'm gasping for breath and so hot, I'd have melted to a puddle on the floor already if it weren't for him holding me up underneath him.

"That's it, let me have it, Ava," he croons, and I whimper as his cock stretches me wide. "There's my girl. You take it so fucking good for me."

"Jesus, Levi . . ."

"Whose girl are you, Ava?"

"Yours," I answer without missing a beat. "Yours."

"Damn straight. *Mine.* Now, arch your back for me."

I press myself further into the bed, allowing him to slip deeper, to hit that spot inside me that only he's ever been able to find. My pussy clamps down on his cock with each stroke of him inside me, and he fucks me deep, picking up his pace until his balls slap against my clit.

It's rough, impatient, and dirty, but it also feels so fucking good, I wouldn't ask him to stop if God himself walked through the door.

His hand slips around the front of my body, toying with my clit, and I swear to God, I see stars.

"Levi, please . . ." I moan, tears streaming from the corners of my eyes from how good it feels to be his. "I'm going to come."

"Not yet, you're not," he grits, pulling out of me completely. I whimper at the loss of him when he tosses me onto my back and stands back to look down at me. He slips his hoodie over his head, and my eyes catch on the sight of his cock, still wet with my arousal, shining in the moonlight. He removes his T-shirt next, and I admire the view of him, completely naked, when he drops his jeans and kicks off his shoes.

Levi Cross may as well be cut from marble. The man is complete perfection.

"Like what you see, baby girl?" He climbs back onto the bed, looming over me. His hands slide up my thighs to my panties, and with a snap, he rips them off. I jerk at the sting, but his fingers caressing my skin numb the pain, replacing it with pleasure. "So fucking beautiful . . ."

He rips the buttons holding my dress, sending a few scattering across the room. He pulls it off and tosses it behind him, leaning back to admire his work. Reaching down, he grips his cock in his hand, and the few strokes he gives it are the hottest thing I've ever seen. Notching it at my entrance, he pushes back inside me, moving painfully slow while he fucks me in long, deep strokes.

"You look so fucking sexy like this, Ava," he rasps. "Waiting for me to fuck you. Begging to come."

He slips his hands around my back, unsnapping my bra and tossing it behind him. I bite back a moan when his fingers toy with my nipples, pinching and teasing until I'm arching underneath him.

He grins deviously in the moonlight, looking every bit like the devil come to steal my soul when the shadows catch his handsome features.

"You like that?" he hums, and I nod feverishly. "Yeah? You like me playing with your nipples while my cock's buried inside this sweet little cunt?"

God, if it were possible to get off on dirty talk alone, I would have by now. My pussy is so wet, I feel it dripping down the curves of my ass. He's doing this on purpose, staving off my orgasm. Driving me crazy with it. It's a form of torture, but even as the desperation takes hold, I find I want it.

I want my pleasure in the palm of his hand. I want him to make me his good girl and let me come on his cock.

"I'm going to fuck you, Ava. You're not going to come until I say so. Understood?"

"I understand," I breathe, fisting the comforter on either side of me.

He takes my hips, angling me so he can fill me completely. He presses my legs further apart, almost painfully, as I stretch to take him.

Then he fucks me.

He ruts inside me, fucking me so hard and fast, I can't think. I can't breathe. I can't *feel* anything but him. My mind goes hazy, the need to come so overpowering I'm sure I'm going to break my promise and come before he lets me, but I force myself to hold off, even as he's hitting the perfect spot.

"Please, Levi," I whine, my nails digging into his hands on my hips. He doesn't stop. His head kicks back as he fucks me deep, hard, and fast. A groan tears from his lips, and he powers into me even harder. The sounds of our bodies meeting fill the room, and I'm sure I'll have bruises on my hips from his touch.

"God fucking damn, Ava. You feel so fucking good on my cock. This tight little pussy was made for me to fuck it."

My back arches, my eyes rolling back in my head with each thrust, and I'm so close, I can taste it.

"You're doing so fucking good. Waiting like a good girl to come. It's going to feel amazing when you do, sweetheart." He leans over me, his hand leaving my hip to grip my chin. His fingers dig into my jaw, pressing my mouth open. "Open wide. Stick out your tongue."

I do, and he surprises me by spitting in my mouth. It's both disgusting and fucking exhilarating.

"Good girl. Swallow," he orders, and I do, my pussy tightening to the point of madness.

"You're so obedient when you want something, baby girl," he rasps, his hand sliding down to pin my throat to the bed. "Do you want to come?"

"Yes," I whimper.

"Say it, Ava. Ask me nicely."

I don't even have the good sense to be embarrassed. I do want it. I want it more than anything.

"Please, Levi, may I come?"

He shudders, looming over me. His fingers tighten around my throat, digging into my flesh. My lashes flutter, but he doesn't take away my breath.

What does it say about me that a part of me wonders what it would be like? To give myself over to him completely.

"Fuck . . . Come for me, Ava."

Like he lit a match after dousing me in gasoline, my entire body lights up. White hot light shoots behind my eyes, and I come hard with a cry. His hand covers my mouth, silencing my cries, but I'm too far gone to care.

"Fucking hell, that's it, baby girl." He thrusts inside me twice more before he pushes himself to the hilt and comes with a powerful groan, his head kicking back as he fills me.

When I float back to Earth, I collapse against the bed, completely spent.

Unfortunately, Levi has other ideas.

Hiking me up by the hips, he flips me back over onto my hands and knees.

"Not so fast, sweetheart," he says, and I can practically hear the sinister grin on his face. "We're just getting started."

CHAPTER
Twenty-Four

LEVI

H ow did you save Hector's life?" Ava asks from her spot on the bed beside me. I look over at her, my eyes roaming over the curves hiding under the blanket.

Fucking perfection.

I just fucked her for two hours, and yet, I could go again.

It's fucking madness. This . . . hold she has over me. It's like she was made for me to fuck her, make her moan my name. Listen to her breathless little whimpers and lose myself buried inside her.

I hate it.

I also can't stop.

I'm addicted, for now, anyway. Sooner or later, I'll tire of her, but at the moment, all I can think about is the next time I can get her underneath me.

Or on top of me.

Or bent over the side of the bed, that glorious ass on display.

How the fuck am I supposed to kick her out of my bed when she looks like that? All soft and warm and fucking *mine*.

I wasn't lying when I called her that at the Tomb. She is mine.

man who even *thinks* about touching her.

"I didn't save *Cheddar's* life."

"Okay . . ." she says, picking up on my attitude. "So, why is he indebted to you?"

"He's not."

She shoots me a look.

"You're being cryptic."

Because I really don't want to think about fucking *Cheddar* when I've got the object of every one of my dirty fantasies in my bed.

"Cheddar is as loyal as they come. Help him, and he'll return the favor tenfold."

"So, you helped him?"

"I guess." When she waits for an explanation, I let out a sigh, scrubbing a hand down my face. "Cheddar was working at a place I took down when I was an agent. He was just a butcher. Didn't realize they were selling drugs out the back door. I went in, realized they were using him as muscle, and he didn't even know it. When I took the ring down, I made sure Cheddar wasn't involved."

She has the audacity to look sad.

"So, they were using him, and you put a stop to it?"

"I suppose so, though, I came to like the big bastard the more times I spoke to him. I trust him more than anyone besides Christian."

"Is he why you go there?"

I shrug. "I go there because I like to fight, Ava."

Something flashes across her eyes before it's quickly replaced with a look of indifference.

"Cherry seemed nice," she says, all of a sudden, and I can't help but chuckle under my breath. "Tell me, does she boil the children first, or is she on one of those raw diets?"

I can't help but smirk down at her.

"Jealousy looks good on you, baby girl."

"I am *not* jealous," she says with a roll of her eyes. "That would

240

imply I like you."

"Don't like me, huh?" I taunt, I place my finger under her chin, lifting her head. "You seemed to like me plenty when you jumped me in the hall."

Her cheeks heat under my stare, and I fucking love how responsive she is to me. I just know she's getting wet again, remembering what we did, and if I weren't so fucking tired, I'd do it all over again.

"You're much more likable when your mouth is occupied," she says, and I grin wickedly.

"Be careful, sweetheart. I've got enough in me to show you what it feels like to have something in *your* mouth."

"Fiend."

"Brat."

She falls silent, and my thumb strokes across her pouty lips. They're still swollen from my kissing her, something I've never fucking done during sex.

Not until her.

"That place . . ." she says after a long moment. "The Tomb?"

"What about it?"

"Why do you *really* go there?"

"Because I like it there."

She looks appalled by my answer.

"So, you fight?"

"Do you care?"

She ignores my question. "That's why you're always covered in cuts and bruises, isn't it? The fighting?"

I grit my teeth, my hand tightening to a fist underneath my head. I drop my other hand to the bed, disappointment crashing through me.

This is the problem with sleepovers. Someone always wants to start discussing the hard shit. Shit, I'd rather bury and lock away.

"Ava, we aren't having this discussion."

"It's just a simple question," she argues quietly. "You could get seriously hurt there. I saw some of those people. Hector was missing teeth."

"Those *people* are none of your business," I grit, a little too forcefully.

"So, why take me there, then?"

"Because word needs to get out that right now, you're my whore, and anyone touching you will not be tolerated.

She grimaces, and I almost hate myself for saying the word. Almost.

She knew what this was when she signed her name on the dotted line.

I made it clear. No sleepovers. No dates. No romance.

If there's one thing this is, it's business. I'm doing what I have to.

"Do I need to remind you of the terms of our contract?"

It's not my fault if she let herself get her hopes up.

At least . . . that's what I tell myself when I watch her face drop.

"You're right," she says, an air of indifference in her tone that I fucking hate. "It's getting a bit *stuffy* in here anyway."

Little brat.

I watch as she climbs from the bed, bending over with that ass on display right in front of me, to shimmy back into her clothes.

My cock, which is protesting that we're letting her out of our bed right now, jumps enthusiastically. I ignore the fucker.

"By the way," she says, holding her head high when she steps over to the door. "His name is *Hector*. If he's so loyal and you care about him so much, you should learn he prefers to be called *that* over a stupid nickname."

I wait until she thinks the coast is clear before I get out of my car and start following her.

For such a tiny thing, she's quick, darting in between people, and I have to work to keep up with her.

The sights and sounds of the city are all around us, but my eyes stay trained on the little brunette ahead of me as she walks, crossing over two blocks before she ducks inside a nursing home off the street.

I give it a few minutes before I follow her through the front door.

She doesn't know I followed her today, but we've already established my girl is oblivious. How she's made it this long on her own is fucking beyond me.

Knowing she was approached outside the nursing home, I decided to follow her. Do I believe she's told me everything she knows? Sure. Do I want proof? Abso-fucking-lutely.

The inside of Pleasant Oaks is exactly what you'd expect. The scent of Vicks VapoRub and that slightly off-putting aroma of urine that seems to hang around in places like this. I look around the lobby, but Ava's not there amongst the dozen pairs of eyes that stare back at me.

A few older women grin at me and giggle. One even winks, waving in my direction. I give her a curt nod and turn my back on them at the front desk, earning me a string of grandmotherly giggles.

"Excuse me?" I greet the clerk, who can't be bothered to look up from her phone. "My wife just came in while I was parking the car. Can you tell me which way she went?"

She glances up at me for only a second before turning her attention back to her phone.

"Who?"

"Brunette. About this tall. Drop-dead gorgeous."

She rolls her eyes and points down the hall. "Room 402."

"Thanks."

She doesn't respond, and I don't wait around to be catcalled by the elderly, stalking off through the halls.

I've always hated nursing homes. I have vivid memories of visiting my great-grandmother's house when I was a kid, and it always felt more like a tomb than a place for people to live. Oddly enough, that's truer now than it was back then.

The halls are barren. With each room I pass, the sounds of televisions filter through the open doors, mixing with the whir of the machines used to keep people alive. There are hardly any visitors, and the scent of shitty food hangs in the air.

Coming to a door at the end of the hall, I pause, listening to the soft sound of Ava's voice from within.

"It's potato soup today," she says, and though she sounds cheerful, I can hear the sadness hidden in her voice. "Yours was better, though."

I peek my head around the corner, seeing her back to me where she sits in a chair beside an elderly woman in the bed.

Her grandmother.

And now . . . everything's starting to make sense.

"I'm not hungry," the woman says, though her voice sounds strained.

She's tiny, her frail body barely filling an eighth of the large bed. If I didn't hear her speak, I would be sure she was already dead.

"You have to eat something," Ava says softly, and I can't take my eyes off her. There's something so vulnerable about seeing her like this that I can't deny there's a part of me—a fucking big part— that wants to wrap her in my arms so nothing can reach her. Protect her from the inevitable.

"Ava . . ." the woman sighs, like she's utterly exhausted. "I had my treatment yesterday. You know it ruins my appetite."

Ava's shoulders sag, and she looks down at the useless bowl of soup in her hand as if it might hold the answer as to what she should do.

"I know," she says, and lead fills my chest where I hide in the shadows. "I just . . . never mind."

I fucking hate this. I hate the guilt I already know she's feeling. I hate the guilt *I'm* feeling for lying to her.

No—fuck that. I didn't do this. I'm merely trying to fix a problem that had nothing to do with me.

Still . . . when I see Ava hastily wipe the unshed tears from her eyes while she turns away to put the bowl down, something unpleasant and tight fills my chest, and I grit my teeth against the sensation.

"How are the treatments going?"

"Ava, we need to talk."

"Nana, I don't—"

"I'm dying, Ava."

I tense, leaning back against the wall beside the door. Just out of sight, the silence in the room couldn't be louder.

"Please don't speak like that," Ava says softly, and I can't lie, there's a heaviness in my chest that I don't care for at the sound of tears in her voice.

"It's the truth, sweetheart. We have to talk about it. I'm not going to be here much longer, and I need to know you're going to be okay after I'm gone."

"I don't want to talk about that," Ava whispers.

"You're a strong girl, Ava. You'll get through it. I know you will."

There's more heavy silence until eventually, a shuffling follows it. I listen to the movement, and I don't have to look into the room to know Ava's lying with her grandmother.

"I'm sorry . . ." she murmurs through tears that I can tell she's barely keeping under control. "I just . . . I don't know how to do it without you. I don't want to."

Her grandmother is quiet for a long moment before her voice

fills my chest with lead.

"You'll always be my girl," she murmurs. "Even if I'm not here."

Fuck this.

Guilt washes through me, and even though I fucking hate the sensation, I'm powerless to stop it. Have I really been that blind to what she was dealing with outside of my house?

Things are so much more complicated than I thought, and now, Ava's caught in the crosshairs.

While I normally wouldn't care, I'm finding it harder and harder to ignore this innate desire I have to shield her from what's to come.

Because we share the same demons. The same past.

The same wishes.

And now I'm realizing, as much as I know I should, I don't want to give her up.

CHAPTER
Twenty-Five

AVA

Following the Tomb incident, Levi and I fall into a routine.

He ignores me.

I ignore him.

Occasionally, one of us says something snarky to one another.

Other than that, the only interaction we have is when he comes to my room each night and makes me come until I pass out.

And of course, when I catch him following me.

It started off as a hunch. A gut feeling of being watched, only to turn around and find no one there.

Now, I'm positive it's him when I step out of the nursing home one night and catch a glimpse of someone across the street in a black hoodie. My stomach dips at the sight of him, even if I can't make out his features with his hood drawn.

He's never been so open about his stalking before, but it's Levi. Does anything he does make sense?

I take a step.

He takes a step.

I pause. So does he.

across the street.

He keeps his hood up, stalking me from the opposite side of the sidewalk, and though I pretend I don't see him, I can *feel* his presence.

Why he's following me, I don't know, but I do know it's getting to be a nuisance.

When I arrive home, I immediately stomp upstairs, but instead of going to my room, I walk straight into Levi's, stopping short when I find him buttoning a pair of jeans after a shower.

My voice gets caught in my throat when he turns to stare at me, my eyes latched on a water droplet that slips down his glorious abs.

"I'd invite you to lick it off, but I don't have time."

Rude.

"I-I . . . why would I do that?" I stammer, blushing because I have to admit a tiny part of me would have considered it.

Okay, a big part, but only because he put the picture in my head.

Levi smirks, his gaze running over me, before he looks away dismissively.

"What do you want, Ava?"

"You have to ask?"

He pauses, cocking a brow at me.

"If you're referring to sex, baby girl, I'd love to stay and fuck you, but like I said. I have plans."

God, could he be any cruder?

"What's her name?"

"Her?"

"Yeah. I assume you're off to see one of your . . . *women*."

I hate the bitter jealousy sliding through me. I hate it even more when he flashes a cocky grin my way.

"Little ghost, are you jealous?"

"No," I lie. "Just wanted to know so I could send flowers to her and offer my condolences. You know, sisterhood of the traveling dick."

"Mmm . . ." he hums. "With any luck, she'll be less clingy. Looks like I got enough on my plate with my housekeeper barging into my room unannounced every day."

What. A. Dick.

"*I'm* the clingy one? You're the one following me."

"Am I?" he challenges, flashing that devious smirk.

"How did you get home so fast?"

The amusement drains from his eyes, and my heart jolts in my chest like he'd stuck me with a cattle prod.

"I've been home all day, Ava."

Ice slips through my veins, and I back up instinctively when he steps toward me, his T-shirt all but forgotten in his hands.

"No, you haven't. You were just in town." I say it slowly, as if maybe he's had some temporary bout of amnesia and forgot. "You were watching me outside the nursing home."

"Ava," he says, like I'm a child who needs coaching. "I wasn't following you today."

I notice he said he wasn't *today*, but if it wasn't him, who was it?

"But . . . but . . . that's impossible," I breathe, tears welling in my eyes.

"What were they driving?"

I shake my head slowly.

"They weren't. They were watching me from across the street."

"What were they wearing?"

"A black hoodie." I glance at the one on his dresser. "Like yours."

"Did they have the hood pulled up?"

"Of course, they did. I didn't see their face."

He stares at me for a beat, probably trying to decipher if I'm telling the truth.

He was there. "I-It had to be you . . . Who else would it be?"

I blow out a shaky breath through my teeth when his phone rings and he steps back. I'm thankful for the space because my mind is going a million miles a minute. He answers, but I barely register his voice as I run over the last three days in my head.

"I'll be there soon," Levi says, cutting the call. He shoves his phone in his pocket and slips his T-shirt over his head, the black making the ink over his muscles more prominent.

Unfortunately, I can't even enjoy the show. I'm too busy thinking about that . . . person. Whoever they were, they know where Gran is, and if they know where Gran is, what if she's not safe?

Is it Donovan? He's always made his presence known. Why hide it now?

Someone else?

"No more trips into town by yourself," Levi says, tugging his hoodie over his head, and it's the first thing that breaks me out of the haze surrounding my brain.

"Excuse me?"

He doesn't even flinch. "You heard me. If you want to see your grandmother, I'll take you."

I can't help but roll my eyes. "I'm not a child, Levi. You can't tell me what to do."

"You're living in my house."

"It's Bella and Christian's, too."

"And they'll back me up if I tell them you aren't to go anywhere."

He steps past me, heading down the hall. I follow after him, ignoring the way his cologne makes my mouth water.

"You can't force me to stay here."

He stops so abruptly that I run into his hard chest when he whirls on me.

"You sure you want to play that game, baby girl?"

Oh, fuck.

I swallow over the thick lump in my throat, falling back a step.

"I have a party to go to this weekend."

"So?"

"So, I want to go."

He chuckles dryly. "Sorry, sweetheart, but what you want doesn't really matter, does it?" He steps closer to me, his eyes darkening. "You signed your life away to me. That means when I tell you no, it means no."

"So, what? I'm just supposed to wait around until you decide you want to fuck me?"

His frosty blue eyes meet mine, and a shiver slips down my spine at the warning in them. "I mean it, Ava. If I find out you went to that party, I'll fuck you right there for everyone to see."

"No, you won't."

I can tell by the look in his eyes that he most definitely will.

He stares at me long and hard for a moment, and I force myself to hold his stare. He's not in control of me. I'm not a child.

"Try it."

Levi Cross is the worst man I have ever met, and I stand by that statement wholeheartedly.

I mean, what an *asshole*.

Not that I really expected anything different. He's been nothing but cruel and rude to me, save for when he wants to fuck me. He didn't come see me when he got home last night. In fact, I didn't hear him return at all.

Well, screw him. I'm not going to wait around for him to decide I'm worthy of his touch again.

It's a nice day when I step out the back door and head toward the hiking paths that weave through the forest. I actually have a day off for once, so I decided to spend it hiking instead of waiting around inside to run into he who must not be named. It's warm, but not hot, and there's a nice breeze blowing through the autumn leaves that makes everything smell like the crisp, mountain air.

I've always loved the trails behind the Cross Estate. The main path cuts right through the tall trees, and it feels like a totally different world from the glitz and wealth that haunt the Oak Ridge Lodge.

I take my time because I have all day, enjoying my stroll and taking paths I've never been down before. One in particular is slightly overgrown, so just because I can, I start down it, with no intention of following a map.

This is what I enjoy. The quiet calm that can only be found when you're alone in the forest.

There's no one to bark orders at you. No one to cast shifty glances your way simply because you exist.

. . . No one to control your every move.

It's just me and nature, and the longer I walk, the more I find myself wishing I didn't have to go back.

It's not until the quiet rumble of thunder sounds overhead, somewhere in the distance, that I pause and look around.

Where the fuck am I?

I'm surrounded by trees on all sides, and when I turn around, I can't for the life of me tell which way I came from.

To make matters worse, the sky overhead is dark, and the clouds are moving rapidly, meaning a storm is coming. A shiver moves through me at the breeze that rolls through the air, and suddenly I'm cold, my light jacket no longer enough to keep me warm.

Well . . . shit.

I look up through the trees, and the thunder grows louder, as if warning me to get home before I'm stranded.

Oh, this is bad.

"Hello?" I call, but it's no use. There's no one around here for miles, and I'm not even on a path.

I'm well and truly alone.

Okay. This is really bad.

I reach for my phone, only to find my pockets empty. And then

I remember . . . I left it in my room so I wouldn't have to deal with Levi today.

"You've got to be kidding me," I growl.

The universe answers me, just in the biggest *fuck you, Ava* way possible.

Thunder rumbles, and it's then that the sky opens up, instantly drenching everything within this forest, me included.

"Oh, fuck you," I growl. Stupidly, I try to cover my head as if that will save me from the torrential downpour soaking me to the bone, and hunt for somewhere to hide.

I'm *so* blaming Levi for this.

With the clouds overhead blocking out a lot of the sunlight in the trees, and the rain making it even harder to see, I stumble through the thick underbrush in the way I think I came from, unsure if I'm going the right way or if I'm heading deeper into the Washington wilderness.

There has to be something nearby. Nowhere in this country is this unpopulated.

Then I remember. The Cross's own at least three hundred acres. The lodge is on the first five of that.

I keep walking, struggling more and more, and getting colder as I go. My teeth chatter, and I tug my jacket tighter around myself, even if it is soaked. I'm coated in mud. Soaking wet to the bone and unable to see anything at all, as the sky only grows darker.

Of course, this storm is one of those storms that wipe out power lines. You know the kind that cause floods and otherwise destroy everything?

I find a large tree, backing up against the trunk, and hold on, like at any moment, the storm will pass, and it'll be back to clear, sunny skies in no time.

It's nearly impossible to keep moving, and my shoes are getting caught in the mud with every step. My choices are to keep struggling in the dark or wait here for the weather to subside, and I think I know which one I'm going to be forced into.

I'm such an idiot. I didn't check the weather before I came out here. I was just desperate to get away from Cross Estate, even if that meant trudging through the forest.

Now, I'd give anything to be warm and dry in my bedroom, even if I did have to listen to Levi and his brooding.

I close my eyes, silently willing myself away from here and suck in a deep breath.

I have to keep going.

I stumble forward, holding onto trees as I go, and just when I'm about to give up, I spot it. A cabin out in the brush. It's dark, and it looks like no one's there, but it's dry. I rush forward, making my way toward the little slice of civilization stuck out in the middle of the forest.

And then my foot catches something hard.

All the air is pushed out of me when I slip down a steep cliff, the mud dragging me down. I attempt to catch myself, fall on my back, and crack my head.

Then everything goes black.

CHAPTER
Twenty-Six

LEVI

Levi: My room. Now.

I sent that text over half an hour ago, and it's been nothing but radio silence on her end since. I can't lie and say I didn't expect it, but she can't ignore me. Regardless of whether she's pissed at me, she can't hide from me forever. I may be patient, but only for so long.

"Open the damned door, Ava."

Which is why I'm at her door the moment the thirty-minute mark hits.

There's no response from the other side. I know for a fact today is her day off, and I'm getting really fucking agitated waiting on her to show up. We have somewhere to be, and we're already late.

After I told her she couldn't go out last night, I haven't heard from her, and I can't escape the nagging voice in the back of my head telling me I need to put a leash on her. My girl likes to be defiant, and I also know she will do anything she can to piss me off. It's part of what's so fucking addicting about her.

There's a part of me that wants to apologize. To tell her the truth about why I'm keeping her at arm's length.

Then, there's that other part that refuses to let anyone see what's really going on in my head. Conceal it. That's always been so easy before. Why's it so damned difficult now?

I try the handle, finding it unlocked. Good thing, too, because I'm this fucking close to breaking it down.

I push her door open, and the scent of her perfume is dull. Like she hasn't been here in a while.

A trickling sense of awareness slips down my spine when I quietly shut the door and start looking around Cross Estate.

She's nowhere to be found, and with today being her day off, I expected to at least find her in the study, reading, or up in her room.

I check with Javier, but he hasn't seen her since last night. I text Mila, but she hasn't seen her either.

I make my way through every room, even going so far as to check the room at the end of the hall—you know, the one I've made it a point to avoid for the last month? She's nowhere to be found, and that's when the quiet alarm bells ringing in my ears turn into a full-on roar.

"Paulina," I snap when I find her in the office at the lodge. "Where's Ava?"

Her brows knit together, and she excuses herself from the guest she was helping.

"Today's her day off."

I grit my teeth, an unsettling sensation slipping through my veins.

"So, where is she?"

"I believe she was going on a hike. I saw her leave a little while ago with a backpack." She looks at the clock on the wall. "She should be back by now."

"Why the fuck didn't you tell me?"

She cocks a brow, clearly unimpressed. "We discussed this.

She's a big girl. If the brat wants to traipse through the woods on her own, let her."

"She's not a fucking brat," I grit. *She's my brat.* "She could die out there, or did you not realize a storm was rolling in?"

She stares at me for a beat, her gaze softening, and beneath that hard exterior, I see a concern that fills my stomach with dread.

My girl's out there in a fucking storm.

"She should be back by now," Paulina repeats quietly.

"I'm going after her."

"You can't go out in a storm like that," Paulina urges, rushing behind me. "It's dangerous."

That's what scares me. Ava is tiny compared to me. I've got at least a hundred pounds on her, and I'm a whole head taller. She's out in a bad storm when even I wouldn't chance that.

"I won't leave her alone out there."

Pushing past her, I hurry out the door as the rain cuts loose, pouring down from overhead. I hurry back to the house, grab a flashlight, and slide a hoodie on—not the best for rain, but it's better than nothing—before I head out into the storm after checking her room one last time.

The rain makes it difficult to see, and as dusk approaches, it's getting darker and darker. She'll be hard to see out in the brush, but I have to try.

Without waiting another minute, I storm through the trees, following the path up the mountain.

It's a gradual climb, but it's long, and I know better than anyone how easy these woods are to get lost in if you stray from the path. If I know Ava, she's so far off the fucking path, she's forgotten it's there by now.

"Ava!" I call out into the rain that falls overhead.

It'll be dark soon, and for all I know, she could be hurt. It's cold, and as the rain pelts down, it's only getting colder.

I can't explain the burn in my chest, nor the panic in my veins at the silence that greets me in place of her soft, sweet voice.

"*Fuck*," I curse, stopping and searching through the trees. "Where are you, baby?"

I walk until it's nearly pitch-black overhead, and though the rain soaked through my clothes long ago, I keep going. I'm going to find her, whether it kills me or not, because I'm supposed to protect her. That's my fucking job.

I'm deep in the trees, and the trail that I thought might be hers died off long ago. I don't stop, though, even as my toes go numb and my mind starts to come up with the worst. It's like my nightmare playing over and over again in real time, only now, it's ice instead of fire that's going to take her from me.

And then I spot it.

A small footprint in the mud that I fucking *know* is hers.

"Ava!"

It's by pure chance that I hear it. A whispered groan carried on the wind whipping through the trees from somewhere nearby.

I don't think I've ever felt pure, unadulterated relief until the moment my flashlight lands on her, lying at the bottom of a steep drop-off.

"*Fuck, Ava.*" I slip down the rocks to land beside her small form, nestled in a bed of weeds and mud.

She's soaking wet and filthy, barely shivering when I reach her. Her face is pale, and her eyes are shut. On her head, a cut oozes blood, and her lip is busted from the fall.

"Fuck," I curse under my breath, trying to shield her with my body. She's in nothing but a thin jacket and leggings, and the rain is heavy overhead. "Sweetheart, look at me."

She doesn't. Not even when I lift her into my arms and cradle her against my chest.

"Ava." I shake her, but she's out of it, her head lolling into my shoulder. "Fuck. Fuck." Struggling to stand in the mud, I hoist her up into my arms, holding her close.

I've got to get her out of the cold, and the cabin isn't far. I cradle her to me, ignoring the answering ache in my feet and hands from the cold, and start the harsh trek toward the only place of solace this deep in the woods.

It's difficult, carrying her small form through the dark and wet night, but I don't let her go. I walk for what feels like hours, but it's probably only twenty minutes until the silhouette of the cabin is lit up by a streak of lightning across the sky.

I sit Ava on her feet on the porch, and she groans, barely able to hold herself up. I pin her to the side of the cabin with my body and fish my keys out of my pocket to unlock the door before she falls over. Picking her back up, I carry her in and kick the door shut behind me.

I lay Ava down on the old couch before I head to the fireplace and toss a couple logs in. Luckily, last time I was here, I left a few stacked to the side so they're dry. I light them, casting the room in a warm glow.

Grabbing the first aid kit I find in the bathroom, I pull up a chair and sit down beside her to clean her cut. She must have taken a nasty fall, judging by the mud caked on her clothes and the cut on her forehead. She won't need stitches, but I clean it, placing a bandage over it to keep it from bleeding.

She doesn't stir the entire time.

"Come on, Ava," I say, but it sounds more like pleading with the ache in my chest. "Look at me."

She doesn't, not even when I start to undress her, hanging her soaking wet clothes on the back of the chairs at the small kitchen table. I remove everything until she's completely naked before I shed my own.

Grabbing the end of the mattress from the bed, I slide it onto the floor in front of the fireplace before I cover it with whatever blankets I can find.

Lifting Ava from the couch, I carry her over to the fire,

wrapping us both inside the blankets and pulling her against my bare chest.

I have no fucking idea what I'm doing, but I've always heard skin to skin is best when hypothermia is at stake, so I hold her tighter, ignoring the way my dick responds and pressing a kiss to her forehead.

"Levi?" Ava breathes, not yet opening her eyes to look at me.

"I'm here, little ghost," I whisper, ignoring the irony behind her nickname and the feelings in my chest.

She shivers, burying her face into the crook of my neck, and I let her, holding her as tightly as I can while I watch the fire over her shoulder.

Fuck, if I hadn't found her, there's no way she would have survived out there through the night. Not with the rain pelting down from above and the cold setting in with the night.

"You came for me?" she says softly, interrupting my thoughts of how I found her, lifeless and freezing on the forest floor.

Leaning back, I look down at her. Her lashes sit heavily on her cheeks, and she's not fully awake, but some of the color is returning to her face, and a shiver of relief rolls through me.

Brushing the still-wet hair back from her forehead, I place a kiss right beside her bandage.

"Always."

The storm has died down to a steady rainfall when Ava stirs against me.

In my sleep, I let out a groan at the feeling of her tight little body running up against my bare cock.

"Fuck," I grit, gripping her hip to stop her.

Her eyes flutter open, and she stares up at me in confusion at first. Then shock. Then horror.

"Levi?" Her voice quivers when she says my name as if waking up naked in bed with me is the worst thing that's ever happened to her.

Can't say I blame her.

"What are you doing here?" Her eyes roam over me to assess the situation. "Why are you naked?" She pauses, seeming to finally come to terms with the fact that her body is pressed against mine. "Why am *I* naked?"

I cock a brow at her, holding her in place when she attempts to wriggle away. Behind her, the fire crackles, though it's died to a warm smolder now.

"Problem, little ghost?" I'm surprised by how rough my voice is. It could be the raging hard on nestled against her thigh, but I'm doing my best to ignore it. This was, after all, about getting her warm. Not fucking her. There will be plenty of time for that later.

"Oh, no." Her voice takes on that air of cynicism that I can't wait to fuck out of her. "I often wake up stark naked, cuddled up with strange men."

"You said it, not me."

She shoves away from me, and this time, I let her, watching as she settles to the back corner of the mattress and wraps a blanket around herself.

Not like it matters, I've already seen everything anyway.

Sliding from the bed, my legs are sore, and my back is tired, but I ignore it. We're both filthy and caked in mud. Stooping down, I slip my arms under her and hoist her up, blanket and all. I carry her toward the bathroom, ignoring her startled gasp and squirming.

"You said it, not me."

"Put me down!" she snaps when I kick open the bathroom door. I've never used the tub in this cabin, but tonight, we will. I want to make sure she's warm.

"What are you doing? Where are we?"

I grit my teeth, turn the water on, and wash the dust out before stopping up the tub.

"You don't recognize the place?" I ask without looking at her.

"Why are we here?" she demands, tugging the blanket tighter around herself.

"Because you were a dumbass and decided to hike through the forest in a storm," I retort, my patience wearing thin.

"Well, forgive my lowliness, my lord. I have but a maid's mind and cannot understand such difficult concepts as the weather."

Little brat.

She turns around to look at herself, wincing when she sees the bandage over the cut on her forehead. Her gaze is shattered, the broken mirror reflecting her image back in a dozen fragments.

"Why is the mirror broken?" she asks, turning back around.

I ignore her question and motion toward the tub.

"Get in the tub, Ava."

"No," she snaps back, her cheeks flaming hot while my blood boils. It feels like an epic wild west showdown, only she's the only one with a gun. I'm just the stupid fuck that decided to mess with her.

Stalking toward her, I don't miss the way her gaze trails down my body, lingering on my still semi-hard cock for only a split second before flicking back up.

So that's what it takes to get her to look me in the eye . . .

"Get in the tub, or I will put you in the tub," I say darkly, stepping right in front of her. "Blanket and all."

She glowers at me, a tremor moving through her when I slip my hand over the smooth skin of her upper thigh, where it peeks out of the blanket.

"Fine," she grumbles. "But only because I'm filthy. I'm not doing this for you."

"Noted," I murmur dryly, stepping away from her to put some distance between us. I cross back to the tub and throw some soap in the water.

She hops down from the counter, but keeps the blanket wrapped tightly around herself while she shuffles to the edge.

I take a breath to calm myself. It's like wrangling a damned toddler.

"I've made you come in every position possible, Ava. It's not like I haven't seen it already."

Her cheeks flame, and she glares my way. In a rush of defiance, she drops the blanket, and my dick twitches at the sight of her standing naked in front of me.

Fucking hell.

I don't bother hiding that I'm staring when she shoves past me and climbs in the tub, sinking into the bubbles.

"Scoot forward," I grunt, and she stares up at me with wide green eyes.

"Why?"

I don't give her an explanation and step in behind her.

In a flash, she slips to the other side, sinking back against the old porcelain and shooting daggers at me.

"Isn't this romantic?" she muses, her arms over her chest. "The lowly maid and the high lord of Cross Palace. I can't wait to tell the other commoners."

I'm this fucking close to dragging her back out to the bed and fucking that little attitude right out of her.

"Anything else?"

I can't tell if she wants to fuck me or hit me. Probably a bit of both, judging by the way her thighs rub together when I place mine on either side of hers and sink down into the water.

When I cut the faucet off, silence rings out in the cabin, the only sound the rain falling on the tin roof outside.

I want to be pissed off at her for going off by herself after I told her not to.

You know what? Scratch that. I am pissed. She could have died tonight.

"What the fuck were you thinking coming out here by yourself?"

She looks at me like I have some kind of nerve, asking her why she put herself in danger.

"Oh, I'm sorry. I didn't realize I needed to check in if I wasn't leaving the property."

"You could have died."

"You're being dramatic," she grumbles, leaning her head back against the side of the tub.

"*I'm* being dramatic?" My temper flares. How the fuck can she not see I'm losing my goddamned mind over her while she barely registers I exist unless I'm making her come? "You're the one who went on a hike and got yourself lost to prove a point."

Instantly, she shoots up in the bath. Bubbles splash over the side.

Neither of us pays attention to it.

"I didn't do *anything* to prove a point," she snaps.

"Then why come out here at all? Especially alone."

"I came out here to get away from *you*."

Her words echo in my head longer than they should.

Probably because I know I'm a fucking idiot for ever allowing her out of my sight.

I've never deserved her. I shouldn't have even touched her. Where hers are pure and clean, my hands are filthy, and I know I'll only spoil her sweetness.

She wasn't made for me.

Unfortunately, I'm still trying to convince myself of that.

"Why am I here, Levi?" she asks when I don't respond. I fucking hate the tears glistening in her eyes more than I hate myself, and that's saying something. "What do you want from me?"

I ignore her question and repeat myself. "You could have died."

"You said yourself, you don't care. Yet, you hunted me down in the woods. This contract—"

"I told you there was nothing romantic about what I want to do to you. You set yourself up with the wrong expectations if you think this will be anything other than us fucking."

"So, you're saying you don't think of me at night?" she challenges, and I'm suddenly *very* aware of the drip in the faucet.

She stares at me—actually fucking meets my gaze—and it's like a thousand hornets just stung me in the chest.

Let her go . . . One voice in my brain chimes.

Fuck her until she's begging to be yours, the other one disagrees.

Fuck . . . am I actually losing my mind?

Carefully, Ava drops her arms and rises in the tub. I sit back against the side, my hand gripping the edge with white-knuckle force when she slips between my legs, her bare pussy hovering just over my cock.

She's so fucking close, all it would take for me to sink inside her would be my pulling her down an inch and giving us both what we want.

Much closer now, Ava's eyes slip up my face until they meet mine, again, only this time, she looks unsure but determined. As if she thinks she can rip down the walls blocking her out with a simple gaze.

I'm starting to wonder if she's right.

"If I mean nothing to you, then why search for me?" she breathes, and my heartbeat hammers in my chest when her hand rests on my shoulder, her body warm and soft over mine.

I don't take my hands off the edges of the tub, but fuck do I want to.

"Or are you just afraid of letting someone see the real you?"

Her pussy brushes over me, and it's like a lick of fire up my spine. My breath catches in my throat, and I clench my teeth on a groan.

Little fucking brat is going to be the death of me.

"Ava," I warn, but she doesn't relent, stroking my cock through her folds.

Her eyes flutter, long lashes casting shadows over her cheeks with the dim lighting in the room. She continues to stroke my cock with her pussy until I'm on the verge of dragging her home and marrying her right fucking now, storm be damned.

"What's the matter, Levi?" she purrs, leaning forward until her lips are at my ear. She presses little kisses along my jaw and neck, and a shiver rolls up my spine. "I thought I had no effect on you?"

She's all over me. Her hands in my hair, tugging the dark strands. Running over my abs, up my shoulders.

Fuck, I need her.

I can't get enough of her.

When her teeth graze my neck, my patience threatens to snap.

"Enough," I growl, gripping the nape of her neck to drag her eyes up to mine.

The little brat smirks.

Fucking smirks at me.

"I haven't been moving," she breathes, cheeks flushed and her voice breathless. "You've been doing that all on your own."

What the fuck?

I look down at my hand on her hip, gripping her against me.

Yeah, definitely fucking losing my mind.

"You're playing with fire, sweetheart."

"Am I?" she taunts, giving me one painfully slow roll of her hips against mine.

"Fuck," I grit, my hand tightening on her hip and rolling her against me again and again. And then my cock notches at her entrance when she lifts her hips, and both of us freeze as the head slips in.

She whimpers. I freeze, groaning so deeply that it reverberates through my body and into hers.

She purses her lips together in a thin line and tries to stop after a few inches, but I grip her hips tighter, pulling her closer.

"All of it."

Her eyes flutter closed, and she gasps as she slides down my length, swallowing me whole. Our breathing is erratic, our bodies melding together like she was fucking made to take me.

My fingers leave her hair, and I use my leverage to move her over me, letting her get adjusted to my size. She's so fucking tight, it feels like she's going to squeeze the life out of me.

"Who's affected now, sweetheart?" I rasp when she bites her lip, rolling her hips over me and riding my cock in slow, delicious jerks. Fuck, I could watch her get off on me all damn day.

"Fuck you," she bites, though it lacks any real heat because it comes out as more of a moan.

"You already are."

Leaning forward, I capture her nipple in my mouth, sucking and nipping a path around the hard peak and making her squirm over me.

"Let me hear you, Ava."

She bites her lip harder, to the point I worry she'll draw blood, but she still refuses to let me hear her sounds.

I take that as a challenge, releasing her nipple and reaching between us and pressing my palm flat on her stomach to roll her clit around with my thumb.

"You want to see the real me, Ava?" I rasp, and her eyes roll back in her head. "You think you could even handle it?"

"You don't scare me," she breathes, and I let out a dark chuckle, fully lost to the feel of her now.

"No? But how bad you want me scares you. How you *crave* to have me in this tight little pussy, fucking you until I'm the only man who will ever do it for you like this. Make you come so many times, you can't think straight."

I strum my thumb faster, pushing her until I know she'll break and let me have her sweet fucking sounds.

"Goddamn, Ava. You're doing so fucking good. Riding my cock

like a good girl."

I thrust my hips into her, dragging her down on me until the water in the tub sloshes over the side. I don't give a fuck. I'm too far gone.

"Ride my cock, Ava. Show me how bad you want it."

Her pussy clenches on me, her head kicks back, and suddenly, her soft cry fills the bathroom. I can't help but grin, even as heat swells up the back of my spine from her clenching around me.

"Good fucking girl. Again."

"I can't," she whimpers, shaking her head.

"You can. You were made to take my cock, Ava." I run a hand through her hair and tug her closer by the messy strands, holding her against me until I can jerk my hip up inside her. "So fucking perfect."

"P-please," she begs, head thrown back and her eyes watery from the orgasm still tingling through her.

"Please, what?"

"Please fuck me," she breathes, and I lose control.

Dragging her against me until her tits are pressed against my chest, and there's not a spare inch of space between us, I fuck her as hard and as ruthlessly as I've been craving.

She takes it all, her nails digging into my shoulders, and when a moan slips free from her lips, I fuck her harder until the base of my cock is rubbing against her clit. She's panting, and I'm out of breath. The bathroom is fucking soaked, but who the fuck cares when I've got her in the palm of my hands?

When I'm inside her, I don't have to worry about where she is. Who might be watching her, just waiting for the opportunity to hurt her.

When I'm inside her, no one else matters.

Her pussy clenches down on me, and she arches her back, clinging to me as desperate whimpers slip past her lips, and it's only a few seconds before she's coming again.

I grit my teeth, powering into her, and push my cock balls-deep inside her when my orgasm finally hits. She's so fucking tight, sucking me in greedily and then refusing to let me go.

I suck in a ragged breath, and she squirms over me, her cheeks flushed and her hair sticking to her wet body.

I reach up and brush the hair back from her face and tighten my hold on her hips.

Tonight, I'll get her out of my system.

I'll find a way to finish this.

"Bed. Now."

CHAPTER
Twenty-Seven

LEVI

I s there a special place in hell for men who pluck off a butterfly's wings to keep her grounded? Make her fall in love and keep her at arm's length so she'll never want to leave?

How about the men who lie, cheat, and steal to get what they want? Do they deserve retribution?

Maybe I'm just reading too much into it. Maybe I've just officially lost my fucking mind.

My eyes ghost over the bed, taking in the soft form nestled into my side.

Ava looks so innocent when she sleeps. It's hard to believe she's here. Her pouty lips, still swollen from my kissing, her parted lips slightly over her even breathing, and her lashes cast shadows over her cheeks. Her hair lies across the pillow, frizzy from my hands. The dark waves form a halo around her face. Like I've corrupted an angel in God's eyes.

Looking at her fucking hurts. Like gutting yourself open from the inside out and watching yourself bleed.

And now I sound like a fucking Hallmark card.

anyone else have her. She's mine. My little porcelain doll to break. To fuck in every way I've been imagining since I laid eyes on her.

Toxic? Yes.

Do I really care? No.

If I'm toxic, then she made me this way. Now she gets to suffer the consequences.

As if Ava knows I'm watching her, she stirs in her sleep, rolling away from me and pressing her pretty little ass against me. Gently, I reach out, tracing the lines of the dimples on her lower back beneath the sheets.

I want to sink inside her just to feel her come for me again, but I know she's not ready. My cock's hard thinking about her body molded against mine. Her nails digging into my back, tugging the roots of my hair while I fucked her like I could engrain myself in every stitch of her DNA. How fucking tight she was, and that throaty voice moaning my name while I fucked her harder than I should have.

A burn slides up my spine, and I shake the feeling off, slowly slipping from the bed so I don't wake her. As much as I'd like to laze around in the cabin with her all day, I've got shit to do, and it would only blur the lines between us even more than they already are.

Fuck knows, I don't need any help there.

I head to the bathroom, catching a glimpse of the scratches on my back, and my cock twitches at the sight.

Fuck. Me.

Cutting on the old shower, I slip under the hot water and place my hands on the shower wall, letting the warmth wash over my neck and shoulders. I'm stiff because I haven't gone that hard in a long time.

I just needed to punish her for disappearing like that. For making me come find her.

She was right when she accused me of caring. I do.

And that's exactly why I need to remind her that I'm not the guy she thinks I am.

When I emerge from the bathroom half an hour later, Ava's sitting up in bed, the sheets wrapped around her as if she's worried about me seeing her naked. As if I didn't just fuck her raw last night in every position I could think of.

"Good morning," she greets softly, her gaze following me when I cross to the dresser on the far side of the room and pull out some clothes. I've got the basics here. A couple pairs of jeans and a few T-shirts. I grab a pair of sweats and a T-shirt and toss them to her. I know they'll be too big, but they'll have to do because her clothes are tattered from last night.

Ava's cheeks flame as the clothes land in her lap.

"They're clean."

Her gaze cuts to mine, then slowly slips down over the low-hanging towel on my hips before sliding back up to the water droplets clinging to my bare chest.

Fuck.

"Keep looking at me like that," I warn.

I drop the towel at my feet, and if I weren't already in a foul mood, I would laugh at the way she quickly looks away.

"How are you feeling?"

Her gaze meets mine once I tug my boxers up my legs.

"A little sore," she concedes. "Hungry."

Hungry. If I had my way, I'd feed her in bed. Spend the day lazing around and avoiding the rest of the world. But I don't have time for that, and shit like that breeds expectations. I'm an asshole. One that doesn't deserve any part of her. I took it, knowing I should have cleaned her up and taken her back to bed. I let her get under my skin, and now I have no fucking idea how to get her out.

"I don't feed, Ava. I fuck," I grunt, slipping the shirt over my head and turning away.

She goes silent, and I can't look at her in the mirror because if I do, I know I'll break. The closer she gets to me, the closer she is to the truth, and I know the moment she finds out what I did, she'll leave. Why would she stay?

Finally, I force myself to look at her and find her watching me with a guarded expression.

"Get ready. I'll take you back to the house. I've got stuff to do."

She opens her mouth to say something, but falls silent instead. Carefully, she slips from the bed, dragging the sheet with her and keeping it tucked protectively around herself like it's a shield. I fucking hate it because I know I'm only pushing her away, but what good is it trying to convince her to stay? She'll always want to know more. She'll want a glimpse into my mind. She won't be able to handle the nightmares or the truth of who I am. A fucking monster that takes and takes because someone took from him, and now, I can't stop.

"Are you okay?" she asks softly when she stops at the door to the bathroom.

Fuck.

I run a hand over my face, my muscles tense.

I definitely need to shoot something. Break something with my bare hands.

I don't deserve her worry. Her concern.

She still cares about me, even after everything I've put her through. Everything I've said to her.

"We both got what we wanted, Ava," I snap harshly, hating myself even as the words leave my mouth. They taste like battery acid on my tongue, but I force myself to fucking say it anyway because I feel like I'm losing my mind. "I don't know what else you think you're going to find."

"Right," she nods and turns away like she can hide the tears in her eyes. Something in me cracks, and I suddenly hate her for her concern. Why can't she just hate me? It would make it so much easier to let her go. If she didn't look at me like there's something good left inside that can be salvaged. Like I need to be saved.

My chest burns, my teeth threatening to crack behind the force of my jaw as I clench them tightly.

I grip the dresser in front of me when she goes into the bathroom and shuts the door, casting a dark cloud over the rest of the cabin in her silence.

When the shower cuts on, something cracks in my hand, and I look down to see that I broke the edge of the dresser with the force behind my grip.

Something cracks in my hand, and I look down to see that I broke the edge of the dresser with the force behind my grip.

The thing was a piece of shit anyway.

Looking down at the splintered wood, though, I can't mistake the irony hidden in the broken surface.

Ava wasn't made for me.

Eventually, she'll see it, too. God fucking help me when that day comes.

"Came alone tonight, I see."

Cherry slides a beer across the counter to me when I sit down on an empty stool at the bar. The place is less crowded today, given it's early, and I can't decide if I miss the noise or not.

Can't have everything we want, can we?

"Got work to do," I answer stiffly, ignoring the question surrounding Ava.

Truthfully, I don't know why the fuck I'm here. I don't want to fight. In fact, I just want to go find the little ghost staying in my house and drag her back to my bed until she doesn't look at me like she hates me.

"Never thought I'd see the day Black fell in love," she smirks.

"The girl seems sweet. In a Care Bear kind of way. Let me guess . . . kindergarten teacher?"

So, the animosity I'd felt in the air the night I'd brought Ava here wasn't just a part of my imagination.

"Never· thought I'd see the day that Cherry was jealous," I counter, tipping my beer back.

"I'm not jealous, Black. I told you I want you to find someone."

"Just didn't think it'd be this soon, huh?"

She shoots me a look, scrubbing the top of the bar.

"I never said that. I just figured you could do better. But hey, if you're into that whole sweet and innocent act, then by all means."

Any other time, I wouldn't care, but now I'm finding myself wondering if anything was said to Ava, and if that's not why she practically jumped my dick the moment we got home. I can't lie and say I'm not grateful, but I also don't want someone putting ideas in her head.

"What happens between me and Ava is no one's business."

Cherry rolls her eyes, vigorously wiping a spot that's already clean.

"Yeah, whatever you say, Casanova."

She stalks off to the other side of the bar, and I sit with my beer, thinking about last night.

The sheer fucking panic I'd felt when I couldn't find her, only to spot her in the overgrowth by some stroke of a miracle.

I don't want to think about what would have happened if I hadn't found her, and I *also* don't want to think about what the fuck that means.

Do I care about her?

Sure. As much as any human being.

Am I in love with her?

Absolutely, fucking not.

It doesn't mean anything.

Needing to see her doesn't mean anything. The guilt I feel for the way I treated her this morning doesn't mean anything. The ache in my chest when she laughs *doesn't fucking mean anything.*

I'm not in love. Love is simple.

This feeling is anything but.

"Thought I'd find you here."

I stiffen. I don't have to turn around to know it's my brother. He has that effect on people—the kind that creeps in just before the storm breaks.

Christian slides into the stool beside me, his presence heavy. He scans the bar with a grim expression, lips pressed tight like he's already made a judgment about the entire place. He's probably right.

Fuck.

"I'm going to need something stronger," I call to Cherry. She flicks a wary glance toward Christian when she hears his voice and sets down the glass she was polishing.

Christian lifts two fingers and gives her a look that says he'll take the same. She hesitates, as if expecting him to flash a badge. Being former FBI, Christian still carries himself like he could ruin your life with a single phone call.

She pours in silence, eyeing him like he's here to arrest her for slinging watered-down drinks before she disappears back down the bar.

Christian lifts his drink but doesn't take a sip.

"Place really suits you. I think the moldy rat carcass at the front door is a nice touch."

"You following me now?" I ask, not bothering to hide the edge in my voice.

"Don't need to follow you when I already know where you are," he replies smoothly, cocking a brow. "If the bruises and cuts you come home with weren't enough, that car may as well be a fucking beacon."

"Should have bought a fucking minivan," I grumble, swallowing half my whiskey in one go.

It does nothing but piss me off because it's not what I want.

No, that unfortunately rests in the little ghost living across the hall from me.

"I don't need a babysitter."

"You sure? You look like shit."

"Thanks," I mutter. "Glad I could be of service."

Christian rests his elbows on the bar, glancing sideways at me. "Mila tells me you've upset her friend."

Tattle-tale.

"Mila needs to learn to mind her business."

"Careful, little brother," he warns, voice dipping low and dark. Fucker's as protective as they come over his wife.

Unfortunately, as much as I fucking hate it, I think I'm starting to understand.

"What's really going on?" Christian asks, nodding at the rundown warehouse we're drinking in. "Why are you here?"

"Got a better idea?"

"Yeah," he says. "It's called therapy."

"Fuck therapy."

He snorts and downs his whiskey, then leans in with a smirk.

"I'd suggest you just fuck the little housekeeper, but it looks like you've already had that idea."

I finish my drink and slam the glass down harder than I meant to.

I don't feel a goddamn thing.

"Did you come to talk about my sex life, or do you want a rundown of my cholesterol levels too?"

Christian's smile doesn't reach his eyes. His stare is sharp—cutting.

"Actually, I came to ask what you plan to do about your little problem."

Of course, he did.

"What do you think?" I murmur, voice low enough to get lost

under the low hum of metal playing over the speakers.

Christian exhales slowly, like he's weighing his next words.

"You sure you want to go down that road? Once you cross that line . . . there's no coming back."

"You're not the only one who's had to spill a little blood, brother."

"I'm just saying," he mutters. "Shit like this? It changes you."

I grit my teeth, jaw tight. Should have had Cherry leave the fucking bottle.

"Why didn't you come to me about this?"

"You've got your own shit. I can handle it."

"Like you've handled it so far?"

"Fuck you," I snap. "You finally have your life figured out, Christian. You think I'm going to let you throw it away to fix my mess?"

He doesn't flinch. Just studies me like he's looking through me instead of at me.

"When I was in your shoes, what did you do?" he asks.

"That's different. I'm single. You've got a wife to think about."

"And now *you've* got Ava to think about."

I swear to fucking God.

"Nothing is going on between Ava and me."

Christian lifts a brow. "Is that why you bolted out of the house like your ass was on fire last night when you heard she was missing?"

I don't answer. I don't need to.

"I'm not saying things have to go the way they did back then," he says, his tone gentler now. "I'm saying we're family. We don't leave each other bleeding in the street. There are only a few of us left."

I swallow hard. His words hit deeper than I want to admit.

Three months feels like a lifetime ago. Like someone else's life.

My phone buzzes on the bar, and I glance at the screen, and the number is familiar—too familiar. My gut clenches, and instantly, I reach for it.

Only to freeze. It's a picture, and I can physically feel the rush of violence that slips through my veins.

It's my girl at that fucking party I told her to stay away from. Only those aren't my hands on her.

I zoom in, and sure enough, Alex has his arm wrapped around her shoulder, as if she belongs to him. A smug grin on his face that I suddenly can't *wait* to wipe clean.

Ava, on the other hand, looks like she's ready to bolt.

I can't help it—I chuckle under my breath.

Oh, baby girl. You've fucked up.

Maybe punishing her is exactly what I need.

Christian smirks from beside me.

"Told you he was after your girl."

I down the last of my whiskey and rise from the stool, my chair scraping loudly against the concrete floor. Christian stands too, watching me with a guarded expression.

"Go home to Mila," I tell him, tossing a few twenties down for Cherry. "I've got something I need to handle."

CHAPTER
Twenty-Eight

AVA

The moment I arrived at this party, I was reminded why I, in fact, do not like parties.

I feel like I'm being watched from all sides, and the more people that bump into me, the more my skin crawls.

It could be because I know I'm breaking the rules, coming to this party when Levi specifically said not to, but it could also be because I'm still wounded from my last interaction with him. That was this morning. He left after he took me home, and he's been gone since.

Not that I noticed or anything. I don't give a flying crap where Levi Cross is. Screw him and his overinflated ego. I'm not a child. I shouldn't have to hide. I've spent most of my life hiding, and look where it's gotten me.

It's just a crush. A harmless little, inconvenient crush that makes it feel like my chest is going to explode when he looks at me.

If he doesn't care, then neither do I. This is just a contract. Nothing permanent.

Then he came along and got me addicted to the way he looks at me. How he growls my name, or how, when he touches me. It's like he's afraid of breaking me, but I'm his to ruin if he pleases.

Now, the silence is maddening.

It's my own fault. I have no one to blame but myself. He made it clear that he will never care about me the way I seem to care for him, and yet, I crawled into bed with him anyway.

The housekeeper and a man from one of the wealthiest families in the state.

It would be a great romance book plot if he weren't such a dick.

"You know you don't have to hide over here," Alex smiles when he returns from grabbing us drinks. I've stuck to him most of the night, avoiding the area in the center of the room where people are dancing. One girl took her top off, and now the whole room is covered in boobs, and that's not something I think I can partake in.

God, can you imagine the look on Levi's face if he came in here and I was free-boobing in the middle of the room? It's almost worth it.

Aside from that, the music is really loud, and I'm getting tired, ready to crawl into my bed in the quiet of Cross Estate.

Maybe I am a recluse, I wonder dryly.

"I'm not hiding." *I totally am.*

Alex grins and holds out a red plastic cup filled with an electric blue liquid.

"Is this *Windex*?"

He snickers, leaning in until his lips are close to my ear so that I can hear him.

"It's punch."

"But what is it?"

"Fruit. Vodka. Try it. You'll love it. The fruit's the best part."

My mouth is dry, and thus far, I've only managed to swallow down one beer, which I must say, tasted like actual butt.

"Do you want to dance?" Alex asks. I reach for the cup, but

before I can take it, it's snatched out of my hand.

"She's good, actually."

I don't have to turn around to know who that voice belongs to. The scent of whiskey and sin is enough. Despite myself, my heart flutters at the knowledge that he's here, even though I know he will try to make good on his threat.

He showed up. That's more than most have done in my life.

I can feel the warmth of him brushing against my back. The electricity that seems to flow through us makes it feel like my body's attached to a live wire.

"I asked Ava," Alex says cooly, his gaze locked on the man over my shoulder.

Levi moves closer, and I can practically feel the hostility flowing between them.

"And I answered you," Levi says darkly.

I've read about this moment in romance novels. The part where the two love interests face off for the main girl. This is just like that, only one is just my friend, and the other has already made it clear he wants nothing to do with me, and I have never been the main character.

Why they're choosing now to compete in their pissing match is beyond me.

—Or should I say, right over my freaking head?

"I'd like a moment alone with Ava."

"I'm not leaving her with you," Alex shrugs, and I swear, I could hit him for continuing this strange caveman-esque showdown with Levi.

"It wasn't a request," Levi counters, and a shiver slips up my spine at the warning laced in his voice.

I swear to God.

"It's okay," I say finally, after the silence starts to hum in my ears. "I'll just be a moment."

Alex is not easily swayed.

"Ava, I don't trust him. What's he got to say to you that he can't say in front of me?"

I pause for a moment, confused, but brush it off. Alex is just being protective, and by protective, I mean overbearing. So is Levi, but one is paying my grandmother's bills, so I at least need to hear him out.

"Well, I *do* trust him." *Kind of.*

That's only partially a lie. Do I trust Levi to protect me with his life? Yes. If he didn't, I'd haunt him with every spare second of my afterlife.

Do I trust him not to completely shatter my heart into a million pieces?

Absolutely not.

"I'll be okay," I tell Alex, softening my tone. I can *feel* Levi's smugness over my shoulder. The two lock eyes, and Alex's lip twitches before he finally concedes.

"I'll be back to check on you."

The moment he's gone, Levi's grabbing my hand and tugging me toward the door.

"Stop," I grit, but I can tell by the stiffness in his shoulders that he's not in a great mood.

Good. That makes two of us.

"Let me go, asshole," I growl the moment we make it out onto the porch, but I may as well be fighting with a brick wall.

The moment my feet touch the sidewalk, I wrench my hand back as hard as I can, snatch my drink from his hand, and storm off toward the trees surrounding the property.

As I suspected, he follows me, though I was really hoping he would just magically disappear.

"Ava."

"Fuck off, Levi."

Outside the party, the music is thankfully a lot less headache-inducing, and I can actually breathe from the lack of smoke in the air.

I step into the trees that border the property, just because I know out here under the full moon, it's a lot better than being in there surrounded by rogue boobs and drunk men getting handsy.

"I will not fuck off, little ghost."

I stop, turning to stare at him. He looks like a god, basking in the glow of the moonlight overhead. He's wearing his familiar black hoodie and jeans, but it's the feral look in his blue eyes and his wild hair that make my heart beat unsteadily.

God, there's no way he's real.

"You know, if you'd peed on me, I think you could have made less of an ass of yourself."

He doesn't acknowledge me.

"Stay away from him, Ava."

I gawk at him.

"He's my *friend*."

Levi cocks his chin up. "He know that?"

I swear to God.

"Why are you here, Levi? I don't need a babysitter."

"Seems you do. Or did you forget someone was following you?" He pauses, cocking his head to the side.

"Yeah, *you*," I snap.

"Sweetheart, I don't need to follow you when I can have you whenever I want you."

In a flash, I toss my punch in his face.

In the split second after, even the crickets know to be quiet.

A predator's on the loose.

It doesn't even faze him. In fact, he grins, and it's both the most terrifying and hottest thing I've ever seen.

The feral smile on his lips is enough to have me backing away when he stalks toward me. Unfortunately, I run right into a tree, effectively caging me in.

"Baby girl, what am I going to do with you?"

"I'm sorry," I rush, flinching when he gets right in my face. He leans in, his hands on the tree on either side of my head, and try as I might, I can't help but breathe him in.

"I don't think you are," he murmurs, his voice barely above a whisper. Heat slips through my veins as if he'd licked between my thighs, and warmth gathers in my core at the dark, low tenor of his voice. "I think you wanted to do that."

"Just leave me alone," I grit, and he smiles. It's devastating.

"I can't do that, Ava."

"Why?" I scoff. "Because of a piece of paper? You could have any girl in the world, yet you're terrorizing me. I do everything you ask, including forgoing any sense of moral dignity I had, and for what? For you to punish me for doing something I want to do for once?"

"Is that why you came here tonight? To piss me off? Did you want me to remind you of our contract?"

"*Fuck* the contract," I grit, tears burning in my eyes. "All you care about is that stupid contract. You're so hot and cold it gives me whiplash. One minute, you make me feel like trash. The next, you're storming in here, demanding I live and breathe for you. What do you want?"

He doesn't respond, and a rush of anger washes over me. I shove at his chest, letting out a growl.

"What do you *want*, Levi?"

Something briefly flashes across his face before it's wiped away. I can't place it, but it's almost as if his gaze softened for a moment.

I know I must have imagined it. Levi Cross doesn't know what guilt is.

"Did I hurt your feelings?" he asks, and despite myself, my chest aches at the mocking leer in his voice. "You want me to care, sweetheart? Is that it?"

"I don't want anything from you," I grit, though it feels like my heart's going to beat out of my throat.

"You do." He steps closer. A shiver slips through me at his

proximity. "Want me to get down on my knees and show you how I worship you, Ava?"

I blink, closing my eyes when a tear slips out of the corner. "Stop."

"Want me to go into that party and tell everyone you're *mine?*"

"Unless you're getting your dick wet, I'm nothing more than a piece of trash, right? Let's not act like you care."

"Oh, sweetheart," he grins, his teeth glinting in the moonlight like a wild animal. "You're going to wish you hadn't said that."

I open my mouth to argue back, but I don't get the chance before he seals his lips over mine and steals my breath.

He tastes like the punch I threw at him, and the taste mixed with him is intoxicating. Despite myself, my body reacts to him. My hips press against his, silently begging him to touch me, right here, where anyone could see us.

It's been less than twenty-four hours, and yet I feel like I've been touch-starved for most of my life.

No . . . scratch that. *Levi-starved.* I need him like my next breath, and I absolutely hate it.

Placing my hands on his chest, I shove him back, but it's like shoving at the side of a mountain. He doesn't budge. I turn my head to the side, gasping for breath, and he takes the opportunity to kiss down the side of my throat, nipping over the racing pulse point in my throat.

"I hate you," I seethe, and he chuckles darkly. He breathes deeply, his face in the crook of my neck like he's inhaling my scent. His lips glide over my racing pulse, and my stomach erupts with butterflies when he lets out a quiet groan.

He presses closer, his cock hard against my stomach, when he pushes his body into mine, and I lose all train of coherent thought.

"I know," he murmurs against my skin. "And it makes me so fucking hard. All I can think about is bending you over the hood of my car and showing this entire party whose cock you're begging for.

But I'm too selfish, baby girl. Only I get to see you come. Hear your breathless little moans. Watch you come alive under my fingers."

My cheeks flame, and my hand falls, my nails digging into the tree bark at my back when he rims the shell of my ear. I don't know if I've ever been this turned on in my life.

All it would take to stop this is my safe word. I know that the moment it left my lips, he'd stop. Still . . . even as I contemplate it, I know I don't want to.

Maybe he's right. Maybe I am pathetic. Pathetic because I want him, knowing he will never feel the same way about me.

Levi aligns his body with mine, shoving his knee between my legs. His denim-clad thigh grinds against my pussy, and I bite back a moan at the delicious friction.

"You think he could make you completely shatter the way I do, Ava?" Levi rasps, rolling me against him so my clit drags against his thigh. It's absolutely maddening.

And then it dawns on me.

Oh my God . . .

"You're jealous."

Levi Cross is jealous because another man is interested in me. I almost can't believe it.

"I'm far from jealous, sweetheart," he lies. He nips my bottom lip to prove his point. "You think he is, though?" He kisses a path down my face to my jaw, then lower to my ear, and his nose brushes along the smooth column of my neck. "Do you think he's behind a tree, watching us while he jacks off like the loser he is?"

"Levi," I growl, but I can't deny that what he's doing feels good. That there's not a soul on this planet that could make me feel quite like he can.

"Tell me, Ava," he breathes. "Do you think I won't break his fingers for trying to touch what isn't his?"

"And who's going to break your fingers?"

His lips tip up at the corner. "You think anyone would have the power to drag you away from me? You think I'd even let them get close?"

"Levi, we can't do this. Not here. We're in public and I'm . . ."

"You're what, Ava? Pissed off? Hurt?"

I shake my head, not wanting to hear what he has to say. I turn my head away because if he's going to insult me again, I can't bear to look at him.

"Why are you here? If you're going to punish me, just get it over with." I force myself to meet those piercing blue eyes. I may as well be staring down the center of the sun with the heat scorching in them. "What do you want from me?"

With a soft chuckle, his fingers tighten on my hip, like he's afraid I might try to run. I would, if I weren't so desperate for his touch.

"Something about you draws me in," he murmurs, low in my ear. Like saying these things out loud is too much. "Something about you is so fucking addictive to me, I can't think about anything other than this. Dragging you to my bed and fucking you until all you can feel is me. Have you moaning my name and begging for me with every breath?"

I try to shove at his chest, but he holds steady, unmoving.

"Say your safe word, Ava, and it all goes away," he growls under his breath.

A shiver slips up my spine with his breath at my ear, his thigh drawing the fire burning in my veins to a scorching inferno. I'm powerless to stop the pleasure coursing through my veins.

His hand slips down my stomach, over my top until he reaches the hem of my dress.

"Or maybe you're too ashamed to admit you want me just as badly. You're craving my touch. My mouth." He enunciates his words with a nip of his teeth on the side of my neck.

Flicking my dress up, he slides his hand into my panties, his fingers slipping through my folds.

"Fucking soaked, Ava," he rasps in my ear. I bite my lip to

silence a moan that threatens to claw its way from my throat. "Is this for me, or for him?"

He pulls back to look down at me, and with him crowded over me, all I can see is him.

"So, what if it's because of him?" I challenge, though my breath hitches when he strokes my clit with his thumb. "What if I'm wishing I was with him right now?"

He bares his teeth, shoving me back harder into the tree. I whimper at the pleasure zipping through me like a thousand volts, my skin burning hot in the cool air from his body pressed against mine.

"Don't tempt me, baby girl. I quite like the idea of cutting his dick off and letting him watch me fuck you while he bleeds out."

His words are filthy and violent. They should terrify me. They should make me want to run the other way, but there's something about his primal need to claim me, even if he's fought it every step of the way, that makes my stomach flutter with the first waves of my orgasm.

"I hate you," I remind him, and he punishes me by withdrawing his fingers with a feral grin.

"I hate you, too, baby."

My stomach clenches at the nickname, then quickly drops to my toes when he kneels in front of me, his gaze finding mine above.

"Levi, someone could see," I argue quietly, but he doesn't seem to hear me, or he doesn't care. Without wasting a beat, he tugs my panties to the side, and the cool air is enough to make me shiver when it hits my skin.

"Let them," he murmurs. "All they'll see is me making you come, proving who owns this pussy. Your pleasure."

I grip his shoulders to steady myself when he pushes my knees as far apart.

"But what if—"

He cuts me off when he licks me languidly from my opening to my clit, and my head falls back to hit the tree on a sharp breath.

Holy. Shit.

"Fuck, that's it, Ava," he growls when a moan slips free. "Let them hear who makes you come."

I'm shivering with the pleasure running through me, and as much as I hate it, his words only fuel the fire.

"You're so much hotter when your mouth is busy," I rasp. It's a lie. Levi Cross's mouth may as well be the soundtrack of seduction.

"Ditto, sweetheart. I can't wait to watch you suck my cock."

Reaching between us, he slides his hand up my inner thigh and slides one deliciously thick finger inside me, curling it up to brush over that sensitive spot only he seems to know about.

The pleasure is enough to make my knees wobble, and he hooks my knee over his shoulder, holding me up completely with his upper body.

"You're so fucking sexy," he rasps against my skin. "It pisses me off. I want to punish you for it. What does that say about me, little ghost? Do you think I'm insane?"

If you're insane, then I am too, because it only turns me on.

"Yes," I breathe instead because the truth is far more dangerous than a little white lie.

"But you enjoy it. You like my insanity as much as you like my tongue on this pretty little pussy. Making you come all over my face. You want my filthy mouth and rough hands. You want my cock inside you, pushing you to your limits and making your legs shake."

"God, Levi!" My body tightens, and my head bashes back against the tree. He smiles, sealing his lips around my clit and fluttering his tongue rapidly. I'm so close to coming that I can't think straight. "Right there, please don't stop."

He spreads me open with his free hand. His tongue continues its movements, his fingers stroke over that perfect spot, and when I can't hold on any longer, he catches me.

I come so hard, my legs give out. Levi holds me to his face, his upper half pressing me back into the tree. A deep groan rumbles through him, and he continues to feast on my pussy, drawing out the orgasm until I'm desperately shoving at him from how oversensitive I am.

With my body still shaking with aftershocks from my orgasm, he climbs to his feet, cradling my face in his hands, and kisses me deeply. His tongue tangles with mine, and I can taste myself on his lips.

My fingers wrap around his wrists, and he presses into me, and for a single moment, I forget that I'm supposed to hate him.

His kiss turns sweet, and suddenly my heart's floating, all manner of irrational thoughts racing through my mind. Like how he tastes like sin and temptation . . . like everything I've been dreaming of and how I would trade a week of my life just to live in this moment for a little bit longer.

"Goddamn, Ava," he rasps when he breaks the kiss, leaning his forehead against mine. His breathing is ragged, matching my racing pulse. "You're the sexiest woman I've ever seen."

That doesn't sound like you don't care, Mr. Cross, I think, but I don't allow myself to dwell on it. Doing so will only drive me crazy.

"Stay away from Alex, Ava."

I expect a threat in his tone, but instead, it's gentle. Almost like he's actually concerned and not just showing his dick again.

"I thought you weren't jealous," I muse, grinning at him when his eyes latch on mine.

Reaching up, he brushes the hair behind my ear, his expression unreadable.

"Protective."

CHAPTER
Twenty-Nine

LEVI

I stay at the party until Ava's ready to come home.

I don't know why, but I don't want to leave her alone. Especially with that dickhead trying to get her wasted. I don't believe for a second he had noble intentions when he gave her that glass of punch. Everyone knows to stay away from the fucking punch at a house party.

Better yet, why did he bring her at all? He has to know she's not the party type. Ava would much rather have a picnic or some shit.

Not that I wouldn't have shown up to that, too, but I digress.

Some might call it hovering. I know Alex definitely would, but it allowed her to have fun with her friends without creeps like him sneaking something into her drink, and that's a price I'm willing to pay to see my girl enjoy herself.

Now, we're on our way home, and she's passed out in my passenger seat after having one too many drinks.

In her sleep, Ava makes a soft noise, and I look over at her. She looks so fucking beautiful, even with her makeup smudged

I park the car in the garage and exit, not bothering to wake her just yet. Lifting her into my arms, she stirs, curling into my chest while I carry her inside and up the back staircase to her room. Once we're inside, I carry her straight to the bathroom and sit her down on the counter in front of me, pinning her there with my lower half so she doesn't fall.

She peeks at me before groaning against the light, and I can't help but chuckle.

"Come on. Let's get you ready for bed."

Her eyes open, finding mine. The soft green is hazy, and her pupils are dilated, but she's got a soft, playful smile on her lips I've never seen before.

"Are you coming?" she reaches for my cock, still hard in my jeans, and I bite back a groan when she strokes me through the material.

Fucking. Hell.

Grabbing her wrist, I pull her off, and my dick protests. Instead, I grab a washcloth from the cabinet beside her and wet it with warm water.

"Don't you want me?" Ava breathes, her words slurred and her soft lips pouty.

"I always want you." *Even though you piss me off more than I ever thought possible from another human being.*

She's quiet while I work on removing the makeup on her face. The shit just smears everywhere, and I grit my teeth.

"I'm doing a shit job at this, baby, but it's better than nothing."

She smirks lazily. "You forgot the girl."

It takes me a minute to register what she'd said before I chuckle under my breath.

"You're drunk."

"I'm not. You didn't call me baby girl. You called me baby, which is different."

By the way she's slurring her words, she is most definitely drunk, but drunk minds speak sober thoughts, so I let her continue.

"Why are you taking care of me?" I can tell by the way her eyes shift and she sways that she's trying to focus on me, but it's not working out in her favor.

I don't answer her. Instead, I toss the rag in the hamper before I take out her earrings and set them on the counter, and reach for her hand.

"You like me," she breathes, and I don't have the heart to tell her I don't *like* anything about her. I'm obsessed. There's a difference. I know because I asked Proctor. "Don't you," she taunts, reaching again for my dick.

Grabbing her hand, I pull it to her lap and take her chin with my other, forcing her to look at me.

"I'm going to say this one time, Ava, because you're too drunk to remember. You are the only thing in my life that I have ever wanted, and the one thing I don't want to lose. Now. You're going to be a good girl and let me take care of you because I have no fucking idea what I'm doing, but I want to do it right."

Her mouth falls open, and she lets out a sharp breath, her eyes widening at my words.

I smirk quietly to myself because at least it shut her up for a few minutes.

"Hold onto my shoulders." I pull her to her feet, and she wobbles unsteadily while I drop down and reach for her shoes. I untie them and toss the sneakers behind me, massaging the arch of her foot with my fingers.

She won't remember any of this tomorrow, and I guess some idiotic part of me is finding excuses to be in her space when I'm not actively fucking her.

It goes against every single one of my rules, but right now, the only thing that comes to mind is *fuck the rules.*

Ava giggles softly, jerking her foot, and I chuckle under my breath. I slip back up her body and lift her dress over her head. When she's in nothing but her—tempting—bra and thong, I spin her around to face the mirror and work on brushing the knots out of her hair.

"Stop giggling at me." She continues, and I swat her ass. Not hard enough to sting. Just enough to get her attention.

Unfortunately, it gets the wrong attention when a soft moan slips from her lips.

"Baby, you're making it really fucking hard to be a gentleman right now," I murmur in her ear, and press a kiss to the top of her head. Hazy, half-lidded eyes meet mine in the mirror, and she bites her bottom lip, grinning. I splay my hand across her stomach, my tanned skin against her creaminess. In the mirror, we look like night and day.

"What if I don't want you to be a gentleman?"

I grit my teeth, my patience wearing thin. Who knew my little housekeeper would be such a dirty girl when she's drunk?

"Too bad. Come on, let's get you in bed."

I tug her hand, and when she opens her mouth to say something, that's when all the vodka she drank tonight decides to get its revenge.

Her face goes pale, and she spins for the toilet, falling to her knees on the tile floor and emptying the contents of her stomach.

"Saw that coming," I murmur, dropping behind her and gathering her hair behind her while she wretches. This isn't my first experience with drunk vomiting, but I can say it's the first time I've ever fisted a girl's hair without my cock buried down her throat.

I do what I think is right, rubbing soothing circles down her back, but I have no fucking idea if it helps. When she's done, she groans and lays her head on her hand and closes her eyes.

"I'm never drinking again," she groans.

"That's what they all say," I chuckle. "Come on. We'll brush your teeth and then you can go to bed."

I help her stand and practically hold her up while she brushes her teeth. When she's done, I stoop down and pick her up, deciding it's probably best if I carry her to her bed. I lay her on the covers, oddly reluctant to let go of her when I grab the sheets to toss over her.

"I'm not ready for you to go yet," she whispers, like the bogeyman is hiding in her closet, waiting for the moment I step out the door.

The air thickens, and I swallow heavily.

Bad fucking idea, Cross.

"Will you stay until I fall asleep?" she asks, and I swear to God, my heart beats unsteadily for a moment. "Please?"

Fuck. If I had more time, I'd find a way to remove that word from her vocabulary. She has way too much power when she uses it on me.

Looking down at her, I push the hair back from her face, and I can see she's fading fast. It's only for a few minutes, so what could it hurt?

"Fine," I murmur, bending down and scooting her over in the bed. I climb on top of the covers, still dressed, and let her cuddle into my arms. This is the first time I've ever cuddled another person, and I have no fucking idea what to do with my hands, so I'm glad she'll be too drunk to remember this.

She falls silent, her breathing soft and slow. I think she's passed out almost immediately, before she speaks.

"I want to ask," she says, her eyes closed as she lays her head on my chest. "Why did you show up tonight?"

It's not until after her breathing evens out and I know she's fallen asleep that I can bring myself to reply.

"I'd do anything for you."

The corridor is dark, nearly pitch-black, save for a faint blue glow at the end of the hall.

I stalk toward it, looking down to find a gun in my hand.

Strange. I hadn't even realized I was holding it.

The hallway isn't long, but each step toward the door seems to carry me further and further away. I keep pushing because something tells me I have to get to that door.

As I draw closer, I realize where I am.

I'm at home, in the same hallway I follow every night, and that door? That's the *door.*

When I reach it, I hesitate. I know I have to go in, but there's a sinking sensation in my chest, and I'm unsure of what I'll find.

Carefully, I push the door, and the old hinges creak from being unused for so long. The door opens, banging back against the wall behind it, and I take in the room. Everything has been stripped bare. The furniture is covered in white cloth. The canopy stripped from the bed.

The only light is from the TV glowing in the corner of the room, cackling with static.

Something's not right.

I glance at the bed, afraid to look, but instead of him, I see her. *Lying peacefully in the center of the bed, her eyes closed and her breathing soft.*

"Ava, wake up." I shake her, but she doesn't wake. She doesn't even stir. "Ava."

"She won't wake."

I spin at the sound of the voice, raising the gun in my hand.

No one.

All that's there are the shadows created by the static and the looming sense of foreboding.

"She'll die here. You know it, and I know it. Everyone who loves you always does."

"Show yourself," I grit, only to be met with a cackle that makes the hair on the back of my neck stand up.

I know that fucking voice.

"Sweetie," my mother purrs, stepping out of the shadows on the opposite side of the bed, only . . . it's not here. Her face—it's wrong. Distorted. Sharp.

Something about it sets me on edge, and I glance nervously down at Ava.

I have to keep her away from Ava.

"What are you doing to her?"

"She's asleep. She's very pretty, Levi. I remember her. She was always a sweet girl. Always had eyes for you, even when she was with your best friend. It's a shame, really."

"Let her go."

Mom cocks her head to the side, flashing sharp, vicious teeth when she grins.

"What's the matter, sweetheart? Do you honestly think she'd stay?"

This isn't real. It's a fucking dream.

"Stop. Don't touch her," I growl, lurching forward, but the moment I do, I'm thrust another foot back.

Mom strokes her long, sharp claws through Ava's hair, and my stomach turns.

"Oh . . . sweetie . . . she doesn't want you. Who could, once they learn the truth?"

"Just leave her alone."

"What do you think she's going to say when she finds out the truth? What you did? Do you think she'll cry?"

"Let. Her. Go."

Why can't I wake the fuck up?

"Or maybe she'll despise you because you're broken? A scared, helpless coward."

"You don't know what you're talking about."

"No?"

"Levi?"

I look down, finding Ava watching me, her eyes the same as my mother's.

It's not real. It's not real.

"He was going to kill her."

"And now you'll be the one to do it." Mom smiles sinisterly, looming over

Ava in the bed. "One day, you're going to snap, kill her too. Why wouldn't you? You're a murderer."

"Levi."

"I did what had to be done."

"MURDERER!"

"Levi, you're hurting me."

In an instant, I snap awake, my mind foggy and full of terror.

"Ava?" I scan the room for her, rubbing my eyes. It's nearly pitch black, and I fell asleep in my clothes in her bed, so I'm disoriented. She finally finds me, her hand coming out to steady me when she places it on my shoulder.

"It's okay," she pants, like she was really struggling. Because of me. "I'm right here."

Her voice is gentle, but there's an edge of fear to it that sends a shot of panic through me. When my eyes finally find hers, her brow is furrowed in concern, and she's kneeling beside me.

"Are you okay? Are you hurt?" My voice is rough with sleep. A tremor moves through my hands. I'm losing my goddamned mind because I could have hurt her in my sleep.

"I'm okay," Ava says, her tone gentler. "You just scared me."

She attempts to push me back to lie down, but I don't let her. There's no way in hell I'm lying down beside her again.

"Fuck," I grit under my breath, rising from the bed to put some distance between us.

"Levi, I'm okay," she says when I start to pace. I pace because if I don't, I'll break something.

I should have never fallen asleep with her. I let her talk me into it, and look what almost happened. I'm so much bigger than her. She's so small. I could hurt her so easily and never know what was happening until I woke up. I feel sick to my stomach at the thought. *This* is why the contract is in place. *This* is why she has to stay away from the real me.

My nightmares are right. I'm no better than what I'm trying to protect her from.

"I shouldn't have slept here," I murmur. I scrub a hand through my hair. "I fell the fuck asleep. I never fucking fall asleep."

"I'm okay. You just squeezed me a little too hard," Ava says gently, rising in her knees to reach for me. "You were mumbling in your sleep. What were you dreaming about?"

"I'm fine, Ava. I'm not talking about it."

"But—"

"I said it's none of your fucking business." I snap, and she falls back to the bed like I slapped her.

I fucking hate that she's afraid of me with every fiber of my being, but I hate myself even more. For wanting her, even though I can't have her. For not realizing sooner that she was in trouble. For not doing anything about it, the second I learned the truth.

I've failed her every step of the way. And now, here I am, disappointing her again because I can't be what she needs.

I'm not gentle or soft. I'm not the type of man you introduce to your parents and family. I'm an asshole. I fuck dirty, and I fight even dirtier.

She'll figure out eventually to stop trusting her heart with men like me.

"Why do you act like this?' she breathes, and something hot and unpleasant slides down my throat.

Releasing her, I step away from the bed.

I shouldn't have fallen asleep.

I chance a glance at her and find myself unable to move.

I've stared down the barrel of a gun. And yet, this is more terrifying. Because for a brief second, I allow myself to picture what it would be like to tell her the truth. Tell her all the things that keep me up at night. Why I'm secretly so fucking scared of everything all the time, and why I'll never be the man she deserves because I turn that fear into anger until it's swallowing me whole.

"I don't . . . know," I admit finally.

My answer feels too honest and open. Like a window to the truth, and my first instinct is to black it out by saying something mean so she can't see what I'm hiding.

"Just stay out of my business. What's in my nightmares is none of your concern."

We've all got secrets. It's just . . . some of us have darker ones, and as far as secrets go, mine are pitch black.

She'd lose her shit if she knew what I really dream about.

In the moonlight streaming through the window, Ava's eyes shine with unshed tears. I think it would be less painful if I swallowed battery acid.

"Go back to sleep. Sorry, I woke you."

"Levi," she rushes. Reaching for my hand when I turn to leave. I look back at the concern in her eyes, and my skin bristles. "I'm worried about you."

"Save your worry for someone who needs it, Ava."

I leave her alone in her bed, and when I step out of her room, I don't go to mine. I wouldn't fall back to sleep anyway.

What do you want from me?

Fucking everything.

Unfortunately, forever's a long fucking time, and sooner or later, she'll learn the truth.

CHAPTER
Thirty

AVA

It's only three days after my argument with Levi that I wake up feeling like I spent the night deep throating door knobs at the Seattle Airport.

My throat is sore. My nose may as well not exist, and I feel like I just barely cheated death with the headache and dizziness I've got going on.

Do I have a fever?

Probably.

Can I afford to take the day off?

Absolutely not.

So, like the pathetic, working-class citizen I am, I force myself to get up and get to work.

The house is nearly empty, although people have been coming and going all day. To my knowledge, Bella and Paulina are at the lodge, and Christian has been confined to his office all morning. Levi, on the other hand, has been MIA for the last three days.

Not that I noticed or anything. I don't give a flying crap where up terrified, holding me like some demonic force was trying to drag me away from him.

People have nightmares all the time. Why should I care about his?

Oh right. Because for some reason, I do.

As brutal as he was when he told me to mind my own business, I can't stop thinking about the fear in his eyes when I woke him. Levi doesn't get scared, so whatever it is, I know it was brutal.

Regardless of how he treats me when I get too close, a part of me aches for him because I know he went through something awful as a child to make him the man he is today. He just needs someone to listen and not judge, and the idiotic softie in me screams *I can help him*, even if he's expressed how much he doesn't want my help.

He still thinks I'm the enemy, even if I've tried to show him a thousand times I'm not, and I know, someday I'll have to accept that and move on. Preferably, before my feelings get involved any more than they already are.

And let me tell you, they're definitely involved.

"Goddammit," I grumble, looking down the ladder attached to the library wall at the duster I'd dropped to the floor. I'm trying to dust, but clearly, it's not working out.

Why couldn't I come from a wealthy family? Why do I have to battle dust bunnies when I'm sick instead of lounging around with an IV of the best antibiotics money can buy?

Looking down turns out to be a mistake because the room sways around me, another bout of dizziness making everything tilt on its axis.

And then the ground rushes up at me.

Uh-Oh.

"What the fuck?"

I stumble down the ladder, barely managing to land on my feet before big arms that can only belong to one person wrap around me, holding me upright.

Unfortunately, I think I would have rather fallen.

"Ava," Levi growls, steadying me. His hand doesn't leave the small of my back.

"I'm fine," I wheeze, pulling back from his grasp and bending down for the duster. I don't want to look at him because I know I look like I just climbed out of a sewer.

Besides . . . maybe I'm a little jaded from the way he acted the other day.

God, why is the room on a tilt-a-whirl today?

I pull out my inhaler, but it may as well be null and void when I take a puff.

"You're not fine."

"It's just a cold," I snap, jerking my arm away.

Wooziness washes over me, and to make things even better, I cough, sounding like an eighty-year-old woman who's smoked three packs a day since she was two.

"Why are you working if you're sick?"

He can't honestly be serious, can he?

"I have bills to pay, Levi. Normal people do that."

"You're allowance—"

"Is being saved to buy a new car."

His jaw tightens, and he looks away.

Oh, right. I forgot. We're not allowed to have any human interactions.

I push out a breath through my teeth, resisting the urge to roll my eyes.

"I have work to do."

"Go lie down, Ava. This shit will be here tomorrow."

"I highly doubt I'll feel any better tomorrow. It's better for me to just do it now."

I move to step back up the ladder, ignoring him completely when he catches me around the waist.

That's when I make the mistake of looking up into his eyes. Two icy blue pools that seem to stretch on endlessly.

I could get lost in those eyes.

Then the asshole stoops down and picks me up.

All the air whooshes out of my lungs on a gasp, and I can't help but cough from the impact.

"Breathe, baby girl."

"I'll get right on that," I wheeze, my head spinning when he carries me through the halls and down to my room. The moment we enter, I'm acutely aware that the last time he was here, it was when we fought over his nightmare, and seeing him here in the daylight feels strange. Intimate in all the ways he and I are not.

Sitting me down on the side of my bed, he pushes the door shut.

"Take your shirt off."

"Why?"

"Because you're lying down. I'll get you something to wear."

"I can take care of myself." *Lie. I couldn't even take care of Sam the Succulent.*

"Clearly," Levi grunts, searching through my drawers. "You have no clothes, Ava."

"I don't need much." *Translation: I'm broke.*

He shakes his head.

"You know, if my employer paid me a little better, I'd probably have better clothes."

He doesn't argue with my joke. Instead, his brows furrow, and he shuts the drawers in defeat.

"Maybe you're right," he grunts before disappearing out of the room and leaving me shell-shocked.

It's not a minute before he returns, tossing one of his oversized T-shirts onto the bed beside me.

"Mine weren't good enough?"

"No," he retorts. "Get undressed."

"You know, you're awfully pushy," I say around another coughing fit.

"And tired of your antics," he mutters, almost like he's pissed off. Just like the night he brought me home after the party, he's all business.

He waits while I sit on the bed and contemplate life.

"Are you going to stay here?"

He cocks a brow, shooting me a look.

Oh, right. He's fucked me seven different ways to Sunday and eaten my pussy at a crowded party.

"Fine," I grumble, reaching for the hem of my shirt. I tug it over my head and toss it to the floor. To his credit, he only looks at my boobs once when I take my bra off.

Once I've shed my shoes, pants, and socks, I slip his T-shirt over my head, and I'm disturbed to find it smells like him, and *my mouth waters.*

Honestly, what has he turned me into?

"In the bed."

"Okay, *Dad*," I grunt, and he swats my ass when I climb up onto the mattress.

"Hey!" I gasp, my cheeks flaming a deep shade of red. Unfortunately, my ire is lost on him because I have another coughing fit shortly after. He steps forward, his hand on the top rung of the four-post bed—I can't even reach that post without standing on the mattress—and his eyes darken when he looks down at me.

God . . . the muscles in his arms could end a war.

"It's Daddy to you, sweetheart." My breath gets caught in my throat, and I swear, my heart doesn't beat for a solid minute. "Now, lie down. I'll be back in a bit."

I'm ashamed to say I listen and that my core tightens when I feel his eyes roam over my ass before I slide under the covers.

I'm betting it's the fever.

"Fine. But if Paulina comes looking for me, I'm blaming you."

His lips tip up at the corner. "Good girl."

I'm almost asleep by the time Levi comes strolling back into my room.

I'm so surprised to see him that I don't even notice the tray he's carrying until he's setting it down on the bed over my legs.

"Soup?"

He doesn't even look at me as he pops the top of a can of ginger ale and then opens a pack of crackers next.

"Eat."

Something shifts, and warmth burns in my chest.

I don't feed, Ava. I fuck.

"You don't feed people."

Still avoiding my gaze, he situates everything in my lap.

"Shut up."

I bite back a smile at his tone and reach for the spoon. I'm not hungry—when I'm sick, I'd much rather starve—but the fact that he went out of his comfort zone in an effort to take care of me feels . . . special.

Honestly, my head feels like it's three sizes too big, and I can't breathe. Not to mention, my eyes are in a constant state of watering, like I'm watching the first nine minutes of *Up* on repeat.

"I'm *not* eating that grapefruit."

"Paulina caught me on the way out of the kitchen. She said they're your favorite," he jokes, crossing the room and kicking his shoes off on the other side of the bed.

"I hate grapef—What are you doing?"

My stomach dips when he tugs his hoodie over his head, and for a brief second, those glorious abs are on display. I'm sure I look like a cave rat next to him right now.

"Making sure you eat," he murmurs, before sliding into the bed beside me.

You have *got* to be kidding me.

"You know I'm a grown woman, right?"

"That much was evident when I had the proof grinding all over my mouth the other night."

"Are you always this crude, or is this reserved special for me?"

"That depends," he counters without missing a beat. "Do you always eat your soup with this much of an attitude?"

I glower at him.

He glowers back.

"If you don't finish that bowl, I'll personally hand-feed you that grapefruit."

I narrow my eyes at him.

"You wouldn't."

"Want to bet?"

"You'll have to kill me first."

"Thoughts crossed my mind," he grumbles under his breath, and we dissolve into silence.

Forcing myself, I eat the soup slowly, and though it's just soup from a can, he tried, and that's more than anyone else has done in a long time.

We sit in silence, both of us watching whatever trashy TV show is on, but it's not as uncomfortable as it normally is. Like maybe we reached some sort of momentary truce while I'm sick.

Truthfully, I've missed him, but I refuse to tell him that.

We left too much unsaid the other night. The way he took care of me. The way he'd kissed me after he'd made me come like he's been dreaming of it all his life.

The way he seemed desperate to protect me in his nightmare.

It all sits heavily between us like the biggest elephant in the room, but neither of us breaches the subject.

Is it bad that I'm thankful?

Is it also bad that, as much as I don't want to, I'm enjoying just having him in my space after two days of radio silence?

"I'm done," I say quietly when the bowl is empty, placing the tray on my nightstand. My eyes are heavy, and I can't help but blush when I blow my nose loudly. Levi doesn't seem to care, but I do. "You don't have to stay."

"In a minute," he grunts, not taking his eyes off the TV. "I'm invested."

"You have a TV in your room."

"It's broken."

I know for a fact that's a lie.

"Fine," I sigh, slipping down into the bed to get comfortable. Suddenly, I'm exhausted. "But don't blame me when you get sick."

"I think if I were going to get it, I would have gotten it by now, baby."

My chest flutters.

He left off the *girl* at the end of that again.

I can't decide if I like it or if it's terrifying.

"Must be hard to catch a cold when your body temperature is the same as the surface of the sun," I muse, hiding my blush by adjusting under the covers.

He chuckles darkly under his breath. "Maybe you just have a weak immune system."

"My immune system is offended."

"Your immune system is a dick."

"Tell me about it," I grumble, and he chuckles quietly.

For what feels like eternity, we just lay there in each other's presence. Neither of us speaking, but not really paying attention to the TV either.

Levi's the first to break the silence, and he swallows hard. "Come here, Ava." His tone is gentler, and for a moment, I almost think maybe I *do* have a fever. Levi isn't sweet. He doesn't do intimacy.

I stare up into his frosty eyes when he opens his arm to me.

"I'm sick." It's a poor excuse. Levi and I don't cuddle. The other night is evidence of that.

He fixes me with a look and tugs at my hand resting between us.

Gingerly, I go, laying my head down on this chest. It's awkward and he's stiff as a board, but there's also a tenderness when he blows out a slight breath between his teeth that I'm not used to. Something warm and sweet and dangerous.

"Thank you for feeding me," I say softly, listening to the sound of his heartbeat. It's beating so fast . . .

"Don't mention it," he says, his voice rough.

The silence in the air hums between us, especially now that the show has ended.

"Have you ever cuddled before?"

He's silent, staring up at the ceiling for a long time.

"Before you . . . No."

My heart breaks for him, and just like that, there's a rush of strange emotions swirling through me that I can't fight. The knowledge that he's not as bad as he wants to pretend he is. That maybe, the big bad wolf has just been misunderstood his entire life and needs someone to show him that not everyone's going to hurt him.

I rise, and he reaches for me, almost instinctually, and I smile softly. His brows draw together in confusion when I roll to my other side and pull his arm tightly around me. He stiffens for a moment but rolls over, his arm around my waist, the other under my neck, while he cradles me close.

I feel his lips at the top of my head, and finally, he relaxes around me, burying his face in the side of my neck. I don't miss the quiet inhale, like he's been starved for my scent as much as I have been for his.

"I'm sorry," he murmurs, after a long time. His voice is so quiet, I barely hear it.

Tears sting in the backs of my eyes because I know what it's like to hide behind anger, because the pain is too much.

"Don't mention it."

CHAPTER
Thirty-One

AVA

Four days after my head cold, I'm finally feeling better. I can breathe without feeling like the air is trying to kill me, and I use my time to catch up on all the housework I've skipped out on—under Levi's orders, of course.

He's spent the last few days force-feeding me soup and lying around in bed with me when he's not working or whatever it is he does all day. He's even taken to watching trash TV with me when I'm trying not to pass out at night. Neither of us mentions the contract, Alex, or even the mystery man following me, and for once, things seem strangely calm.

I can't deny that it feels almost too domestic for Levi and me.

Like yesterday, when he took me shopping for new clothes.

—Then he fucked me in the dressing room with his hand over my mouth and his rough voice growling in my ear.

Or when he took me to finally replace Judith—rest her soul. We christened my brand-new SUV on the way home on a dirt road while it poured down rain outside.

There are other things, too. Like when he takes me to th

wraps me in his arms. It's like there's a part of him that doesn't want to let me go, and I'm spiraling because I have no idea what I'm doing.

He hasn't had a nightmare since we've been sleeping together, but it's because he drinks to chase them away. I worry about him because I see the way his hands shake sometimes. I want to help him, but I have no idea how.

With each passing day, I find myself growing more and more attached to him, and it's starting to become a problem I can't ignore.

Even now, as I make my way down to the security shed, I find myself dreading the hours until I can get back to him, even though I just saw him this morning. It's absolutely maddening.

The Oak Ridge Lodge has ample security, mainly due to its high-dollar clientele. Today, though, the shack is dark and empty when I step inside, the only sound the hum of machines and the typing of Alex's fingers on the keyboard in front of him.

I feel guilty, after the way I left the other night, and because I haven't spoken to him all week with my cold.

He doesn't look up when I knock, stopping at the edge of his desk. It feels strange to be here. I've never been inside, and I hadn't realized just how many cameras were located around the grounds of the lodge and Cross Estate.

Oddly enough, my cheeks heat to a thousand degrees when I wonder just how many of those cameras are hidden outside on the paths through the forest.

"Hey, you," I greet, offering him a smile.

Alex doesn't look in my direction, and his shoulders tense. He doesn't stop typing away, and I resist the urge to snap at him for being rude.

Great.

"Sorry, I didn't come down to see you. I've been sick."

Again . . . no response.

Fine.

"Look, I know you're probably mad I left with Levi that night—

"

"Am I?" he challenges, and I flinch at the bite in his voice. He finally looks at me, and his dark brown gaze roams over me like he's trying to decide if I'm the same person. "You look fine to me."

Okay, rude.

"I had a cold the last few days. I was off."

"I'm sure you were," he murmurs, turning back to his monitor.

"What's that supposed to mean?"

He chuckles under his breath, shaking his head.

"Cross take care of you while you were sick?"

"You seem surprised."

He leans back in his chair, glowering at me.

"Cross doesn't give a fuck about you."

"And you do?"

"Don't act like that.

"Like what? Like I'm tired of being told I'm worthless and no one gives a fuck about me?"

I see him visibly stiffen.

"You know I care about you. I mean fuck, I try to take you out. I try to spend time with you. You shut me down at every turn."

My skin bristles like he'd slapped me.

"I told you I wasn't ready for a relationship," I say quietly, though I can't deny there's a rush of guilt washing over me.

"And yet, here you are, riding Cross's dick whenever he wants," he snaps, working to keep his voice low. His cheeks are red, the little vein on the side of his neck throbbing from how pissed off he is.

Good, that makes two of us.

"I'm sorry, was I supposed to ask permission?"

He scoffs, chuckling humorlessly.

"Maybe I should pay you. Seems you take anyone as long as they're paying you to fuck them."

I freeze, ice washing over me. Bile fills my throat, and I feel sick. Alex notices, a sinister smirk spreading across his lips.

"You think your little contract was going to stay a secret, Ava?"

Tears burn in my eyes, and Alex has the audacity to look away. Like I'd hurt *him*.

"What happens between Levi and me is *none* of your business," I growl, backing away.

"He's not a good guy, Ava," he grits. "I thought you, of all people, could see that."

"You don't know *anything* about my life, Alex."

"I know you're only going to get hurt in the end," he says, like he's doing me a favor. He reaches for me, and I step back away from his touch. His hand falls to his side, and the look in his eyes is defeated.

"The only thing that's going to get hurt is your ego."

"You know what? Fine. You want to run around and be Cross's whore, be my guest. Don't come crying to me when he leaves you when he gets what he wants because that's what he does."

The truth in his words washes over me, and I wish I could say they don't sting, but they do.

I know this thing between Levi and me is only momentary. I know a day will come when I'll hate myself for allowing him to sweep me up in his vortex, but I also know I'm powerless to stop it.

I'm falling in love with Levi Cross—every dark, broken piece of him.

Alex turns away from me, going back to typing on his stupid computer.

"I'd rather be his whore . . . than your wife."

His shoulders stiffen, but I don't stick around to hear what else he has to say.

It's only when I make it halfway across the lawn that I hear the clatter of something crashing into the wall in the security shack.

Fuck Alex. He doesn't get to shame me just because I don't want him. If the roles were reversed and I were sleeping in *his* bed every night, he wouldn't have a problem with it. It's only because I'm with Levi that it's a problem.

I shake my head, growling under my breath when I step into my room.

Right now, my mind is going a million miles a minute, wondering how in the fuck Alex knows about my contract with Levi.

If he knows . . . who else does?

I head towards the bathroom, but I stop short when I see the single blood orange lily resting on my pillow. For a split second, my heartbeat skyrockets.

He used to bring me flowers when he'd done something terrible, only . . . he'd bring roses. I hate roses.

Somehow, part of me knows Levi didn't forget, and my heart blooms in my chest.

He remembered.

I look towards the door, stuck between wanting and Alex's words replaying in my head. I want to see him. What does that say about me?

I get called a whore by one man, only to turn around and find myself desperately craving another.

With a sigh, I give in, needing him to chase away the thoughts clouding my mind right now.

I knock, but he doesn't answer, so I slip inside and close the door behind me. The lock echoes in the room, and in the background, the faint hum of the shower drifts through the bathroom door.

ЯЯ

Carefully, I push the door open, my breath catching in my throat at the sight of his naked body dripping with water. He doesn't look up immediately, his hands on the shower wall in front of him as the water rushes over the dark tattoos inked on his skin.

Heat slides through me, and my mouth is suddenly impossibly dry.

Levi looks like a carefully carved statue of Hades. Like every single line of his body was meticulously crafted to fulfill a woman's darkest fantasies.

My heart bottoms out in my chest when his head turns, his eyes locking with mine. The darkness in his gaze steals my breath away.

My body thrums with my heartbeat, impossible to ignore. Regardless of who he is, there's something about Levi Cross that draws me in and won't let me go.

Sucking in a deep breath, I try to calm my racing heart and remind myself of my mantra.

The worst he can do is say no.

Holding his gaze, I reach for the hem of my T-shirt and slip it over my head, dropping it to a puddle on the floor at my feet. His jaw clenches, his eyes hardening as they lick a line of fire up my stomach before moving to my breasts, where they light with a burning fire.

I slip my pants off, blushing under the heat of his stare. I fight every voice in the back of my head telling me to run back to my room and hide under the covers until either the apocalypse or taxes take Seattle—and me—out.

"Ava," he warns, voice so quiet and dark, I can barely hear it when I stand in front of him completely naked.

Shame envelops me, Alex's words replaying over and over in my head. That Levi is just using me and that when he's bored, he'll toss me to the side, just as he does with everyone else.

But . . . when I force myself to meet his gaze, it's not any of those things I find. There's a possessiveness in his gaze, so scorching hot, my skin burns under its intensity. Dark as night. As death.

Padding over to the shower, I suck in a shaky breath before I open the door. Levi watches me, and his eyes are icy, bottomless pits, deeper than hell itself.

I step underneath his arm, pressing my back flat against the shower wall. Some of the water drips off of him and slips over me, making me shiver.

His eyes open to meet mine—his frosty blue to my peridot green—and he doesn't ask why I'm in his shower. I can't help but wonder what he's thinking when his nostrils flare, his gaze following the movement of my tongue darting out to lick a water droplet off my lip.

Silently, I slip my hand up his chest, looking up at him through my lashes. His breathing hitches, his abs flexing under my fingers. I can't help but feel some sense of pride that I can have *this* effect on a man like Levi Cross. So daringly catastrophic.

"Ava," he warns when I glance down at his cock, sitting hard between us. My mouth waters to taste him, my stomach feels like a thousand butterflies have taken flight. We've never done this, even though he's tasted me a few times now. I've thought about it a lot. What it would feel like. If I would do a good job.

Fuck it.

Sinking to my knees in front of him, he curses under his breath. I look up at him, reaching up and wrapping my hand around his cock and stroking him once from root to tip. He's impossibly hard, and faced with this new, daunting task, he's also huge, and I wonder how he ever fit inside me.

His hand comes up to cup my cheek, his thumb running over my wet lips, and his gaze searching mine. I don't like this look. This serious contemplation of what I mean to him. Like maybe he took it too far and now he's just as far gone as I am, while both of us refuse to admit it.

"Thank you for the flower," I whisper, and his hand moves up to brush my hair back from my face.

"This isn't what it was about," he murmurs gruffly.

"No," I reply, stroking him again. His hand goes back to the wall, and his abs tense in front of me. "This is just for fun."

I feel powerful with him like this. At my mercy, instead of the other way around. I continue to stroke him slowly, agonizingly, and lean forward, the tip of my tongue sliding up the underside of his cock, over the vein there, until I reach the head.

"Fuck," he rasps, his eyes fluttering closed, and I bite back a grin.

I lean back and run my tongue over his head, tasting the precum there. I get drunk on the taste of him, wrapping my lips around him and sucking just the tip.

"Fucking hell, Ava." His voice is hoarse, and my pussy clenches at the bite in his tone. Like he's trying to let me take my time, but he desperately wants to push himself to the back of my throat and fuck me.

My knees are sore from the hard tile, and my back is in protest, but I ignore it all, delighting in the way he groans deeply when I slide him further into my mouth.

It's been a long time since I've given a blow job. My ex always said I wasn't good at it. To Levi, it seems like the best thing that's ever happened to him.

He stares down at me, eyes on fire. Like he'd give me anything if I just kept going. This is what I've always wanted. Someone who makes me feel like I can be comfortable taking what I want.

He may be rough and crude. He may fight in underground fight clubs. He may say the dirtiest things to me when he's inside me, but he's got a soft side that can't be beat, and I'm finding—with some dismay—that he's only soft with me.

I stroke him into my mouth, taking half his length and withdrawing back to the tip. He's so quiet, it's like he's afraid of scaring me off, and my mind is starting to run rampant. Like maybe

I'm not doing as well as I thought, despite how hard he is for me.

"Am I doing a bad job?" I ask, breaking free from his cock. I continue to twist my hand in slow, even strokes, and when he looks at me, his gaze is scorching hot.

"Why the fuck would you say that, Ava?"

I shrug one shoulder.

"You're quiet."

"So?"

"You're never quiet." My cheeks flame, and I fight the urge to look away.

His hand leaves the wall, and he brushes away a water droplet clinging to my lashes.

"I'm completely obsessed with you, Ava Lynn. All I can think about is pushing into the back of your throat and fucking your mouth until you have more of me than breath in your lungs. Seeing your eyes fill with tears and your thighs clench because it turns you on to choke on my cock . . . that what you want to hear, baby?"

Holy. Shit.

My thighs rub together at his words, heat slipping through my bloodstream.

"I want that," I breathe, before I can even think about the consequences.

"You don't want that, Ava."

I nod, suddenly sure of it. Now that he's brought it up, there's nothing I want more.

"Please?" I whisper, stroking him a little faster. His jaw feathers, and when he brushes a thumb across his lips, I catalogue the slight tremor in his hand.

Okay, so maybe I am getting to him.

"Suck my cock, Ava." His voice takes on that commanding edge I've come to love, and my core flutters in response. Leaning forward, I hold his eye contact while I slide him back between my lips. He hisses out a breath between his teeth, his hand resting on top of my head. "Fuck, that's a good girl. Just like that."

He pistons his hips, thrusting in and out of my mouth slowly, but pushing further with each stroke. I *want* him unhinged. I want his roughness and his desire. I don't want him to hold back with me.

When he pushes further back in my throat, half his length in my mouth, I gag around his cock, and he grins savagely.

"There's my girl. You don't know how long I've been waiting to hear that sound."

Oh. My. God.

"You like sucking my cock?"

I moan in acquiescence, and he curses, his body tight under my grasp.

I reach up with my other hand, teasing his balls. I move them around in my palm, and he groans, the sound reverberating through him. He widens his stance, his fingers tightening in my hair until he's controlling the movement, fucking my mouth.

My eyes sting, my tears mixing with the water slipping over us, but all I can think about is making him come. I suck in a deep breath through my nose, pushing further until I can feel him at the back of my throat. He takes away my air, and my body reacts, jerking under his grasp.

"You're going to make me come in this pretty little mouth, sweetheart." I pull back, choking when he releases me, stroking his cock and sucking in heaving breaths. "Want me to fuck your throat?"

I nod eagerly, wanting to feel him come undone for me. Closing my lips around him again, I release my hand on the base of his cock and press my fingers to his thighs. His hand tightens in my hair, and his other comes under my chin to hold me steady.

Then he's pushing past the confines of my mouth and into my throat. I choke around his cock, tears and saliva streaming down my face, but I don't think I've ever been this turned on in my life.

"That's it, baby girl. Open up for me. Make me come."

My stomach clenches at the nickname, and I blink up at him

through tears. He pushes harder, fucking into me deeply, and I only have a split second when I feel him swell in my mouth before he comes.

"*Fuck . . . Ava . . .*"

I swallow everything he gives me greedily, choking as it hits my throat. He pumps his hips into me, and I keep my gaze pinned to his, moaning with the vibrations of his body under my fingertips.

"Goddamn," he rasps, a shiver rolling through him. He lets go of my hair, but before I can fall back, he's reaching down and hauling me to my feet. His hands grip my ass, and he lifts me into his arms, my back hitting the cold tile behind me when his lips meet mine. He kisses me ferociously, both of us breathing heavily when he reaches between us, grips his cock, and slides it inside.

"Oh *my God,*" I whimper, my head falling back against the tile. Distantly, I register his fingers digging into my skin, his cock pushing inside me with a burn.

"Fuck, I love the little sounds you make," he growls in my ear. "Who makes you come, Ava?"

"You," I pant, my hands gripping his shoulders while he moves inside me. "Always you." His lips find mine again, and he swallows my cries while I beg him for more, knowing even as I do, it will never be enough.

CHAPTER
Thirty-Two

LEVI

I've officially lost my fucking mind.

"What's wrong with *The Beatles*?"

"Nothing if you like boring shit."

Ava smiles and swats my arm. I catch her hand and bring it to my mouth, nipping the pads of her fingers.

I can't deny I like the way her eyes light up when she laughs. Fuck, every time I look at her, it's hard to look away. I've caught myself staring, and I don't know if she's noticed or not, but I feel like a fucking creep.

How could I not stare?

She was handcrafted to perfection. Like she was made for me. Soft waves cascade down her back like rich, molten chocolate. Perfect ass underneath my sheets. Pretty green eyes boring into my soul with a lightness I haven't seen from her in a long time.

The once timid, broken girl I'd chased in the forest behind this house is learning to stand up for herself. It's like watching her come alive for the first time since I met her. She smiles more. Laughs more. She meets my gaze.

finding it harder and harder to ignore this innate desire to make her mine. Forever.

I can't, of course, but . . . the thought's there. Fucking festering.

Her fingers trace over the lines of my tattoos, where she lies on her stomach beside me. I don't mind coming home to this place every night, so long as she'll be here, ready to take the edge off.

I know, I know. It's toxic.

She's replacing the liquor, and the irony's not lost on me that I'm fucking addicted.

"What does this mean?" she asks softly.

I smirk, looking down at her fingers.

No one's asked me that question in a long time.

"I got it when I was seventeen. It's Latin."

She peeks up at me, her fingers stalling.

"So, what does it mean?"

"It was a dare."

She fixes me with an amused look.

"It's something vulgar, isn't it?"

"It's supposed to mean 'go fuck yourself'."

To my surprise, she grins, shaking her head.

"I should have known. I wonder how many people have thought it was some profound statement."

"Probably a lot more than I care to admit."

"I always wanted a tattoo," she says with a shrug. "But I'm too indecisive."

"Tattoos don't have to have meaning. It's just skin."

She's quiet, her brows knitted together in thought.

"I always admired my mother's tattoo when I was a kid. It wasn't perfect. Just a heart with a ribbon surrounding it. But it had my name. Ava Lynn . . . I don't know. It just felt special."

"When was the last time you spoke to her?"

She stares at me for a moment, her eyes sad.

"I can't remember. It would have been years ago, at this point."

324

She gives me a soft smile that makes my chest ache. "Since she left me with Gran to go 'find herself', our relationship hasn't been the same."

"So did she?"

"Did she what?"

"Find herself."

She chuckles under her breath. "Yeah, she found herself in Bob and Tim and Domingo. Oh, and some man they called Cookie. Whatever the hell that means." She falls silent for a moment, toying with a loose thread in the comforter wrapped around her.

I slip down the bed, draping an arm over her.

I just fucked her, but the moment her eyes meet mine, soft and warm, I want her again. Just having her in my space fucks with my head. It's never enough. The moment I'm done, I'm already thinking about getting her back in my bed.

I don't want to admit it, but there's something about having her tangled up in my sheets, moaning my name, and clinging to me like I can bring her salvation that makes me think about all kinds of crazy shit I shouldn't.

Like how to keep doing it for the next fifty years while still keeping her at arm's length so she doesn't see the real monster hiding behind my eyes.

Like in those moments where it's just us, she's mine, and the world's not trying to rip her away from me at every turn.

"I'm jealous of you, you know?" she says softly.

"Why would you be jealous of me?"

"Because you have siblings. I was an only child," she says. "I used to dream about having a big family, big Christmases. It was always just Gran and me . . . I envy you."

I brush a lock of hair back from her eyes. *Without my grandmother, I'm alone.*

"Family's not always all it's cracked up to be."

Her brows knit together, her eyes full of sadness. I stroke my hand down her back and over the smooth skin of her ass, ignoring that look in her eyes.

"You never told me why you lost your job," she says finally, her voice soft. "Sorry, *left* your job . . ."

I sigh, looking down into her eyes. I almost lie, but something tells me this is one truth I can give her, so I do.

"I left my job because they made me choose between them and helping Christian save the only person he's ever loved."

"Mila?"

I nod once, brushing the hair back from her face.

"It was family or my career. I'll always chose family."

She's silent for a moment, processing what I'd said. I notice the way her brow furrows at the center like it always does when she's thinking hard about something.

"Who said what, Ava?"

Her brows knit together.

"What do you mean?"

"Today. What made you come find me?"

She blushes a deep shade of scarlet. "Maybe I just wanted to suck your dick."

The dick in question twitches, remembering her on her knees for me. I've been waiting for her to want it. Fucking dreaming of the day when she would willingly get on her knees and fully give herself over to me.

"While I'm flattered, I also know you better than that."

Her smile fades, and she continues to run her fingers over the tattoos on my chest. Like if she doesn't look at me, she won't have to tell me the truth.

"You know I'm going to find out one way or another. I always do."

She lets out a sigh, pursing her lips.

"I tried to talk to Alex today. You know, because I haven't spoken to him all week."

I hate that little fucker.

"And?"

She shrugs as if it's nothing. "He found out about our contract. He called me a whore."

I grit my teeth so hard they threaten to snap. Scratch that. I *loathe* that little fucker, and the day I throw him off my property will be the day I celebrate.

"Don't look like that."

"Like what?"

"Like you're thinking about killing him."

I cock a brow, brushing the hair back from her face. I'm so fucking irritated, I want to leave this bed right now, and dogwalk him off a cliff for daring to say something like that to her.

"Thought's crossed my mind."

She sighs, rolling over onto her back.

"He's not wrong," she muses. "I mean, I *am* technically your employee who's sleeping with you. I left him and came straight up here and climbed in the shower with you."

"Ava—"

"And what does it matter, anyway? Maybe I am. I mean, I agreed to have sex with you for money."

"Shut the fuck up," I snap.

She pauses, her gaze narrowing on mine.

"Don't be rude."

"No, you don't be cynical."

Her jaw feathers, and she looks away.

"He is right," I tell her, reaching for her chin. Looming over her, I turn her face to mine, searching her gaze. She's hurt, but she's trying to hide it. "You *are* my whore." She bristles at my words, her eyes shining in the fading light in my room. "You're also someone I can laugh with. Someone I can talk to—more than anyone else." *You make me want to be better* . . . "You may be my whore, Ava, but only because you want to be."

"You're just saying that to make me feel better," she grumbles, and I push her back, sliding over her to rest between her legs. Taking each of her hands in mine, I raise them above her head, pinning them to the mattress beside her head.

"I don't know what the fuck I'm doing with you half the time, but I know you mean a whole lot more to me than I ever planned."

She swallows thickly, and a shiver rolls through her. I roll my hips into her because even though I came twice, it's never enough.

It will never *be* enough.

"I know," she whispers, and I can feel her heart beating fast against my arm.

"Don't let someone who's not even fit enough to lick the bottom of your shoes tell you who you are, Ava. Not me. Not Mendez. Only you get to decide that."

She smiles softly, reaching up. She brushes her thumb over the scar on my lip, tracing it. I want to nip the pad of her thumb, but I don't, forcing myself to hold still.

"When are you going to learn there's so much more to you than you believe?" she whispers, and apprehension fills my chest.

She shakes her head, but I cut off whatever else she was about to say, pressing my lips to hers. It's different from what it usually is. Sweeter. Deadlier.

"Stay," I whisper against her lips.

"Okay."

The path that leads through the trees behind Cross Estate is a favorite of Ava's. She walks it every day on her break, but today, I'm taking it instead.

I've been watching him all week. Since he called my girl a whore, he hasn't so much as pissed without me knowing about it. There's something about him. Something that makes me uneasy. Like he's the closeted *cut your skin off and wear it as a skin-suit* type.

I don't want him anywhere near her, and today, I'm putting a stop to his little obsession.

I'm walking down the path when I hear a stick snap to my left. Immediately, my hand shoots out, wrapping around his throat and practically lifting him off his feet, where he just emerged from behind a tree.

"Hey, buddy. Fancy meeting you out here."

I shove him back into the bark with a thud, my hands fisting in his collar.

"What the fuck are you doing?" he grits, trying to shove me off. Unfortunately, he's a whole hell of a lot weaker than I am.

"I think I should be asking you that. Is there a reason you're sneaking around, trying to catch my girl alone?"

"Your girl?" he scoffs, jerking in my grasp. "You don't give a fuck about her. Don't pretend like you do."

"Is that so?"

"You only care about yourself and getting your dick wet. Ava means nothing to you. I heard all about your little contract."

"Ah, sneaking around my house often?" I step closer, lowering my voice. With each passing moment, his cheeks grow redder and redder, and I love that I'm getting under his skin. "Tell me, Alex. Have you heard the way she comes undone for me?"

"Fuck you," he growls under his breath.

"Have you listened to her beg for my cock and wondered what it would be like? To have her on her knees for you, willing to do whatever you ask because she wants you that badly?"

My fists vibrate with rage around his collar. I want to snap his neck for what he said to her. I want him crying in a puddle of his own urine for trying to catch her alone.

"What were you going to do when she came down the path?

Hmm, Alex? Going to beg for her to give you a chance? Tell her how bad you miss being eternally friend-zoned by the girl you practically pant after?"

"Let me go," he grits, attempting to shove away from the tree.

I press harder, knocking his head into the bark behind him. Whoops. I'm sure it killed a few brain cells. I'm not sure how many he has left.

"Let's get one thing straight, Alex," I murmur, keeping my voice low. Deadly. Alex actually shivers, his jaw clenching tightly. He looks around us, but the idiot doesn't realize Ava's actually at home getting ready right now, for us to head into town. She won't be taking a walk today. "The next time I catch you fucking with my girl. Waiting for her. Speaking to her. Hell, if you even breathe her name while you're fucking your own pathetic hand . . . I'll be there. Decide if it's worth it."

He doesn't respond, glowering at me like an insolent teenager caught sneaking out at night.

—So, I knock his head back into the tree again.

"Understood?"

He nods, and I release him, watching him fall to his knees and catch himself in the moss. Pity. I was hoping he'd land on a rock.

"You're fired."

"You think you can threaten me, Cross?" he sneers when I start to walk away. "People know where I am. My family will come looking for me."

I turn back to watch him struggle to his feet, a low, dark chuckle slipping past my lips.

The fucker thinks I haven't already thought of this?

"The funny thing is, when they do, there won't be anything left for them to find."

CHAPTER
Thirty-Three

LEVI

So, in this dream, what part do you play?"

Fuck me. Why'd I feel the need to mention the damn dream?

I should have just kept my mouth shut, but it slipped.

"She's yelling at me."

"Which one. The girl in the bed, or your mother?"

I run my tongue over my teeth.

"My mother."

Proctor nods, scribbling something down in his pad.

If you want the truth, I'm ready to get out of here and get back to my girl. The last couple days I've spent holed up in the cabin with her, but it's not enough. It's like my blood can sense her, and all I want to do is forget about this state-mandated therapy and go to her.

There's just one problem.

Every night, she's ripped away from me in my dreams.

"Why do you think your mother was there and not your father?"

"Are you being truthful, Levi?"

Jesus Christ.

I scrub a hand over my face, listening to the sound of the clock on the wall. I swear the fucking thing is the loudest clock I've ever heard.

"I don't know. Mom never did anything to me. She never hurt a fly."

Shouldn't have said that . . .

"Your father, though . . . he's a different story, isn't he?"

"Maybe."

Proctor closes his book, placing it on his lap.

"Levi, is it possible that you're imagining your mother in your father's place because you haven't accepted your father's death?"

"Oh, I know the fucker's dead." *I watched the life die in his eyes.*

"That's not what I mean. It could be that subconsciously, you're harboring resentment towards your mother for leaving you so soon. Perhaps for leaving you with an abusive father."

"I never said he was abusive."

"You didn't have to," Proctor counters.

Touché.

"Look," I sigh, ringing my hands in my lap. "My father was a dick. He used to beat my ass for anything he could. You want the truth? I'm glad the fucker's dead . . . but it has nothing to do with my mother."

"So, if it has nothing to do with your mother, perhaps it has to do with the girl? Do you know who she is?"

I swallow past the burn in my throat. "No."

"This girl . . . it could be a representation of someone you've failed. Perhaps your mother, though you were too young to do anything about your mother's death. This girl could be part of you that you're trying to save."

He has no fucking idea just how right he is. It's almost scary.

"Why would I picture my mother, though?"

I can't believe I'm asking him this, but I have to know. Since having the nightmare, I've thought about it nearly every night. I can't get it out of my head, no matter if I fall asleep next to Ava or alone. It's like my mind is hell-bent on torturing me with the images until I either go insane or drink myself to death.

Lately, the only way I can sleep and make sure I don't do something stupid is by downing a couple drinks before I climb into bed with her. If not, I wear myself out enough that I have no choice but to sleep through the night.

I know she's noticed the way my hands shake sometimes. How I'm never far from a bottle. I fucking hate it, but I feel powerless without it.

"I think you need to address the elephant in the room."

"Which is?"

Proctor eyes me, studying. I fucking hate it.

"Your parents failed you. In return, it created trauma that you are projecting into your life now. I'd say you need to go in that room where your father died, clear it out, and find a new purpose for it."

Immediately, I'm shaking my head.

"I'm not going in there."

"Then it will continue to haunt your nightmares until you do."

Fuck.

It would be simpler to slice that part of the house off. Blow the shit up so there's not a cold chance in hell that it can be used for anything, ever again.

"What am I supposed to put in there instead?"

Proctor shrugs, his eyes twinkling deviously. "Could be a library. A sitting room. Whatever your heart desires. What's important is replacing the bad memories of that space with good ones. Maybe even with this mystery girl you know nothing about."

Dick.

"Have you worked on the homework I gave you?"

No.

"Yeah, uh . . ." I haven't even thought about his bullshit homework. I clear my throat. Five things I'm grateful for. Fuck. "My house. My family. My car—"

Proctor holds up a hand, signaling me to stop.

"I don't want five material things you're grateful for. I want to hear about five feelings you're grateful for. Five things that resonate with you."

Jesus fucking Christ.

"What the hell does that even mean?"

"Think love, for instance. I'm grateful for my wife's unwavering love and support. Those are things that resonate with me on a deeper level than the material objects in my life that any act of God can take away at any moment."

The mention of love makes my skin bristle. Love's a bullshit excuse for two people to stay together even if they're miserable.

"I'm not in love."

"No?"

I don't like the way the fucker smirks at me.

"No."

"Well, perhaps one day."

"Perhaps not."

Proctor eyes me, challenging me. "So, this *mystery girl* . . . She means nothing to you?"

Fucking hell.

"You like to make shit difficult, don't you?"

He chuckles. I don't because I'm serious.

"I think it's important to note that this hatred for your father has built a wall around you. You've closed yourself off from what you think you can't have, which is the idea of love."

"Well, I think you're reading too much into it."

"Answer this for me. If she were gone tomorrow . . . Would you care?"

Possession burns in my chest.

Of course, I'd fucking care. I'd rip the world to shreds until I found her.

But . . . I'd do the same for Mila. Doesn't mean anything.

The buzzer dings, signifying our time is up. I stand, fixing him with a look, needing him to understand before I leave.

"I'm not in love."

He smiles, though I can see the challenge behind it.

"Whatever you say, Levi."

"You don't have to do this."

Ava's voice is barely above a whisper, taut with nerves. She pulls me to a stop outside her grandmother's door, glancing around nervously. Her face has gone a shade paler, like she might be physically ill right here in the hallway.

"Why wouldn't I?"

She opens her mouth, like she might argue, but nothing comes out. Her throat bobs, and for a second, I think she might bolt. But I don't give her the chance. I lace my fingers through hers and gently push the door open.

The room smells faintly of lavender and something sterile, like antiseptic and old cotton. A heart monitor beeps quietly in the background, the only sign of time passing in a place where it feels like everything is frozen. The woman in the bed looks up as we enter. Her skin is paper-thin and spotted, her body so frail beneath the covers that she barely seems to make a dent in the mattress.

She smiles kindly when she sees me, but her face doesn't light up until she sees Ava come in behind me.

"There's my girl," she says, her voice thin but warm. Ava moves past me, going to the side of the bed, and leans in to wrap her arms carefully around the small, fragile woman.

"I missed you," Ava murmurs, her voice caught somewhere between joy and guilt. "How are you feeling?"

"Never mind that," her grandmother says, brushing the question off with a wave of her hand. "Who's your friend, Ava? Don't be rude."

Ava's cheeks flush so bright, you'd be able to see them from space.

"Uh, Gran, this is Levi. My, uh . . ."

"Boyfriend," I finish for her smoothly, offering the old woman a smile as I step forward.

Ava gawks at me, eyes wide, but Gran lets out a triumphant little wolf-whistle.

"Finally," she grins. "You must be the Cross boy. She's told me all about you—"

"No, I haven't," Ava lies, embarrassed. I can't help but smirk at her. It's cute, in an *I want to tie her down and fuck her until she agrees to be mine forever* kind of way.

Gran doesn't miss a beat. "You know, I've been telling her she needs to date you for a long time."

Interesting.

Ava shoots me a look that could peel paint off a car.

"Gran," she groans, her voice laced with mortification. I chuckle under my breath, moving over to the side of the bed.

"Is that right? You and I should talk, Gran," I say, giving the old woman a wink.

"Let's not," Ava mutters, hiding her face behind her hands.

"I can see where Ava gets her good looks from," I add, and Gran gives a tired but genuine smile. It reaches her eyes this time—but only just. There's a heaviness behind it, a shadow of weariness that I couldn't see the last time I saw her.

It hits me then. She looks worse. Paler. Smaller. Like the sickness is winning, and she knows it.

A knot tightens in my gut. I wonder—not for the first time—what it'll do to Ava when she's gone.

Gran's all I have left . . .

"For you," I say, handing her the pink roses in my hand. Ava said they were her favorite. I don't know much about how to keep a woman happy, but I do know most like flowers. Why the fuck do you think I picked up lilies for Ava?

"*Levi* wanted to meet you," Ava says, brushing past me. "I tried to talk him out of it."

"Oh, please," Gran waves her hand. "I'm a national treasure. Of course, he'd want to meet me."

Ava starts to speak, but a knock at the door interrupts whatever she was about to say.

"Ava, good to see you," says a woman in scrubs as she walks in, clipboard in hand. I assume she's a nurse—probably mid-forties. She stops dead in her tracks when she sees me.

"Oh, I wasn't aware you'd brought someone with you."

"Levi Cross," I say, reaching out to shake her hand.

Her cheeks flush slightly, and she gives me a quick, appreciative once-over before smiling. "Well, aren't you the charmer?" she teases, stepping back. "You must be Ava's boyfriend."

"No," Ava chimes, but everyone ignores her.

"Yes."

Ava lets out a strangled sound, her mouth opening in horror as her blush deepens.

The nurse chuckles. "Well, Mr. Cross, it was a pleasure to meet you. Ava, can I steal you for a moment? I've got some treatment information to go over."

Ava looks at me, her expression tightening with concern.

Without thinking, I tilt her chin up gently, brushing my thumb along her jaw before leaning down and pressing a soft kiss on her forehead.

"I'll be fine," I murmur. "Go take care of what you need to."

She lingers for a moment, her eyes searching mine. Then, she nods and follows the nurse out of the room, leaving Gran and me alone.

"Well, you may as well sit down. I'm sure they're discussing end-of-life care, or whatever the hell they call it."

I take the seat next to her, unsure what the fuck I'm supposed to say in a situation like this.

"I want to thank you, by the way."

I cock a brow, confused.

"For taking care of her. She wouldn't come out and say it, but I know she was struggling."

"Don't mention it," I murmur gruffly. I wish I'd done it sooner.

"She's always been a quiet girl. Never was much for parties or crowds. I suppose when the first decade of your life is chaos, you learn to avoid it."

"Sounds like she's only really ever had you."

"And you . . . She likes you," Gran says, her voice softer now. Quieter. Like she's telling me a secret.

I nod slowly.

There's something I want to say—but I can't. The words are right there, burning the tip of my tongue, but they don't come out.

"Some might even say love."

My grip tightens on the armrests of the chair. The word hits me like a sucker punch.

Love.

Why the fuck is everyone accusing me of being in love lately? I'm a grown man, for Christ's sake.

I'm not in love.

I'm obsessed.

They aren't the same.

I'm not planning a future. I'm not building dreams. I'm just holding onto a moment I already know will slip through my fingers. Ava Ryan may be mine right now, but one day, she'll belong to someone else.

I've known that from the beginning . . . so why the fuck does it feel like I took a knife to the ribs now?

"Some might," I grunt, suddenly too warm. It feels like the walls are closing in on me. Or maybe it's just the guilt.

Maybe it's the pit of hell opening up underneath me for ever thinking I deserved her. Fuck, it wouldn't surprise me at this point.

I've never deserved Ava. Especially not with the laundry list of secrets I'm keeping. Sooner or later, she'll learn the truth, and God help me when she does because I don't stand a fucking chance.

Gran watches me closely. She doesn't smile this time. Instead, she twists the rose in her hands—absently, thoughtfully.

"You know, Levi," she begins, voice turning serious, "I remember when Ava was a little girl. She was always so cautious. Always holding back. Even as she got older, she stayed in the background. Quiet and careful."

I swallow against the lump rising in my throat. This is *that* talk—the one I've never wanted to have. The one where you meet someone who finally realizes you're not enough.

"That's changed recently," she says, locking eyes with me. "She's coming into herself. I wonder why that is."

I glance toward the door. Ava's just outside, talking to the nurse, her expression bright and animated in a way I rarely see.

And for some reason, I can't look away.

"She's learning to take care of herself," I say, my voice low.

"When her mother met her father, I was ecstatic. A wealthy heir who seemed to worship the ground she walked on. But . . . like all roses, they have a way of cutting you when you least expect it. That man is trouble. Not only to my daughter . . . but to his, as well."

"What do you mean?"

Her eyes grow wary, and she glances at the door.

"Let's just say money can buy anything, but that doesn't mean it should." She lowers her voice, leaning closer. "You'll protect her, if it comes to that. Won't you?"

I swallow past the lump in my throat as lead fills my chest.

"I will."

"There are things in this life she's not ready for," Gran continues. Her tone has shifted—no more teasing, no more soft smiles. Just raw truth. "And I'm only saying this because I might not get another chance."

Here we go . . .

"She's got a soft heart, Levi. Always has. But she's never quite known where to put it. If you're not going to stick around—if this is temporary for you—then leave now. Because that girl's already falling for you."

She pauses, holding my gaze with iron resolve.

"I'd hate to see her crash."

CHAPTER
Thirty-Four

AVA

I always liked looking at the city from afar."

Levi glances over at me from the other side of his car, the faint glow of the dashboard casting sharp angles across his face. His expression is unreadable, as always — a locked vault behind glacier-blue eyes.

After we left Gran, we went and got cheap fast food and soda that's probably laced with chemicals. Now, we're sitting up on the overlook above the city. The food is delicious and there's a calm I'm not used to hanging in the air. For the first time in my life, I feel . . . normal. Like an average twenty-something-year-old out with her boyfriend for a midnight snack.

Sure, he's not my boyfriend, and sure, there's the distinct crushing feeling of dread always at the back of my mind, but for once, it's not so loud. For once, leaving Gran, I don't feel like I'm leaving behind a piece of myself.

"Just a bunch of buildings," Levi murmurs, leaning against the car door like he's trying to disappear into the night. "I've always preferred the forest."

He doesn't respond right away, but then his voice drops even lower.

"Yeah . . . the silence."

We sit like that for a while — two figures parked on the edge of the world, suspended above the city lights. From up here, everything seems quieter. The chaos is distant, softened into something almost beautiful. But I know better. I know what kind of ugliness hides behind those golden windows.

Like whatever's on Levi's mind. He's been quiet since we left Pleasant Oaks, and I can't help but worry it's too much for him.

My life, my problems. This contract. Maybe the end is close, and I'm just too naïve to recognize when it's time to walk away.

"It's because of your childhood," I say after a long moment. I glance at him, half-expecting his walls to go up. But I need him to know, I see him. That I understand him, even if he doesn't say it out loud. "That's why you prefer the forest. The silence."

Levi doesn't answer right away, but when I look over, I find him already watching me. There's something soft in his eyes — not quite vulnerability, but whatever comes before it.

"I feel the same way."

He turns away, focusing again on the lights below like he's trying to read something in the distance.

"The cabin was always my place when I needed to get away," he says finally. "Still is."

A quiet falls over us again, heavier this time. I shift in my seat, heart drumming with the weight of what I want to say next.

"Your father . . ." I begin, the words cautious, careful. "He wasn't a good man, was he?"

Levi goes still. The kind of still that makes your skin crawl, like something just slipped under the surface.

"If you're asking if he was an abusive prick? Yeah . . . He was."

I shake my head, picturing William Cross in his younger years— bitter, sharp-tongued, hollowed out by his own hatred. If he was that cruel as a dying man, I can't imagine what he was like in his prime.

"Can I ask a question?"

Levi doesn't respond. I take a breath, nerves trembling in my chest. His silence stretches a beat too long before he answers.

"Yes."

I brace myself, trying to make the words come out right.

"How did you . . . survive him?"

Levi's eyes flicker —not in anger, but something deeper. Something like disbelief.

"I'm just asking because he was cruel even when he was sick. The things he'd say to me when I cleaned . . ." My voice catches. "I can't imagine living with him when he could use his fists."

He breathes out through his teeth, slow and deliberate.

"I don't know," he says. "Guess I was just too stubborn. I'd take the beatings, and when I didn't make a sound, it just pissed him off. So . . . he'd go harder."

The image pierces me like glass — Levi as a boy, silent through pain he didn't deserve. My throat tightens, tears stinging in the corners of my eyes.

"That's horrible," I whisper.

He shrugs, like it's nothing. As if it hadn't shaped every piece of who he is.

"It was life. For as long as I could remember." He pauses, jaw tightening. "I think he hated me because I looked like him. I reminded him of everything he couldn't stand about himself. And he couldn't tolerate being wrong. Ever."

I stare at him, seeing that boy — all inky black hair and frosty blue eyes, and my heart threatens to crack open.

"I could never understand why Mom stayed with him."

"She knew?"

He shrugs. "Some of it."

A swell of rage rises in me. Not just at the man who hurt him, but at the woman who let it happen. Who saw and chose to look away. I don't care what reasons she had—fear, money, love. None of them are good enough.

If my child was being abused, there's nothing in the world that would stop me from protecting them. Even their father.

Levi shifts, eyes narrowing just slightly, as if he can read my mind.

"Don't look at me like that, Ava."

I meet his gaze. It's hard and sharp, but I see what's behind it — the part of him that still wants to believe she did the best she could.

"Sorry," I say. "Just thinking."

"About?" he asks, voice lower now.

I shrug. "What it would be like to have a normal family."

"What—two parents?"

"Two *loving* parents," I correct.

Levi says nothing.

"Having a loving family doesn't make life perfect," I go on, "but it makes things easier. At least you'd know someone had your back."

He turns to me then, the shadows on his face deepening.

"People leave, Ava. No one is permanent."

My chest aches. Finally, I understand the contract—the boundaries, the rules. This distance he insists on keeping. It isn't coldness. It's fear. He's been abandoned so many times, he'd rather push people away than risk being left again.

"What about just one person who understands you?" I ask, my voice barely above a whisper.

The silence that follows feels louder than anything else.

I surprise us both when I rise, my breath catching as I shift over the center console and slide into his lap. Levi doesn't stop me. He leans back slightly, his eyes trailing up my body like a flame tracing a fuse—slow and hot. When our gazes finally collide, something unspoken passes between us, electric and weighty.

Then I see it—just a flicker, but it's there. The subtle bob of his throat as he swallows. A moment of vulnerability, as if I've touched something deep inside him. Like he's fighting the urge to give in.

Like I could have anything I asked for, anything at all. All I have to do is say the words.

"Don't you want someone to love you unconditionally?" I ask, my voice barely above a whisper as my hands trail down his chest.

A muscle twitches in his jaw. "Not all of us are so lucky, baby girl."

He says it like it's a fact of life. Like he's already decided that kind of love isn't meant for him. His eyes—ice-blue and to my peridot green—search mine.

The air in the car feels alive, humming with something neither of us dares to name. A quiet moment stretches between us, and then—

"You—"

But I never get to finish.

His mouth crashes onto mine, cutting me off mid-thought, mid-breath. And just like that, my world tilts. Heat blooms through me, scorching and all-consuming. His kiss is rough and hungry, like he's starving. Like this kiss is the only thing anchoring him to the present. To me.

And I realize—this is dangerous. I'm in too deep. I'm slipping into something I swore I'd avoid. I told myself I wouldn't fall. That I couldn't afford to. But how could I not?

Levi Cross is like the first breath after nearly drowning—gasping, desperate, necessary. He's fire in my bloodstream, oxygen in my lungs, a lighthouse in the dark. He's every daydream I clung to as a scared little girl, wishing for someone, *anyone*, to keep me safe. To choose me.

He's everything. And he doesn't even know it.

His hands trail down my back, firm and possessive, before gripping my ass and hauling me closer. He groans into my mouth—a low, guttural sound that shoots straight through me. There's a tremble in his fingers, a tension in his body that says he's holding back more than he's letting on. He clutches me like he's afraid I'll disappear, like he's already lost me once and won't survive losing me again.

I roll my hips over him, sighing softly at the friction.

"Goddamn, baby," he rasps.

When he drags me flush against his chest, his kiss deepens. Hot. Desperate. Like I'm the only thing that's ever made him feel alive.

"Ava . . ." he breathes, lips ghosting down my jaw and to the soft skin of my neck.

"Yeah?" My voice is hoarse, trembling. The windows are fogging up from our breath, our shared heat turning the car into a cocoon.

"I . . ." His voice cracks on the word. He falters. I lean back slightly, fingers brushing the scar etched into his bottom lip—the one I've traced in my dreams more times than I can count.

"I know," I whisper.

His eyes lock on mine, dark and unflinching, and for a moment I swear I see every wall he's ever built start to crack.

There's a softness there—raw, unguarded—that makes my breath hitch.

The tension shifts—still charged, but different now, sweeter and heavier all at once. He exhales like I've just knocked the wind out of him. His thumb traces the curve of my cheek, lingering before sliding down to the corner of my mouth. I kiss the pad of it, tasting the faint salt of his skin.

Levi leans in, so close I can feel the heat radiating from him, his breath fanning over my lips. "Whatever happens, you're not alone. You know that, right?"

My heart beats unsteadily in my chest, my mind at war with itself.

"When will you realize the same thing?"

I lean forward, pressing my body flush against his, while his hands roam. The movement draws a low, involuntary groan from his chest—one that vibrates straight through me.

He kisses me again, slower this time, deep and deliberate, like he's savoring every second. My fingers thread into his hair, tugging just enough to pull another sound from him—half growl, half plea.

"You drive me fucking crazy," he mutters against my lips.

"And you like it," I breathe.

He grins—sinful and tender all at once—before pulling me back into another kiss, one that feels like a promise and a warning tangled together.

CHAPTER
Thirty-Five

AVA

My grandmother's funeral comes on a bleak and snowy Wednesday afternoon.

The flurries from overhead do nothing but remind me that life moves on as I stand and look down at the casket in front of me.

My grandmother's in that box. The vessel that used to hold the most important person in the world now sits empty.

She's gone. At least that's what they tell me. It just hasn't sunk in yet.

When I got the call at three in the morning two nights ago, it woke Levi. I think he believes I'm losing my mind because I haven't cried yet. I can't.

I'm just . . . numb.

The cold on the outside doesn't bother me. The cold on the inside doesn't bother me.

Death has a funny way of showing us what our bodies can handle mentally. Grief is something I've never experienced to this magnitude, and yet, I feel nothing at all.

cry my eyes out, but not being able to shed a single tear.

I'm sure most think I'm heartless.

I've seen the whispers from my family. The people I haven't spoken to in years.

Cousins, aunts, uncles, and God knows who else have gathered today, but there's one person in particular I've steered clear of.

Rebecca Ryan stands across from me with a new boyfriend on her arm, as unfeeling as I am. She's glanced at me one time, though she hasn't said a word to me since I've been standing here.

We may as well be complete strangers standing in line across from one another in a grocery store.

That's fine. She's done nothing to deserve to be here, but who am I to play judge and jury for a woman who's dead and doesn't care anymore?

Still . . . I hate her.

Levi either doesn't notice her or doesn't care. He's been quiet, standing beside me while they read off some pieced-together eulogy of my grandmother's life.

They always leave out the nasty bits. Like how she had to raise me because her daughter failed. How she took in all the local strays because, in her words, no one else would. The way she wasn't like other grandmas who bake cookies and watch Jeopardy every day.

She was completely and authentically herself.

Now she's nothing.

As I'm standing there, Levi's arm wraps around my waist, but he doesn't say a word. I'm grateful for him, though I know his being here goes against everything we agreed upon. He hasn't mentioned it and neither have I, but there's a sinking feeling in my stomach I'd prefer not to dwell on.

It's not until halfway through the service that someone's hand slides into mine, and I look over to see Mila standing beside me. She gives me a soft smile and a gentle squeeze, and for the first time in a long time, I don't feel so lonely.

Beyond her, the rest of the Cross family has arrived, all silent as they listen to the pastor's service. I didn't even see them arrive.

Shamefully, I want to cry because I feel accepted. Not because my grandmother's dead.

I want to cry because even Paulina showed up, dressed in her mourning clothes as she would for someone she's known her entire life.

Christian, Bella, Mila, Paulina. . . the whole family came in support, and it sends a chill through me knowing that at least for these few moments, I'm not alone.

I lean on Mila's support through the service, knowing that if I chose to lean on Levi, it would only cloud this thing between us even more, and I don't need any help in that department.

He remains beside me through the entire speech. Through the harrowing moment when we toss dirt on the casket, then finally, when we make our way across the lawn to the church where the after-party of death is being held.

I don't want to go. I don't feel like celebrating the death of someone who deserved to live for eternity. I'm not hungry. I don't know most of these people, and all I want to do is go home, but I know Gran deserves more than that, so I go anyway.

I feel someone's eyes on me as I make my way through the tombstones, and suddenly, Levi's pulling me to a stop in front of a pair of shiny shoes. My gaze travels over him to the older man standing in front of me, who's looking at me with a slightly disturbed look in his gaze. Like he wasn't expecting to see me here, even though there's nowhere else I'd be right now.

"Ava," he greets, holding out his hand. "Nolan. I was a friend of your grandmother's. I wanted to offer my condolences."

I pause, letting him shake my hand, though I feel like I'm under a stormy cloud that's threatening to drown me at any moment.

All I can do is stare blankly at him.

"Ava's had a long day," Levi grits, his voice rougher than usual, as if he's conveying some secret message to the stranger. "I'm sure she appreciates your presence."

I don't understand the meaning behind that statement, but I don't care either. Right now, all I care about is getting this done and over with so I can go home and climb into bed.

The two men stare each other down, but I'm in no mood to play peacekeeper, so I release Levi's hand and walk away without a word.

Sometimes, you just don't feel like speaking to anyone.

It's not until I'm in the bathroom, taking a few moments to breathe and clear my head, that the door opens and I finally come face to face with my mother for the first time in six years.

"Ava," she greets, as cold and unfeeling as ever on the day we buried her mother.

"Mother."

"It's good to see you." I can tell by the tone of her voice that it's not.

Rebecca Ryan was never meant to be a mother. She hates children with a fiery passion, and she hated *me* even more because I was a reminder that my father didn't stick around.

"I was surprised you came," I say without thinking. Is it rude? Yes. Do I care? Not anymore.

"She's my mother."

"She was sick for two years. Was she not your mother, then?"

"You don't understand the bond between a mother and daughter."

"You're right," I retort. "I don't."

"I see you've found another family to mooch off of."

"I see you haven't."

She glares at me. I glare back.

"Why are you here, *Rebecca*? To stir up trouble?"

"I'm *here* because my mother died, Ava. Do I need a reason?"

"You two haven't spoken in years, and you expect me to believe you care *now*? After you told her you hoped she'd rot in hell for embarrassing you when she took me?"

"Yes, it's always about you, isn't it?"

"On the contrary, I think it's always been about *you*, hasn't it?"

"You don't know what I had to put up with from you."

"No, I guess I don't. In between your stream of men and your neglectful parenting style, I'm guessing I must have forgotten to remember how I ruined your life when Dad left."

"You know *nothing* about your father," she hisses. "He was a spineless narcissist who knocked me up and left me with *you*."

"Well, I guess it's a good thing you no longer have to worry about me, isn't it?"

"Of course," she snaps, and although I'm used to the animosity in her words, I have to admit, the bitterness still stings. "Sign over my rightful property, and we'll be done here. You'll be free to go back to your party, and Brad and I will leave."

I freeze. "What property?"

She looks at me like I've grown three heads.

"The house, of course."

We both turn to look at the door, and Brad's stepping inside. It's the women's restroom, but he doesn't seem to give a damn.

He looks like he's around my age. Maybe a little older. Regardless, he's half my mother's age and looks like the type that would buy minors beer at the local liquor store. Not to mention, he smells like he lit a pack of cigarettes and smoked them all at once.

"Your mother is Della's next of kin, is she not?"

"No," I snap, shooting him a look. I mean, honestly, who does he think he is? "She's not. Gran named me her power of attorney." I turn back to my mom, tears burning in the backs of my eyes. "The woman just died three days ago, and you're already homing in on her house?"

"Don't act like you've got the means to use it. It should go to me. I grew up there."

"So did I," I fire back.

Mom takes the rolled-up papers out of Brad's hand and steps over, placing them on the counter in front of me.

"Just sign the papers, and we never have to see each other again."

I take a step back. Both advance like vipers ready to strike.

"No."

Brad moves closer, a sadistic glint in his eyes.

"Just do it for your mom, sweetie."

"Get the hell away from me."

"Sign the papers, Ava," my mother growls, while Brad inches closer, crowding over me.

Sickness pools in my stomach, and I jump when I'm backed into a corner.

Oh, this is bad.

A shadow passes over us, and I flinch.

One moment, my mother's boyfriend is in my face. The next, I'm staring at the broad shoulders of a man who shouldn't bring me this much comfort, but who feels like a life raft in the middle of the sea.

Levi . . .

"Ava's not signing anything for you," he says, his tone laced with darkness.

Relief washes over me, even as he gets right in Brad's face, forcing him to back up.

He falls back a few steps, glaring at him, but even I can see the fear in his beady gaze.

"Give me the contract."

"This doesn't concern you," my mother snaps, her cheeks flaming red.

Levi chuckles darkly, taking another step forward. Brad falls back into the wall.

"*Everything* she does concerns me. You've got DEA and FBI here, right now. You really want to fuck around?"

Christian stands at the doorway, blocking Brad from leaving, and he cocks his head as if daring him to try.

My mother glares at both men before she shoves the contract into Levi's chest. I watch in awe when he takes it, holding it up in front of her face, and rips it right down the center.

He drops it at his feet in a desecrated pile, his voice dropping so low, I can barely hear him.

"Let this be a warning. Don't come near her again."

Both my mother and Brad freeze, neither moving. The only sound in the room is the racing of my heartbeat and the steady drip of the faucet.

It's the most human I've felt in two days.

"Come on," Levi says, finally stepping back. He holds his hand out to me, which I graciously accept. "I'm taking you home."

───────────

The ride home is silent, filled with nothing but the steady whir of the heat going in the car.

It's hot, but I barely feel it. Unfortunately, the cold lies somewhere much deeper.

Levi keeps glancing at me, that indifferent look I've come to grow used to doing nothing but grinding my nerves because he doesn't seem to understand I don't want him to look at me.

I don't want anything. All I need is to sink inside myself and huddle up in bed, ignoring that the world exists.

I don't know how to navigate this . . . this *hole* that's aching in my chest.

No one ever tells you how to handle death. I don't think anyone honestly knows. Even if it comes slowly, it's a shock every time.

I didn't even realize we hadn't gone home until Levi put the car in park and I looked up to see the cabin.

I'd dozed off on the ride, my head resting on my elbow on the window.

I can't even be angry. With any luck, he'll leave me here and let me wallow in my own self-pity because I don't want him to see me this way.

See the broken girl that I hide so well. The one whose mother is an awful person, and whose father couldn't even be bothered to stick around.

I don't want Levi to know *that* Ava. The one who hated her life growing up because it was never hers. The one who was so scared of anyone and everything that she would rather hide out in her room than chance facing the world outside.

I don't want him to know the real me.

"Come on," he says, his voice quiet and rough. He slides out of the car without another word, and he's already at my door by the time I reach for the handle.

He holds out his hand, helping me out of the car, and I release it the moment I have my footing.

His touch *burns*, and for the first time, I'm realizing it's not because I need him to fuck me.

It's because I need him to *love* me.

God . . . how pathetic.

I've fallen in love with Levi Cross.

The only problem is that he will never love me back, and that might be the hardest pill to swallow.

Not everyone you fall for is good for you. Just like not everyone you fall for will feel the same.

Sooner or later, he'll realize and send me on my way. Just another statistic in the long line of women who thought they'd be different, and in the end, found out they're nothing more than a number.

Levi leads me into the cabin and immediately crosses over to the fireplace. With the overcast day outside, the cabin is dark, but I don't mind because it matches my mood.

When he's done, he stands back and crosses back to the door, stepping back outside without a word.

I stare at the flames crackling in the fireplace, my feet rooted in place while a few stray tears manage to break free and slip down my cheeks.

I'm alone.

Gran's gone. I'll never get to hear her sing along to Elvis anymore. I'll never hand out Halloween candy and dress up with her. She'll never get to see me get married or meet her great-grandchildren.

She won't exist in my life after this.

"*Ava.*"

I hadn't even realized Levi was standing behind me.

I don't care.

I think it's finally hit me.

I turn over my shoulder, and his stare is dark as he watches the tears cascade down my cheeks.

"Gran's dead," I croak, my voice barely above a whisper.

And then I break down.

Everything I've been ignoring the last couple days finally hits all at once, and I can't hold back anymore.

Pain, unlike anything I've ever felt, blooms in my chest, and my throat closes up when a sob breaks free.

Levi is by the door one second, and the next, he's grabbing me around the waist, hauling me up into his arms.

I don't want to cry on him, but I can't help it. I sob against his chest when he sinks to the couch, and cling to him like he's a life raft that will save me from drowning.

"Shhh . . . baby," Levi breathes against my hair, unmoving as he holds me. "I've got you."

I close my eyes, finally succumbing to the anguish, the dull roar drowning out everything else.

Levi doesn't speak, even if I could have sworn I heard him say, "I'll always have you."

God, I wish that were true.

CHAPTER
Thirty-Six

LEVI

I open my eyes to the sound of the fire crackling in the fireplace in front of us. I'm lying on my side; one arm draped over Ava's waist while the other is underneath her neck. She sleeps softly, breathing even, and her back pressed against my front.

Looking at the old clock on the wall, I can see I've only been asleep for an hour. When she stopped crying and fell asleep in my arms, I couldn't bring myself to give her up, so I just held her while she let me.

I bury my face in the side of her neck and press a soft kiss to her skin, committing the scent of lavender and citrus to memory in case someone tries to steal her away from me.

Ava's always been the unobtainable. The woman put on this earth to remind me I'll never be the man she deserves.

It's never bothered me as much as it does right now.

"Levi?" she breathes, her voice soft and full of sleep. I tighten my arms around her, knowing now that she's awake, she'll try to pull away from me.

It seems the only time I can give in to the fantasy that she's

Surprisingly, though, she doesn't pull away. Instead, she turns over in my arms to face me, her gaze shining in the moonlight streaming through the windows.

The couch is small and old. Highly uncomfortable, and there's definitely not enough room for both of us, but I still pull her closer, not quite ready to give her up.

Reaching up, I brush a lock of hair back from her face.

"Hi, little ghost."

Her lips purse, concern etched into her pretty face while she studies me. Her hand slips up my chest, and I hope to God she can't feel my heart racing under her fingers.

"I'm sorry for crying all over you," she says quietly.

I have no idea what to say to make her feel better, so I say the only thing that comes to mind.

"It's okay."

She doesn't seem to like that answer and frowns, a crease forming between her brows.

Her hand cups my cheek, her thumb brushing over the scar on my lip.

I know what she's thinking. How much she doesn't know about me. How much I've kept hidden from her. It's for the best, but she doesn't see that.

Her eyes are half-lidded and hazy when her tongue darts out to lick her lips, and I can't help but follow the movement with my gaze, desire slipping through my veins.

Without a word, she leans up and presses her lips against mine. I'm still trying to decide whether I should let this continue or be the good guy and stop it.

My hand slides into her hair, angling her head back, and I press my lips fully against hers, drinking her in.

She moans quietly against my mouth, and I know without a doubt, she's got me by the fucking balls.

She attempts to slip her hand down my chest, going for the

button on my jeans, but I catch her wrist, stopping her.

"Ava."

"Please," she whispers, trying to press her lips to the hollow below my jaw. A shiver ghosts through me, and I force her back.

"This isn't what this was about," I grit, trying to keep my voice gentle.

"Please, Levi," she whispers, and I watch a tear slip down her cheek. "I just want to forget."

"Baby girl, you're playing a dangerous game."

"I just want to forget," she whispers, again, tugging her hand away from me.

She slips it down, cupping my cock through my slacks, and I grit my teeth at how fucking good it feels. I'll never push her to do anything but fuck if I haven't missed her these last three days.

"Just for a little bit."

"Ava," I grit, laying my forehead against hers. *Christ, this woman's going to be the death of me.* "I can't take the pain away."

"No," she breathes, stroking my cock in slow, painfully fucking slow movements. "But you're the only one who can make me forget . . . even if only for a little while."

And then it occurs to me.

I'd take everything she's feeling right now, if I could. All the pain, guilt, shame, sadness. Fucking all of it, and it wouldn't matter to me because she'd be happy.

Fuck, what has she done to me?

"Please," she exhales against my lips when I catch her hand.

"Shhh . . ." I slip down on the couch, pressing a kiss to her cheek, her neck, the top of her breast peeking out from underneath her dress. I move lower, climbing down the couch until I'm sliding my hands up the outsides of her thighs. She's so soft and warm, all I want to do is slip inside her and forget the world exists, but that isn't what this is about.

I slip her dress up to bunch around her waist, and the moment my tongue slips through her folds, I let out a groan. Ava's breath stutters, her body arching off the couch and into my mouth.

I swirl my tongue through her sweetness, nibbling on her clit and drawing those little sounds from her that drive me fucking crazy.

"Levi," she murmurs, her eyes finding mine.

I break away, slipping a finger inside her and grinning at the way her eyes threaten to roll back.

"What, baby?"

"You're being so sweet."

"Am I not allowed to be sweet to my girl?" I rasp, angling that finger up to brush over that sensitive spot inside her.

"Not right now," I shudder, and I notice the way her hand fists in the material of the couch. "Right now, I want to be your whore."

Fuck. Me.

I run my tongue over my teeth, slipping my fingers out of her.

"You want to be my whore, baby girl."

Instantly, her eyes change. From sad and soft, to warm and needy.

"Yes," she breathes.

"Then sit on my face."

She freezes, her eyes widening.

"What?"

I fall back against the other side of the couch. "Get up here." I don't leave room for any arguments.

Heat floods her gaze, her cheeks darkening in the pale glow of the lamp in the corner of the room.

Carefully, she crawled up my body, and when she gets close enough, I grab her hips and tug her onto my mouth.

She yelps, her hands fisting the shoulder of the couch above my head, and just when she's about to open her mouth to speak, I silence her by tugging her up by the hips and sucking her clit into my mouth.

"Oh my fucking God," she gasps, scrambling to find purchase while I feast on her.

I fight a smile on my lips at her dirty words, and swirl my tongue through her wetness, devouring her in the only way I know how.

Her hand winds into my hair, fisting on the dark roots, and she meets the thrust of my tongue. Her breathless little moans fill the cabin, met with my rough breaths as I give her exactly what she needs. What we both need.

The need to claim her, show her she's mine in every way, as much as I'm hers, burns through me, so hot that I don't even stop when she's grinding against my tongue. Her thighs clench around my head, her hand tightens in my hair, and her arousal coats my tongue.

"Levi, I'm going to come," she whimpers desperately, but I don't stop. Not until her sweet moans fill the cabin and her legs are shaking with the orgasm that rips through her.

"That's my girl," I coax, dragging her back down to the couch cushions.

She's still shivering when I roll her onto her back and slip between her legs. My lips crash against her, and her tongue dances across her wetness on my mouth.

"Levi," she breathes against my lips when she slides her hand between us.

"I know, baby," I murmur, pressing my lips back to hers with a groan when she manages to wrap her fingers around my length.

I barely get my cock out before I'm falling back over her and pushing inside her.

Fuck, it'll never be enough.

Clenching my teeth, I fill her until there's nothing left of me to give. Until my balls brush against her ass and she's whimpering beneath me, her back arching off the couch.

"So beautiful," I murmur, taking her hands in mine and pressing them against the cushions beside her head.

Leaning down, I press my lips against her racing pulse and start to move, loving the soft moan that slips from her lips.

"Whose pussy is this, Ava?" I ask, my voice breathless in her ear.

"Yours."

Her body shivers against mine, and I thrust harder, the sound of my balls hitting her ass filling the room.

"Who fucks you?"

"You."

Who do you belong to?

"Fuck, Ava."

I release her wrists and grip her hips, tugging her up into my lap and pressing her front to mine. My hand fists in her hair and holds her there while I piston my hips upward, using my free hand to pull her down on my cock. I fuck her hard enough that the couch slips across the floor with each stroke, but I don't care.

"You feel so good," she breathes, and the sound goes straight to my fucking chest. "Please, *Levi*."

"I know, baby," I murmur in her ear, feeling exactly what she is.

I hold her tightly, watching her eyes screw shut, my hand in her hair pulling her towards me while I nip and suck the flesh of her neck. Kiss her racing pulse and get so fucking lost in her desperate little pleas and the way she gives herself to me that I couldn't stop the aching need in my chest, even if I wanted to.

I've tried. Fuck, have I tried.

Tugging her face back to mine, her mouth falls open on a desperate little cry while her pussy tightens around me.

"Give them to me," I order roughly, and capture her lips with my own. My balls draw up tight with the need to fill her. To do something irrational, like make her mine for the rest of our lives. Put a baby in her so she'll never want to leave. "Come for me, Ava."

She meets my thrusts, her nails digging into my shoulders while she rides my cock, and when her pussy clamps down on me, I lose it with her.

"*Fuck*," I grit, peppering her damp skin with kisses and filling her with everything I've got until it leaks down her thighs. "Fuck."

She shivers in my arms, her eyes half-lidded and hazy when I slip out of her.

"Thank you," she breathes, and just like that, I know what I need to do. She has no idea how deep this runs.

She doesn't know that possession burns in my chest, thinking of someone coming for her.

How, before her, I've never held someone. Never taken care of someone when they were sad or sick.

To her, this thing between us is murky. To me, it's never been clearer.

I'm in love with her.

—And now I need to tell her the truth.

Fuck.

CHAPTER
Thirty-Seven

AVA

As December rolls around, the cold settles in, blanketing everything in a layer of snow. I don't mind, mostly because I spend all my free time in Levi's bed, either in the cabin or in the house.

I'm not ashamed to admit I'm healing myself in a non-conventional way. One orgasm at a time. When he's touching me, I don't have to think about anything else. Only him and what he wants me to do for him. Whether that's making him come with my mouth, my hands, or my body.

I've had so many orgasms, I've lost count of them, but I know I must have a strong heart from how hard it's been working recently.

Levi and I don't talk about my mother and Brad. We don't talk about Gran's death, or how I fell apart after she died.

We just live. One day at a time.

"I'll only be a moment," he says, pressing his lips to my forehead. He's dropped me off at the bar, again, while he goes back and talks with Deigo. "Cherry's here, and if you need anything, I'm north, but I force a smile on my face.

"I'll be okay."

He stares at me for a moment, his eyes bouncing back and forth between mine like he doesn't believe me.

Something briefly flashes across his features before it's replaced with indifference.

"I'll just be a second," he reminds me.

"She'll be fine, *Casanova*," Cherry chimes from behind me. I can't help but cringe at her voice. "She's not a baby bird."

Levi looks over my head at her, and something unspoken passes between them. I get the sinking suspicion there's more between them than what Levi told me, and I can't deny I feel like the fool willing to turn a blind eye.

Finally, Levi nods and releases me.

I watch him walk away, my stomach sinking as he goes. I push it down and slip into an empty stool at the bar. Cherry doesn't ask, sliding a soda across to me without a word.

"Thank you," I say quietly.

"Don't mention it," she says, equally as awkward.

She's quiet for a while, washing the bar. Drying glasses. Otherwise, ignoring my presence.

Then finally, she speaks.

"It's strange, isn't it?"

I stare at her for a moment, swallowing my drink slowly.

"W-what?"

She glances up, and I follow her gaze across the room. Levi's speaking to a woman. I can't hear what they're saying, but I also can't deny the twinge of jealousy sliding through me.

"Bringing the current girl here to be babysat by the former girl at the bar while you meet with the next one behind her back."

"He came to speak to Deigo."

"Don't shoot the messenger," she says, holding up her hands in self-defense. "I'm just making an observation."

"He's not like that," I grit. "If you knew anything about him, you would know that."

"I know him better than you think," she says, wiping down a glass. "Who do you think was there for him when his father died?"

I think it would hurt less if she'd just stomp on my chest, rather than ripping my heart out.

I look back across the room, and he's chatting with the woman, his arms crossed over his chest. He seems interested in what she has to say, and there's a sick and twisted part of me that wishes I could hear what they're talking about.

And suddenly, without a doubt, I know.

"You're . . . Cherise."

She grimaces at the name, but sighs with a shrug.

"Guilty."

It's why he didn't want me present when he was speaking with the police. Because the girl he was with is the same one who makes his drinks every time he comes to this stupid club.

"You were . . . with him before."

"Ava," she says, like I'm a child who needs coaching. "I was where you were, at one point. I thought I was high on the world being the girl in his bed. I thought I could change him. It's not real."

It's not real.

It's not real.

"It's men like that who always get what they want," Cherry continues. My gaze locks on Levi across the room, and I can't fight the disturbing pang in my chest. "They take and take and take, and when they're done with you, they throw you to the wind."

Without looking at her, I shake my head.

"Levi's not like that."

I hear her humorless chuckle behind me.

"Is that what you really think?" she asks quietly. "Or is that what he told you to believe?"

A pit opens up in my stomach and threatens to swallow me

whole.

She's right.

Of course, I know she's right, but I don't want to believe it.

He cares about me. He has to. Otherwise, why would he have come to Gran's funeral? Why hold me while I cried?

Hell, he even went so far as to threaten my thieving mother and her new boyfriend for me.

"In the end, it's the girls like us that get forgotten,' Cherry says, her words sliding over me like hot tar. "I'm just sorry no one told you sooner."

Sickness pools in my gut, and my heart feels like it's trying to claw its way out of my chest. Without knowing where I'm going, I climb from my barstool and walk away from Cherry and her stupid red hair. I make my way towards the long line at the bathroom, only when I spot the neon exit sign, I follow that instead.

Once I'm out in the night, I realize the wetness on my face is tears. Angrily, I scrub them away as I make my way down the sidewalk.

Why was I so stupid?

I let him pull me in. He told me from the beginning this was just sex, and like the idiot I am, I let myself get caught up in the little things.

Like the way he holds me in his sleep. Like I might run away or disappear.

Or the way he made me soup when I was sick and brushed my hair with his fingers until I fell asleep in his arms.

Or the way he calls for me in his nightmares. Like I'm the only one who can stop them.

I hate him.

I hate him because he made me love him. I'm a walking oxymoron with a penchant for falling for men who should come with a list of trigger warnings.

I ignore my phone buzzing because I don't have to look to

know who it is. Part of me wants to answer because I have no idea where I am, but the other, stupidly irrational part of me is pissed off and hurt like a child.

I keep walking, and the further I get from The Tomb, the colder it gets. The sun is starting to set, and the streets are growing quieter.

It's not until my phone stops buzzing for the seventh time that I stop and look around.

Nothing looks familiar, and I realize what a grave mistake I made.

I'm lost and alone.

The wind blows my hair around me, sending a shiver down my spine.

The shadows grow darker from the alleyway to my left.

The silence hums around me.

I'm well and truly alone.

At least . . . until someone whistles behind me.

"You alright, sweetheart?" a man asks, his back pressed into he bricks of the alleyway. He's got a cigarette hanging out of his mouth and a smirk on his face.

I keep my arms wrapped tightly around myself, glancing into the man's dark brown eyes.

"I'm fine, thank you," I respond, though my voice cracks as a crawling sensation slides up my spine.

I continue past him, but I can feel his presence behind me. I resist the urge to run, holding my bag tightly to my chest.

"You sure?" he asks, his voice too close for comfort. My stomach sinks with each thud of his footsteps behind me, and my breathing grows tighter and tighter with anxiety. "Pretty girls shouldn't be out this time of night. It ain't safe."

Wonder why that is? I think dryly.

"My boyfriend's on his way," I lie. I have no idea if Levi's looking for me or not. He's not even my boyfriend.

"Oh, come on," the man slurs, and I can tell he's been drinking.

369

"Don't be like that. Let me take you home. I can protect you."

"No, thank you."

He chuckles, and the sound turns my chest to ice.

He doesn't stop.

In fact, he only gets closer.

"Please leave me alone," I gasp, but when his hand wraps in my hair and *tugs*, I can't do anything but fall backwards.

The man catches me, and all the air is pushed from my lungs. I fight in his grasp, pure, icy panic sliding through me like water.

"*Bitch!*" he snarls when I swing, managing to hit him in the nose despite the tears clouding my vision. For a split second, he releases me, and I tear strands of hair free to run.

And when I start running, I don't stop.

His footsteps pound after me as I race down the sidewalk, bag clutched tightly to my chest and my knuckles smarting from the impact against his face.

Please. Please grant me a miracle. Please.

"Get the fuck back here. I want to play," the man growls from behind me, quickly catching up to me. I may be small and fast, but it doesn't beat his long legs as he thunders down the sidewalk after me.

Levi. Find Levi.

Surprisingly, I didn't expect to run right into him.

The impact of my body against his knocks the wind out of me, but I don't have time to register that it's him before he's moving me behind him and grabbing the man by the collar and yanking him forward.

The look in his eyes is murderous, and if I didn't know he wouldn't hurt me, I'd be fucking terrified.

Kind of like the man who was chasing me.

Levi grins down at the man with a wicked smile that sends a shiver down my spine.

The man looks like he might piss himself.

"Oh, you really fucked up now."

Jessi Hart

CHAPTER
Thirty-Eight

LEVI

I'm going to fucking kill him.

Grabbing the piece of shit that had his hands on my girl by the shirt collar, I shove him forward into the bricks of an old, abandoned building.

I don't even know how the fuck she got here, but I'm half-tempted to bend her over the hood of my car and spank her ass right here for running off like that.

She's shivering against the side of the building, her wide eyes filled with tears when I punch the asshole so hard, my hand aches afterward.

The dumbass tries to swing, but he only manages to stumble, nearly falling off the curb. I grab him by the back of the neck, spinning him around towards the brick wall, and shove his face into the stone over and over again. Blood from his broken nose sprays the bricks, but I don't stop until I know he's close to passing out.

When I'm done with him, he'll wish he'd died.

Dropping him, the asshole doesn't move an inch while my

was going to do to my girl.

My girl.

My hands are vibrating with rage, and I clench them at my sides, my split knuckles cracking under the pressure.

"Levi," Ava breathes, and my head snaps in her direction.

She's huddled against the wall, her back pressed against the bricks and her arms wrapped protectively around herself.

"Get in the car."

Her gaze widens, but for probably the first time since I met her, she doesn't argue with me.

With the little stunt she pulled, it's probably a good thing.

"Mr. Black," Cheddar wheezes. Poor fuck has been running since the moment we found out Ava was missing. "Did you find her?"

"I did," I tell him.

"I'm . . . sorry . . . I didn't see . . . what happened."

I want to be pissed off at him, but even I know it's not his fault. I hired Cheddar to keep a watchful eye on Ava when I'm not around, but I know her.

She's slippery. At the first sign of something rejection, she bolts.

Guess that's why I'm too busy raging at myself to worry about Cheddar.

"Go take a breather, Cheddar."

He shakes his head.

"I'll wait here for Mr. Christian, so you can take Miss Ava home."

I look back at the asshole passed out on the ground. If there's anyone besides my brother I can trust, it's Cheddar.

"You sure?"

Cheddar smiles through broken teeth.

"It's the least I could do."

I nod once, scrubbing a hand through my hair. I'm still pissed off, but it's not Cheddar's fault.

It's *hers*.

"Thanks . . . Hector."

He looks pleasantly surprised that I'd used his real name, and it only makes me grit my teeth harder because she was right.

I'm about to climb back in the car when my cell rings, piercing the night air.

"Did you find her?"

"Yeah."

"And?"

And I want to rip the man limb from limb.

"Cheddar's waiting for you."

"Splendid. How is the big bastard?"

"A big bastard. Christian?"

"Yeah?"

"Make the call."

Christian chuckles under his breath, low and dark.

"Happily."

I'm about to hang up when his voice rings out again.

"Levi?"

"What?" I growl. I'm in no fucking mood for a lecture.

"Go easy on her."

He hangs up without another word, and I suck in a deep breath.

Go easy on her? Fuck that. It's one thing to throw a tantrum. It's something else completely that she *fucking scared me*.

Scratch that. She didn't just scare me.

She made me fucking panic.

I don't panic.

Yanking the door handle open, I fall inside, the blazing against my already hot skin. I'm burning up from the inside out and trying to reel in my temper. My hands shake on the steering wheel, my mind going a million miles a minute over what could have happened.

I want to punish her. Tie her up in my cabin and fuck her until she's coming over and over for me. I want to brand my name on her goddamned ass so everyone will know who she belongs to.

He touched her. He would have hurt her, had I not found her in time. Maybe worse.

He touched her.

"I'm so—"

"*Don't.*"

Ava jumps at the tone of my voice, falling silent. With a growl, I put the car in drive and start towards the house.

She doesn't try to speak again until we're out of the city and into the forest.

"Look—"

"Not the time, Ava."

"Then when? I get you're angry with me, but you can't silence me, Levi."

Oh, there are ways . . .

Fine, baby girl. You want to play, let's play.

"What the fuck were you thinking?"

She sputters from the passenger seat, her cheeks flaming red.

"I was . . . I was thinking I didn't want to sit around and watch you flirt with another woman while I looked like a fool," she snaps, pretty little head shoved high.

I chuckle darkly.

She really has no fucking clue, does she?

"You mean the informant who's been keeping tabs on *your* name?"

"Why is she keeping tabs on me?"

"Because, Ava, someone was fucking following you. Or did you not think they were still watching you?"

She putters, falling back in the seat like I'd slapped her.

Finally, she shakes her head, looking anywhere in the car but at me. "It doesn't matter."

Jesus fucking Christ.

"What the fuck's gotten into you?" I grit. I hear what she's saying, but I don't fucking like it.

This isn't my Ava. These are the lies someone's put in her head.

She scoffs, chuckling humorlessly.

"You made me sign a contract that I would leave if I developed feelings for you."

"So, are you?"

"Am I what?" she fires back.

"Developing feelings?"

She looks like she's been caught with her hand in the cookie jar.

"That's not what I said."

"It's what you implied," I challenge, and she falls back at the bite in my voice.

"I'm not a charity case, Levi. If you want me gone, then man up and tell me."

I scoff at her boldness.

"What the fuck did Cherry say to you?"

I know exactly what it is, and I'd bet a grand that it has something to do with whatever Cherry said to her after I walked away.

I fucking *knew* it.

My knuckles crack with the force of my grip on the steering wheel.

She shakes her head, looking out at the road. I fucking hate it.

"It doesn't matter."

"Of course, it fucking matters!" I snap.

"Okay, Levi. You want the truth? Maybe I'm just waiting for this thing to be over."

Silence is the only sound despite the blood roaring in my ears.

"Come again?"

"You and I were never meant to be forever, Levi," she says, her voice cracking despite the determination in her gaze. "I know the contract I signed. I also know I have to protect myself, and leaving tonight was just that. An act of self-preservation."

I pull the car to the side of the road, down a dirt path that leads to an old, forgotten campsite, and shove the car into park.

I hear her sniffle and realize she's crying, but I can't do anything about it.

Not this time.

The last three weeks have shown me what loving someone means. It's not cheesy one-liners and dinner dates with wine. It's the real, hard shit. The nasty shit no one wants to talk about.

It's holding her while she silently cries at night when she thinks I'm asleep.

It's brushing her hair when we take a shower because she's too tired.

It's fucking coming home to her. Not someone else every night. Her.

It's doing what I have to do to protect her, even if she may hate me in the end.

The laugh that escapes me sounds bitter even to my ears.

Imagine that. I was worried about her developing feelings, but as it turns out, I'm the one who fucked around and fell in love.

I pull the car to a stop in front of the house. Neither of us moves.

"You really think you've got this all figured out, don't you?"

She narrows her pretty gaze on me, and suddenly, I want her to fight me.

I want her to tell me what a piece of shit I am. Shove me away. Tell me she hates me.

Maybe then, I could let her go.

"Screw you, Levi."

She reaches for the handle, but I reach across her, pulling it shut, and get right in her face.

"No, screw *you*, sweetheart. You think you can just walk away from this? You don't know a fucking thing."

"I know you murdered your father."

A calm falls over the car, so silent, even the snow stops falling for a moment.

"Excuse me?"

"What the fuck did you just say?"

She swallows heavily, and those pretty green eyes finally meet mine.

"I know about that night, Levi," she breathes, and I feel like the world is crashing down around me. "I watched you murder your father."

Tears burn in her eyes, and I watch the descent of one as it slides down her cheek.

"I know what you did, and I know you think punishing yourself for it is going to make it better, but it's not."

"Stop," I growl, but she doesn't.

"—It's not your fault. You didn't deserve the way he treated you. He was an evil man—"

"I said *stop*!"

She jerks at the violence in my voice. I've never yelled at her. Never. Even as it leaves my mouth, I feel guilty because a flash of fear crosses her pretty face.

I should have fucking known she'd seen me that night. I should have made sure. I should have *checked*.

Before she can continue, I get out, slamming the door hard enough that it rattles from the impact. I stalk down the path a few feet in front of the car, trying to get my adrenaline to go down.

My hands are shaking when I run them over my face. My mind is going a million miles a minute with all the things that could have happened because Ava decided to listen to *fucking Cherry* and ran instead of coming to me.

I, who hasn't gone a single day without her by my side for the last two months.

I should have known it wouldn't be that easy, because moments later, the passenger door shuts behind me.

"I strangled my father in cold blood, Ava. I watched the life bleed from his eyes for what he did to my family." When I turn around, she's hovering by the car, her eyes guarded. "And you know the fucked-up part, baby? If someone were to come for *you*, I'd do worse."

She closes her eyes for a single second, and a tear slips down her cheek. I watch its descent, the meaning behind it burning like battery acid in my chest.

"So, yeah. You can tell me I'm a monster. You can hate me for making you sign a contract. Fuck," I chuckle darkly. "You can hate me for how badly you crave me, but don't you *ever* pull some stunt like that again. I'm a patient man, but you almost got yourself fucking killed today. If you think I'm going to let someone rip you away from me, you're wrong."

"Why?" she sneers through the tears on her face. "Because you'd lose your contract?"

"Because *you're mine.*"

The silence in the space between us is so thick, you could cut it with a knife.

"You don't mean that?"

I step closer to her. She backs up. I step closer still, and she falls back against the hood of the Aston.

It's not until I'm looming over her that those pretty green eyes meet mine and I realize I'm fucking done for.

Losing her is going to kill me.

I grip her hips and lift her onto the hood of the car so fast, she lets out a tiny gasp. I grip her chin, and she shoves my hand away, but I don't let go, forcing her to look at me with those tear-filled eyes. I lower my lips to hers, close enough to kiss her, but I don't.

"You're mine, Ava. Today. Tomorrow. For the next one hundred lifetimes. I won't let someone take that away from me."

"Levi—"

I press my lips to hers, cutting off whatever she was about to say. My hands wind in her hair, angling her head back so I can devour her. She slides her arms around my neck, and I hoist her up against me, letting her wrap her legs around my waist.

This kiss is different. It's a promise.

I'll do whatever it takes to protect her . . . even if it means breaking both of us in the process.

"Tell me you hate me," I whisper, sliding my hands under her shirt, teasing her nipples through her bra. I feel her heart racing against my palm, matching my own. "Tell me you're better off without me."

"Levi," she gasps when I stoop down, nipping the flesh over her collarbone. "Stop saying those things."

I move my hand to the button on her jeans, sliding the zipper down. She lets me spread her legs with my hips, forcing her back into the car so I can rip them down her legs.

"It's crazy how pissed off you get me," I rasp, sliding my fingers along the seam of her wet thong. "Like tie you up and make you scream my name until you lose your voice, pissed off." Her head falls back when I swirl her clit through the material, and I take the chance to press my lips to her racing pulse. "Does that sound sane to you, baby girl?"

"Levi, please . . ." she begs, her lashes fluttering heavily against her cheeks. "I want you."

"You've got me, Ava," I whisper against her throat. "Do you trust me?"

She nods feverishly when I slip her panties to the side and slide a finger inside her, testing her. She's soaking wet, dripping into my palm, and my mouth waters to taste her. I want to, but not right now. I'm too fucking far gone. The knowledge of what's to come only furthers my need to own her as completely as she owns me.

"Use your words, Ava."

She melts at her nickname, moaning. The sounds of my fingers moving inside her fill the clearing, and all I can think about is getting her underneath me.

"Yes, I trust you," she breathes, reaching between us for my zipper. I groan when she fists my cock, and push her back, withdrawing my fingers from her.

I'm hard as fuck when I throw her legs over my shoulder and notch myself at her entrance. I'm not gentle when I push inside her. She cries out as I stretch her, and a growl rumbles up from my chest with the way she's squeezing the life out of me.

I should take her back to my bed, spend the night showing her exactly what I can't say, but there's no time for that.

I lean back, taking her hips in my hands, and spread her wide for me. Her legs are on my shoulders, and I thrust inside her, my cock bottoming out halfway.

"*Fuck* . . ." I growl, sliding out and looking down to where her pussy coats my cock. "So fucking perfect, baby."

I thrust against her, watching myself disappear inside her. When I look up, she's watching me, her expression cloudy with lust and need and something else I don't want to acknowledge.

Something that looks . . . a whole lot like love.

My control slips, and I can't help but move faster, my body slapping against hers. She's trembling, and my fingers dig into her thighs, pounding into her while my balls slap against her ass. She takes it all, arching her back to suck me in deeper. Begging for it like the good girl she is.

Our heavy breathing fills the air, cloudy in the cold, but neither of us stops.

She feels too fucking good, and I'm too far gone.

"Oh God . . ." she moans, her eyes rolling back when I stroke that deep-seated place inside her, making her dig her nails into my hands. "Please, you're going to make me come."

I fuck her harder, needing to brand myself on her. The sound of our bodies slapping together fills the clearing, mixing with her soft cries.

It's not enough. I'll never get enough.

"You feel me, Ava?" I grunt as my hips slam into hers. "Feel how fucking deep I am?"

A shudder rolls through me, and I groan deeply. She moans in return, and then the brat does something I never expected. She grins. Fucking grins.

That's when I know I'm fucked.

I'll give her anything she wants. All she has to do is ask.

"That's my good girl. Such a good little slut for me," I grunt, placing my hand flat on her stomach. I drag my thumb through the wetness covering her pussy and use it to stroke her clit in time with my thrusts.

"Levi," she cries, body spasming as her pussy clenches around me. I grunt, shoving deep inside her, owning her with every stroke.

She sags on the hood when I pull out, only to grip her hips and drop her to her feet on the ground. I spin her around, pushing her flat to the hood, before I slide back inside her.

I slap her ass hard enough to turn it red, and in the falling snow, she moans, arching back into me for more. I grin and do it on the other side, before taking her ass in my hands and fucking her hard and rough.

There's no gentleness in the way we fuck. I'm not sweet with her like I have been. It never occurred to me that she craved me as violently as I craved her. I've been too soft on her lately, and she's forgotten who owns her. That contract signifies that she's *mine*, and I'll be damned if Cherry, the DEA, or even the entire state of Washington fuck with it.

"I'm going to remind you who I am, Ava. And when I'm done with you, you're going to feel me for days."

She moans, and I grip her shoulder, using it to pull her back on my cock as I fuck her fast and hard, not giving either of us room to breathe. Lowering myself, I press my chest to her back and slide my hand around her, my throat going to her throat and squeezing. I've never taken her this far, but judging by the way her pussy clenches tighter, it's turning her on.

I test her by squeezing, stealing her breath for a moment, and I'm met with a tremble that slides through her. I can't help but grin.

"I think she likes it," I say in her ear, doing it again, fucking her while I steal her breath. When I release the pressure, she gasps, sucking in a lungful of air.

She cries out, eyes clenched shut and pussy dripping in my hands while I growl in her ear.

"You're doing so fucking good, baby girl," I rasp against the side of her throat. "You were made to take my cock. Give it all to me."

She moans, and a tear slips down her cheek. Her nails dig into my hand and for a split second, I'm fucking terrified that I hurt her.

"Please don't stop," she begs, gasping for breath, and I can't help but grin wickedly.

"That's my girl. Take a deep breath for me, baby. I'm going to show you who owns you."

She sucks in a heavy breath, and I tighten my hand, stealing her air and driving my cock inside her. At some point, I black out, the only feeling is her squeezing me like a fucking fist, and the need to rut inside her until she shatters for me.

Until she no other man will ever be able to make her come again.

Her hand falls from mine, and just when she's about to go slack in my arms, she comes. I release my hand, and she gasps, her cries silent as her entire body vibrates beneath me.

I fuck her through her orgasm, powering into her until she's shaking in my hands, back bowed, and her pussy leaking down my fingers. I don't stop, even when she comes, I push her forward and power into her again and again until I can't hold back anymore.

"Fuck, *Ava!*"

With a guttural groan, I spill inside her, my entire body vibrating above hers. I've never come so hard in my fucking life, and I'm not ashamed to admit it's got nothing to do with what we just did.

It's her.

It's *always* been her.

With her orgasm fading, she shivers in the cold. The snow blankets her hair, and I brush it off her face when I turn her around to face me, keeping her pinned to the hood of the car with my body because her legs are shaking.

Gently, I brush a lone tear off her cheek, and her eyes meet mine.

There's a new feeling in the air. Almost like the sinister silence in the calm before the storm.

I may not have it all figured out, but if there's one thing I *do* know, it's that when they learn your weakness, people will use it against you.

And unfortunately, staring down into the soft green eyes in front of me, I now know . . . Ava Lynn Ryan has become my weakness too.

CHAPTER
Thirty-Nine

LEVI

As gently as possible, I slip my arms under Ava and lift her from the car. She's still trembling from the last orgasm I gave her when I carry her into the cabin, bridal-style.

"I can walk," she says softly, but I pretend I don't hear her and hold her tighter, not willing to let her go.

It's only been ten minutes, and yet I feel like I'm fucking starved for her touch.

Me.

Starved for the touch of another person. I don't know what the fuck she's doing to me, but I'm powerless to stop it. This need I've grown accustomed to for her body was never really that at all.

All this time, I've been madly fucking in love with this girl, and fighting it every step of the way.

"What are we doing?"

"We're going to shower, and then we're going to bed."

Outside, the snow is falling, but the fire is still warm in the fireplace inside. It's dark now, and we're both too exhausted to talk things out tonight.

She winces from the brightness, and my eyes rake over the damage. She's got three hickeys on the side of her neck. Her lips are red and swollen, and her hair's a tangled mess, but she's never looked more beautiful than she does right now when she peeks up at me through her clumped lashes.

Turning away from her, I cross the room and turn on the shower. Steam fills the room, and Ava shivers from her spot on the counter when I step up in front of her.

"I look like I was fucked by a tornado," she grumbles out of nowhere, and I can't fight the laugh that rips free. Ava looks at me like I've grown an extra head. "Are you feeling okay?"

I slip her shirt over her head and toss it to the side before I move to her jeans and sneakers.

"Okay, brat." I hold out my hand to her, and for a moment, I think she's going to deny me. "Ava, get your ass over here."

Something soft crosses her delicate features, and she slowly slips her fingers in mine, letting me help her down from the counter.

I let out a sigh of relief and lead her towards the shower, letting her get in while I finish undressing.

Ava crosses her arms over her chest, standing under the warm water, her eyes latching onto my abs when I slip the shirt over my head.

I chuckle darkly under my breath. Some things never change.

"Like what you see, baby?"

I expect her to look away, but for the first time since I've known her, she lets her eyes travel over me. Like she's devouring me.

Fucking hell, that's hot.

"Careful, baby girl," I taunt, climbing in the shower behind her. "You're going to start giving me ideas."

"You just made me come half a dozen times, and now you're getting hard, again," she points out, and I shrug.

"Want me to make a full dozen?"

She shakes her head and bites her lip to hide her smirk, but there's something else there. Her eyes fall to her toes, and I catch the tear slipping down her cheek.

Fuck.

"Hey . . ." I reach for her chin, tilting her face to mine. Her eyes are bloodshot, and tears cling to her lashes. "Talk to me."

"I just . . . I'm sorry for not listening to you."

My chest grows tight with the sob that wracks through her body. With a sigh, I pull her from the wall and press her against me. She shivers in my arms, so I hold her tighter.

"That man . . ." She tries to pull back, but I don't release her.

"I'll handle it, Ava."

"But—"

"Don't worry about him." I catch a stray tear with my thumb. "He was going to hurt you, Ava. It can't go unpunished."

She shudders at the darkness in my voice. "What are you going to do to him?" she asks quietly, pulling back enough to look up at me. I brush her dark hair back from her face, my thumb brushing over her lip.

"Nothing you need to be a part of."

"I can handle it, Levi."

That's the problem. I know she can. I can't.

My girl is soft. Gentle. I'm rough and jagged. I can't watch that softness turn to stone. I'd rather take a bullet first.

"Why didn't you tell me? About that night?"

Fuck. I feel like she's sand slipping through my fingers. The tighter I try to hold onto her, the faster she falls.

She swallows hard, her tongue darting out to lick her lips.

"Because it wouldn't have changed anything." She glances down, and when she looks back up at me, her eyes are swimming with tears. "Does that make me a bad person?"

Cautiously, I lean into her, running my nose up the side of her throat, and despite the warmth of the water cascading over us, she shivers.

"Nothing about you is bad, Ava Ryan," I whisper against her ear.

She stiffens, but she doesn't pull away. I don't know why, but whispering it makes saying shit like this a whole lot easier than having to look into those pretty green eyes and say it aloud.

When I pull back, there's a look I can't place in her eyes.

I swallow past the burn in my throat and pull her under the warmth.

"One day at a time, baby."

"Don't call me that," she mumbles, her cheeks flaming red.

"Why not?"

"Because it makes me feel things I shouldn't."

I'm so surprised by her answer that my voice gets caught in my throat. My blood roars to life, and my cock twitches.

Suddenly, I'm thinking about all kinds of stupid shit. *My* ring on her finger. Her carrying *my* baby. She and I in bed every night and coming home to her every evening.

It can't happen, but fuck if the fantasy isn't tempting.

My hands take her hips, pulling her closer to me, and the water covers us both. I dip my head, my lips only inches from hers, and we share each other's air.

I kiss her, drinking her in. Before the kiss can go too far, I pull back, forcing some distance between us. I just fucked her seven ways to Sunday, and yet, I could keep going. There's no limit to my desire for her. To feel her coming undone underneath me. It's maddening, but who the fuck cares? She stole my sanity a long time ago.

I reach for the shampoo on the ledge, and she shivers under the warm spray, letting it coat her cool skin. Motioning for her to turn around, I lather up my hands and take my time washing her hair, reminding her of everything I can't say out loud.

"Mmm . . ." she moans while I massage her scalp.

"Baby, you've got to stop that." She blushes when she realizes my cock's hard against the small of her back again, but I notice the small smile tugging on her lips.

"I don't know what you're talking about."

"I'm sure you don't."

Once her hair is clean, I condition it. When I'm finished, I move on to her body, washing her. When I'm satisfied, she reaches for the shampoo and repeats the process for me, though it's much harder for her to reach my hair, and I have to stoop down for her, making her laugh under her breath.

The sound hits me right in the fucking chest, and I have to remind myself not to stare at her too long because it's like staring into the sun. Eventually, you'll get burned.

There's nothing sexual in the way we clean each other, and it strikes me that this is the first time I've taken care of another person like this. There's this heaviness in my chest that refuses to leave and a desperation in the pit of my stomach that's got me ready to give it all up if she'll agree to stay. Strangely, there's also the desire to do this again and again. Take care of each other.

When we're done, I help her from the shower and dry her off before brushing out her hair.

She yawns at her reflection, watching as I work the knots out of the dark strands. When we're done, I take her hand and pull her back out into the cabin and to the bed.

Sleepily, she lets me pull her to the bed and under the covers, her head resting on my chest like she's afraid to put too much weight down. Tonight is no different than the last three weeks, but at the same time it is. There's something . . . more.

She stares at me, her eyes studying mine.

"Are you okay?" she asks finally, and though there's a sinking feeling in my gut telling me to run in the other direction, I force myself to meet her gaze head-on. I reach up and brush the hair back from her face, my chest tight, and when she looks up at me, I'm overwhelmed with shit I've never felt before.

Her hand comes up to my cheek, brushing over the bruise

forming there from the one punch the bastard was able to land on me tonight.

"I . . ." Fuck. Why is this shit so hard? "Let's go to sleep."

She's silent, her breath catching, and her lips parted ever so slightly.

Leaning forward, I lay my forehead against hers, closing my eyes.

I take her hand in mine, holding it up to the moonlight. She's so much smaller than I am that her hand looks childlike next to mine.

"One day at a time," she whispers, before she falls asleep.

"Yeah," I murmur, dread filling my chest. "One day at a time."

The man wakes with a scream that could break the sound barrier.

"There he is," Christian mutters, smacking the side of his face to wake him up.

Dale, who I suspect is shitting himself right about now, stares up at me from where he hangs upside down.

"What the fuck?" he slurs, still drunk off his fucking rocker from where Christian found him in the alleyway.

I have a feeling he'll be sobering up pretty damn quickly when he gets a look at what's waiting for him below.

"Good morning, princess," I greet, letting him sway from the rope attached to the tall tree overhead. "Sleep well?"

"You're that whore's boyfriend?"

"Wrong choice of words, bud," Christian chuckles darkly, stalking over to the other end of the rope.

It's a pulley system. The more he lowers his side, the higher mine goes. The opposite is also true, but a whole hell of a lot more fun.

"Oh, I'm a whole lot more than that." Kneeling beside him, I allow him to get a good look at my face. The one that's going to make him pay for all the shit he did to my girl. "Do you know why we're here, Dale?"

"That little fucking bitch," he spits, his face getting redder and redder by the second. "I promise she's making shit up. I just wanted to help her."

"Well, in that case, we should probably let him go." I look to Christian, who shrugs. "What do you think?"

"I think we should figure out if he's lying first. Can't be too sure nowadays. A criminal's word doesn't really mean as much as it used to."

"Good point."

"What the fuck is wrong with you? You going to kill me? Over a fucking lie?"

"Is it a lie, Dale? I saw you chasing my girl. She was terrified."

I nod once to Christian, who lets the rope go slack just a hair, dropping Dale an inch with a harsh lurch.

Dale gasps, flailing, though his arms are tied behind his back, so it's really not much use.

"That looks uncomfortable, Dale."

"Let me down from here. I did my fucking time."

"You did time for drug paraphernalia." His eyes widen the slightest bit. "Oh, yes. I went through your file. Petty burglary. Sexual assault when you were younger. Pretty much the bottom of the barrel as far as citizens go."

He has the audacity to spit, and it lands on the side of my face.

"You don't know shit about me."

Gripping his shirt, I wipe the spit off my face and stand.

—Then I punch him in the dick.

Dale cries out in pain, his screams echoing in the clearing around us.

"You can scream all you want. No one will hear you. Even if they did, I'm not sure anyone would care."

"What are you going to do to me? I've got a family, you know. They need me."

"They survived without you for nearly ten years. I'm sure your absence would be a blessing for them." I stand back from the large pit in the ground that Dale's dangling over. Dangly Dale. Seems like a fitting nickname. "As for what I'm going to do to you? Well, I'd rather show you."

Dale opens his mouth to say something else, but before he can, the sound of a metallic door sliding open from the pit below silences him.

Dale's eyes go wide at the man who stalks into the clearing.

And then they nearly fall out of his head when he looks below and sees the big ass grizzly bear pacing around beneath him.

"Dale, I want you to meet Smokey. He hates men."

Smokey grunts in response, pacing around underneath Dale like he's a hanging filet mignon.

"That's a-that's—"

"A bear," Christian finishes for him. "In case you couldn't tell."

I kneel back down in front of Dale, taking his chin in my hand and squeezing until he stops spinning. He sputters, struggling to breathe from the angle he's been dangling at for the last ten minutes.

"Now tell me, Dave—"

"His name's Dan."

"Oh, right," I smirk. "Doug . . ."

"*Fuck you!* You aren't going to feed me to a fucking bear."

"Well, that depends. We're going to play a game of Russian Roulet . . . only with a bear. You tell me the truth, and I don't shoot. You lie, this revolver has one shot, and I'm going to point it directly at the line holding you over Smokey's pit. Whether you fall in and become a chew toy is up to you."

"You're a sick fucking bastard, you know that?"

I shrug.

"Funnily enough, that's what my girl says you are." I grin at him, a genuine toothy grin so he can see how fucked he is. "Shall we begin?"

"Help!" he screeches the moment I stand and walk back a few feet out of the clearing. "Somebody help me! He's going to kill me."

I almost roll my eyes. We're at least ten miles from any civilization. No one's coming to save Dale.

"Smokey's pretty hungry, Dale."

"And pissed off," Christian murmurs, joining me with an amused look in his eye. "You see, Smokey can't hibernate, Dale. Not like the rest of them."

"Which makes him a very angry boy." Smokey huffs in response.

"Shut the fuck up and let me down from here!"

"Alright, Dale. Question one. What were you going to do to my girl when you caught her?"

"Fuck you!"

I'm so sick of this fucking guy.

I raise the gun, point it directly at the only rope stopping him from being Smokey shit, and pull the trigger.

Blank.

Honestly, I'm glad. The fun continues.

"I was hired to follow her!"

My grip tightens on the gun, and I have half a mind to shoot him where he hangs.

That wouldn't be nearly as painful, though.

"Very good. You're learning."

"Please," he whimpers. "Don't do this—"

"Question two. Who hired you to follow her?"

"Please . . ."

With a huff, I point and fire a second blank.

"Odds are getting slimmer, Dale," Christian calls, lighting the end of a cigarette and blowing out the smoke into the damp night. "Smokey sounds like he's getting pretty pissed off down there."

"I don't want to die."

Too bad, asshole.

"Last chance, Dale." I step back over to him, lowering my voice and getting right in his face so only he can hear. "Who hired you?"

His eyes widen to saucers, and I think it's at that moment he realizes he has no choice.

He rattles off a name, and it's not the one I was expecting.

A cold chill runs up my spine at the information he gives me. I watch him speak, hear what he's saying, but my mind can't wrap around it.

I'll fucking kill him.

At the same time, Dale screams in fear, I fire the shot directly at the rope. The bullet hits, and with a crack, Dale falls into the pit with a heavy thud.

All three of us step over to the side, watching as Smokey charges. Dale's screams are unlike anything I've ever heard, and the noises emanating from the pit send a shiver down even my spine. Abruptly, the screams stop, and then in the blink of an eye, all that's left of Dangly Dale is a few spare body parts that Smokey will take care of and a pair of workless work boots.

Christian is the one to break the silence, pointing to the hand that lies discarded off to the side.

"Need a hand?"

I shoot him a look.

"Good to see you practicing your dad jokes. Can't wait to be an uncle." I pat him on the back when he chuckles under his breath and head over to where the man, they call the Butcher, is leaning against a tree.

"Thank you for this."

He's silent, the black skull mask covering his face offering no explanation as to who he really is. They're like this, and the only reason we're standing here right now is because of a job I did a few years ago as a favor to *them* under the DEA.

"I didn't do it for you," he says finally.

"How the fuck did you catch a grizzly that size, anyway?" Christian asks when the Butcher pushes off a tree.

"A year ago, a zoo had scheduled to put him down because he ate his trainer. The trainer had a history of abuse." He shrugs. "The zoo thought he was dangerous. I felt he was justified."

And with that, he turns and walks off into the trees without another word.

Christian and I watch after him, but like the ghost he's meant to be, he disappears into the overgrowth without so much as the rustle of leaves.

"You know, this may be a first," Christian murmurs. "But that motherfucker creeps me out."

I can't help but smirk.

"He's harmless." I glance back at the pit where the metal door is opening, and Smokey is licking his paws. "Unless you're someone like Dale."

"Don't be like Dale," Christian says as we walk back towards the car. Unfortunately, it's at least a mile walk, but at least we don't have Dale to worry about. Hauling a knocked-out Dale here in the dark was a fucking treat. "Great life motto."

CHAPTER
Forty

AVA

It's official. I'm screwed.

Against my better judgment, I've gone and fallen in love with Levi Cross, and there's not a single thing I can do to stop it.

He winks at me across the room, where he's speaking with Christian and Paulina. Neither of them seems to notice that his eyes haven't left me for the last twenty minutes.

As if he knows I'm thinking about what he did to me in the shower earlier, his gaze travels over my body, down the emerald green silk of the dress he picked out. I'm sure it cost a fortune, and I've been wary of getting even a speck of dirt on it the entire night.

Heat travels through my blood. It's insane. I just came three times this afternoon, and yet, I want him again. I always want him. It's like my libido is on steroids, and nothing can satiate the hunger burning inside me.

Shifting nervously from foot to foot, I turn away, my cheeks hot to the touch. I'm trying to pay attention to what Bella and Mila are saying. I just can't. It seems I can't focus on anything other than

It's Oak Ridge's Annual Christmas Party, and the ballroom is packed. Crowded with wealthy guests who spend their holidays here.

Bella and Mila did a phenomenal job. I just don't think large parties are for me. Especially surrounded by enough wealth to purchase the state of Washington.

I sip my champagne and mingle. Do my best to ignore Levi Cross staring me down across the room, but it's no use. I'm enthralled with him. Like we're two magnets drawn together.

Life has been . . . strange. It's been a week since I was chased, and a week of constant whiplash. One moment, he's laughing or fucking me. The next, he's quiet, lost in thoughts he refuses to clue me in on.

I can't escape the feeling that he's hiding something from me. Something about my past that he doesn't want me to know. I don't want to believe that he could be lying.

—I'm also realistic.

Even if I'm falling for him, he's still hiding a piece of himself, and I'm struggling to decide if I'm willing to accept him without that missing piece or if I need it all.

I've never been in love. To me, love is accepting another person for all their flaws. Every negative characteristic. Every curse or sin. It's trusting someone to love you so completely that you can show the ugliest parts of yourselves, knowing they'll take those parts and make them beautiful.

With each passing day, I find myself wondering what could have happened to make him shut the world out. If he'll ever really let me in, or if we'll continue this song and dance for the rest of our lives until one of us gives in or ends the contract.

Something tells me it won't take long.

His gaze finds mine across the room, and I can't fight the longing in my chest to go to him. I want to be by his side, on his arm. We've spent most of the evening together, but it's not enough.

I want to be in his bed with him on top of me, making me come until I can't remember my name.

Holding his gaze, I look back at his sister and Mila.

Then, I start heading for the back hall of the lodge.

I'm only out of sight for a second when I feel his presence.

"Miss me, baby girl?"

I don't answer him, instead, turning and raising to my tiptoes before crushing my lips to his. He groans, his hands instantly coming to my hips before slipping lower to cup my ass. His tongue collides with mine, and he pushes me back into the wall like he doesn't give a single fuck about where we are or who could see us.

"Fuck sweetheart," he rasps against my neck.

"I want you," I breathe, my head falling back to give him more access when he sucks on the pulse point below my ear. It feels so good that the heat already rushing through my veins turns to a full-on ache.

"Thought we were going to wait until tonight? Make it last?"

I shake my head, reaching between us to cup him through his pants. He hisses out a curse under his breath when I find him long and hard.

"I don't want to wait," I breathe, nipping the scar on his lip when he lifts his mouth back to mine.

His gaze searches mine for a moment, almost sinister. Like he's captured heaven in the palm of his hands and now he's planning to ruin it for anyone but himself.

In a lot of ways, he already has.

"You're dangerous, Ava Lynn," he mutters gruffly.

My stomach bottoms out at his words, my body hot and feverish. This is absolute madness, but I blame him for my lack of self-control where he's concerned.

I don't know what's gotten into me, but I need to feel his hands on me. I need him to claim me.

Mostly, I just need him to fuck me and remind me who I belong to.

Hauling me to him, his lips crash against mine, and he lets out a groan. Hoisting me up into his arms, his hands fist the material of my dress. Anyone could walk around the corner and see us, but I'm past caring. I know he won't let anything happen to me.

"This dress . . ." he rasps. "I want to fucking burn it.

"Don't," I whisper in between kissing him and slipping my tongue along his scar. I've found he secretly likes it, and when he shivers, a rush of triumph consumes me. "I like it."

"I'll like it better when it's on my floor tonight," he rasps, nipping and sucking a path up the side of my throat.

I arch in his grasp, pressing myself against him, and he chuckles darkly in my ear. He pulls back, cupping my face with his fingers.

"You're so fucking perfect . . ."

My breath gets caught in my throat when he searches my face. It's right there on the tip of my tongue, but I know admitting it out loud makes it real. Too real.

"Levi . . ."

He lifts a hand, slow and deliberate, and tucks a loose strand of hair behind my ear with a tenderness that feels completely at odds with the darkness in his gaze.

"Let's get out of here," I whisper, and relief flashes in his eyes.

"You're serious?"

"Yeah," I breathe, and he chuckles under his breath. "As much fun as I'm having, I'm tired of wearing heels."

He shakes his head, chuckling in disbelief.

"What?"

He steps back, taking my hand. "Nothing."

If you had told me four months ago that I'd be walking down the halls of the Oak Ridge Lodge, hand in hand with none other than Levi Cross, I would have laughed in your face.

Now, when I try to pull away, he tightens his hold, shooting me a look.

"Someone might see."

He cocks a brow at me. "So?"

His hair is mussed from my fingers, and I'm sure my lipstick is all over my face. We may as well have a neon sign over our heads that reads, '*We're leaving early to go have sex*', but I don't care.

Not when he looks at me like I'm the only girl that's ever walked the planet.

"You don't care?"

His hand grips my waist, and he pulls me into his front, his lips at my ear.

"Are you implying that you're embarrassed to be seen with me?"

I pull back, shoving at his chest, fighting back a smile.

"I have to use the restroom," I say quietly.

He leans in and places a soft kiss on my forehead before stepping back and finally releasing me.

"I'll go tell Christian we're leaving."

I nod, and I can't fight the stupid grin on my face when he pulls away, walking backwards down the hall.

I feel like we're two teenagers in love for the first time. Like I'm made of air.

I practically skip into the bathroom and quickly clean myself up in the nearest stall. I'm standing at the counter, reapplying my makeup when the scuff of heavy boots sounds at the door.

"You can't be in here," I smirk, but when I turn to lock eyes with the man at the door, it's not Levi like I'd thought.

"What are you doing here, Alex? If Levi sees you in here, he's going to kick your ass."

"We need to talk."

"About? You pretty much said everything you wanted to say. You know? When you called me a whore."

He shakes his head and sighs.

"I was just trying to tell you the truth. Cross isn't who you think he is, Ava."

A laugh bubbles up my chest even as apprehension sets in.

"Apparently, neither were you."

"He's dangerous."

"Yeah, to *you*." I glance towards the door. "He's going to come looking for me."

"I just need a moment. If you don't want to speak to me ever again after this, then fine, I'll leave you alone, but I can't just walk away without telling you the truth."

My pulse is racing, and my throat feels like there's a golf ball lodged behind my tonsils.

Of course, Levi is dangerous. It's part of what drew me to him in the first place. But he'd never be dangerous towards me. Never . . .

"Fine, but make it quick." I'm not kidding when I say that if Levi catches him cornering me in the women's restroom, he'll rip him limb from limb.

"I didn't want to have to be the one to tell you this, but I care about you, Ava, and I'm not about to sit back and watch you get hurt."

"What are you talking about, Alex?" I snap. I've had about enough of his cryptic nonsense.

He lets out a deep breath, scrubbing a hand through his hair, and looks anywhere in the room but at me.

That's . . . never a good sign.

"Cross is using you to get closer to the Burelli's."

I freeze, my entire body rigid like I just fell through the ice in a lake.

I can't do anything but stare at him blankly. "I don't know what you're talking about."

"He's being paid, Ava," he interrupts impatiently. "He's been playing into your feelings because Cross knows you're his only shot at getting his miserable job back. Making you think he wants you is the best way to do that."

My eyes sting when I shake my head and back away.

"No. You don't know Levi," I whisper. "He wouldn't do that."

Boring.

Prudish.

Whore.

Alex takes a step forward.

"Do *you* know Cross?"

No. It can't be true.

I refuse to believe the same man who made me soup and held me while I cried when my grandmother died and panicked when I disappeared is only entertaining me because he's using me.

But all the signs are there . . . the little voice in the back of my head whispers.

The contract. The flash drive. Not wanting to get any closer to me than he had to.

"Why would I have information on the Burelli's?" I whisper, my voice barely audible.

"Because, Ava. Who do you think your father is?"

"No."

Alex doesn't have to speak to confirm what I already know.

Oh my God.

I stumble back, clutching the counter beside me for support.

He used me.

I fell for the man who's using me like a tool in his game.

The room tilts, my breath coming shallow and uneven.

He's lying. He has to be lying.

But his eyes—dark, gleaming, far too steady—don't waver.

"You've felt it, haven't you?" Alex presses, stepping closer, his voice low and coaxing, like a snake slithering through the cracks in my defenses. "That nagging sense that something was missing. That someone was keeping things from you. All those years of wondering who your father is. Did you really think it was for your protection?"

My throat closes. "Stop."

He doesn't. "Your father isn't some ghost story, Ava. He's alive.

And very much involved."

I shake my head so hard it makes my vision blur. "You're wrong. He loves me," I whisper, but the words feel thin, fragile, like glass ready to shatter.

"Or maybe he just loves what you represent. A bargaining chip. Access. You're not a lover, Ava. You're leverage."

The word cuts straight through me, colder than a blade.

I grip the counter until my knuckles ache, staring at him, desperate to find the lie in his face. But he doesn't blink. Doesn't soften. He waits, patient and sure of the poison he's planting in my chest.

"I'm sorry to be the one to have to tell you," Alex says, interrupting the thoughts spiraling in my head. When I meet his gaze, it's full of pity.

"Get out."

He reaches for me, and I bristle at his touch. "Ava—"

"Get. *Out.*"

Alex grimaces, his hands falling to his sides. He heads towards the door, while I stay frozen in shock.

"Ask him who Nolan Marks is, Ava . . ." he says quietly. "Then tell me that he cares about you."

He walks out, leaving me staring at the door while the world comes crashing around me.

He lied to me. Every person I've ever loved has lied to me.

My eyes burn before I realize I'm crying.

I clutch the counter, feeling like I'm going to be sick, and when I raise my eyes to meet my reflection in the mirror, they're bloodshot and smeared with makeup.

Levi Cross made me fall in love with him, then he used me.

Once the tears start, I'm powerless to stop them. Every single emotion I've been holding back for the last three months crashes through me like a tidal wave. Nana. The Burelli's. Levi. The loneliness aching in my chest.

Suddenly . . . it's all too much.

With some dismay, I realize the reason I've been so drawn to Levi from the moment I met him. It's because when he looks at me, it's not indifference I see. It's reverence. Desire. Need so potent, it pisses him off.

Levi Cross isn't indifferent towards me at all.

And that pisses him off.

Too bad it wasn't enough.

"Ava, get the fuck back here," Levi growls from behind me when I hurry up the stairs to the second story of Cross Estate. My heart bottoms out when he catches my hand, then it turns to something much more dangerous when I realize the unsteady ache in my chest is because I know we can't come back from this.

Levi grips my hips and pushes back against the wall. My tongue darts out to lick my lips, and I'm so confused, I don't know whether I want him to take me to his bed and hold me like his baby girl or bend me over the side of it and fuck me like his whore.

In a flash, he spins me around, pushing me back against the wall. His hands press into the wall on either side of my head, caging me in.

"Why are you hiding from me?" he asks, and the deadly edge to his voice is suddenly much softer.

It's unfortunate because it will make it that much harder to deny him in the end.

"I . . ."

A tear slips down my cheek, and he watches its descent, his thumb coming up to capture it like it's made of gold.

"Talk to me," he says softly in my ear, and a shiver moves

through me. I lay my head back against the wall, closing my eyes. "What happened?"

The scent of whiskey washes over me, and a fresh tear slips down my cheek.

When I force my eyes open, the eye contact sears. I want to look away, but I need to know the truth.

My mind races a million miles a minute, unable to comprehend that this entire thing between us has been nothing more than a lie.

—So, I ask the question that I know will either make or break us.

"Who is Nolan Marks, Levi?"

His entire body stiffens against mine, and that's when I *know.*

I watch as realization crosses his handsome features, each passing moment more devastating than the last.

Then, in the silence of the hallway, he lets out a dark chuckle.

"This is great," he mutters, pushing away from me. "Real fucking great."

"You lied to me," I breathe, tears stinging in the backs of my eyes. "Who is he, Levi?" When he's silent, my patience snaps. "Who is he?" I screech, shoving at his chest with the anger coursing through me like hot water.

His gaze meets mine, and the darkness there makes it feel as though all the air has been sucked from the room.

His jaw tightens, and he looks away.

"The head of the Burelli crime family."

"And?"

"Your father."

My knees wobble, weak as my body vibrates.

My father.

His silence stretches, heavy enough to crush me. I search his face for the man who once steadied me with nothing but his touch, but all I see is stone and shadows.

Finally, he exhales through his nose, the sound harsh. "Because you were never supposed to know. Not like this."

My chest twists. "You knew the entire time?"

His jaw feathers, and I feel like I'm looking at a stranger. The Levi I know is gone, replaced with one far more deadly.

"From the moment I met you."

I think it would hurt less if he'd slapped me. My chest feels like it's been flayed open, my heart ripped out and stomped on before being haphazardly sewn back into place.

"You were just using me . . .?"

"It's not fucking like that," Levi grits. "Your father is a dangerous man, Ava. I'm trying to protect you."

"Bullshit!" I turn away from his piercing blue gaze because it hurts too much to look at him right now. Knowing that every interaction between us has been a lie from the moment I met him. "How could you do this to me? I trusted you. I . . . fell for you."

"Ava," his voice softens. He reaches for me, but I tug away from his grasp, backing up into the banister behind me. He takes my face in his hands, and this time, I slap him so hard my hand stings. "*Goddamnit*, listen to me."

"Why?" I growl, tears mixing with my makeup and blurring my vision. "How would I even know it's the truth? You've lied about everything from the start."

His eyes burn with a venom that sends a chill through me.

"Everything I have done, I have done to protect you."

"*Don't touch me.*"

I push away from him, and he lets me, though he doesn't let me get far. His hand reaches for my waist, and I almost back out right there.

"Just fucking listen to me, Ava. Your father isn't a good man. He murdered Wright, and now someone is trying to use you against him. Against *me* because it was my job to stop it, and I couldn't. I walked away because my brother needed me, not realizing I was putting you in danger with each step."

I shake my head, completely overwhelmed.

"Ava, look at me," Levi growls. "You know this is more than that. You know that. You *know me*."

I suck in a deep breath, watching his hands clench before my eyes slide back to his. Something brief flashes across his features, but I saw it. A kind of desperation only someone who's about to lose everything would feel, all while telling themselves they never wanted it anyway.

"You're making me regret you."

He winces at the way my voice cracks, taking a single step towards me. It's the first time I've ever seen him indecisive.

"Can you not feel everything I do? Can't you see I'm fucking desperate for you? Me? I've never been weak for anything in my fucking life, but you? I'd go to war for you, Ava. I *have* been fighting for you. I . . ." he stops and scrubs a hand through his hair. "Fuck," he curses.

"Goodbye, Levi."

I hurry towards my door, but he's there, catching my wrist and tugging me back to his chest. In a split second, his hands come to either side of my face, and he crushes his lips to mine.

Pain, unlike anything I've ever felt, blooms in my chest.

God, I want to sink into him and forget the world exists. Go back to that cabin and spend weeks memorizing every detail of his body and soul.

It won't be enough, though.

He lied. He hid the truth from me. He knew who my father was from the start, yet he didn't feel like I deserved to know.

There will always be a part of him that he keeps hidden from me. Shunning me for reminding him of anything he deems off-limits. Refusing to accept that I'm not the bad guy in his story and merely the stupid girl falling completely, madly in love with him.

I rip my lips away, putting a hair's breadth of space between us. "Purgatory."

He releases me as if I'd burnt him, and falls back, his hands fisting at his sides and his eyes wild.

In the time that I can remember since I met Levi, I've never seen that expression on his face. Uncertainty. Hopelessness.

"Try and leave me, Ava." His voice is rough and unhinged, but there's something else underneath it all. Something like pure fear.

"Consider this my resignation." I keep my eyes trained on the wall. I can't look at him now. If I do, I know I'll break. "I don't expect anything from you."

"*No.*"

"You can hide behind your walls, Levi. I still see you. You'll let me go because it's what I want, even if it kills you."

And then I leave him standing in the hall alone, trying not to break down before I make it to my room and lock the door behind me.

"Carry her in here."

Christian lifts me like I weigh nothing, like I'm not completely falling apart. He carries me into their spare bedroom, laying me down on the bed gently. Mila trails silently behind him, her face pale, eyes wide.

She found me curled on the hardwood floor of my room, too empty to move, too shattered to care. I don't know how she knew. Maybe something in her chest tugged the moment mine broke. Either way, she came. And I hate how grateful I am because I ruined their night.

When Christian steps away, I don't even wait. I curl into myself like something wounded and small, wishing I could fold myself out of existence. My body aches, but not in any way anyone can fix.

I think I'm numb. Or maybe just ruined. His words keep playing in my head, looping like a cruel lullaby. But it's not like it matters anymore.

I signed the contract. I agreed to the rules.

I just didn't expect to lose myself along the way.

I didn't think he'd tear my walls down so gently . . . and then obliterate everything left.

"Give us some space," Mila says softly, her voice so careful it barely stirs the air. Christian hesitates, then the door clicks shut.

I hear her come over, the soft sound of her steps, then the dip of the mattress behind me. A moment later, arms wrap around my body—warm, steady, undeserved.

She holds me like someone who still sees something worth saving.

But I don't feel worth saving.

Unlovable. Unworthy.

Disposable.

Trash.

"I'm so sorry, Ava . . ." Mila whispers, and her voice cracks like she's breaking with me. But I can't speak. My throat's raw, closed. I can't even beg her to stop being kind.

The only thing I can do is cry—quiet, helpless tears that slip down my face and soak into the pillow like they've been waiting their turn.

"I'm sorry," she says again, softer this time. As if maybe she knows I'm not just crying over him.

I'm crying because in the midst of it all, he'd helped me find myself.

Even if it was all a lie.

CHAPTER
Forty-One

AVA

Day one, post-Levi, I wake up feeling like I've been hit by a truck—sore, achy, sick to my stomach from crying myself to sleep. My eyes are swollen, my throat is raw, and my pillow is still damp from last night. I drag myself to the bathroom and catch a glimpse of myself in the mirror. It's so jarring, I flinch. My skin is blotchy, my hair's a tangled mess, and I barely recognize the person staring back at me.

It's humiliating.

But it's my fault.

I knew what this was. As if I could separate my heart from my body and be the girl who doesn't get attached.

But then he started saying things that made me feel safe. Doing things that made me feel wanted. Like I mattered. And I let myself believe that I could be the exception.

It all happened so fast.

Falling for him.

Losing him.

There's no one defining moment I can point to. No single

moments—each one carving his name deeper into my heart.

It was the way he was with Gran, bringing her flowers and making jokes.

The way he held me in silence when she passed, letting me cry until I had nothing left in me.

The way he made me soup when I had the flu and how he'd cleaned me up when I'd had too much to drink.

The way we laughed. Really laughed. Shared stories about our pasts, confessed our secrets like we were the only two people in the world.

At least—I thought we both did.

Now I realize the secrets we shared were mine alone. His stayed hidden behind that carefully constructed wall of iciness and deflection.

By day two, post-Levi, I'm angry now. Tired. Emotionally drained.

Why did I let him lie to me? This entire time, he was using me, and I was too stupid to see the signs. And for my father, no less. A person he *knows* I have always wondered about.

I'm staying at Mila and Christian's place, under Mila's strict orders, but it feels like I'm a ghost haunting someone else's life. I move through the rooms without touching anything. I barely speak.

Christian keeps himself busy, probably because he doesn't know what to say. Mila tiptoes around me like I'll break if she looks at me too hard. Maybe she's right.

The house is too quiet. I spend most nights staring at the ceiling, replaying everything over and over like some sick highlight reel.

Still, I can't help it. I keep waiting.

Waiting for the sound of footsteps on the porch.

Waiting for the scent of whiskey and longing to wash over me.

Waiting like an idiot for Levi to show up and say he was wrong. That's he's sorry. That he *needs* me.

Is that toxic? Delusional?

If it is, then he made me this way.

I want to ask Mila if she's heard from him, but I don't. Because if she says he's been out at the Tomb with Cherry and her neon-red hair, I might lose it. I might actually show up just to get under his skin. To prove I'm not the girl everyone abandons.

Like maybe if I can piss him off enough, he'll realize what he lost.

It's childish.

It's petty.

It's human.

By day three, post-Levi, I've stopped waiting.

It's over. And I know that now.

There's no grand gesture. No apology. Just silence.

By day four, one million and *one* dollars show up in my account.

One dollar to show he remembers.

One dollar to twist the knife just a little bit deeper.

I rejected it immediately. I couldn't follow the terms of his cold, transactional little arrangement, and I don't want his or my father's money anyway.

I've survived without it my entire life. I'll keep surviving.

What I wanted—what I still stupidly want—is *him*.

But that part of me is starting to die, little by little.

On day five, I tell Mila I'm moving. I spend the rest of the night moving into Gran's old cottage in the woods. It's off the beaten path and just isolated enough that I don't have to worry about being friendly with the neighbors.

Everything is covered in dust and cobwebs. I haven't been able to come back since I moved into Cross Estate. Mainly because it feels hollow without her. But, now . . . so do I.

I start by cleaning out the bedroom as best I can. I'm still surrounded by Gran everywhere I look, but at least now, I can breathe enough to sleep.

And somewhere along the way, I go numb.

Not in a peaceful, I'm-healed-now kind of way. More like my emotions have finally short-circuited.

I hate him.

I hate him because he made me fall in love with him. I'm a walking oxymoron with a penchant for falling for men who should come with a list of trigger warnings.

It's pathetic.

I want to cry and scream and throw things. I want to break someone else's heart because mine feels like it's been ripped out and stomped into the dirt.

It wouldn't change anything. I'd still be just as miserable without him as I am now. So . . . I accept it.

Not because I've moved on.

But because I've run out of ways to resist.

On my sixth and final day, I find myself in my old room, packing what few things I have. I hate that it doesn't smell like him when I pass his door. Almost like he hasn't been there since I left him.

I'm nearly finished when a sharp knock breaks the silence, echoing through the room like a gunshot. My heart lurches, skipping a beat. I freeze, unable to move. For a moment, it feels like time holds its breath with me.

My mouth is dry when I swallow hard, each step toward the door feeling heavier than the last. I suck in a deep breath and grip the handle like it might anchor me to reality. With a trembling hand, I pull it open—

Only to find Paulina standing on the other side.

My stomach sinks violently, as if I've just stepped off a ledge. I don't even know why I allowed hope to get the better of me. Of course, it wouldn't be him.

"Can I help you?" I manage, my voice flat, stripped of emotion. Whatever opinion she has of me doesn't matter anymore.

"Actually, yes," she says, lifting her chin with that familiar arrogance and brushing past me like into the room.

I stand there, stunned, the door still open behind me as I watch her stride into my room like she's got every right to be here.

"I didn't invite you in," I mutter when she drops into the chair beside my bed, poised like she's settling in for a long chat.

"That sounds like your problem," she shoots back, eyes flicking around the room with thinly veiled judgment.

This bitch.

I exhale sharply and push the door closed with more force than necessary, crossing my arms over my chest as I glare at her.

"What do you want, Paulina?"

I know I'm being rude, maybe even cruel, but I'm done playing nice. I've bitten my tongue for too long, swallowed too many words. And after tomorrow, I won't be under her thumb anymore.

She has the audacity to look me dead in the eye. "I want you to take Levi back."

Her words hit me like a freight train. My heart jolts violently, the air knocked from my lungs. It's been days since I've heard his name out loud. Just hearing it feels like ripping open a wound I've barely managed to stitch shut.

My legs give out beneath me, and I collapse onto the edge of the bed, clutching the mattress for support. My heart pounds in my chest, loud and erratic.

"If you've come here to bargain for him . . . save it."

She tilts her head like she doesn't understand the problem. Like it's a detail that can be easily brushed aside.

"Whatever happened, fix it."

"I'm sorry," I say, sarcasm sharpening my voice. "Did I miss the part where you were allowed to barge in here and start making demands? I already quit. I'll be gone tonight."

"Despite everything, I like you, Ava," she says unexpectedly.

"Yeah," I snort, "that was always really obvious."

She ignores the bite in my tone. "Something about you changed him. I don't know what it was, but he softened. You made him different. Better. I've never seen Levi care for someone the way he did for you."

My chest tightens, the pain almost unbearable. I remember that version of him—the one who held me like I was his lifeline, who whispered things in the dark that he couldn't say in the light. The version who tried so hard to be more than the pain he was born into.

But that was all a façade. Just like everything else, he made me feel.

"Paulina . . . " I sigh, pressing a hand to my sternum, as if I can keep my heart from shattering again. "It's over."

She goes quiet. So quiet that for a moment, I think she's stopped breathing. I wouldn't be surprised—these days, the universe seems to take every opportunity it can to screw me.

"Where would you go?"

"I have a house. My Gran's house. I'll find a new job," I shrug. "Does it matter?"

"You can't."

"I can," I snap. "And I will. It's for the best. There's nothing left for me here."

"You have us," she says, softly—so unexpectedly soft that it actually hurts.

But I don't have him.

"That's not enough," I whisper.

Paulina exhales slowly, and for the first time since I met her, there's no smugness in her expression. Just sadness. A hollow sort of regret.

We sit in silence. A shared, heavy acceptance settles over the room like a cloud of dust.

It's a clean slate. A new beginning.

God, I need that.

"How is he?" The words tumble out before I can stop them. It's the only thing I've wanted to ask since she walked in.

Paulina studies me, and then finally—finally—she answers.

"He's hurting, Ava. He's broken. I've never seen him like this. He won't say he misses you, but it's written all over him. I can see it."

I wish she hadn't said that.

"Goodbye, Paulina."

I stand abruptly, heading for the door before the ache in my chest can turn into action. Because if I stay here, I'll go to him. And I made myself clear—he and I are through.

"When I became the caretaker for my niece and nephews, I had no idea what I was doing," she says, voice quiet behind me. "I've made a lot of mistakes. But my biggest regret?"

I turn, just enough to see her watching me. And for once, there's guilt in her eyes. Real, human guilt.

"Being an asshole?" I offer dryly.

She ignores me. "I was too easy on him."

I blink, stunned. "Excuse me? He was beaten by his father his whole life. How is that 'easy'?"

"I let him shut everyone out," she says, her voice cracking. "I thought I was protecting him, giving him space. But I was enabling him. I should've made him talk. I should've helped him face it instead of hiding from it."

I shake my head, that familiar dread creeping over me like a storm tide. "You didn't know."

"Don't give me excuses, Ava. I was too busy to see how his father was hurting him. And now? He destroys everything he loves."

A tear slides down my cheek before I can stop it.

She stares at me, long and hard. Like she's peeling back layers I didn't even know I had. I feel stripped bare beneath her gaze.

I swallow over the lump in my throat, tears stinging in the backs of my eyes.

"What's done is done," I say hoarsely.

It sounds final. Heavy. Like a door slamming shut in the distance. And maybe that's what this is. The end of something I'll never get back.

Will I ever feel again? Will I find anyone like him?

A quiet voice in my mind whispers, *NO*. And my knees almost buckle under the truth of it.

Even if what Paulina says is true . . . Even if he's hurting . . .

There will always be something missing.

Something lost.

Something Levi took with him the day he let me go.

"I'll say this . . ." I pause, reaching for the door handle. I have to get out of here. "I wish I could hate him, but . . ." I shrug. "I just can't."

She doesn't respond, staring at me with guilt.

"Goodbye, Paulina."

CHAPTER
Forty-Two

LEVI

O f all the things you could've fixed around here, you chose the biggest piece of shit on the island. Congrats."

Christian's voice slices through the air like a switchblade. It echoes off the warped wooden beams of the old barn, sharp and smug and laced with that brand of brotherly disappointment I've known since we were kids—sharp enough to sting, familiar enough to burn.

I ignore my brother when he steps up to the engine I've got torn apart in front of me. I just needed something to do, and working on engines has always calmed me when my mind was a warzone. It's the only kind of broken I've ever known how to fix.

I'm fixing this damned boat whether it likes it or not.

"What part of 'I want to be alone' didn't you get?" I mutter, not bothering to look at him when he leans back against the side of the old, beat-up boat that rests in the barn on Shipwreck Island. I can't help but see the irony in the name.

Shipwreck Island is where he disappeared when life got too loud. Where he dragged Mila after saving her from whatever old, haunted cottage, a stubborn lighthouse clutching a cliff, and a few decaying shacks.

Well, and this piece of shit boat.

Shipwreck Island is quiet. Empty. The kind of place people can come to fall apart in peace.

—Unless, of course, your brother is named Christian Cross.

"Right," he says with a smirk. "I forgot. You're deep into your tragic lone-wolf phase."

Fucking dick.

"Did you come out here to be a jackass, or do you want something?"

"You're avoiding your problems," he grunts.

"I'm not avoiding anything."

"Bullshit. No one gives a flying fuck about this boat."

"Maybe I do." *Maybe it's the only thing left that I haven't completely ruined.*

Christian doesn't seem to take the hint, instead falling into the old lawn chair beside the boat and kicking his feet up.

Jesus fucking Christ, why can't he just leave me alone?

"Don't you have somewhere else to be annoying?"

Christian meets my stare—steady, cutting.

"Right now, I've got a wife ready to murder my brother, a brother hiding out on my island, and a sad little brunette who cries herself to sleep every night, occupying most of my wife's time. The least you could do is offer me a drink."

Ah, of course. This isn't a visit. It's a goddamned siege.

My grip tightens around the wrench in my hand until my knuckles throb. That guilt I've been choking down for days swells, bitter and thick, rising like smoke.

I grab the bottle. Take a long pull that scorches my throat and does jack shit to ease the ache. Then I pass it to him. .

It's not a comfort. It's a distraction that I thought I'd moved past, but it's all I've got right now.

Christian drinks too, slow and thoughtful, then sets the bottle down with a soft *clunk*.

"How is she?"

The words come out like glass. Fragile. Dangerous.

He doesn't answer right away. Just studies me with that unnerving stillness of his, like he's peeling back layers I thought I buried deep enough.

"Not great. I'm not supposed to tell you this, but she just moved back to her gran's house," he says finally. "But of course, you already knew that, didn't you?"

Of course, I did. I've only spent the last three nights waiting outside in case anyone decides to show up.

"I told her not to get attached," I mutter, and it sounds pathetic—worse than an excuse.

It's also hypocritical.

From the moment Ava stepped into my life, it was like the world made sense. Something mattered, and it wasn't just my family or my job. Fuck, *I* mattered.

Not that it makes a damn difference.

Christian's brow lifts. "Yeah. I'm sure that really softened the blow."

The silence afterward is like a weight on my chest. It presses on my ribs until every breath feels like penance.

I sigh, turning back to the boat. "Doesn't matter. It was going to happen eventually."

Christian chuckles under his breath, shaking his head.

"You're really committed to being the biggest dumbass this side of the Pacific, huh?"

"Fuck you."

The asshole doesn't know what the fuck I'm dealing with. He doesn't know the only sleep I've gotten all week is when I've passed out, only to wake up from a nightmare, reaching for the empty spot next to me.

He doesn't realize that I've watched the cameras at the house every. Fucking. Day. Just waiting to catch a glimpse of her, only to come up short.

He doesn't realize I'm fucking dying without her.

"No, fuck *you*, Levi."

"What do you want from me, Christian?" I snap. My voice cracks as I hurl the wrench. It hits the far wall with a hollow clang and vanishes into the dark. "You want me to say you're right? Want me to stroke your ego?"

"I want you to realize you're ruining your life by being a pussy."

"Fuck you," I snap. "You don't know half the shit I've dealt with. You were too busy running off after Mila to even think about what was going on here."

"You think I don't know what Dad did to you?" His face is growing redder and redder by the moment. "You seriously think I don't realize you went against what I said and murdered the fucking bastard?"

Well, fuck.

We stare each other down—the only sound the heavy rain outside and our heavy breathing.

"So, what? You want to lecture me? Want to turn me in?"

"Of course, I'm not going to turn you in. I wanted to do the same thing. What I *want* is for you to get your head out of your ass and realize you're going to die a sad, lonely, pissed off old asshole if you don't fix this shit."

"I don't want to fix things, you big asshole," I snap. "She was a good fuck, but it's over. We had a deal, now it's done. She knew what she was getting into. I didn't fucking force her."

He opens his mouth to argue back, but stops abruptly, cocking his head to the side.

"Well, I'll be damned . . . you're in love with her."

"Fuck you."

"I never thought I'd see the day," he murmurs, shaking his head.

"Does it matter?"

He fixes me with a dark look. "It always matters."

I shake my head, grab the bottle, and turn away from him. I swallow half of it and don't feel a thing.

"She doesn't need to be a part of this."

"She already is. And now you've abandoned her."

"I didn't fucking abandon her," I snap. "She fucking left. It's better this way."

"Bullshit," he scoffs. "You think she gives a fuck that Dad used to beat you? Or that you have nightmares some nights? She fucking loves you, for some goddamned reason. You know how hard it is to find shit like that? Especially for assholes like us."

I shake my head. He doesn't get it.

"She doesn't fucking want me," I grit. He says nothing. "What about when Palmer shows up? What then?" He doesn't respond when I stare at him. "Yeah, sure, I fucking love her. I love her so much that I'd rather live a life without her than a life with her fucking dead, even if it fucking kills me. Do you not understand that?"

The silence between us is heavy.

"Everyone's willing to break the rules for someone . . ." he says finally. "Are you willing to let her walk away?"

I shake my head, turning away so he can't see the agony coursing through me.

It's been a week without her, and I feel like I'm going through withdrawals day in and day out. It's like I need her to breathe, and I'm slowly suffocating without her.

It feels like she's stolen the man I used to be, and now, I don't know how to live.

"I loved Mila for years . . . Even when I knew I shouldn't. It didn't stop just because I said goodbye."

I don't know what to say, so I don't.

"I know Dad did horrible shit to you. I know he beat the fuck out of you."

"We can save this trip down memory lane. I'm really not in the mood."

"Too fucking bad," he grunts. "Bad shit happened, and you have to accept that you've got things you need to figure out . . . but don't punish the girl for it."

I grip the edge of the counter in the old barn, my hands tightening until my knuckles turn white.

He's right. I've always been a stubborn son of a bitch. So much so that it's fucked me over a fair few times.

I scrub a hand over my face, trying to push the image of her tear-streaked face out of my head. It's haunted me since I came to this goddamned island, and nothing will chase it away.

From the moment I met her, I've taken from her and taken from her, while keeping her at arm's length because I knew the moment I let her get too close, I would be fucked.

Now, I have to live with the consequences.

"Love isn't all about protecting them," Christian says, breaking through the tirade of thoughts swirling around my brain. "Sometimes you have to accept that they're going to see your dark parts, and hope that they can still look at you the same after."

I scoff under my breath.

My dark parts.

Fuck, where do I even begin?

I finally toss the wrench down on the counter, looking at the broken engine torn apart in front of me, and silence fills the barn.

"You sound like a Hallmark card," I grunt eventually.

Christian shrugs. "Sometimes Hallmark cards are right."

Fucking hell.

I scrub a hand over my face. Look out the barn doors to the sky. Wonder what the fuck I'm doing.

"You think she'd even want me back . . . after what I did to her?"

Christian cocks a brow. "You'll never know unless you try."

Pain lances at my chest, and I rub over the spot absentmindedly. Maybe I'm getting old. Maybe it's just the thought of her disappearing from my life.

I love her. That's enough, right?

Fuck, I can't believe I'm about to do this.

"Takes a half hour to get to her house," I grunt, looking at the time on my phone. "Think you can get me there in the next twenty minutes?"

Christian grins.

"Make it ten."

The ride to the little cottage in the woods feels like it lasts a lifetime. My head's a fucking mess. My sanity is even worse.

I keep thinking about the outcome. If I manage to convince her to take me back, how the fuck am I supposed to keep her safe?

Lock her away in the cabin until this ends? Keep her prisoner in my bed so she can never see the light of day?

Fuck, I wish this shit were easy. I wish I could fucking find him, but there's been no leads.

Even the shipments have stopped, though I know there's just something I'm missing.

If I could, I'd give it all up. Just to know she's safe.

If love means you're willing to sacrifice the best parts of yourself to save even the darkest parts of them, then yeah, I guess I love her. Do I understand it? Fuck no. Does it matter? Not anymore.

We're racing down the backroads, Christian driving my car while my mind works overtime with a plan.

What the fuck am I supposed to say?

Sorry, I fucking suck. Please don't go?

I've gone toe to toe with some of the world's most dangerous criminals.

Why the hell is it a little five-foot-three brunette that scares the fucking piss out of me?

When he pulls down the drive to Ava's cottage, the place looks empty. If it weren't for her car out front, I'd think it was completely abandoned.

Christian pulls to a stop beside the SUV, but I'm too busy staring at the slight crack in the door to notice when he shoves the car into park.

"What the fuck?" Christian murmurs under his breath while I climb out of the car.

I march up to the front door, hesitant at first, before I reach out and knock.

The door swings open.

"Ava!" I call out to the emptiness of the house. The scent of mothballs greets my nose. None of the familiar citrus I've been salivating for in the last week.

Behind me, Christian gets out of the car, hanging back, but I can see the look in his eyes, and I don't fucking like it.

Something isn't right.

I step inside, my boots creaking against the worn hardwood floor. The place is cold—too cold. A chill seeps in through the open door, but it's more than that. It feels... wrong. Hollow. Like all the life has been sucked out of it.

"Ava!" I shout again, this time with more edge.

Still nothing.

The living room is a mess. Not in the way it would be were no one living here for years—no, this is different. A chair was knocked over. A shattered glass on the floor, tiny fragments glittering like a threat. Her coat is still hanging by the door, her sneakers neatly lined up beneath it.

She didn't leave willingly.

Christian moves in behind me, slow and cautious, his hand drifting toward the gun in the back of his waistband.

"There was a struggle," he mutters, eyes scanning the room. "That's blood."

My head whips toward where he's looking—just past the kitchen threshold. A dark smear on the edge of the counter. Small, but fresh. My pulse kicks up, hammering in my ears as I cross the room in two long strides.

I reach out and touch it.

Still tacky.

"Ava . . ." I whisper, this time like a prayer.

Christian's voice is low, urgent. "Levi."

I turn.

He's crouched by the coffee table, holding something up. A phone. Her phone. But it's the picture still frozen on the cracked screen that fills me with lead.

As if on cue, my phone rings, echoing in the silence of the house.

I stare at it for a moment, rage bubbling through my veins like poison.

Lifting it to my ear, I almost snap it in half.

"Where is she?"

I can practically hear his sinister grin through the phone.

"Hello, golden boy."

Iciness slips through my veins, my hand shaking with the effort to contain the blistering rage sliding through me.

She's gone.

She's. Fucking. Gone.

"If you hurt even a single fucking hair on her head, I promise I'll be the last thing you see before God."

He chuckles menacingly. "God doesn't want me, Cross. It's the devil I'll see, and when I do, I'm taking your pretty little whore with me."

This is all my fucking fault.

I fucking failed her.

Visions of what he could do to her flash through my mind like a fucked-up zoetrope. My entire body stiffens, my mind screaming in agony until it drowns out the heavy beat of my heart.

"You know I'm going to hunt you down," I growl, a calm clarity settling over me. "And when I find you, I'll feed your balls to you like hors d'oeuvres while you bleed out in whatever cesspool you're hiding out in."

"Relax, your little pet is alive for now. See?"

A soft sniffle comes through the line, and my chest tightens painfully.

"Levi?" Ava's voice filters through the phone, and I nearly drop to my knees.

"Baby, I'm coming for you."

"Levi . . . I'm scared," she breathes, and I can hear his laugh in the background.

"I know, baby. Just hold on. I'll explain everything to you later, just don't—"

"Time's up. Sorry, I'm a very busy man," he muses. "You have one hour to get me Marks. If you fail, I'm slicing her throat."

Click.

Rage bubbles through me—a quiet storm brewing on the horizon.

My girl.

"There's something else," Christian says quietly, holding up his phone for me to see.

It's an email from an encrypted number. One of his old contacts with the FBI.

It's what's in the email that fills my chest with lead.

My blood runs ice cold.

Christian sees it too. "A body just washed up on the south shore . . . It was Palmer's."

I blow out a breath through my teeth. Scrub a hand through my hair. Suck in a shallow breath through the rage bubbling through me.

I lift my head—slow, deliberate. Eyes cold.

I chamber a round with a snap. The sound echoes through the cottage like a promise. Then I shoulder past Christian without a word.

"Mendez just signed his fucking death warrant."

CHAPTER
Forty-Three

AVA

I'm ashamed to admit I've let my grandmother's house go.

The place is a wreck. Cobwebs hang from the corners, the fridge smells like death's cousin, and it's so cluttered, I don't even know where to begin.

Luckily, it's enough to keep my mind occupied on my first day on my own, leaving me little time to think about Levi, my mysterious father, and the threat of whoever is hunting me looming over my head.

After all, cleaning is my specialty.

Except when I start, I find a picture of Gran and me and end up in a puddle of my own tears on the floor.

So . . . in the silence of my new home, I cry as loud and obnoxiously as I want. I cry for Gran. I cry for Levi. I cry about a cat I had when I was twelve, who went missing one day. I'd found him in the window, too young to realize until I tried to pick him up that he was already dead.

I cry for every version of myself I've ever had to bury just to survive.

for a long time, cheek pressed to the dusty hardwood, arms curled around the frame like it's the only thing anchoring me to the earth. The picture is old—faded at the edges—but Gran's smile is just as I remember. Warm. Fierce. Like she knew all my secrets and loved me anyway.

God, I miss her.

Eventually, I sit up and swipe my sleeve across my face, smearing tears and dust together like war paint. I'm not done grieving. I don't think I ever will be. But grief doesn't get to rot this place to the ground. Not while I'm still standing.

So, I get up.

I toss the picture on the counter, blast an old playlist Gran used to love—some mix of Patsy Cline, Fleetwood Mac, and angry woman country that I've never listened to in my life—and start scrubbing like it's going to save me. Maybe it will.

Each cabinet I empty, each surface I wipe, feels like reclaiming something. My sanity. My life. My strength.

But that doesn't mean I'm not still haunted.

Levi's voice echoes in my head sometimes when I reach for something high up or when I slam a drawer too hard. His laugh. That quiet growl he made when I said something that pushed his buttons. The way he'd look at me like I was the only thing he'd ever been sure of.

And then there's the other voice, colder and sharper—Alex's. His words echoing back to me, reminding me that I will never be anything more than a pawn in someone else's game.

But not today.

Today, I scrub blood off the metaphorical walls and sing horribly along to the music until my voice gives out. Today, I let myself be a little broken, a little brave, and a little pissed off at the world.

And when I finally let myself collapse on the couch, covered in sweat and dust and whatever the hell that black goo in the sink was .

. . I don't feel *good*, exactly.

But I feel something like hope.

Tomorrow, I'll figure out how to change the locks. Tomorrow, I'll go into town and get supplies. Tomorrow, I'll try to remember who I was before all of this. Or maybe I'll start deciding who I want to be now.

Tonight, though?

Tonight, I'll wrap myself in Gran's old quilt, heat up a questionable can of soup, and let the silence hold me without crushing me.

And that's enough.

At least for now.

When I climb under the spray of the shower, it's near dusk, and a quiet calm settles over the clearing outside. The snow has started to accumulate, but it will be a few weeks before it becomes a problem. For now, I've got enough old, dry wood stored to last, at least until I can muster up whatever strength I can find to go out and chop wood.

Maybe that could be my new calling. Lumberjack Ava.

Okay, maybe not, but I'll make it work.

By the time I climb out of the shower, the house is cast in shadows, and the sun is beginning to dip below the trees. I slide on a pair of jeans and a fresh T-shirt because I have every intention of heading into town to get some supplies for the house.

It's not until I'm brushing my hair that I realize the music in the kitchen has stopped.

I freeze, brush mid-stroke.

The silence is sudden. Suffocating. The kind of silence that doesn't just fall—it *lands*. Hard. Like a warning shot.

At first, I try to rationalize it. Maybe the playlist ended. Maybe the power flickered. Maybe I accidentally hit pause with my elbow when I passed by the speaker. But I know I didn't.

The cottage is old, but she's reliable. And I know what silence sounds like when it's natural. This isn't that.

I set the brush down carefully on the bathroom counter, every nerve ending in my body going on high alert. The kind of instinctive awareness that settles in your bones after you've been hunted before. And I *have*.

I pad barefoot to the doorway and press my shoulder against the wall, straining to hear *anything*. A creak. A footstep. The whoosh of the heater kicking on.

Nothing.

Which is somehow worse.

Slowly, I reach for the small drawer under the hallway table, where I tucked my grandmother's old revolver earlier today while cleaning. The handle is cold and familiar in my palm, the weight grounding me just enough to keep the panic at bay.

I inch toward the kitchen, heart thudding against my ribs like it's trying to warn me of something my mind hasn't caught up to yet.

When I round the corner, everything looks the same—except for one detail.

The back door is cracked open.

Not much. Just a sliver. Barely enough to notice unless you're looking.

But I *am* looking.

And I know damn well I locked it earlier.

The cold air creeping through the opening brushes against my bare arms, and suddenly I'm not sure if it's the chill or fear that raises goosebumps along my skin.

I lift the gun and take one step closer, peering out through the gap.

The clearing looks empty. Still. Snow dusts the back porch, undisturbed.

But that doesn't mean someone didn't already come in.

I step back and shut the door quietly, clicking the lock into place. Then I twist the deadbolt for good measure. My breath catches when I turn and notice—

One of the mugs from the drying rack is missing.

It had been there earlier. I remember. Blue ceramic with a chip along the rim. Gran's favorite.

Now it's gone.

Which means someone was here.

Maybe still is.

My grip on the revolver tightens. I move quickly, silently, checking the rest of the cottage room by room, until I reach the last place—Gran's old bedroom. The door is mostly closed, just barely ajar.

I swear I didn't leave it like that.

I don't breathe as I nudge it open with the toe of my shoe.

Inside, the bed is untouched. The closet door is open an inch.

My heart pounds so loud I'm sure whoever might be hiding inside can hear it.

I raise the gun, hand steady, voice low and hard. "If you're in there, you've got three seconds to step out before I put a hole in the door."

Silence.

Then—

A soft creak.

I don't wait. I kick the closet door open and step back, gun raised.

Empty.

Just coats and old blankets and the musty smell of cedar and time.

I stand there for a long moment, pulse still racing, before lowering the weapon.

There's no one here.

That is, until they wrap their arms around me from behind.

I try to scream, but a gloved hand slams over my mouth, dragging me back before the sound can leave my throat. My feet skid across the floor, kicking wildly, and my elbow connects with something solid—but it barely slows them down.

They're strong. Too strong.

And silent.

The revolver clatters to the floor just out of reach, spinning across the wood like it's mocking me.

I thrash harder, desperation overtaking fear, nails clawing at their hand, trying to twist, bite, *anything*—but they've done this before.

I'm thrown forward onto the bed, and my hands are ripped behind my back and cuffed. I wince at the pain of the metal digging into my bones, and try to fight them off, but it's no use.

Then a voice—cool, calm, and far too fucking sinister—slithers out of the darkness like a blade against my spine.

"You're making this harder than it needs to be."

I twist onto my back, dazed—and freeze.

"Hello, Ava," he says, voice smooth and low. Too calm.

My eyes dart to the object glinting in his hand.

A syringe.

No. No, no, no.

"You," I whisper, voice barely audible. My entire body seizes with instinctive terror. "Don't—don't do this."

He tilts his head, black eyes glinting as he studies me like something beneath glass. "They warned you, Ava. You should have listened."

I push back against him, trying to kick, trying to move, but I'm boxed in. There's nowhere to go.

"Don't," I breathe, trembling so hard my teeth chatter.

But he's already lunging. The needle sinks into the side of my neck with a sickening sting. I scream—but it's already fading into a slur.

Fire spreads from the puncture down my spine.

I gasp, trying to fight it. Trying to move. My limbs go numb. My head spins. My tongue goes thick and useless in my mouth.

"Levi . . ." I slur again, desperate. My vision wobbles, tunneling at the edges.

He leans in, brushing hair from my face with terrifying gentleness. "I told you Cross would get you killed."

The world is spinning.

Levi was right . . .

I want to scream. Fight. *Do something.*

I want to tell him to go to hell.

Unfortunately, all I can do is black out.

The first thing I notice when my senses crawl back from the void is the sickness.

It doesn't just settle in my stomach—it *ravages* it, twisting and roiling like a nest of snakes. Acid claws up my throat, leaving a trail of fire as I shift on the cold, unforgiving concrete floor. Pain radiates from every point of contact. My joints groan, stiff from whatever cocktail of drugs Alex injected me with.

The air is heavy. Wet. Foul. It clings to my throat, thick with the scent of mildew, rust, and something unmistakably iron—*blood*. It coats the back of my tongue with every breath I take, and I gag before I even open my eyes.

When I do, it's like peeling open wounds.

Light blisters against my vision, too bright, too raw. The room spins in nauseating circles, the walls pulsing with each throb of my skull like they're breathing in tandem with me. It takes everything not to retch on the floor. Tears sting at the corners of my eyes. My lungs flutter, struggling to draw in air that won't come clean.

Then the world sharpens—painfully, cruelly—into clarity.

"Well, well, well . . ." The voice slithers out from the shadows, oozing satisfaction. "Look who's finally decided to wake up."

The nausea spikes so hard I nearly lose it right there.

Alex.

He's draped in a rusted, cracked metal chair in the corner like he owns the fucking world, one leg crossed lazily over the other, arms spread like a bored king surveying his new toy.

"Sleep well?"

"You . . ." My voice scrapes out of my throat like broken glass. I can barely form words through the fury threatening to combust inside me. "You fucking *asshole*."

He smiles, completely unbothered. "I tried to help you, Ava. I really did."

With a lazy nudge of his foot, he kicks a filthy metal bowl across the floor toward me. Water sloshes inside, bits of dirt and hair swirling on the surface.

"Go on," he says. "You're probably thirsty."

Like I'm a fucking dog.

I grip the bowl and hurl it across the room with every ounce of strength I can muster. It bounces off the ground, spilling water over his boots.

"Drink it yourself, dickhead."

His jaw ticks. The gleam in his eyes dims, just a fraction, replaced by something hungrier. Meaner.

"Tsk-tsk." His voice takes on that condescending lilt, like he's scolding a child. "See? I told you Cross was a bad influence. Listen to that mouth. Not very becoming, Ava."

He reaches beside him and lifts a tray—dry toast curled at the edges, pale and lifeless like it died weeks ago.

"Hungry?" He tosses it at me, and it lands with a soft *plop* at my feet.

"Fuck you."

His grin widens. Predatory. All teeth, no soul. "We'll get there."

Something icy unfurls in my chest.

"Eat," he orders.

"No."

His expression hardens. The playful cruelty drains away, replaced with something colder.

"Ava, Ava, Ava . . ." He stands slowly, his boots echoing against the concrete. "You're not making this easy."

Then his hand cracks across my face.

My head snaps to the side, the sound of it echoing off the walls like a gunshot. A flash of white heat bursts across my cheek, blooming into sharp, stinging pain. I taste blood—warm and metallic, in my mouth.

"I don't want to hurt you," he says, but his voice is hollow. Mechanical. Like he's rehearsed that line a hundred times. "But I gave you an order."

"Go to hell," I hiss, copper on my tongue.

"Sweetheart," he says, crouching in front of me, voice almost tender. "Can't you see? You're already there."

His cologne hits me—sickly clean, sharp, and artificial. It doesn't cover the rot clinging to the walls. It makes it worse.

I try to shrink back, but the wall is already against my spine. My body trembles. Ice coats my veins.

"Are you doing this because I rejected you?" I ask, trying to buy time, to *breathe*. "Or because you're working for my father?"

He laughs—a low, cold chuckle that guts the room of warmth.

"Poor, simple Ava. You really don't know anything, do you?"

His gaze sharpens as confusion tightens my gut.

"Why do you think I took the job at Cross Estate, Ava?"

My stomach sinks as realization sets in.

"It . . . it was you." The words barely escape my lips. "This whole time . . ."

"You didn't know?" Alex raises an eyebrow, feigning surprise. "Come on, Ava. You're smarter than that."

"You set us up," I whisper, the truth slipping through me like poison.

"Very good, beautiful."

He leans forward and brushes hair from my face. I flinch, every inch of my skin crawling.

He pulls a knife from his pocket. Cold steel catches the light, flickering like lightning across my vision. "Your father murdered mine, and you want to know the truth?"

I swallow past the lump in my throat, closing my eyes and praying to whatever power is in the universe that I could be anywhere but here.

"I was happy to watch the old bastard die. He was never a father to me, but . . . with his death, the connections died too. Everything I'd worked for under my pathetic, miserable excuse of a father, and for what?" I shake my head, but he grips my chin tighter. "I lost everything because of your family. Now . . . I'm going to pay him the same respect."

He runs it along my thigh absentmindedly, his gaze searching mine.

"I always found you so beautiful, Ava—such pretty eyes. I can see now why Cross is so obsessed with you. That's what makes this part so tragic."

Then he *stabs* the knife into my leg.

I scream when the sharp end of the blade pierces my skin. Pain explodes through my leg, hot and unbearable. My jeans darken as blood seeps from the wound, the sight of it making my vision sway.

"Where is he?" he asks, calm and emotionless, like he's asking for the weather. His voice carves through the pain, razor sharp and unrelenting.

"I don't know!" I sob, my voice cracking. "I *don't know!*"

He twists the blade, digging it deeper.

The world implodes into white-hot pain. I scream, raw and primal.

"I don't think you're telling me the truth, Ava." He tilts his head.

Jessi Hart

"You see . . . I know Cross. He wouldn't let you out of his sight. And your father's paying him oh so well to keep an eye on you. So, either you've run away like a naughty little pet, or he's dead."

"We're broken up," I choke. "I haven't seen him in a week."

Alex takes my face in his hands, suddenly soft as he brushes a tear from my cheek—like a mockery of tenderness.

"Shhh . . . I don't care about Cross. Where is Nolan Marks?"

I jerk away, but he grabs my chin, fingers turning to iron.

"Where is he, Ava?"

"I don't know," I whimper, every nerve screaming. My body feels like it's been lit on fire, like he's melting me from the inside out.

"Just tell me, Ava, and I'll set you free. You won't have to see me ever again."

"You're a fucking monster."

Alex has the audacity to look bored.

"Yes, but of course, you already knew that . . . Didn't you, sweetheart? Or do you only respond to *baby girl?*"

I glare up at him.

"*Fuck. You.*"

Alex grins.

"You know, I really enjoyed the little show you put on at the cabin." His voice turns cruel. "Tied up and begging for Cross to fuck you. I was surprised. But then, I always knew you were a whore."

"I hope he finds you," I spit through my teeth. "And when he does, I hope he rips you apart piece by piece until you *beg* for death."

"Sh, sh, shhh . . ." He taps my cheek gently. "Poetic justice, isn't it? I'm going to kill your father. Cross next, and you—well, you're the icing on the cake. I'll make him watch while I fuck you. Then he can sit in a pool of your blood while you bleed out. And when I'm done, I'll take my time finishing off the youngest Cross brother."

"You're pathetic," I whisper, forcing every ounce of venom into the words.

The flicker in his eyes—rage, sharp and unrestrained—tells me

I've struck the nerve I was aiming for.

"See? That's the problem with you, Ava. You still think someone's coming to save you. Cross isn't a hero. He never was. He's just a man who likes to pretend he's better than the rest of us."

I shake my head, my voice hoarse. "He's not you."

That earns me a sharp laugh. "No. He's worse. At least I don't lie about what I am."

He pulls out a phone, and my stomach clenches as he hits a button.

"Don't worry, sweetheart. I'll get what I need one way or another."

The dial tone rings.

"No," I breathe.

Please, God—

"No!" I scream when he stands.

The line clicks. The ringing stops.

And then—

"Where is she?"

I close my eyes, tears slipping down my cheeks at the sound of Levi's voice. Dark and sinister. Deadly.

Alex looks over his shoulder at me and grins. I glare at him through the tears in my eyes.

"Hello, golden boy."

My vision swims. Just the sound of him makes my chest ache. I want to crawl through the phone and fall into his arms. Hearing his voice, my body aches for him like it's next breath.

"If you hurt even a single fucking hair on her head," Levi says, venom in every syllable, "I promise I'm the last thing you'll see before God."

Alex chuckles menacingly, his menacing smile widening to show his teeth. "God doesn't want me, Cross." He squats back down in front of me, eyes black and soulless. "It's the devil I'll see, and when I do, I'm taking your pretty little whore with me."

"You know I'm going to hunt you down." Levi's voice drops to a whisper, more terrifying than a scream. "And when I find you, I'll feed your balls to you like hors d'oeuvres while you bleed out in whatever cesspool you're hiding out in."

Alex shrugs. "Relax, your little pet is alive for now. See?"

He thrusts the phone in my face, and I suck in a shaky breath, my throat cracking with emotion.

"L-Levi?"

"Baby, I'm coming for you." I blink back tears, knowing that there's no way we both make it out of this alive.

His voice is rough, vehement on the other end, and suddenly it's like the last week didn't happen. All I want to do is go to him and let him hold me. Forget everything that happened and just soak in the warmth and safety of his touch.

"Levi . . . I'm scared," I whisper, and Alex laughs sadistically.

"I know, baby," Levi says. "Just hold on. I'll explain everything to you later, just don't—"

"Time's up. Sorry, I'm a very busy man." Alex steps back, and I let out a hoarse scream of anger. "You have one hour to get me Nolan Marks. If you fail, I'm slicing her throat."

Click.

Then silence.

Alex slides the phone back into his pocket and steps over to me. I shrink away from him, but he's faster, grabbing the handle of the knife and ripping it out of my leg. I scream at the pain, arching against the brick wall behind me when he steps back, as nonchalant as if he were contemplating taking a walk.

"I'll be back in a bit," he says as he heads towards the door. He turns back to me, smiling with his hand on the handle. "Don't forget to finish your dinner."

CHAPTER
Forty-Four

AVA

"Looks like your little boyfriend isn't going to show," Alex says, glancing at the Rolex on his wrist, his voice casual—mocking.

I don't know how much time has passed—hours? Days? Time's been eaten alive by the dread pounding in my chest—but I know my jaw aches around the gag, a dull, constant throb that's begun to blur into the rest of the pain.

I glare up at him, defiant through tear-clumped lashes. My cheeks are raw, streaked with salt and desperation, but I don't look away. I *won't* give him that.

Alex exhales as if bored, stretching like he's just gotten out of bed, and rises to his feet with a grunt.

"Well, I guess that's that," he says, almost disappointed. "I gave him a chance. Unfortunately, you'll pay for it with your life."

Panic claws at my throat when he steps forward. I jerk back instinctively, a strangled cry caught behind the gag. The rope around my wrists bites deeper into my already raw skin as he hauls me up like I'm made of rags.

like I'm disposable.

I twist violently in his grasp, and the back of my head slams into his nose. The sickening crunch of bone meets my ears, followed by a sharp, guttural curse.

"Fuck," he growls. "You're more trouble than you're worth."

He lunges again, grabbing a fistful of my hair and yanking me backward until my spine hits the unyielding steel of his chest. I cry out, breath stolen from my lungs. The gag is ripped from my mouth, and I sputter, choking on the bitter taste of cloth and fear.

"Ava Lynn," he hisses, breath hot against my cheek. "You're going to pay for that."

A cold kiss of metal slides across my throat—his knife—angled just enough to remind me how close I am to the edge.

"I wouldn't do that if I were you."

The voice is low and controlled.

—But it hits like a fucking lightning bolt.

"Levi!" Alex clamps a hand over my mouth, pulling me back into his front.

He came . . .

No, no, no, no . . . why is he here?

"I'm here, baby girl," Levi says, stepping out of the shadows like a god of vengeance, eyes stormy and jaw clenched so tight I swear his teeth might crack.

I want to sob in relief, to collapse into him and let this nightmare fade. But I can't. Because I know something he doesn't seem to. There's no way in hell we *both* make it out of here alive.

"Isn't this sweet?" Alex chuckles, voice curling with venom. "Come to join the fun?"

"Let her go, Alex." Levi's voice is calm and collected, but I can see the tightness in his shoulders. The way his knuckles are nearly white from how hard he's clenching his fists.

He looks awful. Like he hasn't slept in weeks. Dark circles ring his eyes, and he hasn't shaved.

My heart sinks, knowing that he's been struggling by himself. Knowing that even if everything between us started out as a job, he's just as lost without me as I am him.

Paulina was right. He destroys everything he loves before it can destroy him. He was just too late this time.

"She's not a part of this."

No, no, no, NO . . .

"Let her go."

"Don't come any closer," Alex orders from over my shoulder, the tip of his blade digging in deeper. I feel the warm tickle of blood slide down my throat. "You know I love the sight of blood spilling from pretty little women."

Levi's face is unreadable. He doesn't look at me, but I can't take my eyes off him. My hands shake where they're tied behind my back, my eyes swimming with tears that threaten to spill down my cheeks.

"This is between you and me," Levi continues, his voice eerily calm. "Ava has nothing to do with this."

"Is that so?" Alex laughs through his teeth. "I think we both know she has everything to do with it, doesn't she?"

My eyes fall closed, all the blood rushing to my head with my ragged heartbeat.

"Tell me," Alex starts, his hand brushing down the other side of my neck. Levi keeps his gaze on Alex, never once looking my way. "What was your plan? Send her away and hope I didn't see the depths of your loyalty to your little whore?"

As he speaks, he digs the blade into the side of my throat, and a whimper manages to slip free from the pain.

Finally, Levi's eyes cut to mine, and there, hidden in their frosty depths, I can see something I've never seen in his eyes before.

Pure, unadulterated fear.

"You had to know I'd take her simply because she was his. He had to know when he ruined my life, I'd ruin the only thing worth a damn in his."

"What happened to your father happened because he was a criminal. Ava has nothing to do with this."

"My *father* was pathetic," Alex spits. "Marks ruined my future."

Alex jerks me back, and the tip of the knife nicks me. It hurts, and I gasp at the sting. Levi's expression slips—just for a second. But it's enough.

Alex sees it too.

"Ah, yes . . ." I can practically hear the smile in Alex's voice. "There it is. I never thought I'd see the day. Levi Cross in love with his mousy, little whore." He flicks the blade, digging it deeper into my skin, and a cry rips free.

"You son of a bitch, let her go!" Levi growls, surging forward, but Alex holds the knife up.

"That's the problem with you Cross siblings," he hisses. "Always so hellbent on being right that you never care to see what's right in front of you." Alex removes the blade from my throat, sliding it instead down my cheek. "How I was able to take your whore, right out from under your nose. How I was able to infiltrate your house, watch your every move . . . It was too easy, really."

"Let. Her. Go," Levi urges. "Take me. I'm right fucking here."

"I'm afraid I can't do that, Levi. You see, I'm going to make you watch while I fuck your whore. Then I'll slice her throat and let you suffer helplessly while she bleeds out. Just. Like. My. Father." Alex turns to grin at me, his hand fisting in my hair. "And you're going to love every second, aren't you, little mouse?"

"Go fuck yourself," I grit through my teeth, but he only chuckles.

"My, my, Cross. She is feisty. I can see why you're so obsessed. She was never this vibrant with me." I whimper when his knife slips down my throat, over my racing pulse.

The blade digs into my flesh, slicing my skin as it goes. Levi's wild eyes meet mine, and through the blurriness of my tears, I can see he's panicking.

"Damnit, Alex! I'm right fucking here. You can have me! Just let her go!"

"How pathetically poetic. Willing to sacrifice yourself for her," Alex tsks. "It was always going to end this way. You and me." Alex leans down, his tongue sliding along the blood on my neck. Disgust recoils through me, and I try to move away, but he tightens his hold. The world starts to spin around me, the pressure in my skull setting off a throbbing tempo in my head that matches my heartbeat. "All the while you were worried about Palmer, I was right there under your nose. At the Tomb. At the funeral for your spineless father. I'm everywhere, Cross!" he bellows, and I jump.

"Let her go."

Everything falls silent as Christian steps into the room, Nolan Marks in front of the gun in his hand.

My father.

"Finally," Alex grins. He lowers his lips to my ear, his breath hot on my cheek. "Daddy's here, little mouse."

I blink through the tears as the man who's supposed to be my father comes into focus. Levi's eyes never leave mine, his chest heaving with each breath.

"I'm the one you're after. These two have nothing to do with it," Nolan says, stepping further into the warehouse.

"Mmm . . . but she does, doesn't she? Tell me, Nolan, does Ava know the truth?" Alex asks, and the silence in my ears is deafening.

"Ava," Levi says, his rough voice breaking through the haze. "Look at me, baby."

Nolan doesn't answer, his gaze unreadable as it sweeps over me.

"*Ava*," Levi growls, and my gaze cuts to his. "Keep your eyes on me, baby, *please*."

I wish someone would tell me what the hell is going on. I shiver when Alex's hand slides down my face, to my throat. He swirls the blade along my skin, not slicing, but close enough to threaten.

A silent sob slips free from my lips, and Levi's face grows redder and redder with suppressed rage.

"What's the matter, little mouse?" Alex says softly in my ear. "Oh, that's right. This is the first time you're really meeting him, isn't it?"

"Ava," Levi barks when I look away. My gaze shoots back to his, and the desperation there is enough to frighten me.

"Did you know your daddy was in on it? See, it wasn't just my father who had deals with the Russians. No. It was yours too," Alex sneers, his voice maniacal in my ear. "Then your father screwed mine over. My father was murdered."

"Let her go, Alex," Marks says from the door. "It's over."

"Daddy left when you were just a little girl, didn't he?" Alex sneers. "He left you all alone with Mommy and her shitty boyfriends. He never cared about you. Not the way you want him to. Who do you think the favorite was?"

"Ava," Levi growls, but realization is dawning on me.

Alex presses closer to my side.

"Did you really think you were an only child, Ava?"

No.

NO.

Alex grins in my face when reality comes crashing down on me.

"That's right, sweetheart. Donovan Palmer is your brother."

Time stands still, and my heartbeat ticks like moments on a clock.

My brother.

Donovan is my brother.

"Why do you think he paid Cross to watch over you?" Alex continues. "Daddy screwed me over and thought he could save the only thing he has left. Doesn't that piss you off?"

"Fuck you," I breathe, and he just chuckles.

"Good idea. What do you think he'd say about that?" His free hand starts to roam, while his knife stays against my throat.

Disgust coils through me when he grips my breast through my

clothes, and I surge in his grip to try and get away from him. A cry slips free when he tightens his hold on my hair, no doubt pulling strands free.

"Or maybe the boyfriend . . ." he chortles in my ear, moving lower and laying his hand flat over the center of my thighs. "Mmm . . ." he moans, staring pointedly at Levi. Levi takes a step towards us, his gaze murderous, but Alex digs the knife into my throat, and I gasp at the pain. "She's nice and warm. Tell me, Cross . . . how does she feel? Soft and sweet?"

"Let her go!" Nolan roars. Taking a step forward. Alex drags the knife closer to my throat, hauling me back. I wince, feeling the blood slipping down my skin and soaking the collar of my shirt.

"I'm going to fucking kill you," Levi says, watching the trail of blood, his voice holding a deathly calm.

"I'd love to see you try," Alex sneers, and unfortunately, it's the straw that breaks the camel's back.

Everything happens so fast.

A shot rings out, and my eyes shoot to Donovan Palmer emerging from the shadows. His eyes meet mine, but it's only a split second before the most heart-wrenching sound fills the room.

Alex is the first to be shot. He crumples to the floor, and suddenly, I'm released. I fall to my side on the broken concrete, and Levi lunges for Alex, pinning him to the ground.

The two men struggle, and the sickening sound of bone meeting metal fills the air when Levi plunges the knife directly into the side of Alex's throat.

"No!" I snap when someone tries to tug me away.

DEA, FBI, and the Seattle police department swarm the scene, and Levi's lost in the sea. I fight to get to him, searching for him in the swarm of bodies.

Levi's eyes find mine, and I reach for him, everything moving in slow motion.

"Come on, Miss Ava," I hear, and the hands that can only

belong to Hector grip me tighter, attempting to drag me towards the door, but the flash of a gun catches my eye.

Alex may be bleeding out on the floor, but the gun in his hand . . . it's pointed right at the back of Levi's head.

This world means nothing without you in it.

I shove away from Hector and dart to Levi, just as the shot rings out through the air.

Our gazes meet.

—Frosty blue and peridot green.

In a flash in time, I knew I'd gladly give my life to save his.

—And then everything fades to black.

CHAPTER
Forty-Five

LEVI

He slips a picture out of his wallet and hands it over to me.

The soft green eyes staring up at mine are like a punch to the chest.

"No."

He doesn't respond, but he doesn't have to. It's the eyes. The same ones that haunt my fantasies match the eyes of the man standing in front of me.

"You're her father . . ."

"If you can call it that," Marks grunts, snatching the picture out of my hand as if it's his most prized possession.

"So why am I here?"

Marks looks away.

"I made a mistake."

"Doesn't explain what you want from me."

He cocks a brow, cocking his head to the side in thought.

"You're a very hard person to read, Cross."

"Your point?"

"Just that. You're a very hard person to read . . . except," he holds the picture up in front of me. ". . . When it comes to my daughter."

from the photograph.

Fuck.

My mind is reeling, and I'm having a hard time wrapping my head around the woman in the picture being the same woman who's plagued my mind for the last three months.

"What the fuck did you do?"

Something dark flashes across his gaze.

"No."

My gun's out of my pocket in the blink of an eye, aimed directly at the center of his forehead.

"You can shoot me, if you need to," he says, so nonchalant, I debate on doing it for the fucking hell of it. "It won't change anything."

"I could just end it right now," I spit, venom coating every word.

"You could. Though, do you really think it would save her? Wright's son is looking for her, as we speak. He'll use her against me regardless of whether I'm alive or dead."

"And who is his son?"

"That's the problem. We don't know."

"Jesus fucking Christ." I scrub a hand over my face. "You're a real fucking asshole, you know that?"

"Of course, I know that. Why do you think I've never been a part of her life?"

"Yeah," I grunt. "Father of the fucking year."

I can't fucking believe I'm considering this.

"And what's going to stop him when he decides to come for her?"

"You."

I should walk away right now. Leave him to figure it out on his own.

But . . . can I live with the alternative? Knowing what I know?

Fucking hell.

"If I do this . . . I have some demands."

Marks cocks a brow, pulling out a letter from his jacket.

"This is a letter of release, stating you're restored to your former job title. No therapy. No warming the bench. Fully reinstated agent status."

I grit my teeth, my blood burning in my veins.

I should take it, get my life back.

There's just one thing that's standing in my way.

"No."

"No?"

"I don't want it." I take a step towards him, ignoring the burn in my chest. *"One million."*

Marks stares at me, his eyes dark and foreboding. I think he's going to deny me before he finally speaks.

"One million is nothing."

I shrug.

"It's what I want."

One million for being a shitty fucking father. One million for all the times she's gone without because of him.

One million because that's exactly what she told me it would take, and God knows I need all the help I can get.

Marks pauses for a moment before a grin spreads across his face.

"You've got yourself a deal."

The blood that stains the bandage over Ava's shoulder makes me sick.

I've been around it all my life, yet the sight of it now, knowing it's hers and that I failed her, makes me wish it were mine instead.

It *should* have been me.

She's out of it. Has been for hours, and yet, I haven't moved, sitting in the hospital chair beside her bed despite everyone coming in and out of the room.

It would take a fucking nuke to move me now.

Call it what you want, but I'm just crazy enough to light this city and watch it burn to the ground before I'd leave her side again.

I thought I was doing the right thing, giving her the space she asked for. I let them trick me, and for that, I feel like I deserve that bullet they dug out of her side.

I never would have guessed Donovan would be her brother. Never could have imagined it when Marks came to me. All the signs were there. I should have fucking realized what it all meant.

She paid the price. The love of *my life* paid the price. And for that . . . I'm not sure I'll ever forgive myself.

"You going to sit here all night?" Christian asks, stepping quietly into the room. His voice is low, aware of the heaviness already thick in the air. My family left over an hour ago to head down to the cafeteria, while I stayed behind, unwilling to leave her side.

He places a tray of food on the small stand beside me. I don't look at it. I'm not hungry. The smell alone turns my stomach.

"Mila," he explains, and I grunt in response.

He sighs and lowers himself into the seat beside mine, the one that's barely been empty since we got here. For a long moment, neither of us speaks. We don't need to. The silence says more than words ever could.

He's thinking the same thing I am.

"Any word on Mendez?" I finally ask, my voice like gravel from disuse.

Christian nods once, casting a quick glance at Ava to make sure she's still asleep. She is—her chest rising and falling under the hospital blankets, her face pale but peaceful. It's the most deceptive kind of calm.

"I was hoping he'd bleed out before he made it to the hospital, but he's stable." He leans forward, elbows on his knees. "They got everything they need to put him behind bars for the rest of his miserable life."

I shake my head, violence filling every vein in my body.

"I want to kill him, Christian."

"Well," he mutters, "I think you're going to have to accept that he's going to rot in whatever federal hellhole they throw him into. Slowly."

I should feel some satisfaction about Alex's fate, but I don't. I wanted more than a quick end. I wanted to hurt him the way he hurt her. But I didn't get the chance—not when she was in danger.

Definitely not after she took a bullet for me.

Fuck, it pisses me off so badly my hands shake when I think about him drugging her and pulling her from her cottage. Stealing her right out from under my nose.

All this time, I was worried about Palmer, but as it turns out, someone else was pulling the strings.

Palmer was just as much a pawn as the rest of us.

"I wanted to make him suffer," I say quietly, staring straight ahead, my voice flat. "I wanted him to choke on his own blood while he begged for death."

Christian doesn't say anything at first. His silence is agreement enough.

"She almost died," I whisper again, the words cutting me open from the inside. "She almost fucking died, and it's because I wasn't careful."

He doesn't argue. He doesn't try to soften it. That's not who he is.

"You know this only ends one of two ways, right?"

I nod slowly, clenching my jaw so tight I feel it crack. Of course I know. I've been sitting here with the weight of that truth pressing into my spine since they wheeled her out of surgery.

"You going to tell her the truth?"

"She knows everything," I grunt, but we both know that's not what he means.

He chuckles under his breath, shaking his head like I'm a stubborn child. "I meant about you being in love with her."

I go completely still.

Fuck.

I don't answer. I don't have to. It's written all over my face, carved into every raw, panicked decision I've made in the last seventy-two hours.

"She's better off without me," I mutter finally, bitterness thick in my throat. "I almost got her killed. That's not love, Christian. That's carelessness."

He leans back in his chair as he watches me with quiet, relentless judgment.

"You did what you thought was right."

I shake my head. "It's too late for that."

Christian lets out a soft snort. "It's never too late," he says. "Not unless you don't say it at all."

I shake my head, but I don't disagree. I'm not sure I can.

Because as much as I want her to stay—as much as I want to believe there's a future for us after all this—I know what I am. I know what I've done.

And as I sit here, staring at her fragile, bruised body in that hospital bed, it hits me like a fucking freight train: I have no idea what I'm doing. I have no clue what the next step even is. Everything I thought I was—everything I built my life around—feels hollow now.

I thought the DEA was my purpose. But maybe it was just a distraction.

Because now, all I want is her.

And I'm not sure if I have the right to ask for that.

I feel like she's stolen from me. Ripped something out of my chest and made off in the night. I want to punish her and worship her at the same time.

"Why did you give up the FBI?"

Christian thinks for a moment, quiet.

"You're wondering if you want to go back to being an agent." It's not a question.

I don't have an answer for him. Not one that doesn't sound like a weak excuse or a coward's confession.

"When I stepped back," he begins, his voice low and coarse like gravel underfoot, "it was because I found something that meant more to me than whatever criminals are in the world. I found I didn't give a fuck what they were doing, so long as she was safe . . ." He looks at me then, really looks, and for a second, I see our mother in his eyes—dark and blazing, carved from a grief we both carry in different ways. "If you're asking these questions, I think you know your answer."

I look back at Ava, curled up beneath the tangle of pale sheets. She's sleeping softly, her lashes creating a heavy shadow on her cheeks. She looks so small. Fragile. Like if I blink too long, she might vanish. And maybe that's the point—maybe she will.

He's right. I do know my answer. I've always known it, buried beneath pride and fear and the blood I've spilled for less worthy things.

"What . . ." I hesitate, jaw tight, shame crawling up my spine. "What do I do when she leaves?"

It's a coward's question, and we both know it. Because she will leave. Because I've given her every reason not to stay.

He doesn't respond right away. Just studies me with that same unreadable stillness that used to scare the shit out of me as a kid. When he finally speaks, it's not soft. It's not cruel, either. It's honest—even if I fucking hate it.

"Give her the time she needs," he says, voice thick with something unspoken. "And when she's ready for you, make sure you're ready to be the man you want to be."

I swallow hard. The weight of it settles in my chest like stone. I don't ask what happens if I'm not ready. I already know the answer.

CHAPTER
Forty-Six

AVA

I'm in a hospital. I can tell because of the smell. That sterile, chemical stench that clings to everything. It smells like Pleasant Oaks, and I hate it.

There are voices around me and the steady, mechanical whir of machines that beep like a countdown. My head is pounding, like someone's taking a hammer to the inside of my skull, again and again. I want to cry out, to scream, but my mouth won't move.

God, why won't they shut up?

"I told you to protect her," a voice growls, sharp and livid. "No matter the cost. She was fucking shot."

Shot. The word rattles through me. I was shot?

Oddly enough, I don't feel a thing.

"What the fuck do you think I was doing?"

That voice—rough and ragged. Familiar.

Levi.

My heart jerks toward him like a tether pulled tight, but my body stays frozen, limp beneath the weight of the drugs or trauma—or both. The voices blur, dipping in and out of clarity, dragged back down again.

"You let her out of your sight. What the fuck were you thinking?"

"I was thinking I fucking love her," Levi snarls. His voice cracks, barely contained emotion slipping through the edges. "Or did you forget that they planned to use her to draw you out from the beginning because of *your* stupid fucking 'mistake'?"

"It doesn't matter."

"If it has to do with her, it *always matters.*"

"You want to blame me," the man scoffs. "It was your own selfish desires that almost got her killed."

That other man—who is he? The anger in his voice is volcanic, but it's not impersonal. It's tight with something deeper. Guilt maybe.

"You think I wanted to do that?" Levi growls, pain threaded through every word. "I played your game, Marks, and it almost cost me everything."

"I told you we had no leads on who Wright's son was. He was right under your nose and yet you missed him. Mendez is still fucking breathing. And *my daughter* is bleeding out in a hospital bed because *you* let him slip past you."

"She's alive," Levi grits.

"Barely," the man bites back. "She's in a fucking hospital bed and it's your fucking fault."

. . . Please don't blame him . . .

I want to tell my father not to blame Levi. That he was only trying to save me.

He was trying to save me . . .

"I know," Levi says, voice low and hollow now. Defeated.

There's a beat of silence. It's loud with pain.

"Enough," a third voice cuts through the tension. Christian. He sounds like hell—like gravel and smoke and a week without sleep. "You two want to do this, go outside. Not here."

"She's stirring," another voice adds gently, and I know it's Mila. I'd know that softness anywhere.

I try to wake up. I really do. I claw toward the surface, toward the light, toward the voices that matter.

I feel air shift beside me—a subtle breeze brushing my skin— and I know it's him. I *know* it's him.

"Baby," Levi whispers, his voice resolute. "Wake up."

I can't. I can't move. I can't speak.

It's like my body's buried in snow—paralyzed under a sheet of ice, my nerves frozen, my voice lost in the cold.

But I know that smell.

His scent wraps around me like a blanket—familiar and warm, and so *him* it makes something in my chest crack wide open.

We're alive . . . At least I think so.

I push against the weight pinning me down. I just want to see him. Just one look. Just one glance to prove he's real, and okay. But my eyes stay closed, and the voices begin to drift, like I'm being pulled away again.

No—wait—please . . .

My consciousness frays at the edges, slipping from my grasp like sand through trembling fingers. And in the final moment, when everything else fades, a calloused hand closes gently over mine, and a rough voice breaks in my ear.

A single word. Cracked. Desperate.

"Please."

A while later, I jerk from sleep, the nightmare still hanging on the far reaches of my mind.

"You're safe."

My heart jumps in my chest, hammering when I spot the dark figure in the chair beside my bed.

Levi's watching me, his shoulders slumped and his eyes distant. He looks . . . broken. A man robbed of life.

Neither of us moves for a long time. Somehow, I know he's been by my side the entire time I've been unconscious. Silently watching over me like he has so many times before.

The swell in my chest steals my breath away. A mixture of agony, love, and desperation that feels too good to be healthy.

He loves me. I love him.

—But we are going to destroy each other.

"How long have I been asleep?" I ask, my voice gravely with sleep.

Levi hands me a glass of water that sits on the hospital tray beside him.

"Twenty-two hours," Levi says emotionlessly, as if he's been counting down the exact time.

I swallow down the water, grateful as it wets my dry mouth. Looking around the room, there are flowers, cards, and stuffed animals, but not another soul in sight.

"It's late," Levi says, glancing at the flowers beside him. "I sent everyone home."

"Who are these from?" I ask, confused. I'm not sure I even know this many people.

"Your family," he answers finally, his expression dark. Troubled.

"You mean your family," I say, halfheartedly. There's no use trying to lighten the mood, but that doesn't stop me.

A hush falls over the room, the only sound the whir of machines and the distant hum of someone else's television.

"So . . . what happened to Donovan?"

Levi lets out a deep sigh, rubbing a hand over his eyes. I can see he's tired, like he hasn't slept in weeks.

"No one knows."

"And . . . Alex?"

"Alive. For now."

I shake my head, lying back in the bed. I feel like someone put me in a washing machine on the bulky setting. Everything hurts.

"Guess you were right," I say after a long time. "Alex was dangerous."

Levi looks like he might break something.

"I should have known, Ava. I should have seen the signs. I'm sorry."

I shake my head.

"The money from the contract . . . it was my father's, wasn't it?"

He clears his throat, his voice husky and thick. "All except for one dollar."

I don't know why I'm relieved, but I am. In some cruel twist of fate, I realize he'd done this solely to protect me. Not for money.

So why do I still feel like the line between us has been severed?

The weight of reality crashes down on me like a ton of bricks. I can't do anything but stare at the wall in front of me and hope I'll wake up back in his cabin and this will all have been a bad dream.

Who am I kidding?

I could never get that lucky.

"Why . . ." I can't finish that sentence. The why doesn't matter. Just that he didn't tell me.

"He asked me not to."

My heart cracks a little bit at that statement.

I want to snap back at him and ask why Nolan Marks deserves loyalty, and I don't, but I keep my mouth shut. Arguing about it won't do any good.

The damage is done.

I shake my head, ignoring the sting of tears in my eyes.

"Was . . . anything the truth?"

Levi looks as broken as I feel. Like he wants to reach for me, but he's holding himself back. Paulina's words come to mind, and my chest aches, wishing I could wrap myself around him and forget any of this happened.

Start again from the beginning.

"Every time I touched you," he says, voice barely above a whisper. "That was real." My heart quivers, and my eyes fill with tears that sting in my eyes. "Every time I held you . . . that was real. Everything I said or couldn't say about how I felt? That was real, too."

"You hid things from me. Big things, Levi." I shrug, sadly. "I don't know if I can trust you again."

"I'm not sorry for what I did," he says finally, his voice rough like sandpaper. "I'm only sorry . . . that I didn't tell you that I'm in love with you sooner."

I don't like this side of him. How sad he is. I want to erase his pain. Swallow it all myself so he doesn't have to feel it anymore, but I know that's not possible. I'm hurting too, and for the first time in my life, I'm realizing that's okay.

"Why the contract?"

He finally meets my gaze head-on, those icy blue eyes boring into my soul.

"Because I knew there was no way you'd let me love you if you knew who I really was."

"You're a good person, Levi. One who had horrible things happen to him. I'll never fault you for the things you did to protect your family. I wasn't lying when I said I fell for you. Hard." I shrug, giving him the most unhappy half-smile to ever exist. "I still am." I shake my head. "Even if I know I shouldn't be."

"Ava—"

Levi is cut off by the shuffling of feet when Nolan Marks steps into the room, his eyes raking over me in the bed.

My heart catches in my throat at the little stuffed dog in his hand. Like I'm a child. I suppose, in his eyes, I still am. When he left,

I was only four years old.

"You're awake," he says distantly, and my throat swells. I'm not sure if it's from being asleep so long or the pain radiating through my chest.

"You're my father," I say quietly.

He looks both guilty and ashamed. I don't understand. Why leave if you're going to feel bad about it?

"I am."

"Why are you here?"

Surprise crosses his face before he accepts what I've said.

It's funny . . . his eyes. They're nearly the same shade of green as mine. That's the only similarity that I can see, and yet, looking at him, I know.

"I shouldn't be," he admits finally.

"But . . ." I finish for him.

"But I am still your father. By blood. There was a time when that wouldn't mean much to me, but now . . ."

"Why did you leave?"

He winces, refusing to meet my eyes.

"I haven't lived a good life, Ava. You deserved a father, and I didn't deserve a daughter . . . When I found out your mother was pregnant, I was engaged to someone else. I wasn't sure I even wanted to be a father," he murmurs. "For four years, I tried to be good to you, but I was only making you sad. Showing up when I could get away from my life. Leaving you crying when I had to go back. I realized you were better off without me, even if it killed me to watch you go."

The soul-crushing truth in his words feels like spikes digging into my heart. It's true, in a lot of ways.

That doesn't make it right, but dwelling on it doesn't change anything. The past is the past. I've lived twenty years without him and survived.

"Why did you find me now?"

"I had no idea Wright was Alex's father. If I had, I would have stopped it before he could reach you. Luckily, I knew you were working for Cross, and I met with him, asking him to keep an eye on you." Nolan has the audacity to stare pointedly at Levi. "I didn't expect him to take me so literally."

"Why would he use me against you? You were never a father to me. Not like you were to him."

He soaks in the silence of my words, his face grim. I suppose I'm being harsh, but I'm just so tired. Tired of fighting for my spot in people's lives. Tired of wishing someone would choose me. *Really* choose me and not just when it's convenient.

"I've always watched over you, from afar. I was there the night your mother lost you. I was there when you broke your arm at nine years old . . ." He clears his throat of the roughness in his voice. "It might not mean much, but I've changed. I'd like to be there when you get married and have babies of your own . . . if you'll have me."

Tears burn in my eyes, and I know without a doubt what I need to do.

The life I've lived has been for everyone else around me. I've never given much thought to what I wanted to do with my life. I've never experienced anything. I've never been out of this corner of the country.

From my mother to nursing Gran, to loving Levi, to discovering I have a father, I had forgotten that there was still a person inside me who deserved to dream. I forgot to figure out who I was when everyone else was away.

Like the flip of a switch, my heart sinks, because at that moment, I realize exactly what I need to do. Judging by the look on Levi's face, he does too.

"I forgive you," I say finally, and in my father's eyes, I see myself. He knows too. "But, for now . . . I need space."

It surprises me that I don't feel the crushing weight of the world around me in that statement. I had to know I could be alone in the world without relying on Gran, my friends, or even love. I have to be able to make the decisions on who is allowed in my life and who isn't.

Starting with my father.

If I don't, I'll be a shell of a person—someone just like my mother.

Nolan nods once, looking down at the dog in his hands. Silently, he places it in my lap before he bends down, pressing one kiss to my forehead.

Almost twenty years, and all it took to win his affection was a near-death experience.

"I'll always watch over you, sweet girl."

Then he walks out of the room, leaving behind a heaviness that I hadn't expected. I didn't know the man, yet it feels like I'm saying goodbye to the little girl who rests inside me, who always wished for a big family. Cousins, aunts, and uncles. A mother and father who loved each other.

From the time I was six years old, it's always been my deepest wish. To feel that kind of love and acceptance.

Now that the possibility is there, I'm finding I'd much rather learn to love myself than settle for the scraps of someone else.

Which brings me to my next heartbreak.

Levi's eyes meet mine, and I think he knows. His head cocks slightly to the side, like he's studying me, waiting for the other shoe to drop.

I know I'm reaffirming his darkest fear. He doesn't like to be left behind. The knowledge that I'm hurting him feels like I've swallowed glass.

His gaze meets mine, and the darkness there makes it feel like all the air was sucked from the room.

I almost back out, but I know that if I do, he will *never* get better. He'll never learn to let people in. Paulina is right. Everyone else around him is enabling him. Allowing him to keep up with this façade that he's fine and everything's okay, when deep down, the voice inside him is screaming for help.

I can't be just another enabler. I love him too much.

Tears well in my eyes, and he blinks, looking down at his hands in his lap.

"I'm guessing I don't need to explain to you why I did what I did," he says finally, his voice quiet.

Love. It's such a fickle thing, isn't it?

It's elusive, but when you find it—and I mean *really find it*—it can tear your soul straight from your chest with just a few words.

Tears sting in my eyes, and I fiddle with the stuffed dog on my lap, so I don't have to see the pain in his gaze.

"I'm also guessing this is the part where you tell me you forgive me . . . but that you need space."

No, no, no. I want to scream at him. Fight with him. Listen to him say he loves me again, and let myself give in to the idea that I can accept the parts that he *will* give to me.

But I know I can't.

He broke my heart because he thought it would save me. Now I'm doing the same for him.

He nods once, and I can't help myself. I meet his gaze, and the turmoil there matches the pain radiating through me. This hurts so much more than I could have ever imagined. More than hearing about his secrets. His lies.

I knew he did it all to save me. It didn't make it any easier.

"From the moment I laid eyes on you, I think I knew you'd own every piece of me for the rest of my life," he says. "There won't ever be a moment when I'm not madly fucking in love with you, Ava. In this life and every single one that follows. . . I belong to you. I'm going to earn you back."

A tear slips down my cheek, and I can't look away from those frosty eyes.

The bullet wound in my shoulder is nothing compared to the pain of watching him get to his feet. Gently, he stoops down, mirroring my father and pressing one soft kiss on my forehead.

The scent of him washes over me, and desperation burns through me. Heartache blooms in my chest, sending a ripple of pain through me that has nothing to do with being shot.

I feel like I was ripped to shreds.

Levi walks away from me, towards the door, only to stop and look back at me, his hand on the handle and his eyes clouded in darkness.

"Whenever you're ready to come home, baby . . . I'll be ready for you."

And then he walks out the door.

And out of my life.

CHAPTER
Forty-Seven

AVA

I n the weeks following my release from the hospital, I spend the first two buried in my bed, hiding away from the world.

I'm exhausted. Whether from the hole in my shoulder or the one in my heart, I don't know.

Mila and Bella stop by and try to coax me out of bed. They bring food and cheap wine, even though I can't drink it because of the pain medicine, but it's their presence that makes it worthwhile. No expectations. Just company in a world that feels empty since I left half my heart behind in the hospital the night I told Levi I needed time.

Even Paulina showed up and, bless her soul, helped me wash my hair. I was so grateful to her that I forced a hug on her, which she eventually softened to.

Bella and Mila begged me to come to Christmas, but it didn't feel right, showing up there knowing I can't look at Levi and not think about how much I ache for him. My body literally craves his. His warmth, his scent. Knowing that no matter what, there's still a huge part of me that wants nothing more than to crawl into his

Instead, I spent the day binge-watching horror movies and eating junk food on my couch without a care in the world.

Christmas is easier to ignore when you're all alone.

I haven't heard from him in three weeks, nor have I seen him, and I'll panic if I think about it for too long. Like maybe he's decided I'm not worth it and that he'd much rather move on.

It's not constant, but when those moments strike, it feels like a knife twisting deep inside. Half of me vanishes, a part of my soul carried away on some cruel wind, and I'm left groping blindly in the dark, grasping at nothing but shadows. I wish I could say each day gets easier, but the truth is, every night when I lie in bed, staring at the ceiling, it's not nightmares of what happened that haunt me. It's him.

His scent, his laugh, his strength.

Part of me wonders what would happen if I showed up at his doorstep tomorrow. Could I forgive him for everything he did?

The other half is terrified—terrified of his rejection, of the cruel finality it would bring. I don't know if I could survive that pain a second time.

And then, like all things when it comes to Levi Cross, I'm right back where I started.

It's early in the morning on a Tuesday in January when I'm woken by the sound of someone banging around outside.

For a split second, a shot of panic slides through me, before I remind myself that Alex is dead. I'm safe.

Then, I force myself out of bed.

Pulling on a robe, I head towards the front door and peek out the window beside it.

My heart stops beating when I see the familiar black car parked out front next to my SUV, and the inky black hair that haunts my dreams just past that at the wood pile.

Swallowing over the lump in my throat, I tug my robe tighter around myself and step out onto the porch, wondering if I should have at least brushed my hair first.

But then he turns, and his eyes find mine, and suddenly, I forget about everything.

Those eyes . . . God, I've missed those eyes.

"W-what are you doing?" I ask, more confused than anything.

His answer is simple. "You need wood."

"Y-you don't have to do that."

He's right, I did need wood. I just wasn't expecting him to come and chop it for me.

He shrugs. "It's my job."

Then turns and resumes chopping. I stand there frozen on the porch for what must be an eternity. The wind whips around me, cold enough to chill me to the bone. I wrap the robe tighter around myself as a myriad of emotions swirl through me.

Confusion, distrust, desire, hunger, insecurity.

"Go inside, Ava. It's cold."

My gaze snaps back to his, and his gaze holds something I'm not prepared for.

It's not possessiveness or sadness or anything I was expecting. It's longing.

I know that feeling all too well.

I'll earn your trust, one day at a time . . .

I want to ask him to come inside, but I know I'm not ready for that. Instead, the words get caught on my tongue until I'm forced to nod at him and turn to head back into the house.

It takes me a moment to gather my bearings, but eventually, I manage to brush my hair and teeth and change my clothes before I brew some coffee.

I'm just about to head to the living room to resume my cleaning from the day before when I pause, staring at the pot on the counter.

Five minutes later, I'm trudging out into the snow and carrying a thermos full of hot coffee. I have no idea how he drinks it, or if he drinks it at all, but I can't have him freezing out here on my account.

I keep my distance, placing it on the old tree stump near him, before backing up.

"In case you get cold," I say hurriedly, before rushing back towards the house.

"Ava," he calls out, and I freeze at the bottom of the steps. Turning around, I find him watching me.

"Thank you."

I suck in a shallow breath, a shiver moving through me that has nothing to do with the cold.

"Don't mention it."

Every day for the next two weeks is the same. Levi comes over in the morning and works on something around the house. I don't invite him in, and he doesn't ask, though it's right there on the tip of my tongue every day.

He chops enough wood that I won't have to worry about it until next winter. He fixes the leak in the porch roof and the loose floorboard to the left of the stairs. He shovels the front walk and makes a path out to the old garage in the back. He even goes so far as to repair Gran's old rocking chair, which, I won't lie, made me shed a few secret tears when he left.

We're getting more comfortable around each other. I bring him coffee every day, and he drinks it black. He never says if he likes it or not, but I bring it anyway.

I think a part of me doesn't want him to find a reason not to come back because when he runs out of things to fix outside, I ask for his help with the leaking drain under the kitchen sink.

—Then the back door that doesn't like to shut properly.

—Then the fireplace in the living room, which I have no idea how to work.

I keep finding things, and he keeps fixing them, and I can't deny that one night, I briefly contemplated breaking something so he could fix it the next day.

We start to talk more. About trivial things. Music and movies. Things that don't really matter because talking about those things is easier than talking about *us*.

I learn he secretly likes *Fleetwood Mac*, though he'd never tell his brother because he'd never live it down. He learns I went through a *Slipknot* faze and still listen to them in the car when I'm alone.

I learn his favorite Christmas movie is *Die Hard*—shocker—and he learns mine is *The Grinch*, because I love how stupid the *Who's* look.

I learn he wants to get a dog . . . He learns that I do too.

Life moves around us, but in the comfort of Gran's little cottage, it feels like it's just the two of us left in the world.

And that's when I learn I don't want him to leave.

Nearly every night after he leaves, I find myself lying awake at night in the quiet of the house, wondering what he's doing in that very moment. If he's thinking about me, too, or if I'm reading too much into his helping.

Then I kick myself for thinking anything but.

Of course, he's helping to win me back. It's working. Slowly, but surely, he's moving back into my heart, though I don't think he ever really left.

I want to forgive him, but I don't know how. After everything, I know I can trust him with my life, but my heart?

I'm not sure I could survive losing him twice.

I'm starting to settle into my new life, going out with Mila and Bella for dinner, and searching for job opportunities, though I have no idea what I want to do with my life. A week after my hospital visit, I received another transfer from an anonymous account for the sum of one million dollars. My hands trembled when the lady on the phone told me, and I swear I threw up in my mouth because that kind of money isn't something that ever remotely crossed my mind.

The same day, an envelope arrived, but instead of a long letter detailing more reasons why he left, it was a simple picture of my father and me from the day I was born.

My heart swelled, looking at the photograph and the sprawling writing on the back.

Forever my retribution.

—Nolan Marks

I framed it and put it on the mantel in the hopes that someday, I can make amends and find the same little girl who used to dream of her father, and tell her that he might deserve a chance, after all.

And that's when I realize, while watching Levi patch a hole in the drywall in the hallway, that everyone makes mistakes. Even ones they think are for the greater good.

The weeks pass, and eventually, I finish cleaning the living room. I move onto the kitchen and don't even notice that Levi's not fixing random broken things anymore. He's just helping me pack up everything I don't want and clean what's left.

Life feels . . . normal. Like the last six months didn't happen. Like falling in love all over again, even though you know that at any moment life could rip the rug out from under you.

It feels like meeting him for the first time, and I can't deny that my heart has already forgiven him, even if my mind can't.

It's not until February that I offer to let him stay for dinner.

He hesitates, his gaze searching mine for entirely too long. I almost back out, my cheeks flaming red, before he finally agrees, a devious glint in his eyes that makes my stomach dip.

"Whatever you want."

We end up ordering pizza and sitting on opposite sides of the couch, watching *Die Hard*, and otherwise trying to navigate this new territory.

"This isn't really much of a Christmas movie," I joke somewhere halfway through.

Levi grins. "Takes place on Christmas. That makes it a Christmas movie."

I roll my eyes, though I can't hide the grin that spreads on my lips.

"You're impossible," I murmur, shaking my head.

"You're perfect."

Somewhere near the end of the movie, I must fall asleep, because when I wake up, I'm in my bed and he's sliding the blankets over me.

He pauses when I peer up at him, too exhausted to fight sleep.

Neither of us says anything for a long moment, both of us frozen. It's the closest we've been in months, and yet, I can't deny there's a large part of me that wishes he would stay.

But he doesn't. I guess both of us realize we aren't there, yet.

"Goodnight, Ava."

I swallow past the lump in my throat.

"Goodnight, Levi."

Levi and I are at a comfortable distance, with me hiding out in the living room while he fixes a cabinet in the kitchen, when a knock sounds at the front door.

I freeze, my heart plummeting to my toes, and I glance at Levi, who steps into the doorway of the kitchen.

"Relax," he says calmly, before crossing to the front door and opening it. I stay back in the living room, listening to the sound of whoever's at the door, but I'm unable to picture who it could be.

It's not until Levi steps around the corner, into the living room, that I scramble backwards.

"It's okay," Levi says, holding up a hand while Donovan Palmer looks as cold and unfeeling as ever.

"I'm not here to hurt you," Donovan says, stepping cautiously into the room.

"Forgive me, but that's what Alex said right before he stabbed me in the leg."

"I just want to talk."

"Did you know he was coming?" I ask Levi. Donovan winces, while Levi looks away, jaw tight.

I can't believe him.

I shake my head, angrily swiping at the tears on my cheeks.

And to think I was starting to trust him again.

"Get out."

"Ava . . ." Levi says, taking a cautionary step towards me. "Just hear him out."

"I don't want to."

"Ava—"

"No," I snap, hair flying around me when I whip back around. "I don't even know him."

"And yet, he's still your brother," Levi snaps back, and my heart takes a tumble in my chest.

Both of us stare at each other, chests heaving, while Donovan doesn't move.

"Right, this has been fun, but I only came for one thing."

I step back, crossing my arms over my chest. "Your ego."

"The truth."

My lips clamp shut, and I lean back against the wall. There's nothing saying I *have* to speak to him. This is *my* house, after all.

But . . . I do want answers.

I have a right to know who I am and where I came from, even if that isn't a very good place.

"Talk."

Donovan lets out a heavy breath and sinks down to the couch. Levi relaxes visibly, though he stays back, crossing his arms over his chest and leaning against the doorway.

I remain rooted in place across the room from both of them like they're infected with a flesh-eating parasite.

"As you know, our father, Nolan Marks, is the head of the Burelli crime family."

"So what, you guys are big, bad mobsters?"

Donovan doesn't appreciate my sense of humor.

"Something like that," he says, but there's a faint smile at the corner of his mouth, like he wishes it were that simple. His eyes aren't cold—not right now. They're far away, somewhere I can't follow.

"As you know, I own the Tomb. I bought it as a way to break off from my—*our* father and do something that no one else was doing. An outlet."

"Okay?"

"And that's how I met Cross. Our family comes from money, Ava, but one thing it's lacking is stability. I never knew my mother."

The admission tugs at something in my chest. "Why not?"

He shrugs, but it's not careless. It's tired. "She died during childbirth. A few years before you were born, I guess."

For a moment, neither of us speaks. The room feels smaller somehow, wrapped in the weight of things neither of us got to have.

"I didn't even know about you," I say quietly.

Donovan's gaze finds mine again. "Yeah . . . I know. But I knew about you. I always knew."

There's no accusation in his tone—just a kind of wistful sadness, like he's mourning something that never had the chance to exist.

"Why me? I didn't even know about you. Or Nolan, for that matter."

Donovan chuckles under his breath.

My throat feels tight, a sharp ache pressing against my ribs.

Donovan smiles faintly, but there's no joy in it. "You were the only thing he ever kept close that didn't have a price tag on it."

I look away, blinking hard as tears threaten to spill. I don't know what hurts more—the thought that my father cared, or that I never got the chance to see it for myself.

"I don't understand. Why would he think Alex would come after me if the deal went bad? I mean, you're the one he chose to stay with."

"And yet, the only picture in his wallet is of you."

Something hot pricks at my eyes, and I press my lips together to keep them from trembling. I don't know if the tears are for the father I never knew . . . or the pieces of him I'm only just now finding.

"I hated you," Donovan says, as if I need to be convinced. "I hated him *because* of you."

I shake my head. "I don't understand."

"Because you got all the best parts of him, even if you never knew it."

And for the first time, I realize we're not just two strangers bound by blood. We're two people who grew up missing the same thing.

Donovan shifts, his tone gentling. "We didn't get to choose the family we were born into, Ava. But maybe . . . we can choose what we are to each other now."

Donovan stands, the chair scraping lightly against the floor. He holds out his hand to me, palm steady, fingers open. I hesitate for half a beat before taking it. His grasp is firm but not crushing, warm but not lingering—like we're just any two strangers passing in the street, and not a half-brother and sister meeting for the first time under the shadow of a man we both have reason to hate.

And maybe . . . maybe I wouldn't want it any other way. A clean handshake feels safer than a hug I'm not ready for. Forgive me, but I'm still tainted by the way our first meeting unfolded.

"Whatever happens from here, Ava . . . you're not alone in it."

The words are simple, but something in the way he says them makes them feel like a promise. And for some strange reason, I believe him.

Donovan lingers for a moment in the silence of the room. Then, finally, he heads towards the door and leaves without another word.

As February rolls around, so does the cold. The wind cuts through me every time I leave the house, and I can't wait to return and stay in front of the fireplace.

The cottage has come a long way, and it's starting to feel like home again. With each passing day, the dust and cobwebs disappear, and a bit more of the character I grew up with shines through.

I can't deny Levi has been a big part of it, and I know without his help, I would have played hell trying to keep the place warm.

He still comes every day, but there's something new in the air between us. Something warm and new and vibrant that steals my breath away when I catch myself staring at him.

There are moments when we accidentally brush hands or bump into each other, and he steadies me with a hand on my waist that I feel like I might combust if I don't get his hands on me.

There are other moments when I still want to blame him for what happened, even knowing the true reason behind his actions.

I'm finding it difficult to trust at times, and at others I want to throw caution to the wind and leap into his arms.

I'm a walking contradiction, and it's giving me a headache.

It's not until the coldest day of the year that he doesn't show.

My heart sinks every time I glance at the clock.

It's stupid, the ache in my chest when it dawns on me that he's not coming. I can't expect him to spend every day hanging around my house waiting for me to forgive him. He has a life, and so do I. It's better this way.

At least . . . that's what I tell myself until I hear his car coming down my drive.

Instantly, I dart off the couch and head to the window, peeking out through the curtains to see him climb out of the car.

My heart flutters in my chest, knowing he came, but I'm also angry that he chanced it with the big snowstorm coming through.

"Get inside, it's freezing," I call out when he comes up the slick sidewalk.

"Miss me, baby girl?"

My heart does a somersault at the familiar old nickname, and I open my mouth to tell him not to call me that, but the devil-may-care grin on his lips has the words dying before they ever reach the surface.

"Just get inside, you psychopath."

He follows me in, kicking the snow off his boots in the doorway, while I shut the door behind him.

"Why would you come out here in this? It's crazy outside. You could have wrecked."

Amusement lights his gaze, and he holds out a small box. I stare at him blankly before he takes my hand and places it in my palm.

"What is this?"

He shrugs, moving past me towards the living room.

"It's Valentine's Day."

I pause, falling short. I look down at the box in my hand, and my heart beats a little faster. How did I not realize? How did he?

He heads over to the fireplace, messing with it like he does every day. I swear I'm not doing something right because it's never as warm as when he does it. I'm starting to think he's rigged it, so I need him to come over and fix it every day.

Carefully, I slide open the box, and my voice gets caught in my throat.

It's Gran's old Tiffany necklace we found the other day, broken in a drawer in the bathroom. Only now . . . it's fixed.

My fingers graze over the metal chain, my eyes filling with tears. I hadn't even realized he'd taken it, and now, it's fixed and shining like it's brand new.

I thought I'd done a good job at hiding how much it upset me to find it broken, but I should have known he'd see right through that.

"*Ava.*"

I look up to find him watching me, his expression serious.

I place the lid back on the box and join him in the living room, stopping just beyond the couch because the closer I get to him, the less my brain wants to work.

"Why are you here, Levi?"

He's quiet, studying me. A tear slips down my cheek, and he watches its descent, his eyes dark.

"Because there's nowhere else I'd rather be."

God, why can't I give in to him? I want to. My heart longs for his. It's my head, that's the problem.

"I told you I'd wait for you, Ava. I meant it."

I glance back up at him, unsure what to say. It's the first time we've talked about us since he started coming here.

It's stupid, but I can't help the laugh that comes out more like a sob.

"You drove here in a snowstorm, you idiot."

He shrugs. "And I'll do it a thousand times more."

He takes a cautious step towards me, stopping just close enough that the scent of him washes over me. My body aches for his, but I stay rooted in place.

He reaches for my hand, and I let him take it, cautiously stepping just a little bit closer. He doesn't push me any further, and his hand feels so good around my cold fingers that I want to sink into him.

"If you think my feelings have changed, you're wrong," he says quietly. "I know I hurt you . . . but I'll spend the rest of my life making it up to you, if that's what it takes."

I don't know why a bitterness unfolds in my chest. Maybe it's because I can't get my head to cooperate, but a small part of me wants to lash out, even if I hate myself for it.

"And what if it doesn't work?"

His lips tip up at the corner, and that's when I know. "Then, I'll find another way to make you love me again."

I can't bring myself to tell him I never stopped.

"I'm starting to think you're letting me win."

He smirks. "Maybe I'm just shit at *Uno*."

The power went out—surprise, surprise—three hours ago, and for some odd reason, I just wasn't ready for him to go. He taught me how to make chili over the fire, and after, we dissolved into playing *Uno* at the coffee table with nothing else to do.

"It's *Uno*. Kids play this game," I laugh, and he throws a piece of pre-made popcorn at me.

"Alright, brat."

I reach for my wine glass and find it empty. There wasn't actual wine in it, I just don't have any other cups. When I'd offered, he'd held up his hand, telling me he's sober. I can't lie, I may have teared up a little at that admission. So . . . we'd both opted for soda instead.

The sun set a while ago, and outside, I can hear the wind

whipping against the side of the house. It's snowstorms like these that make me wish I lived somewhere warm, like Hawaii, but then I remember the warmer the climate, the bigger the bugs are, and that's just not something I think I'm up for.

"I should get going," Levi says quietly. My gaze cuts to his, and I find him watching me, a carefully guarded expression on his face.

My heart hammers unsteadily in my chest. I look past him out the window, watching the snow fall.

Cross Estate is only twenty minutes from here, but the roads will be icy. Not to mention the blistering cold.

"Y-you can stay," I say, so quiet I'm not sure the words make it past my lips. My throat feels tight, my breath shallow.

He doesn't answer right away. Just studies me, his gaze steady but unreadable, as if he's weighing the risks. The silence stretches until I start to wish I could take the words back, as though saying them might have shifted something fragile between us.

"It's dangerous out there," I murmur, trying to fill the space. "And slick. I can make up the couch."

His jaw tightens—just barely. His eyes linger on mine like he's searching for something, some hidden meaning I'm too afraid to put into words.

He doesn't move toward me, but I see the way his fingers flex at his side, like they're fighting the urge to reach for me. My own hands are clenched in my lap, every muscle coiled, waiting for him to decide. The storm outside presses against the glass, but it's nothing compared to the one sitting between us.

I almost think he's going to deny me, and embarrassment floods through me at the prospect of his rejection.

"You sure that's okay with you?" he asks finally.

I try to come up with a reason why it wouldn't be, but I only come up short.

"Yeah."

"Okay."

"Okay," I repeat, and neither of us moves.

God, what am I doing?

I hop up before I can make a bigger fool of myself and head towards the bedroom.

"I'll get some blankets."

The wind beats against the side of the house, the sound howling in the night outside my window.

I'm lying on my side, watching the snow fall. Reminiscing about the life I thought I wanted, versus the one I have now.

Oddly enough, I wouldn't ask for anything different.

These budding feelings in my chest, reminding me that Levi is out on my couch, are intense. New and vibrant and so much more than I bargained for.

Can I forgive him?

He protected me from the shadows lurking around me, shielding me from so much that even when I wanted to hate him for it, I couldn't. I still can't.

The man I met almost a year ago at Cross Estate isn't the same one asleep on my couch tonight. He's so much more.

Patient and gentle. Strong and steady when the rest of the world feels so unstable. He's the rock that held me up when Gran died, and the same one that cradled me when I crumpled.

I keep waiting for the moment when my heart is no longer broken, but the problem is that it never really was. Because deep down, no matter why he did it, he did it because he loved me.

So the question 'Can I forgive him'?

I already have.

Without thinking, I climb from the bed and hurry towards the bedroom door. An intense ache burns in my veins, knowing the only solace is him.

Levi and I aren't black and white. We're every color of the rainbow that doesn't make sense, but somehow turned into something beautiful anyway.

I rip the door open, and my breath gets caught in my chest when I see him standing there, dark eyes and tousled hair, and God, I think it just hit me how much I miss him.

He had been about to knock because his hand drops to his side.

"I . . ." he starts, unsure what to say.

So, I make sure he doesn't have to.

I throw myself into his arms and drag his lips down to mine, kissing him feverishly.

And for the first time since I moved back to Gran's, it feels like coming home.

His groan rumbles through me, and I climb up his torso, allowing him to lift me off my feet and cradle me in his arms.

This kiss is desperate and full of everything neither of us has been able to say.

My heart does cartwheels in my chest, while my mind comes up with every possible scenario. One after another. Good. Bad. Beautiful.

They all lead me back to the same place.

Him.

It's always been him.

"Fuck, I missed you," he rasps against my lips, his hands trembling where he touches me. His fingers slide up into the back of my hair, pressing me closer to him until there's not an inch of space between us. My body vibrates. My heart may as well take a leave of absence. I'm not sure it's even functioning properly with how hard it's beating.

I keep kissing him, not ready to give him up. It's been such a long time, the nights stretching endlessly without him. I crave him with every fiber of my being.

Everything else can wait.

When the kiss breaks, Levi's eyes never leave mine as he carries me deeper into the room. There's something primal in his gaze—something possessive, almost reverent. Like he can't believe I'm real. Like he's afraid I might disappear if he lets go.

"Tell me this is real," he says, his voice rough and low.

"It's real," I whisper, threading my fingers through the hair at the nape of his neck.

"Tell me not to touch you, Ava, and I'll stop. I don't want to do this if you aren't ready."

"I'm ready," I breathe. Reaching up, I trace the scar on his lip with my fingertips, and he closes his eyes against my touch. "I'm tired of living without you."

"You've always had me, Ava."

He groans and his mouth crashes down on mine before I can say anything else—hungry, claiming, desperate. I taste the fire in him. The restraint barely leashed. The heat that's been simmering between us for far too long.

He sets me down, but only so his hands can roam. My T-shirt hits the floor, and his jeans follow. He lays me back on the bed and looms over me, watching me like I'm the most goddamn beautiful thing he's ever seen.

Like I'm his religion now.

His shirt drops to the floor, revealing skin I've touched a hundred times but never like this—as his. Every hard plane, every muscle shifting under ink and scars, is mine now. And God, the way he looks at me, like he's starving, sends a wicked thrill down my spine.

Levi crawls onto the bed, slow and predatory, and settles between my thighs like he belongs there—because he does.

"I've missed you so fucking much, baby girl . . ." he breathes, his hands roaming my body. "And I'm going to spend the rest of my life showing you just how much you mean to me."

The night passes in a blur. I can't tell where his body begins and mine ends, but I know I never want to give him up again. Never want to feel like half my heart is missing.

I claim every inch of him the same way he claims me. Feverishly. Hungrily.

"Say it," I whisper, so lost in riding him, all it would take is a breath of air, and I would come.

"Fucking hell," he curses, his head falling back to the pillows. He drags his hand through my hair and tugs me down, pressing his lips against mine. "I love you, Ava. Is that what you want to hear? How fucking desperate I am for you?"

"Yes," I whimper, unable to do much else but roll my hips against him. His groin brushes my clit, and he holds me there, one hand in my hair and the other on my ass, moving me over his cock. "I love you," I gasp, and that's all it takes.

I splinter around him, crying out his name as I clamp down hard, the orgasm ripping through me like lightning. My vision whites out. My body bucks.

I feel him everywhere—under my skin, in my blood, deep inside me.

Levi flips us in a blur of motion, like instinct takes over. He drives into me once, twice—and then he's coming with a low, feral growl. His body tenses above mine, his head buried in my neck as he spills into me with a broken curse and my name.

The only sound is the wind howling outside and the ragged rhythm of our breathing. His body is still pressed against mine, skin slick with sweat, hearts pounding in sync.

And then he leans down, brushing his lips over mine, so soft it breaks something inside me.

"I love you, Ava," he breathes against my lips, like it's sacred. He tucks a strand of damp hair behind my ear, the pad of his thumb brushing my cheek. "I will love you until I take my dying breath," he continues, his hand snaking up and his finger under my chin. "In this life and the next. I love you, Ava Ryan. So much so that being without you feels like someone robbed half of who I am."

The words are a vow and a warning, dark and absolute.

I should feel trapped by that kind of promise.

But instead?

I feel free.

This man—this psychopath—is mine.

And I have no intention of giving him up ever again.

EPILOGUE

F uck, *Levi . . .*"

    I grin against her, sliding my tongue through her slickness as she comes undone for me for the third time today. Even after a year and a half, and spending nearly every night inside her, I still can't get enough.

Ava shudders underneath me, and I press kisses up her stomach, then to her tender breasts, before I reach her lips. She's flushed, so pretty, and panting in the wake of her orgasm when I press my lips to hers.

"You're going to kill me," she breathes against my lips.

"I'm innocent." *Lie.* "I'm just trying to keep my girl happy."

Her cheeks flame, and she smiles up at me from the bed when I force myself to break the kiss. She looks so beautiful with the new glow in her skin.

"We're late," she grumbles when I help her stand, though the grin on her face tells me she's not all that upset about it.

I scrub a hand over the back of my mouth and help her right her dress. It's just big enough that it hides the small bump there,

I smirk, dipping my head so my lips graze her ear. "Sweetheart, I'd make us late every damn day if it meant seeing you like that."

She places her hand over mine, interlocking our fingers on her stomach. Her smile softens, and for a moment, the chaos of everything outside these four walls doesn't exist. It's just her, me, and the tiny life growing between us.

"Careful, baby. You keep eye-fucking me like that and we'll never make it to this thing."

She swats at my chest, laughing, but the sound breaks into a nervous little sigh when she catches the weight in my stare. I don't look away. I can't. The sight of her—glowing, carrying the proof of us—is more than I ever thought I'd deserve.

"You're staring again," she whispers, cheeks flushed.

"Can't help it," I admit, squeezing her hand on her stomach. "Every time I look at you, it feels like the first time. And now…" My voice cracks, and I clear my throat. "Now I know you're carrying my kid, and fuck, Ava—it's like my whole goddamn world's right here."

Her eyes glisten, and she presses her forehead to mine. "Are we going to tell your family?"

"Soon."

"They're going to figure it out eventually. Paulina's been hovering lately. She probably already knows."

I meet her gaze, dead serious. "I want to enjoy you. Us. Before everything changes. Once people know, it won't just be ours anymore—it'll be everyone's business."

Her lips part like she wants to argue, but then she exhales slowly, nodding. "Okay. Our secret. For now."

Her brows furrow in that familiar way they do when there's more on her mind than she's willing to let on. If there's anything I've come to know in the last six months we've been married, it's that my wife likes to worry about things that don't need to be worried about.

I lean back, taking her face in my hands. "What is it, Ava?"

Her throat bobs as she swallows, but her doubt lingers, written all over her face. "Are you sure?"

"About what?"

She glances around nervously, biting her lip.

"All of it."

My chest tightens because I know exactly what she means. She isn't just talking about the baby. She's talking about me. About us.

"Sweetheart, you're the only thing in this life I *am* sure about."

She smiles then, and it's like looking into the center of the sun. Fucking breathtaking.

I glance at the clock on the bedside stand behind us. We were supposed to be at the family reunion twenty minutes ago, but she was just too fucking tempting in her little yellow sundress. I had to have her—again—before we left.

"Come on, Mrs. Cross. I know you're hungry."

She smiles, letting me take her hand and pull her towards the door.

"There had better be chocolate cake, or I'm starting a riot."

I pull her out to the car, helping her get situated before I cross to my side. The little cottage where she grew up is coming along nicely. We spent the last year renovating it. Adding another bedroom and an office. We installed new flower beds and even repaired the old, busted garage out back.

It's become more than just a house. It's a home—our home, and it's more than either of us ever imagined we'd ever have.

Fuck, looking over at Ava—*my wife*—I still have a hard time believing it's all real.

The leather creaks under me as I slide behind the wheel, but I don't start the engine right away. Instead, I glance at her—bare legs tucked under her, one hand resting over her stomach like it's second nature now. The late afternoon sun filters through the windshield, catching the tiny gold flecks in her eyes, and damn if it doesn't knock the breath right out of me.

She turns, catching me staring again, and that slow, knowing smile spreads across her face. The one that says she sees right through me. The one that undoes me every single time.

"What?" she teases softly, brushing a strand of hair behind her ear.

I lean back, taking it all in—the woman who survived hell, the woman who chose me anyway, the woman who somehow became my wife. "Nothing," I murmur, even though it's everything. "Just can't get over the fact that you're mine."

Her eyes soften, but there's a spark there too, like she knows exactly the power she has over me. "Forever," she whispers, lacing her fingers through mine on the console.

Forever. A word I never believed in until her.

I finally twist the key in the ignition, but my chest feels too full, like it might split wide open. The little cottage behind us isn't just walls and paint and flowerbeds—it's proof. Proof that no matter what we went through, no matter who tried to tear us apart, we built something no one can take away.

It doesn't matter what comes next. We'll figure it out.

The drive to Cross Estate is short, and by the time we pull down the long drive, the party is starting. The family reunion was Mila's way of bringing together all the people that she cares about, and I guess, I'm happy to be a part of it.

We've become a family. One big, messy family, but family all the same.

Her siblings from all over the country flew in, and now they're staying at the newly renovated lodge. Her mother, Monica, is fussing about, trying to ensure everything is perfect, while Mila rolls her eyes at her.

It's normal. I fucking love it.

"There's Donovan," Ava points out her brother, where he's talking to Jake, the husband of Mila's sister's best friend. Cherise is on his arm, looking at him longingly. I've got to say, that's a couple I never saw coming, but I'm happy about it. Mainly because, as much as both of them have pissed me off in the past, I know they're good people, deep down, who deserve some joy in this life.

"Oh my God, you've finally made it," Mila groans when I open Ava's car door and take her hand. "I thought I was going to have to deal with my mother on my own."

Ava laughs and lets me lead her to the party while Mila talks our ears off.

"She just won't stop. Do you know she brought my daughter *six* bags of new clothes? *Six*. No eleven-year-old needs that many pairs of shoes."

"By the way," Ava says, grinning. "I've got Lily some new shoes I saw at the shop the other day."

Mila looks like she might lose it.

"I swear," she chuckles. "You're all going to spoil her."

"Let them," I smirk. "Kid's had a hard life. It's time she felt some love."

Mila stares at me like I've grown an extra head.

"Who are you and what have you done with my brother-in-law?"

"Okay, brat."

"About time you showed up," Donovan greets, sliding out of nowhere. He hugs his sister, but gives me a handshake. "I've been waiting on you two."

"We got tied up," Ava rushes, totally not ratting us out.

Donovan smirks as Cherise joins us. He knows what tied up means.

"Got some news."

She holds up her hand, and Ava gasps, taking it to look at her ring. I'm glad the two of them have made amends. I think a large part of that is because of Donovan, but the fucker's head is big enough, so I'd never tell him that.

Over the last year, Ava and Donovan have been steadily working towards building a relationship. I suppose when you learn you have a sibling in your twenty's it's hard to adjust, but I'm proud that she's trying.

As for Marks? The Burelli's have since been disbanded. We see him every now and then, but he mostly keeps to himself. I think almost losing both his kids was the wake-up call he needed to figure some shit out. I know it bothers Ava that he's not around much, but it's for the best.

He did hold up his end of the bargain, though. I was offered my job back at the DEA, but I declined. I'd rather work here with Ava and my brother. Sure, it's not exciting like it was when I was an agent, but I'd become a fucking accountant if I could just come home to my wife every night.

We've taken the lodge and turned it into something we can be proud of. It's no longer the upscale, wealthy retreat it was and is now a place where everyone can bring their families. Our guest list has increased, and I actually enjoy showing up every day, as opposed to avoiding it like the plague.

Ava became the event planner, and she's been doing a damn good job of it. I'm so fucking proud of everything she's accomplished, and everything we're doing as a team. This place has become something I'm actually proud to call mine. A legacy I can leave behind for my kids one day.

We all take our seats at one of the many tables set up, just as Lily and Christian emerge from the forest. I know for a fact, she was hiding out in her treehouse. Christian built it for her so she'd have a place to go when the world was just a little too much. The kid's a miracle, and the fact that she's so happy and carefree after everything she's lived through astounds me.

I have to admit, when he first told me they were thinking about adopting her, I was on the fence, but watching the three of them blend into the perfect family? Well, it gives me hope for the life growing under my hand.

My fingers flex over Ava's stomach when Christian takes the

seat across from us, nodding once. It's subtle. No one else would notice it but me, but the meaning behind it is clear.

We've come a long way.

From a family in pieces to one that can withstand anything. And looking around at everyone gathered for our late September family reunion—the first of many, I wouldn't have it any other way.

Ava glances at me, eyes shining, and I can feel her gratitude even without words. Her hand finds mine under the table, fingers threading together like they've always belonged there. The squeeze is gentle, almost unspoken, but it says everything: we've survived, we've chosen each other, and we're not letting go.

Cherise nudges the side of her glass, breaking the hush. "So… who's going to start the food fight this year?" Her grin is infectious, and suddenly laughter ripples across the table, washing away the heaviness of unspoken memories.

Even Donovan cracks a smirk, shaking his head as if he's resisting joining in, but I know better—he's only holding back for dramatic effect.

I glance around again, taking it all in: the easy chatter, the shared glances, the laughter that reaches into the corners of the yard and bounces off the trees. This is more than a family reunion. It's proof. Proof that the pieces can fit together, even after the messiest of storms.

And for the first time in a long time, I let myself believe that this is how forever feels.

I haven't spoken to Proctor in nearly six months. Once I'd figured it all out, there just wasn't a need for me to keep going. I've put the past behind me, and I'm building a future with my wife. I have everything I could ever want, and even more than I ever thought possible for a man like me.

If I could see him, though, I'd let him know I've found five thousand things to be grateful for. Not just five. And all of them rest in the girl beside me, bearing my last name and carrying my baby.

I squeeze Ava's hand under the table, a silent vow passing between us. No matter what storms come next, this moment, this family, this fragile, beautiful peace—we'll protect it.

"I love you," she whispers underneath the chatter, and my chest swells with pride.

"I love you, too, *Mrs. Cross.*"

She grins, and for the first time, I stop thinking about what could go wrong. Instead, I just breathe it in, letting it settle over me like sunlight through the trees. Watching the stars shine in my wife's eyes and hear our family's chatter.

And in that quiet certainty, I realize: this is home. This is forever.

The End

Thank you so much for taking the time to read Never Die for a Sinner. If you enjoyed reading this book, please consider giving it a review on the platform(s) of your choice.

Reviews are like tips for authors, and let us know how we're doing, as well as spread the word of our work. Your opinion matters.

Love,

Jessi

JOIN THE CLUB

If you want to follow along for future updates, secrets, or just want to read the ramblings of a tired, book-crazy writer, click the link below to sign up for my newsletter.

Love Always,

Jessi

jessihart.com

Tiktok: jessihartauthor

Instagram: jessihartauthor

Facebook: jessihartauthor

ALSO BY JESSI HART

NEVER EVER SERIES–Series Complete
Never Kiss and Tell
Never Wake Up in Vegas
Never Deal with the Devil
Never Dig Beneath a Grave
Never Fall for an Angel
Never Die for a Sinner

STANDALONES
Forget Me Not

TVD–Series
PLV (Coming soon)

MEN OF MADNESS
The Reaper (release info coming soon)

ABOUT THE <u>AU</u>THOR

Hey everybody! I'm Jessi Hart, writer of contemporary and dark romance stories that will probably make you fall in love, cry, laugh, and want to throw the book across the room, all in a few chapters.

I like my hero's grey and my heroine's sassy and full of wit. My characters are human with human flaws that might make you angry, sad, or maybe, relate to them a little more than you thought you would. In the end, though, you can't help, but love them. Because even if they're just on paper, they're real, just like you and I.

-Jessi Hart lives in Ohio with her partner and dogbaby, Rylie. When she's not daydreaming up the perfect scene, you can probably find her gaming, binge-watching a spooky show or pranking her partner, Nick.

Made in the USA
Monee, IL
23 December 2025

40227682R00282